A Rainbow
Murder Mystery

Rave Reviews for *Pharmacology Is Murder*

"First-time novelist Dirk Wyle skillfully pairs the tone of the hard-boiled mystery with the intricate scientific detail common to the medical thriller. The result is an excellent whodunit. . . . a first-class mystery that combines elements of Michael Crichton, Patricia Cornwell, and even Edna Buchanan."

– *Booklist* Mystery Showcase
American Library Association

"Collectors should jump on this one . . . by an author with a promising future . . . a good solid interesting mystery in the traditional style of literate storytelling. . . . very smooth and intelligent. . . . I read it straight through, as slowly as I could manage.

– Sharon Villines,
Archives of Detective Fiction

". . . very obviously written for the intellectual who loves mysteries . . . the murder involving, and the characters well presented. It is far more than just a 'mystery,' it depicts the evolution of a young man's life. Congratulations, Mr. Wyle, I'm expecting your literary star to shine in the same firmament as Michael Crichton's."

– Under the Covers Book Reviews

"... one fine debut mystery, combining scientific method with a quirky, humanistic scientist/detective and resulting in the perfect compound ... inventive, intriguing, and, most importantly, evocatively drawn. If you like a puzzle, you'll love this one."

— Les Standiford, author
Presidential Deal

"When the chairman of the pharmacology department of a Miami medical school is murdered, Dade County medical examiner Geoffrey Westley recruits Ben Candidi to infiltrate the department as a student and gather information. But in the pseudonymous Dirk Wyle's debut ... Candidi's venturing forth from his houseboat may be more hazardous than he thinks."

— *Publishers Weekly*
"Mystery Notes"

"... amazed at the author's ability to create tension, introduce a little love-making along the way, and tell a good mystery story ..." — BookBrowser

"... a delight for those of you who love lots of technical information. And for those who like a good regional mystery, this one offers a love affair with Miami."

— Black Bird Mysteries

"... Here's a murder mystery with the intellectual, educated appeal of a Michael Crichton story."

— *Publisher's Report*

"... an informative mystery novel. His dialog would delight even Charlotte MacLeod. His characters are well delineated, and the time spent reading the novel is actually educational rather than 'killed.' The book is as good as a Florida vacation. Perhaps we have a successor to Travis McGee in Ben Candidi, the bemused protagonist. We await the next Candidi novel."

— Sandra Weinhardt,
Magna Cum Murder Conference Webmistress

Pharmacology Is Murder

Dirk Wyle

Library of Congress Cataloging-In-Publication Data

Wyle, Dirk, 1945-
    Pharmacology is murder / Dirk Wyle.
        p.   cm.
    ISBN 1-56825-038-X (acid-free paper)
    I. Title.
PS3573.Y4854P48   1998
813'.54--dc21   97-40637
                                                                    CIP

Pharmacology Is Murder © 1998 by Dirk Wyle

ISBN 1-56825-038-X

Publisher
        Rainbow Books, Inc.
        P. O. Box 430
        Highland City, FL 33846-0430

Editorial Offices and Wholesale/Distributor/Retail orders:
        Telephone/Fax: (941) 648-4420
        Email: NAIP@aol.com

Individual/Retail Orders:
        Telephone: (800) 356-9315, Fax: (800) 242-0036

Cover and interior design by Betsy A. Lampé

Manufactured in the United States of America

Dedication

I wish to thank Carlisle, Yvonne, Karl, Ellen, Larry, Elena, Gisela, Mary, Daniel, Henry, Winona, Ed, Mary-May, Charles, Ira, Paddy, Sandra, Cynthia, Nancye, Lenore and Douglas (Miami bicyclist, historian and photographer) for their candid reactions to my work while in progress.

This novel is dedicated to all who have known a true love of science – the solitary pursuit of Nature's secrets in the laboratory at three o'clock in the morning.

Prologue

It seemed a most attractive offer: a chance to earn a Ph.D. in pharmacology with no loss of income. Just what the Good Doctor would order for an underachieving 28-year-old techie working a dead-end job in the coroner's laboratory doing routine assays. Good Doctor Westley said he'd have to lay me off anyway. I should be doing something important; while studying pharmacology, I could "unwittingly" pass on scientific information – which would help him with a murder case.

Yes, Dr. Westley was right. I couldn't spend another six years sitting on my boat gazing at Coconut Grove and letting the world pass me by. So I accepted his challenge and "took the King's Shilling." Later, he explained the expression was the three-centuries-old metaphor for a binding recruitment.

I quit my job and entered the pharmacology Ph.D. program. I studied the 12 professors who taught the program. And I spent day and night trying to figure out which one of them used what poison to kill their chairman.

With the optimism of a raw recruit I had marched off to battle. But I soon learned it would be a long campaign, a one-man mission with no backup. The handbook for the clandestine investigation of a murderous pharmacologist had not been written. Dr. Westley never said anything about searching a professor's lab at night like a cat burglar. And he didn't say the list of deadly drugs would be impossibly long.

"Innocently and unwittingly," I was supposed to deliver Westley the name of the professor and his poison. Then he would check my theory by testing the corpse. If I was right, they would indict the renegade prof. Unfortunately, scientific proofs have never been 100 percent clear. But I did deliver.

Once uncovered, my "scientific information" quickly lost its innocence – and so did I. In the language of my newly learned specialty, the information became "potent" and intrinsically "adrenergic." Inject it into the system and blood pressures rise.

Things got nasty, PDQ. The wrath of an insulted faculty and the fury of a wounded institution are difficult to imagine until experienced first hand. So I had a second campaign to fight – an all-or-nothing struggle to avoid checkmate in an N-dimensional board game played by rules I had yet to learn. I was unprepared when the process server came knocking. Must I run away from everything, including the woman I love?

If I had foreseen the demands of the campaign, the King's Shilling would have never touched my flesh. But after months clutched tight in my hand, it became a talisman for personal change. I returned from my last battle a different man.

– I –

On the Carpet

I WAS OFFERED THE KING'S SHILLING on one of those steamy, mid-August Miami days when you thanked God for your nice, white-collar job inside an air-conditioned space. While the central air conditioner fought the late-morning sun, I sat at my small desk nestled between analytical instruments in the laboratory of the Dade County Medical Examiner's Office. It wasn't a bad job for me, Ben Candidi, that "gifted" techie with a six-year-old B.S. in Chemistry from Swarthmore. I had no ambition to get a Nobel Prize or become a millionaire before reaching 30. Some people might say I had no ambition whatsoever.

Six years ago, I thought the job might be exciting – doing chemical analyses to determine cause of death. But after a few months, it proved hopelessly dull. When the docs down in the morgue suspected death by poisoning, they sent up blood samples and orders for standard assays. We technicians performed assays for street drugs, prescription drugs, insecticides, poisons, household chemicals, or all of the above. We sent back reports and heard nothing more. I was rarely involved in an exciting investigation.

Over the years, I carved out a niche as specialist for maintaining and troubleshooting the analytical instruments. That saved me having to perform routine assays with the seven other technicians. And it left me lots of time for dilettante pursuits.

I had just typed in the "start" command on a high-pressure liquid chromatograph, putting the chemical bloodhound through a routine maintenance check to ensure that he could still sniff out "serotonin" in blood extracts at concentrations down around five nanograms per milliliter. The test tubes clinked in the sample changer and the desktop computer-sized instrument sucked on the first sample. In 45 minutes, I'd know if Old Blue could still sniff, or if I'd have to clean his electrometric nose. I settled into an interesting *Scientific American* article titled, "Raising the *Vasa*: The Swedish man-of-war which slept for three centuries at the bottom of Stockholm Harbor."

Then I heard the approaching footsteps of my supervisor, Dr. Steve Burk. His heels clicked in a parade-ground cadence, telling me he was in one of his supervisory moods. I quickly closed the *Scientific American.*

"Candidi," he barked. I got to my feet as he came to a halt at an uncomfortably close distance. He would have made a good Army major with his six-foot, athletic frame, officer's haircut and intimidating dark moustache. He held five red-stoppered tubes of blood.

"Unexplained death. One sample and four controls. Run them. They've been screened for the usual stuff, and all tests came out negative. And they're negative for food poisoning toxins. We've also sent samples over to the clinical lab at Dade County General for a multi-drug screening. Now let's see what *you* can find."

"Sure, Dr. Burk. And what are we looking for?"

"Anything that might explain the death. Look for anything the other tests might have missed. We're under direct orders from Dr. Westley on this one. Probably one of his pet projects. Just do it." He handed me a test tube. "This one's the subject, cause of death unknown. These four are controls to use for comparison."

"What can you tell me about the controls?"

"This one's a motorcycle accident. This one's a coronary from Dade General. I'm not sure what these other two are supposed to be – probably nursing home cases they're doing downstairs as part of the Alzheimer's project."

So it would not be a dull day after all. These few and far-between special projects for Chief Medical Examiner Geoffrey Westley were my chance to shine. But I didn't appreciate the unceremonious way Burk handed me the project. Sure, Burk had a Ph.D. in toxicology from the University of Kentucky and had worked here for 15 years. But he would have been lost trying to do this project by himself. And he would have been twice as lost if he'd delegated it to his flunky, Jake Brown. By way of reminder, I politely asked Burk if he had any specific technical suggestions. Did he want me to use any particular detectors . . .

He frowned. "Sure, Candidi. Use all the detectors you want. Run all the HPLCs at the same time, *reading that magazine and standing on your head!* If you find anything, we can always rerun the samples ourselves, for certification purposes."

Before Burk had marched his butt back to his office, I was already at work extracting the unknown molecules of death from the victim's blood. My organic solvents gave off an interesting variety of smells as I pipetted them into rows of test tubes and added the blood samples. They reminded me of cheap perfumes and of the chemical plants back in New Jersey. And they brought back fond memories of my last special project for Dr. Westley, a year or two ago.

The inner workings of a high-pressure liquid chromatograph might be a big mystery to Dr. Burk and his crew, but to me an HPLC is nothing more than a collection of pumps, thin metal tubes, and columns that separate molecules in solution. It's connected to an ensemble of shoe-box-sized detectors that absorb light or electrically react with the molecules when they come out the other end. The detectors report to a desktop computer.

I took out my precision wrenches and hooked up five different types of detector module to the HPLC, reconstructing the old "Ben Candidi Rig." My innovation had delighted Old Man Westley a couple of years ago. Last time, the results were important enough for Dr. Westley to publish in a forensic medical journal. At the end of the article he thanked "Mr. Benjamin Candidi for valuable technical assistance." Maybe he'd be grateful enough this time to keep me around a few more years.

I set a quinine test solution in the sample changer and typed in the start command. The HPLC machine gave a soft, willing, precision whine as it pumped the quinine solution through its narrow metal tubes. Everything worked perfectly. The hydrophobicity column held back the quinine for the expected 3.297 minutes. The detectors responded, as the quinine came out the other end. The flat red, yellow, white and pink lines on the bottom of my computer screen started traveling up and then down, leaving "peaks" which told me that four out of the five detectors had sensed the quinine molecules. The green line stayed flat because the electrical conductivity detector cannot "smell" quinine.

It's heady stuff, seeing your data come out in multicolored computer traces. Every time Dr. Westley brought down a group of distinguished visitors, I would play back one of these multicolored runs on the computer screen. The yokels thought the experiment was running in real time. Like a whiz kid at a science fair, I'd tell them how quinine makes your tonic water taste bitter and how it makes your gin and tonic glow blue under the "black" lights at the disco. I'd explain how my detectors can tell whether the deceased had drunk a gin and tonic 24 hours before he died. And I'd tell them quinine is chemically related to the heart medicine, quinidine.

Working in my spirited, whiz-kid mode, I set up a second HPLC machine with a different type of separating column. It was nice to see the two machines working side by side, the little robot arms of the "autoanalyzers" dipping their hollow needles into arrays of test tubes, and slurping up little hummingbird-sized drinks of blood extracts which would set in motion the multicolored traces, telling the chemical stories of the deceased, the motorcycle casualty, the coronary and the Alzheimer's patients. What nicer music than the clicks and whine of a well-oiled and intelligent machine? And my little robot friends would produce a load of answers in a few hours.

Then Burk's flunky, Jacob Brown, came in to bitch about how I'd modified the machines. He'd have to recertify them when I was done. Jake was a 35-year-old Senior Lab Tech who didn't know shit about troubleshooting HPLCs. He wore a white shirt and tie, and enjoyed playing the company man. He had me pegged as a techno-nerd and pushover. He'd been trying to get Burk to make him my supervisor. So far, Burk had shown enough sense to resist the notion.

This started me brooding. It's an unpleasant fact of forensic laboratory life that bureaucratic paperwork is just as important as properly running instruments. Prosecutors and defense attorneys are sticklers for paperwork. Forget to dot your i's or cross your t's, and they'll crucify you.

Burk liked to make jokes comparing our facility with a MASH unit. At least once a day, we'd hear the beat of helicopter blades, as fresh casualties of the gun, knife and highway were delivered to the roof of the Ryder Trauma Center across the street. Blood samples often arrived an hour later.

I couldn't survive in a real MASH unit because I hate regimentation. Tennis shoes, blue jeans and T-shirt are the proper uniform if you're working with your body and mind. My clothes were never dirty, and I always came to work clean-shaven and well-groomed, so Burk couldn't complain. But he would have liked to write a lab regulation outlawing my ponytail, although it's only three inches long. The guy's a cube who can't stand anyone who's moderately hip.

I like to think of myself as a nineties kind of guy. Since I'm four inches short of the six-foot masculine ideal, I've never been tempted to strut around like Dr. Burk and his macho friends. My greatest claim to masculine vigor is my thick black hair, inherited from my mom and dad who are both second generation Italian. A well-timed smile will often earn me a second glance from certain types of girls. Some find me charming and don't seem to notice that my teeth aren't perfectly straight.

This reminded me that help was available for my project.

I walked over to the main lab with the samples.

"Carmen, could you run these for water-soluble chromophores? It's a special case for Dr. Westley."

"Sure, as soon as I get through with this series," she said with a twinkle of the eye and a friendly smile. Carmen was one of those girls who felt I rated a second glance. She was close to my age and we understood each other well. But she had a husband and two children, so a romantic interest was out of the question.

I spent some time in the main lab, running the five samples on the gas chromatograph. That instrument reported traces of gasoline in the blood of the motorcycle fatality. Had he been working on his engine or tailgating a clunker with loose piston rings and three dead sparkplugs? Unfortunately, I didn't find anything in the blood of the deceased subject.

Returning to my lab, I sat at the HPLC computer and ran my custom-designed program to flag differences in the peaks of the deceased and controls. Oh, it found differences all right: The deceased's blood was cleaner than the controls!

So I searched manually, spending an hour flipping through screens and screens of red, yellow, green, pink and white peaks, trying to find any evidence of unusual molecules in the deceased's blood. I found nothing useful. The motorcycle fatality had breakdown products of cocaine. One of the nursing home patients had been taking a lot of aspirin-type drugs. And the coronary patient had a whole mountain range of peaks. What else is new?

I checked back with Carmen. Her runs didn't show anything, either. It was beginning to look like the subject had died a disappointingly natural death.

As I sat down at my desk, my stomach growled, reminding me that it was past two o'clock, and that I'd forgotten lunch. Then Dr. Burk's footsteps approached from behind.

"So, how's it doing, buddy?" He always called me "buddy" when he wanted something. Sometimes he was even halfway friendly.

"Not so good," I replied, deciding to give him a full technical answer. "I extracted with five solvents, ran them with two types of column and used five detectors. That makes fifty combinations. The subject is cleaner than the controls! Only one of the controls was clean enough to – "

"Okay, I hear you," Burk interrupted, half turning away. "I'm going to see the Old . . . I'm going to report your negative findings to Dr. Westley. Finish up and let me know if you find anything positive. And write me a two hundred-word Executive Summary before you leave."

A fine way to treat a guy who just performed 25 mandays of work in a single day. Ganging those detectors together was my idea, and it increased my power of analysis by an order of magnitude. Couldn't the bean counter see that?

I must have been stewing over this stuff for 10 minutes when the phone rang. It was Doris, Dr. Westley's secretary of over 25 years. "Ben, Dr. W would like to see you in his office. Could you come now?"

"Sure, I'll be right over."

Only three times in the past six years had Chief Dade County Medical Examiner Geoffrey A. Westley called me into his office. When he wanted information, he usually strolled over to my lab bench and chatted it out of me. Sometimes he wanted the low-down on a new instrument that The Suits were peddling, or the scoop on a new toy his counterparts up in Fort Lauderdale or Palm Beach had just purchased. Why should they have fancier toys when they didn't have half as many drug-related deaths?

To Dr. Westley, I was just a whiz kid for analytical instruments. He wasn't an unsociable guy, but he did come across as a little stiff in his expatriate English way. This time he would question me about what chemicals I'd found in the deceased subject. Sorry to have to disappoint him.

In honor of the occasion, I put on a lab jacket. I walked up three flights of stairs to his office.

"You can go right in," Doris said, with a motherly smile. "Dr. W and Dr. Burk are waiting for you. It seems like something important has been going on."

How extraordinary! Never before had I been called in by *both* bosses. Short, pudgy Dr. Westley rose slowly from behind his desk to greet me. Dr. Burk sat in the corner like he wasn't too happy to see me there. Dr. Westley gave me a soft handshake and asked me to sit down. His skin had the texture and feel of blue cheese wrapped in cellophane − soft, pale white, almost translucent. Small veins and arteries were visible along the stretch marks in his cheeks. He sank into his well-stuffed leather chair with a somewhat theatrical sigh.

What pleasantry would he use to start this interview? He always awakened in me a feeling of *deja vu*, as if I'd seen his pale face, framed by thin white hair, in a 1950s movie. Dr. Westley's Oxbridge speech and manners had not been corrupted by thirty-some years of life among a lesser sort in Miami.

He dispensed with the pleasantries.

"Dr. Burk reports that you have gone to great lengths to improvise an extensive chemical screening of the blood sample of interest and have been able to find nothing."

As always, Dr. Westley spoke in soft, yet well-enunciated tones which resonated at a pitch considerably higher than his natural voice. His speech was so cultivated, he would sound intimidating reading "Mary Had a Little Lamb." Actually, *Winnie the Pooh* would have suited him better. He could so skillfully modulate tone and volume for emphasis. He dropped his pitch as he ended with "able to find nothing."

"Well, sir, not all the results are in yet, and it might be possible that − "

"I quite understand. I am assured that you have applied yourself to this project with your usual alacrity. And we will proceed on the assumption that there is nothing to be found by purely chemical methods."

Did I detect an almost fatherly smile?

"My purpose in summoning you is not to *pick fault*, but rather to *pick your brain*. You see, Mr. Candidi, a rather challenging case has been brought before this office. It may be an untimely death; it may be a most clever murder."

This promised to be exciting. The Old Man never discussed new cases with me, although he often conferred with Burk on such matters. Dr. Westley was a living legend in Miami. He was frequently in the newspapers and on the evening news, stating an opinion on a perplexing murder. Miami, the drug smuggling and crime capital of the U.S., had furnished him bizarre cases.

"Gee whiz," I said. "Must be some case!"

(*Great exclamation, Ben. Right out of an Archie comic book!*)

Dr. Westley had that effect on me. I never knew what language to use with him. Cop-chemist Burk shook his head like I'd just fouled the air. The Old Man rewarded me with a prolonged, full-body scan, his gaze starting at my tennis shoes, working its way up to my blue jeans and ending with my T-shirt. I'd forgotten to button my lab jacket. He slowly shook his head as if questioning why he'd invited me into his office in the first place.

"Mr. Candidi, what I tell you is, as always, to be held in the strictest confidence."

"Yes, sir," I affirmed in a military tone.

"I shall tell you only the barest medical details and you will give me only your technical comments. You and Dr. Burk will consider yourselves sworn to secrecy. Any discussion of the matter outside this room could have disastrous consequences for the – for the case."

"I understand, sir."

Dr. Westley continued, saying, "The facts are as follows. At about six o'clock, two evenings ago the deceased, a forty-eight-year-old biomedical scientist, was found lying on the couch by his wife as she came home from work. He complained of general malaise. Without eating anything, he went to bed around eight, but could not sleep. His condition deteriorated. He became incoherent and finally delirious. At ten o'clock he went into a state of shock. The paramedics found no pulse and could elicit no response with defibrillators and intracardiac injection of adrenaline. He was pronounced dead on arrival at Dade General."

Dr. Westley laid in a dramatic pause, glancing first at

Burk, then at me.

"The emergency room reported a swollen black tongue and noted massive intravascular coagulation – Candidi, that would be clot formation – and a purple coloration of the skin. There was also massive hyperkalemia – meaning high blood potassium. They considered the cause of death to be cardiac fibrillation – uncoordinated contraction of the heart – but we're perplexed by the extensive clot formation."

Dr. Westley threw me glances and dropped the pitch of his voice as he translated the medical terms for my benefit. I nodded to indicate understanding.

"There was no sign of pathogenic organism, and we are doing an extended toxicology screen on his blood sample. And of course, Mr. Candidi, your investigation has also come up negative. It would not seem to be poisoning by a *simple chemical* because simple chemicals must be present at high concentrations in the blood to elicit such bizarre and complex symptomatology."

"Sir," Burk chimed in, "can we be sure that every simple chemical could be detected at a lethal concentration?"

"Well, Mr. Candidi," the Old Man said, "am I correct that you have screened for the presence of chromophores?" He knew the meaning of all the laboratory terminology.

"Yes. I used the usual ultraviolet absorption detector and also ran the fluorescence detector."

"And did you test for chemically reactive species?"

"Yes, I used the redox detector."

"And you also looked for volatile agents?" He pronounced volatile as "vola-TILE," with an elegant upward inflection of the second syllable.

"Yes. I did a gas chromatogram and found traces of gasoline in one of the controls."

"And thus," he said, turning to Burk, "Mr. Candidi seems to have done his job quite well. So what other means of detection would you propose for a simple chemical?"

"Well – "

Burk did not like to be on the spot, so I quickly interjected, "I also did a light scattering analysis of particulate solids for the case that the lethal compound didn't have a chromophore or a chemically reactive species."

The Old Man processed my technical jargon without a blink and said, "And that also came up negative, I would assume."

"Yes."

"So now we must come up with a second theory. We must ask if the lethal agent was a *protein or glycoprotein toxin.* When injected, they make beautiful murder weapons. Extremely nasty. The kiss of death, like a cobra's bite. But there are so many proteins in the body that one can't just go looking for them at random like Mr. Candidi looked for chemicals with his HPLC. One must know exactly which protein to look for. And when it comes to protein and glycoprotein toxins, your conventional HPLC machine is, of course, quite helpless – quite blind actually. To your detectors, all proteins look the same. One can't find thirty milligrams of protein toxin lurking in a corpse which contains thirty pounds of protein already."

He told us that the lab had already tested the deceased's blood for a number of common protein and glycoprotein toxins using antibody-based assays, and that Fort Detrick just faxed back negative results for biological warfare toxins such as "yellow rain toxin." It was like searching for a certain straw in a haystack. "One must know, beforehand, the amino acid sequence of a protein toxin to make identifying antibodies against it."

He pronounced "amino acid" as "a-MINE-o acid."

Then he reasoned, "Perhaps we will not have to look for protein toxins, since there was no evidence of needle marks. We checked the corpse all over for needle marks, square inch by square inch. Not a mark to be found. And the murderer could not have been effective giving protein toxins by mouth because the stomach digests them."

He and Burk kicked these ideas around. Burk asked dumb questions and Westley gave elegantly phrased, intelligent answers:

No, the deceased could not have been shot by a hollowed-out BB containing the potent toxin "ricin" like the Bulgarians did to the BBC journalist. Westley's medical examiners didn't find any BB or any puncture trauma.

No, there isn't any known toxin so potent that you could deliver a lethal quantity in an undetectable scratch.

No, it could not have been an oral dose of cholera toxin.

"Even if the protein had survived in the stomach, it still would have wreaked havoc on the intestinal lining. The poor fellow would have contracted a most severe case of diarrhea. The lack of such GI upset was most remarkable. Before one dies by protein or glycoprotein toxin in the intestine, one goes skipping to the loo every ten minutes."

I sensed that Dr. Westley was becoming impatient with Burk. He had taken an American folksong, had made a word play on "water closet" and had insulted Burk's Kentucky background in the process. Westley glanced at me with a wry expression and caught my smile of appreciation. Then he settled back in his chair, subsiding into bemused distraction. All this was lost on Burk.

In absence of any ideas from Burk or myself, the Old Man launched into a mini-lecture on orally-active protein toxins. "Cholera toxin kills third-worlders when given off by bacteria living in the intestine – attacks the intestinal lining, causing what you call 'the drips.' It kills by simple dehydration and electrolyte imbalance. One can keep the poor beggars alive with that popular 'alligator' athletic drink, if one had a mind to it." The Old Man was noted for his derision of American commercialism and popular culture.

Burk asked what would happen if you ingested cobra toxin.

"It would be digested in the stomach. Bill Haast over at the Miami Serpentarium used to swallow *glasses full* of deadliest venoms that he milked from those ugly creatures. He never experienced the least discomfort."

Dr. Westley seemed disappointed in Burk as he sank deeper into his leather chair, dejected and oblivious to both of us. It was now Benjamin Candidi's turn to come up with something. But I had nothing to add. I decided to play the interested student.

"You used to collaborate with Haast back in the sixties?"

"Yes. He helped me with snake bite cases and I put him in touch with some biochemists at the two medical schools, helping him with his research aspirations. He packed up his operation and headed out West some years ago."

The Old Man sounded weary. The Serpentarium, with its 20-foot-high cement cobra, coiled in a striking pose with bared fangs, had been a landmark, giving that section of U.S. 1 the feel of a theme park. Mr. Haast had been a living legend who hand-caught and milked cobras three times a day before a live audience. He had been bitten so many times that he was immune to every type of venom. He had saved many lives by donating his plasma to snake bite victims.

I remembered Haast's last performance, when he arranged his audience in a big circle around an enormous wicker basket, let out a 12-foot king cobra, wrestled it down and milked it – theater-in-the-round, Miami style. Some people said the guy was a little nutty, but you could say that about everyone who came down to Miami before 1960. His leaving marked the end of an era. The cement cobra crumbled when they tried to move it. The bank bulldozed the buildings, putting in a shopping strip. How long had I been stupidly day-dreaming?

"Benjamin," the Old Man said, "we are under considerable pressure to do something about this case. You are one of our brighter young lads, and I was wondering if you could lend your mind to it. You are, after all, a member of that *society* . . . What do they call it?"

"Mensa." Six years ago, I'd mentioned my membership in Mensa. I was still trying to live it down.

"I thought it might appeal to your 'Mensa interests,' so to speak. And you *do* know a great deal about assaying chemicals."

I didn't really know much about biomedical science beyond what I'd learned from my B.S. at Swarthmore and from my pleasure reading in the *Scientific American*. But I could talk the stuff. "If the poison was a protein, I might know a way to get it past the stomach. In the aspirin commercials on television they talk about an 'enteric coating' which keeps the aspirin from dissolving in the stomach, but releases it when it gets to the intestine. But then the murderer would need some clever way to get the protein across the intestinal lining without the protein getting chopped up or the victim getting diarrhea."

"This is precisely the type of thinking we need to bring to the case!" But Dr. Westley's enthusiasm rapidly faded. "An oral protein toxin theory may be untenable. Scientists have not yet learned how to direct proteins across the intestinal lining and into the bloodstream. Were it otherwise, the pharmaceutical companies would already be peddling enterically coated, orally active insulin. And they would be making hundreds of millions of dollars with their insulin pills, since the poor diabetics are loathe to inject themselves with a needle twice or thrice a day."

We spent a long time discussing the science underlying the case. I'm good at logic, so I could hold my own. Finally the Old Man cleared his throat and said, "Benjamin, would you be good enough to summarize the characteristics of Molecule X?"

I thought for a minute, then said, "It must be one of three things. One: A very poisonous chemical that is not destroyed in the stomach. It must be poisonous in such small quantities that I would miss it with my HPLC machine."

"Or?" Westley asked, watching and listening very carefully.

"Or, two: A protein toxin that is much more poisonous than ricin, so that all you would have to do is dope the point of a tiny needle with it, and barely pricking his skin with it would introduce a lethal quantity."

"Yes, conceivably. But more importantly?" His eyes locked on mine, demanding to know if I understood.

"Or, thirdly and finally: Any protein or glycoprotein toxin that can be enterically coated and that can get across the intestinal lining and into the blood but without causing diarrhea, using a molecular delivery system which hasn't yet been invented."

"Well stated! That is the problem exactly."

"And," I continued, "you have no idea what this chemical poison or protein toxin could be?"

"Unfortunately, that is our predicament."

"Sir," Burk chimed in, "how do we know that the deceased was poisoned?"

"The hypothesis is supported by the symptoms. It was a most bizarre death. And the widow suspects a deliberate poisoning."

Burk squirmed in his seat and protested, "But, sir, a widow might not – "

"The widow is also a biomedical scientist," interrupted Westley.

"And the last meal?" asked Burk.

"American fast food, carried in, and eaten together with colleagues, who are biomedical scientists, as was the deceased. I used to know two of those scientists back in the old days."

"Wow!" Burk's mouth opened wide.

"You both are to limit your interest in this case to the scientific question which Mr. Candidi has so ably paraphrased. Further laboratory tests will be of no use without a short list of likely agents. Please give this matter your deepest thought. Please come back to me if you have any inspiration. And not a word to anyone. This goes for your 'scientific inquiries' as well. This matter is very, very close to home. At this time, there have been no overt police inquiries. Their very presence might serve to alert the murderer. Have I made myself clear?"

"Yes, sir," we answered in unison.

The Old Man waved off Burk but indicated to me that I was to stay. After Burk closed the door, the Old Man said, "I wonder if you would care to join me for dinner this evening. I have a little proposition I would like to make. The restaurant at the clubhouse of *Faire Isle*. Shall we say at seven?"

The Old Man said it as if there would be no question as to my availability.

"I would be most honored and delighted," I replied. Flabbergasted was a better word. The Old Man had never even invited me to lunch before.

"Cheers," he said, dissolving into reverie and sparing me worry about how much deference to show while exiting.

– II –

Proposition

BACK IN THE LAB, I PORED OVER my data and still didn't find a clue how the scientist was poisoned. If one of his colleagues poisoned his coffee, you couldn't prove it by me. No Boy Scout merit badge for Ben Candidi today. According to my HPLC analysis, the deceased should still be walking around. At a quarter 'til five, Dr. Steve Burk marched in.

"So what's the story, good buddy?"

"Same as before, Chief. There's nothing to find among the ground clutter." Perhaps a weather radar analogy would strike a chord with him.

"Okay. Just finish it off and don't forget the report."

"Dr. Burk, could I have until tomorrow morning? I just have enough time to finish up here before . . ."

I trailed off, not wanting to tell Burk about the dinner invitation. After one-upping him in Westley's office, I almost felt sorry for him. Of course, Westley would always like him because he was predictable and reliable.

"Sure," Burk said. "First thing tomorrow morning." He left for the day.

After straightening things up, I went to the locker where I kept my computer, my important personal records and other water-sensitive stuff. I pulled out a light blue dress shirt and my sports jacket. These came in handy for emergencies, like when dignitaries from Dade County government drop in. Punching out on the time clock, I walked out to face another hot, humid mid-August, Wednesday afternoon. Carefully folding the jacket, I put it on the rat-trap carrier of my 10-speed bicycle, chained to a tree. Luckily, the dinner invitation would not take me out of my way. The *Faire Isle* condominium complex was only a few hundred yards from my home. Dodging hospital visitors and employees on the pedestrian mall, I rode out of the Medical campus and down 12th Avenue.

I'd like to shake the hand of the man who invented the bicycle. It's the right conveyance for an athletic, ecologically-conscious man or woman. You move efficiently under your own power, as free as the wind in your face, at a speed that won't kill you or anyone else. The scenery moves by slowly enough for you to enjoy it. In the winter I ride fast for the sheer thrill of it and for aerobic exercise; but in the summer I pedal just hard enough to be taken seriously by the cars, but slowly enough to keep from working up a sweat.

In the middle of a heavily travelled section of Little Havana, I stopped and bought a cola at a cafe. In the winter I drink *café cubano*. I chatted with Isabella who worked behind the sidewalk counter. It's part of my daily routine. With a dozen open-air cafes on my route, I visit each one only twice a month. I have a certain affinity for the Little Havana milieu.

Leaning against the counter, contemplating the traffic moving south along 12th Avenue, it occurred to me that my ride home through Little Havana was like the ride that the molecules take through the separating column of my HPLC machine. Different molecules get held back for different amounts of time – all according to their affinities for the packing material in the long, narrow column.

My affinity for Isabella and the cafe slowed down my trip through Little Havana by 15 minutes. I mounted up and reentered the stream. After crossing that ugly highway named U.S. 1, I was in Coconut Grove. The trees, tropical overgrowth and proximity to the Bay made for a cooler ride. After a mile on Tigertail Road, it was time to turn off and coast down to the Bay.

The *Faire Isle* complex sits a quarter of a mile out in Biscayne Bay. About 20 years ago, some rich people decided there wasn't enough waterfront property to go around. So they filled in part of the Bay to create their own island with five enormous high-rises, swimming pools, tennis courts and clubhouse. And the rest of us lost a portion of the bay.

I pedaled along the private causeway and over the bridge, arriving at the guard house by which the cars must pass in single file. I glided past a half-dozen assorted Mercedes, BMWs and Jaguars to the front of the line, falling in behind the leader. This provoked a few lower-class honks of protest from the upper-class cars. Luckily, the guard knew that I was expected and let me through without causing the gentry much delay.

"We don't have many guests come here on bicycle, mon," the guard said with a Jamaican accent and a toothy smile. Both features went well with his abbreviated khaki uniform and pith helmet.

I chained my bike to a convenient tree, sat down next to it and contemplated the milieu for the hour I had to kill. Yes, the black Jamaican with his Colonial uniform would suit the Old Man just fine when he drove up in his Rolls Royce Silver Cloud. Over the years I had glimpsed him a few times, driving that 1959 relic, with its rounded fenders emphasizing its white-walled tires and with its winged nymph on the hood. Did her elfin bottom inspire sexual fantasies in the old boy as he motored along, sitting in his overstuffed, leather-appointed seat behind his cherished wooden dash panel?

It was just the car for an English fat cat to drive on the French Riviera – a definite plus for *Faire Isle's* snob appeal, which was every bit as phony as English accents you hear in commercials for luxury cars. But how would the average *Faire Isle* resident relate to Dr. Westley, the genuine article?

How would the average Miamian relate to Dr. Westley? There was a story that, in the old days, Westley had considered the only thing at this latitude worthy of Her Majesty's visit to be the Bahamas, 50 miles due east.

Professionally, he cut a fine figure in criminal court with his expert opinions on cause of death. The *Miami Standard* once described him as one part emergency room physician, one part scientist, one part detective and one part English gentleman. And he had an illustrious history solving Miami Beach Mafia murders, Cuban "political" assassinations, and cocaine- and designer drug-related deaths of every kind. "He has kept pace with every step of Miami's growth from tourist town to major metropolitan area," the *Miami Standard* once stated.

I could imagine him impressing the indigenous southern gentlemen, and other folk who ruled the roost 30 years ago, down here in Miami. But as the years rolled on, Cubans, Haitians, Nicaraguans and many other groups were added to the list. How did the new groups like the patronizing English gentleman? Could snob appeal and competence keep his career alive for another decade?

And what was I to make of this dinner invitation? I sensed a fatherly interest behind his stiff formality, but I have a very sensitive antenna for this kind of signal. Would he protect me against the budget crunch that Burk had been talking about?

Sure, I was in the doldrums with my job, but I'd been very idealistic about it in the beginning. In my second year, I suffered a major setback which held me back professionally. In a murder case, the defense had subpoenaed me to testify on my HPLC analyses on cocaine and its breakdown products. The defense attorney used country-boy tactics and sophistic arguments to make hash of my work. Afterward, Burk said my testimony was so bad that it threatened to destroy the State Attorney's case.

I am too honest in reply and often crumple under the force of certain people's will. After that day, I was no longer a signatory on forensic assays. The other technicians handled all of the formal bullshit, leaving me the role of special projects boy wonder and occasional trouble shooter. And did the Department really need a trouble shooter? For $150 per hour they could fly in a factory technician from Atlanta. How much was their pony-tailed Mensa genius in blue jeans actually saving them?

I put on my sports jacket and went to the clubhouse. The maitre d' expected me and directed me to a secluded table.

Dr. Westley would be with me shortly, and I should order a drink. A gin and tonic sounded fine. I could contemplate the quinine standard and my beloved HPLC machines. The Old Man appeared at about the same time as the drink, voiced his approval, and told the waiter to make it two. We started off with some small talk about his Silver Cloud and his experiences in Miami – stuff I knew he'd like to talk about.

After we ordered dinner, Dr. Westley got around to the special project. His proposition would be to our mutual benefit and would advance my professional development.

"I must first tell you more about the case. Please remember, Ben – I would like to call you Ben – that what I am about to tell you is to be kept in the *strictest* confidence. Not even Burk knows all of what I am going to tell you. The deceased is Dr. Charles D. Cooper, Chairman of the Department of Pharmacology at the Bryan Medical School. As you know, it is a private medical school located a scant 300 yards from our building. The widow is Dr. Jane Goddard Cooper, Professor of Epidemiology, at the same institution."

"I see what you mean about the case being 'close to home'."

"The following is a matter of record: Dr. Charles Cooper ate at a faculty meeting a fast-food lunch procured by his secretary. The meeting took place in his office at twelve noon. At least half of his faculty hated him. Mrs. Cooper, oh dear, what shall we call her? Dr. Mrs. Dr. Cooper, I suppose. In any case, *she* thinks that one of the faculty poisoned him. Let's simply call her 'the widow'. She isn't just some hysterical female. She is a biomedical scientist, albeit a dietician. But she does have a Ph.D. She is an extremely well-connected individual, who is presently making life very difficult for me."

Dr. Westley went on to say that the County Manager was pressuring him to solve the case. The County Manager and the deceased Dr. Cooper were buddies on the vestry of St. James Episcopal Church. At church, Dr. Cooper had confided to the County Manager that he was despised by certain members of his Pharmacology Department. The widow had confirmed it.

Westley reiterated that, at the slightest hint of an investigation, the perpetrator would destroy all the evidence and forever destroy his chance of learning how the crime was committed. Dr. Jane Cooper and the County Manager were behaving accordingly.

I asked, "Does she suspect a particular professor?"

"She thinks three capable of having done it. She suspects one in particular, but I cannot tell you which. She can supply nothing in the way of proof. Our problem is that she and the County Manager expect us to *solve* this thing. Given my circumstances, I have no way of doing it. When it comes to modern pharmacology, I'm a bit out of my depth. And it's precarious just existing in this office with all this political intrigue. Some of the commissioners are conducting a campaign to have me removed. They can't forgive me for telling the truth about the blood cocaine level in the floozie in the Gettis case."

The Commissioner-Gettis affair had been big-city politics at its worst. It had ended when Gettis fled to an undisclosed Latin American country.

"A couple of the commissioners are still treating that pistol-packing cowboy like a *cause celebre!*" Dr. Westley said, alluding to an earlier incident where Gettis brandished a pistol in the faces of security guards at the High Point Condominium. It had something to do with valet parking.

The Old Man talked about recent efforts to sack him. He lamented the low quality of Miami political life, with politicians carrying on like irresponsible louts but expecting public servants to oblige their every whim. He intimated that his impeccable reputation was somehow catching up with him.

"People think that we can do anything, including raising bloody Lazarus from the dead!" Maybe he just needed a sympathetic listener, but he was speaking and gesturing with more candor than I'd never seen in him.

"You see, Ben, I told the County Manager that we can't simply confiscate the contents of every one of those twelve professors' freezers and subpoena their notebooks. Yet we can't let the murderer get away with it. A healthy forty-eight-year-old man doesn't simply drop dead. But with this collection of suspects, a meaningful investigation has to be every bit as clever as the crime itself. We can't send in a mob of police detectives to trample about."

"Yes, Dr. Westley, I understand. You need a short list of molecules which were available to those professors."

"Quite. But even then we might have enormous problems with detection and analysis."

Dr. Westley dropped back in his chair and began massaging his flabby biceps through his blue blazer, while staring silently at the floor. He looked up for a second as if beseeching me, and then dropped his gaze to his plate. We were halfway through the main course.

"I must weather this one as I have survived such storms before. It is simply that – in our own medical community – this infernal backbiting – and the fact that they can criticize me silently, leaving me no means of defending myself. Oh, damn this city, anyway!"

Why was he telling me all this?

After a long silence, he began reiterating his difficulties, counterbalancing them by subtle jabs at me, emphasizing my lack of career plans. He described the severity of the English university system in which he had studied, lamenting that excellence is not appreciated anymore. The Canadian Consul stopped by our table for a minute and Dr. Westley half-introduced me.

With dessert and coffee, Dr. Westley's behavior became downright odd. Forgetting his English manners, he paddled his coffee with his swizzle stick. Then he put it down, staining the white table cloth. He wrung his hands and avoided my eyes. His voice, usually so controlled, took on an almost whiney tone. He told of grave budgetary problems in the department, that the county bureaucracy was giving him trouble and that Dr. Steve Burk was not my greatest supporter. Painfully and inarticulately, he told me that, with a non-engineering bachelor's degree, I was "betwixt and between" and that I was demonstrably ill-suited for positions requiring "supervisory skills."

"You know . . . these job descriptions . . . personnel reports . . . bloody bureaucracy . . ." His voice trailed off. He twisted the table cloth. "And you don't even bother to dress for the part!"

Involuntarily, my toes curled up inside my tennis shoes. Dr. Westley was silent for a few seconds as if deciding whether to take back these words. He looked me in the eye for a split-second.

"Ben, you should not fritter away your life as a laboratory technician. You should receive further education and advance yourself. It is often a good turn for a lad who's come of age, to throw him out of the house." He said this emphatically, but then practically buried his face in his empty dessert plate. I felt as sorry for him as for myself.

He rattled on about my being "ideally situated" to solve this "unprecedented intellectual problem" which might appeal to my "Mensa interests." Hovering on the brink of his proposition, Dr. Westley wrung his hands so hard I thought he would pop the veins in his blue-cheese skin.

"More coffee, sir?" asked the waiter.

"No, George," he said as if shaken from a trance. "Not tonight. We will be retiring shortly. Sherry on the balcony with Mrs. Westley . . . " His voice trailed off.

As the waiter walked away, I took two deep breaths and said, "Dr. Westley, I'm intrigued. What do you propose?"

"What I propose is that you become a graduate student in pharmacology at the Bryan Medical School. I propose that my department continue to engage you, but as an independent contractor to keep our instruments in good repair, at half your current salary. I suggest that *while* you are pursuing your Ph.D. degree, you may turn up information which might be useful to the present case." He searched me with pleading eyes.

"I will need to think about it."

"Why, most certainly. A doctorate in pharmacology that will carry more weight in this world than membership in that oddball society of yours. Mensa, is that what they call it?" he asked, chidingly.

I grimaced. He'd known for six years what to call it and he didn't need to insult my friends to make his point.

"Toxicology is very closely related to pharmacology," he said in persuasive tones. "After receiving your degree, we could bring you back in a permanent position. Look here," he said, pulling a fountain pen from the inner breast pocket of his jacket and scribbling on a cocktail napkin. "The University gives a $12,500 fellowship to the pharmacology graduate students. Add the $12,500 that you will bill us for your time as an independent contractor, working a few hours a week on our instruments, getting the cobwebs out of the organ pipes, so to speak. You would have your current salary. I will keep your bread buttered during the four years that you will need for your Ph.D."

"How do you know they'll take me?"

A sly smile crossed the Old Man's face as he shook his head and said, "Oh, they'll take you, they will. My sources say they're taking students from all quarters of the compass, even from remote corners of the world."

"It sounds very interesting."

"Oh, I am *so* glad that you will consider it," he said warmly. "Now, may I invite you up to our apartment? I would like you to meet Margaret."

For six years he'd kept me at arm's length. Now he was firing me for my own good and bringing me upstairs to socialize with his wife, whom I'd never met. Of course, I couldn't refuse. "Margaret has more than her share of the infirmity of age, but she would so much like to meet you."

He continued with this line of gab all the way up to the apartment. The metallic-sounding music in the elevator added a surrealistic touch. We walked down a hallway papered with an indestructible sharkskin plastic material of hypnotic design, past several painted sheet metal doors of his condo neighbors until we reached Dr. Westley's. His was made of oak and displayed a large, engraved brass knocker. He opened the door to reveal an interior suggestive of an English country house, with a long mahogany dining table and matching high-backed chairs, and a tall wood-and-glass china cabinet to the side, displaying tastefully designed, old and expensive porcelain. It also held glasses for wine, champagne, brandy, cocktails, and plain water, all of the most elegantly-shaped and refractive crystal.

I was greeted properly but warmly by a frail Mrs. Westley, gray-haired, wrinkled, short and bent over with a pronounced "dowager's hump." She smiled up at me, expressing a curious mixture of friendliness and vulnerability as she offered her hand and said a few words of greeting. I tried to say the right things but was distracted by the frailness of her hand and the deep folds on her pale face. She was very English, the sort of upper-middle-class lady whom you would see in an Alfred Hitchcock movie. Her voice and its inflection fit the part. She spoke with a high-pitched warble. Half of the quaver seemed intentional and the other half must have come from the ravages of age. I had never been to England, and I was surprised to learn that such people really do exist.

"Wessie tells me that you are one of his brightest lads . . . a genius with the gadgets that he uses to solve heinous crimes, murders foul in the night!"

With the words "genius" and "gadgets," her pitch rose half an octave. At the word "murders," her voice dropped deep, with dramatic conspiratorial effect. It would take me a long time to get used to her conversational cadence, with choice of emphasized words seemingly determined by momentary whim. Her sentence endings were determined as much by the need to breathe as by logic.

Fascinated by her language, I almost forgot to reply. "I try to give him my best, Mrs. Westley."

She pressed on, saying, "When I *imagine* how complicated and technical life has become, with *machines* to find out why you died, machines to *keep* you alive, machines to peek *into* you, it boggles the mind. But I *do* try to keep up with these things. We had a wonderful presentation by a most *clever* young scientist at the Ladies Auxiliary of the Bryan Medical School! You know, old faculty wives and wives of rich benefactors and that sort of thing. Last *Tuesday,* I believe. He was a most clever young man. He actually *nudges* along the divine act of conception in *test tubes*! Japanese or Chinese. Ikemoto, I think was his name."

Turning to Dr. Westley, she asked, "Darling, have you heard of him?"

"I am afraid not," replied Westley, slightly bemused.

How did it serve Dr. Westley's purpose to engage me in such outdated and useless conversation?

Margaret thought for a minute and then fluttered on. "Yes I believe he was Chinese. Yes, Ikemoto. It is very fascinating and I should say strangely wonderful – what they can do in their Petri dishes and with their lasers. They are working on ways to tell by just looking at the seed whether they would be girls or boys. And how they can literally blast away the ones deemed unsuitable. To think, that one might be able to order a boy or a girl."

"Very Huxleyan" interjected the Old Man.

"But I shouldn't very much want to order up a child from a Chinese or Japanese as some people order up a motor car," she said, glancing at the Old Man, who sadly shook his head. "Life can be very disappointing without having to suffer with all those Petri dishes and lasers."

She sighed, lost in thought. The Old Man wrung his hands, as if hopeless to make up for some past disappointment. Margaret continued:

"Happily, I shan't live to see the day. But I will continue to see their little 'fiber lens' television pictures of my creaky old joints. And I will continue to devour their pills to my dying day, which may not be too far away."

I muttered something. Margaret ended up telling me that she hoped that the future belongs to nice young men like me, and that she did not know what the world was coming to, with the teeming masses springing up like weeds among the roses. Good manners were being lost, even in the Royal Family.

The Old Man changed the subject by showing me, with a certain measure of pride, the rest of the apartment. The furniture, overstuffed chairs, end tables, reading tables and lamps defined the apartment as a little piece of England. All that was missing was a fireplace. The walls held paintings of English countryside reminiscent of Carpenter. The Old Man narrated and interpreted:

"Penrith, Lake District, you know; Yorkshire moorland in autumn, fogs as messy as the bogs, they say; Clipper ships under sail; Thames Estuary." Walking into his study he said, "And here is where I hold forth."

On the wall behind his mahogany desk were his diplomas and certificates of completion of Public School. ("Of course, not to be confused with the truly public schools in this country.") Next to it hung a framed portrait photograph of Queen Elizabeth the Second on the occasion of her coronation. The other side of his study was dedicated to a collection of Egyptian artifacts and framed antique photographs of what appeared to be a British Museum expedition.

Under an oversized black-and-white photograph of the Sphinx, was a most unusual chair of ancient design but modern construction, painted in a hideous red-and-orange pattern. The back was straight and tall. The non-upholstered seat and arm rests were uncomfortably high. A pair of 10-inch jackal heads rose from the forward-most portion of the armrests where you would put your hands. Granted, the Pharaohs used to sit in those things. But 15 minutes in Dr. Westley's chair would be enough to drive me nuts. Dr. Westley was standing nearby, vocalizing sub-audibly.

Of course, coroners are attracted to the occult, so I decided to humor him. "Dr. Westley, I knew you were interested in Egyptology. It seems that you have also been to Egypt."

"Yes, on more than one occasion. As you perhaps do not know, Egypt was the site of one of my more interesting autopsies, performed at the behest of the Egyptian department of antiquities. A question of possible skullduggery four millennia ago. It proved closer to skull surgery, although one can only speculate as to their motives. Clear, straight cuts on the roof of the skull, lines true as the base of the Great Pyramid.

Done with the help of opium, as we can suspect from their hieroglyphs and from the morphology of seeds found elsewhere. Of course, we didn't have chromatographic analysis back then, so there was no chance of any chemical detection even if the opium molecules had survived the mummification and four thousand years of oxidation."

"That sounds like it should have been in the *National Geographic* magazine."

"It didn't appear there, but it did appear in *Endeavour*. Yes, we acquitted ourselves well. We turned over the medical evidence to the higher court of archeologists and anthropologists who can decide these things. It was all good fun! The Egyptian chaps were most appreciative of my help with the case," he said gesturing to a photo of a much more youthful version of himself in khaki, in a rather slumping pose next to Gamal Abdel Nassar. He ushered me out to the balcony.

"I should have submitted it to the *Guinness Book of World Records*, I suspect. Which brings us to the modern equivalent: the demise of Dr. Cooper. These days we have the use of liquid nitrogen freezers, which gives us the advantage of stasis. So we have time, but do we have enough material? And, of course, you will help me by showing us *what* to look for."

How could I say "no" to such a polished Englishman, after he offered me the chance to perform noble service?

We sat in comfortable chairs on Dr. Westley's balcony on the 43rd floor of the building, facing out toward Biscayne Bay. He spoke about his old cases, about education and about his role as a mentor. The breeze was comfortably warm and gentle. Margaret pushed out a wooden trolley with glasses and bottles of wines and liqueurs. The wheels squeaked, reminding me of her arthritic joints. The glasses tinkled like the test tubes on my shaker several hours earlier. Three glasses of sherry were poured and some cordial words were said. Then Margaret returned to the kitchen, leaving me alone with Dr. Westley.

From the marina below, halyards were gently beating against the masts of the docked sailboats, sounding like alpine cows at pasture. Lights flickered from Key Biscayne, three miles across the bay. Although the Old Boy made me feel welcome, my thoughts turned to getting home to the *Diogenes*. After a quarter of an hour, I thanked Dr. and Mrs. Westley and told them I must go.

"I'll think it over very carefully and talk to you about it tomorrow," I promised him.

He plodded to his desk and produced a glossy brochure titled *Graduate Study in Pharmacology at Bryan Medical School.*

"Take this home with you tonight and look it over. You do have electric lights on that vessel, don't you? Tomorrow morning, first thing, you can come to my office and tell me what you make of it."

"And we would so very much like to have you for dinner in the near future," Margaret added.

- III -

The Road Not Taken

IT WAS ONLY A FOUR-MINUTE RIDE south along Bayshore Drive
to my doorstep, the Dinner Key Marina, where I did the usual:
I locked up my bike, unlocked my little dinghy and rowed
out past the spoil islands to the "Price is Right Anchorage,"
where the *Diogenes* was faithfully riding on anchor. The *Diogenes*
is the Choi Lee ketch I rescued five years ago. At $10,500 for 38
feet, my seagoing apartment compares favorably with a studio
condominium apartment. The maintenance costs are lower.

And the pool is bigger. Half an hour of swimming the
Australian crawl around the boat does wonders for the circu-
lation and appetite. My neighbors are a mixed bag, but so are
Westley's. The 20 minutes of rowing out is a bit inconvenient,
especially in stormy weather, but I don't have to wait at a
gatehouse or in elevators.

The breeze off the bay was comfortable and mosquito-
free. I deactivated the alarm, opened the cabin, tossed some
cushions into the open cockpit to the stern, plugged in my
reading light and settled down to browse the glossy brochure
Dr. Westley had given me.

The front cover proclaimed its purpose in bold letters
and pastel colors, reminiscent of a once popular Miami television cop show. The background was a colorful Miami sunset with palms. The second page displayed a large photograph
of the deceased Dr. Cooper: Big head, rather gross features
and a businesslike but not unattractive smile. The photo inspired neither great sympathy nor antipathy.

Under Dr. Cooper's photo they made their pitch: "Pharmacology is a crossroads discipline forming a junction between biochemistry, physiology, chemistry and molecular biology." It described how pharmacologists (not to be confused with pharmacists) study drug interactions with living cells and tissues. It described career patterns in universities, government and industry.

The following 13 pages described the faculty and their research interests. Each page displayed an action photo of a prof, a description of his or her educational background, research specialization and citations of two publications. They used state-of-the-art techniques to study drugs, proteins, nerves, heart, muscle and blood. Their ages ranged from about 30 to around 60.

I recognized the name of one of them: Donald Fleischman. Yes, he was *the* Donald Fleischman who discovered the sodium-potassium ion pump in nerve membranes. Back in biology at Swarthmore they had assigned us a *Scientific American* article written by him.

As the sky darkened, the brochure under the small focussed light became the center of my universe. I flipped pages, thinking about the prospect of graduate study. How would I feel about taking up Westley's proposition and going back to school? My watch said ten o'clock. I switched off the light and waited a few seconds for my eyes to dark-adapt. The gentle offshore breeze pointed the stern of the boat toward shore. High tide had been at seven o'clock. A one-half knot, outgoing tide was gently struggling against a 10-knot incoming breeze, causing the boat to drift from side to side, shifting about 90 degrees like a pendulum with two-minute swings.

How many nights had I spent gazing out over the stern, sailing on anchor, just as now? At the northern extreme of the swing was Westley's *Faire Isle* condominium complex. On the southern extreme of the swing, glowed the halo of the tourist drag in the "Coconut Grove Business District." Between the two extremes rose a peculiar office building with 20 stories of receding terraces, planted with shrubs and trees. It looked like the ruin of a Mayan temple.

Between the Australian pine-inhabited spoil islands, I had a broken view of the cavernous Pan Am seaplane hangers, used now by the Merrill Stevens boat-repair facility. Next door was the two-story art deco terminal building for the old amphibious Pan Am "Havana Clipper." The terminal now serves as the Miami City Hall. Yes, in this location I had it all: high rise luxury, hip counterculture, tourist center and remnants of a bygone era — Eddie Rickenbacker, Howard Hughes. It brought to mind that corny old song, "I've flown around the world in a plane . . . but I can't get started with you."

That's what the Old Man had been trying to tell me: I couldn't get started with my life. I could charm a gas-chromatograph/mass spectrometer like Bill Haast could charm his king cobra. But I had no real career. Maybe Good Doctor Westley had secretly diagnosed my malady: the soul of a teenager, in the mind of a cynical 40-year old, in the body of a 28-year-old man. Maybe the glossy brochure was the Good Doctor's prescription for getting my life organized.

Solving a murder in my spare time wasn't so bad. My Mensa friends were always bragging about their far-out hobbies. But what would happen to my plans to sail around the world? I was putting that off until I found the perfect girl. And why hadn't I found my longed-for perfect girl? Well, the *Diogenes* and I had certainly hosted enough girls over the years — artsy girls from Coconut Grove, intellectual girls from Mensa and some nice ones from Little Havana, too. I'd even dated a fashion model from South Miami Beach, renting a car for a couple of months to keep up with her. I often rented wheels when things got hot and heavy. But the bottom line was always zero. Years of searching and trying, yet never once a spiritually viable relationship that could endure. Maybe I should have been looking in graduate school.

Wavelets lapped against the *Diogenes* and the music from the rock cafes became louder with each port-side swing of my vessel. Earning a Ph.D. couldn't be any harder than restoring this boat that I bought as a sinking 38-foot hulk. I'd rescued it, stopping leaks, pumping two feet of water from the bilge, and washing off 40 pounds of pelican droppings. And I rehabilitated it, patching broken fiberglass, replacing cables and fittings, resetting the two masts, and rebuilding the diesel engine. And I restored its original beauty, lovingly scraping away layers of rot from the teak deck planking and repainting the fiberglass hull. And I rechristened it the *Diogenes*.

If I could restore this boat, I could earn a Ph.D. In fact, that was probably Dr. Westley's half-spoken message in his sarcastic mention of "that vessel" and "that oddball society." I couldn't have impressed him with my Miami history and photography project, even if I had put it together as a book. He would classify it as adolescent escapism, like my wearing jeans and commuting on bicycle.

"Double or nothing." That was Dr. Westley's rude challenge. Get a Ph.D. and pull yourself to the level of Dr. Burk or slide to a level below Mr. Jake Brown. Stand up and be a man. Brilliant analysis, Dr. Westley. Thanks for the "tough love."

I hadn't actually thought of the M.E. job being permanent when I first hired on. And during my senior year at Swarthmore, I'd been thinking about graduate school. I had even taken the Graduate Record Examination. Had I fallen into a spiritual stupor during these six years?

I went below, lay down in my berth, and clicked on the mini-fan. The wavelets rocked me to that state of dreamy sleep where I received answers to my questions.

– IV –

Application

*W*AKING A HALF AN HOUR BEFORE dawn, I found my anchorage quiet and peaceful. I could make out the purposeful roar of cars and trucks on U.S. 1, a mile behind Coconut Grove. Feeling clarity of purpose that had been absent for years, I knew my decision was made. Over a bowl of cereal wetted with condensed milk, a hard-boiled egg and a cup of coffee, I studied the brochure with growing enthusiasm.

The Old Man seemed to know my decision before I crossed his threshold.

"I'm ever so pleased that you have decided to have a go at it! Of course, our conversation of last night really didn't take place . . . just rest assured that I'll keep up my end of the bargain. Yes, I am so pleased! And I do think that it will benefit your professional advancement. Of course, the first thing to do is to *apply* to the department. Consider yourself excused today so that you can get busy with it."

"So I start working on the application this morning?"

"Yes, with all due speed. Once accepted in Pharmacology, you can tender your resignation to me, and we can proceed as discussed. You would need to be available here three evenings per week for your 'independent contractor' duties."

"What if they don't have a slot for me in September?"

"Well, you could perhaps suggest starting with a single course. Getting the camel's nose under the tent, so to speak."

"Sounds fine."

"Yes, swimmy! One final thing. We shall have no more

communication on these matters in my office – deniability and that sort of thing. Nothing should appear irregular. But Margaret and I would be most delighted to have you for dinner as soon as you learn where you stand with those folks."

Yes, Bryan Medical School was a "scant 300 yards" from our facility. It occupies a wide and long nine-story building, painted in the same battleship gray as all the other buildings of the Dade County General Hospital complex. The portal to my future was a pair of glass doors obscured by the same corrugated sheet metal canopy system which covers all of Dade General's walkways.

I opened the door and stumbled onto a guard station where I was asked to show my badge. My Medical Examiner's badge didn't do the trick. It just made the guard a little suspicious. The Medical School belongs to a private university and is not connected to Dade County General Hospital or the M.E. Office. The guard called ahead to the Graduate Office and then gave me directions. It was a small office, staffed by a single worker.

Half an hour later, I was back at the M.E. facility working on my application packet for Pharmacology. By two o'clock I had completed it and confided my aspirations to Doris. She insisted on seeing the application package and suggested some modifications which made it look more professional. She was able to drag up a copy of my Swarthmore transcript, going back to my original application to the M.E. Office.

With two copies in hand, I went over to the Medical School. I gave the originals to the woman at the Graduate Office and was given directions to the Pharmacology Office on the fifth floor to deliver the copy.

I quickly did my homework, reading the page of the brochure which described Dr. Gordon Taylor, the head of the graduate program. His picture showed the sternest, most unforgiving face of the whole bunch. He had received his Ph.D. from the University of Cambridge in 1965. His research topic was the "electrophysiology of squid axon," which meant that he stuck electrodes in squid nerves to study their signalling.

I knew that the squid axon was a "good model" for the nerves in the brain. Taylor's two cited publications had to do with "noise analysis of the sodium channel at low temperature."

On the fifth floor, I found a cluster of Pharmacology mailboxes and searched for Taylor's name. Someone was waiting behind me. I quickly put the letter in Taylor's box and stepped to the side. With one spritely step and a long reach, the person pulled out my letter. It was Taylor himself. His eyes, blue-gray and penetrating, were as stern as in the brochure, but in real life he looked slightly comical. Maybe it was his rumpled shirt or his dark brown hair, so thick and unruly on the bottom but thin and wispy on the top.

Half embarrassed, attempting to break the ice, I said, "Now there isn't any question that you've gotten my letter."

"No. Now the only question is as to its contents," he said, stroking his well-trimmed beard in mock contemplation. "Let me think: It's too early to complain about my annual lectures on nerve conduction being too hard. The Medical Sophomore Course hasn't started yet."

With this, he broke into a boisterous laugh and a sympathetic smile. He spoke with an unmistakable English accent, undiminished by some 25 years in Miami. Although his enunciation was like Westley's, his delivery was quite different. Westley's words resonated softly in his upper nasal passages; Taylor's words resonated loudly in his chest.

"No, I'm not a medical student. The envelope contains my application for admission to your Ph.D. program," I said nervously.

"Just one week before the start of the semester! Well, just in time for the new campaign. We are always looking for cannon fodder!"

He sounded like a British sergeant major mustering a squad in Sudan. Almost every sentence was punctuated by boisterous laughter.

"I know that the timing is tight," I replied. "If you have to delay consideration of my application until January – "

"By no means! Step with me into my recruiting office.

Let's place your pint of ale before you and get you to touch
the King's Shilling!"

While tearing open the envelope and skimming its contents, he ushered me down the hall, all the while keeping up a
curious line of stentorian chitchat. He led me into a laboratory, better described as an attic filled with scientific paraphernalia – hand-assembled electronic consoles, connected by
tangles of wire to 1950s vintage oscilloscopes, microscopes sitting on tables, with small glass Petri dishes and bundles of needle-
thin glass pipettes, all enclosed in large screen-wire cages.

Dr. Taylor's office could have once been an oversized
mop closet. His desk fit snugly against three walls. Over it
hung several wooden shelves, bolted into the wall and sag-
ging from the weight of hundreds of pounds of books. What
floor space remained was sacrificed to two file cabinets on
which tottered a three-foot stack of *Nature* magazines.

Taylor entered the office first and sat down with his chair
facing outward and his back to his desk. He indicated that I
should take his "guest chair," a lab stool with wheels. With
me sitting in the middle of the narrow doorway, there was
just enough room for the two of us to converse at a less-than-
comfortable distance. The stack of *Natures* towering over me
might have required no more provocation than one more
boisterous laugh to bury me in an avalanche.

"Well Mr. Candidi, your application's quite interesting,"
he said, flipping through the papers. "Some lab experience, I
see. Oh, yes, here's the transcript. Swarthmore. Fine college.
Chemistry and physics. Finished in 1986. Been out for a while.
Late bloomer, are you? Good grades, though. Awards, honor
societies and a senior thesis? We'll need an original transcript,
of course."

"It has been ordered."

"What's this? A post office box as an address?"

"It's the most reliable way to get my mail," I equivocated.

"And I see you had quite a bit of chemistry. Good grades
there too. But no Graduate Record Exam score. What a shame."

"I took the test right after graduating and did well on it.

I have ordered the results to be forwarded to you."

"Yes, yes. Instrumental analysis, application of chemical principles to life science. Excellent. And your essay: 'Science is a most interesting and useful human pursuit'; you work on 'ultrasensitive methods of quantitative analysis of organic chemicals.' And you read journals such as *Science* and *Nature.* Did you, by chance, see in the latest *Nature* – that exciting article on prions?"

"No, but I read about them a couple of years ago in the *Scientific American.* I subscribe to it."

"Hobbies of sailing, photography and literature? German and Spanish as foreign languages? *Sprechen Sie Deutsch?*"

"*Jawohl.*" (I barely spoke it.)

"And Spanish just as well, no doubt."

"*Es mejor,*" I said. I hadn't written that I was fluent in Cuban Spanish. I also omitted any mention of my membership in the Mensa Society.

"Well, fine. And you write that you 'wish to become an academic research scientist or an industrial scientist engaged in drug discovery and development.' Now I need to ask a few questions. Are you applying to medical school? Do you harbor any secret desire to become a physician?" His blue-gray eyes scanned me carefully, waiting for an answer.

"No. I am more interested in studying things in depth. I'm going for the Ph.D., not the M.D." This pleased him.

He lectured me that getting a Ph.D. is a long arduous process requiring high-level thinking.

"I think I can do it. I have good quantitative and deductive skills. I can express myself pretty well. I have a broad range of interests . . ."

"Yes, I see," he said flipping back to my transcript. "You also received an 'A' in philosophy. Say, tell me, Mr. *Candidi,* what philosophy did they teach you in that course? That it is the Best of All Possible Worlds!" His laugh rattled the file cabinets.

A flash of inspiration furnished a reply. "Yes, that's exactly what they did teach. The prof's name was *Dr. Pangloss.*" Dr. Taylor smiled at my snide answer, so I upped the ante.

"At this point could I ask *you* how well am I standing up to the *Grand Inquisitor of Lisbon?*"

This brought out another booming laugh. His chest heaved, and he literally bounced in his chair. The stack of *Nature* magazines didn't fall. It was my lucky day.

"Mr. Candidi! You are the right fellow who has come at the right time."

He sent me to interviews with two colleagues.

I quickly consulted the brochure before walking into the lab of Dr. Robert Sturtz. He earned his Ph.D. in 1987 from Rensselaer in Upstate New York, had been a post-doctoral fellow at Cal Tech. He was studying how growth factors turn on the genes in "fibroblast" cells to make them multiply. So he should know what makes skin grow back over a wound.

Dr. Sturtz had a narrow head, short curly black hair and seemed to be in his thirties. Standing next to his technician in front of a bank of compact fluorescent lights, he held what looked like an X-ray negative with a dozen oversized bar codes – the type that the laser scanner reads at the supermarket – but larger and longer. A bumper sticker on the door asked, "HAVE YOU READ ANY GOOD DNA LATELY? Eta Chemical Company." I guessed that was exactly what Sturtz was doing – reading DNA.

He handed the film back to the technician and said, "These sixty-six bases are fine. Add them to the sequence and then analyze the next stretch."

He greeted me with a self-satisfied smile, and we went into his office. While heavy-metal rock music wafted in from the adjoining lab, Sturtz read my application. He intimated that I didn't have enough biology to study pharmacology.

Dr. Robert Gunnison from Stanford Medical School (Ph.D., 1988) and U.C. Berkeley (post-doctoral) wasn't any friendlier. I figured he was also in his thirties, but his narrow, gaunt face could have belonged to a 50-year old. Science can do that to you. While he read my application, I read his blackboard:

Androgen –> Nucleus –> Receptor –> mRNA –> Protein –> ???

Across from his desk was a poster of a long-haired girl in a bikini, riding a sailboard, with everything blowing and bouncing in two-foot waves. It was captioned: "CALIFORNIA GIRL, Catalina Sailboards, San Diego, CA."

Gunnison's lab uniform was a Hawaiian shirt over an old pair of faded blue jeans with sandals. He subjected me to some stiffly-phrased questions about my education and listened impatiently, stroking his closely-cut blond beard as I answered. Luckily, his phone rang, putting an end to the interview.

I handed back my application to Dr. Taylor. He had been staring at a computer screen, manipulating a joy stick like he was playing a video game. A single line traced across the screen, drawing rock formations like in a *Roadrunner* cartoon.

"Each one of these blips is the electric current going through a *single* sodium channel in a nerve membrane," he said in a much softer and more natural voice.

I had enough dilettante knowledge to understand in a general way. Dr. Taylor could actually "see" the activity of a single molecule. He explained the workings of his "micro-electrodes" and sensitive amplifiers, and how he digitally-recorded the data on "miles and miles" of tape when squid were in season up in Woods Hole, Massachusetts. "You see, there is limited time and a limited number of squid. So you run day and night to stock up on data. Rather like a cow hastily devours grass in the meadow and chews her cud elsewhere." The stentorian voice had returned. "You might say that I come back here to *ruminate*." The boisterous laugh returned in full strength.

My physics background proved strong enough for me to play the interested student to his lecture on "open state probability," "noise analysis" and "ensemble averaged behavior." He warmed up to me. Slowly, the conversation returned to my application. I was in luck, they were having a faculty meeting next Monday. They would probably render a positive decision at that time, pending transcripts and GRE score.

The next day was a Friday. The M.E. lab was still doing a lot of extra work on what I guessed was Cooper's blood

samples, but Burk told me to stay away from it. I spent the
dead time browsing the pharmacology brochure. Based on
their scientific research, the deadliest prof was George Ashton,
M.D., an aristocratic-looking full professor who was specialized in neurotoxins.

Doris always read the *Miami Standard* on her coffee
breaks. When I went to ask if she had copies from the last
several days, she was making a long-distance call. I waited
around and overheard an interesting conversation. She was
calling the Institute for Scientific Information in Philadelphia,
ordering for Dr. Westley all the scientific publications of Dr.
George Ashton. No, she didn't want to order publications from
any other authors.

Doris had the right newspapers. In a three-inch column
under "Death Notices," I learned that Charles David Cooper, Ph.D., had tragically and unexpectedly passed away, being survived "by his wife, Dr. Jane Goddard Cooper and two
sons, Charles D. Cooper, Jr. (22), and James L. Cooper (19)."
The Notice stated that he was a prominent molecular biochemist, Chairman of the Department of Pharmacology at the Bryan
Medical School and that he had made major contributions to
the understanding of heart disease. He was a member of many
community organizations and was a vestryman at St. James
Episcopal Church. His funeral was to be held there and his
ashes were to be "scattered at sea." Instead of flowers, his
friends were asked to make a contribution to the Florida Af-
filiate of the American Heart Association, in his name. I hoped
that the Old Man had gotten some good blood and tissue
samples before the cremation.

My Friday evenings are usually devoted to bar hopping
in Coconut Grove, but this time my heart wasn't in it. No use
searching for girls in the bar scene when graduate study promised to introduce me to girl scientists. And I might as well get
a head start on the investigation.

Early the next morning I was dodging cars and the dangling air roots of the enormous ficus trees along the narrow
and historic Main Highway in Coconut Grove. Then I ped-

aled north through tropically overgrown "South Grove," crossed a dirty carbon monoxide canyon called U.S. 1, and took in the well-manicured lawns and expensive Mediterranean-style houses of stately Coral Gables.

The Coral Gables Library is a historic building of quarried coral. I locked my bike by the fountain and entered through the massive wooden doors. Microfilms of the *Miami Standard* yielded what I was looking for: a Sunday supplement story describing how an upstate coroner may have killed his wife with an injection of potassium chloride. I checked a physiology book and was pleased to learn that high concentrations of potassium in the blood mess up the electrical impulses that make the heart contract.

It wasn't a particularly clever murder because the potassium had to be injected. If you take it by mouth it upsets your stomach and you throw up. So the unimaginative upstate coroner injected his wife, leaving a needle mark which was detected.

A back issue of *Time* magazine yielded a slightly more clever example of murder by a physician. This guy injected his wife with the drug called "succinylcholine." The physiology book told me that the compound works like acetylcholine, opening up the sodium channels, but overstimulating them so they eventually shut down. At low doses it relaxes your throat so the anesthesiologist can insert the breathing tube. At high doses, it relaxes your diaphragm muscles and you can't breathe at all. The wife died of asphyxiation.

But the coroner noted the needle marks and became suspicious upon learning that the doctor was an anesthesiologist. Hell, I knew enough biology to study pharmacology! As a further exercise, I looked up "ricin," the poison that the Bulgarians put in the BB to kill the BBC journalist. I learned that it is an "enzymatic peptide" that cuts in half the "ribosome" inside the cell. And, of course, it had to be injected to be lethal.

Did all protein toxins have to be injected? I vaguely remembered a *Scientific American* article on "proteins as drugs" and found it on the shelf. The article said it was virtually impossible to deliver proteins orally. The protein would have to be modified so that it could cross the intestinal lining which was there for the express purpose of keeping foreign proteins from getting into the blood stream. So the Old Man was right. The article said that there was a tremendous need for an oral delivery form for insulin, because most diabetics hate to inject themselves.

So I should concentrate on nonprotein molecules which do not get digested. I got real excited about the project – too excited for my own good, actually.

– V –

Acceptance

OH, HOW THE TIME DRAGS WHEN your life is on hold. I spent four depressing days hanging around the Medical Examiner's lab waiting for Dr. Taylor's call. It finally came late Thursday afternoon. In formal tones he told me I was accepted and would be awarded a fellowship of $12,500 per year. The program required each new student to conduct 30-minute get-acquainted interviews with all the profs. I should arrange these myself. The first official event would be a get-together luncheon, coming Tuesday. I told Doris the good news and asked to see the Old Man. He was pleased and not the least bit surprised. When I started to sit down and discuss strategy, he made a sour face and said I was invited to dinner for that purpose, that evening. Burk wasn't surprised either when I handed him my letter of resignation.

When I told Carmen, her eyes moistened.

"But, Carmen, it's not like I'm going to another city. I'll be stopping in here every once in a while."

"You had better, *viejo amigo!*" she said.

I told her I'd be doing occasional maintenance on the instruments.

Suddenly, Jacob Brown became very interested in trouble shooting. I acted like I had no time for him, until he said "pretty please." Giving him a crash course tied me up until five o'clock. Then I began clearing my personal stuff out of the lab, stuffing it into a backpack. By a quarter to seven, I was riding to Dr. Westley's, compiling a mental checklist of

everything we needed to talk about. What should I tell him
about Drs. Taylor, Sturtz and Gunnison? Which two or three
profs should I concentrate on? With proper guidance from
Dr. Westley, I could do a good job for him and probably start
delivering answers in a couple of weeks.

At the guardhouse at *Faire Isle*, I repeated the scene with
the luxury automobiles. This time, the guard was a Haitian
who announced with an authentic-sounding "*Oui, Monsieur*"
that I was among The Expected. Like his Jamaican counter-
part, he commented that bicycles were an oddity in these parts.

As I tramped past the reception desk with my backpack,
I was detained by a good-looking American brunette who politely but firmly asked me to state my business, which she
then verified, telephonically, with Dr. Westley. I had no trouble
finding Westley's oaken door on the 43rd floor. He opened it on
my second stroke of the brass knocker and graciously ushered
me into his English country house some 400 feet over Miami.

"Ben, I am so pleased to have you visiting us. I chanced
to see you riding up on your bicycle. I hope it was not too
exhausting. In the summer, Miami is so dreary, with its heat
and humidity. You can put that backpack by the door, and
you shouldn't be wanting the jacket until dinner, so let me
take it. I thought we might sip a good sherry while Margaret
is putting the finishing touches on the evening's repast."

He produced a bottle and two glasses. He poured the
sherry with a certain understated flourish, handed me a glass,
toasted me with a subtle movement of his glass and said,
"Cheers. I do hope that you share my little weakness for eccle-
siastical music. It goes back to my childhood, so to speak."

In the corner were piles of records in dusty-looking al-
bums. The jackets showed cathedral spires and organ consoles. He carefully took out a record from its jacket and placed
it lovingly on the turntable of an ancient phonograph housed
in a cabinet of polished mahogany. Deep within this fine piece
of English cabinetry the turntable began to spin and music
issued from the large fabric-covered speakers in a slowly-
developing crescendo. I could practically smell the dust burn-

ing as the vacuum tubes heated up to power that antique.

Dr. Westley provided slow-paced, absent-minded chatter, explaining in bits and pieces that he had once been a choirboy at Exeter – "The Cathedral." He still had a hobby interest in music ("but completely vicarious and sedentary, I am afraid"). I committed the *faux pas* of sipping my sherry too fast and responding too slowly to his conversational offerings. Why couldn't we get down to business?

Dr. Westley finally talked himself out. Our silence was filled by a sonorous boy's voice singing a solo passage in Latin. How irrelevant, listening to this stuff when we should be talking about the investigation.

"Dr. Westley, I'd like to talk about how we're going to solve the murder. There's so much to discuss, and . . . ."

"I quite understand. Perhaps you would permit me to refill your glass," he replied in an even voice, but with raised eyebrows. My glass was completely empty and his was still three-quarters full. As he slowly picked up the bottle and refilled my glass, it became apparent that I was being mildly rebuked.

"Dr. Westley, I just feel like the guy in Kafka's novel, *The Castle.* He couldn't get in to do his job."

"Perhaps Kafka's very point was to describe an exercise in patience."

"Or an exercise in futility?"

Dr. Westley slowly shook his head.

"You see," I plunged on, "there is so much that I need to know. Take the widow, Dr. Jane Cooper. You said that she suspects two or three profs. Which ones? She must have known everyone at Bryan. Knowing who she suspects would be very helpful to me."

"No, Ben, it wouldn't. It would bring absolute disaster to your efforts."

"Look, there are twelve professors in that department. I can't investigate them all. Which one is the suspect? I haven't thought of anything else since you made your proposition to me." I caught myself just in time. I had gulped down half of the newly-filled glass of sherry and was becoming forceful.

Westley sank deeply in his leather armchair. He stared va-
cantly at the floor a full minute, then slowly rose from the
chair. For a dreadful second I thought he was going to ask me
to leave. But he wandered to the corner of the room, opened
the mahogany lid and pulled out the record.

"You wouldn't mind bearing with me while we play the
other side, would you?" he softly chided. "As you Yanks are so
fond of saying, particularly your Southern variety, 'I hear you
talking.' I can sympathize with you, but I cannot agree with
you. It would simply not do for me to give you specific information on the personalities of this case. You must trust me to have
put the pharmacological problem into stasis, so to speak."

He signalled with one bushy eyebrow and contemplated
me in the diffuse gaze of his cloudy blue eyes. I put the damp-
ener on my emotions and set my brain in gear. So he was telling
me that he had put a big chunk of Dr. Cooper in the freezer
where all the chemicals and protein toxins would stay frozen
until we know what to look for. I nodded in understanding.

"And you might also give me credit for having taken
certain steps to put the wrongdoer at ease."

This must have been the obituary which implied that Dr.
Cooper's remains were being cremated.

"But I shall give you no specifics, Ben. Any information
which you receive, you will receive indirectly. As to why we
must carry on in this indirect, inefficient manner, I shall answer you by analogy."

He carefully closed the lid and once again the boy choir
filled the room.

"Ben, some fifty years ago I was honored to sing in the
choir at Exeter. We were all so motivated in our choirboyish
ways, wanting to please the director, who was quite a perfectionist. But there could be but one lead boy – the one with the
best voice." The Old Man's tone became so friendly, and a
relaxed smile came to his face, as if he were recalling fond
memories.

"The lead boy sang the part the most perfectly, enunci-
ating correctly, with all the right nuances, and with perfect

control of crescendos and diminuendos."

He blathered on about perfect pitch, holding memory of a note and making strong entrances in the correct pitch.

"Thus, the sound which issues from your mouth will be at once correct and beautiful. Ben, I sense you are becoming impatient," he concluded, in the tone of an offended schoolmaster.

"I'm sorry. It's just that I don't see what this has to do with solving the murder." I probably sounded like an offended schoolboy, myself.

"Ben, it has everything to do with the murder. Your first step should be to refrain from speaking the word 'murder.' It is a most wretched and ugly-sounding word. Let us return to the youthful Geoffrey Westley and his fellow choirboys. We were all, in our own ways, striving for the perfection of the perfect solo – like the solo that we hope you will sing for us, Ben."

This time it was I who raised an eyebrow. The Old Man nodded in acknowledgment.

"The choirmaster told us about a perfect boy soprano who had once sung for him. He described all his attributes, but left him unnamed. We listened ever so closely, because we wanted to become that boy."

Dr. Westley chortled on about how a perfect choirboy always listened carefully, perceived nuance and never made the same mistake twice. He said these lessons served him well throughout adult life. He talked about learning to sing harmony when your voice turned alto, and having to sing your part as written, even when it didn't make sense.

His message was that I didn't know the whole score. I wouldn't be "singing lead." I would "unwittingly" act as his eyes and ears in the Department of Pharmacology.

"You will see things which I would have no chance of seeing. You will obtain information in ways that the police cannot. Through polite and innocent conversation with me over a good English dinner, you will slowly reveal to me the realm of scientific possibility – the possible means by which one of those professors could have killed another, using the tools of his trade."

Hell, I could go along with his subterfuge. From over-
hearing Doris, I already knew that Dr. George Ashton was
the one to investigate. I could play the good choirboy, pick-
ing up nuances in the Department of Pharmacology and "unwittingly" passing on "innocent" information at dinner. Afterward, I could truthfully tell police, prosecutors and defense
attorneys that I had nothing to do with it. There would be no
grounds for throwing the case out of court on constitutional
technicalities.

The old ecclesiastic had a dandy circumlocution for the
constitutional problem. "If we have lived our respective parts
in practice, then we should be able to sing our respective parts
from the depths of our souls. One must make a righteous and
joyful noise unto the proper authorities. Do you understand?"

Well, it was a gray area since I would no longer be an
employee of the M.E.'s Office. I gave Westley my assurances,
adding that I'd already forgotten the conversation with him
and Burk.

"Good. That fits with my memory of it. You would have
made a good choirboy. Now that I have treated you to a 'farewell dinner' and have found I like you, I have taken a fatherly interest in you. Margaret also likes you. We lost our
only son at a very young age, and it broke both our hearts.
You are a sort of surrogate son to us. It has become habit to
invite you for dinner once a week."

I asked, "But what happens if I come home empty-handed:
A prodigal son." Dr. Westley smiled at my New Testament metaphor matching his Old Testament metaphor on "joyful noises."

"Well, we might not go as far as killing the fatted calf for
you, but I wouldn't disown you either. Possible failure? That's
the chance we have to take. We would at least have a better-
trained Ben Candidi, who would hopefully receive his Ph.D.
and return to my employ in a higher capacity. But I know
you to be an intellectually curious fellow, and I know that
you will, as they say in this country, 'give it your best shot'."

As he chuckled over this witticism, Margaret came in
from the kitchen.

"Margaret, have we killed the 'fatted calf' for our adopted son?"

"No veal tonight, Wessie. But I have just roasted a nice rump of beef, with potatoes, carrots and gravy."

"Well then, let us repair to the dining room and let the feast begin!"

Over a relaxed dinner, Margaret became less of an enigma to me. She grew up in a suburb of London as the daughter of a schoolteacher who eventually rose to the level of assistant principal. She married "Wessie" a few years after the war, and had "followed him through thick and thin." She said her first years in America were "rather like a Rudyard Kipling story."

"Our way of life is much different back in England, and I must say, please forgive me, more civilized – although Miami has certain organizations which help me to while away my time until I can return to England to further cultivate my arthritis."

This affliction did seem quite serious, and I felt sorry for her as she hobbled around slowly, bent over. Blue veins stood on her neck and head, suggesting a generalized circulatory problem. She had pronounced edema around the ankles, and I probably would have seen varicose veins if she hadn't always worn three-quarter length dresses.

My visit seemed to make her happy, and she often leaned over to tell me something about "Wessie" in a conspiratorial tone. When speaking to him, she referred to me as "our fine young visitor." The Old Man seemed to be enjoying himself immensely.

Dessert was accompanied by the reflected orange of a glorious sunset. Then the Old Man and I "went to vespers" on his balcony, which we approached through his Egyptology-laden study. An old, framed, black-and-white photograph caught my eye and brought to mind the Old Man's choirboy lecture. There they were: thirty young boys, a handful of teen-agers and a dozen men, robed and posed in four tiers on the steps before a cathedral chancel.

Around the seated choir director/organist stood his boys,

dressed in black cassocks, white smocks and ruffled collars, ages between eight and 12. Some of the older ones had ribbons around their necks holding medallions the size of silver dollars – obviously hard-earned awards. The boys' faces ran the gamut from conscientiously correct to mischievous to lackadaisical to carefree to intense to insouciant. Could I find the young Geoffrey Westley?

"Could a perfect choirboy be found among them?" asked the Old Boy, apparently reading my thoughts.

"Yes, I believe that it might have been this one," I said, pointing to a slightly obese 11-year old of serious demeanor. The boy stood in the second row, center, his left elbow practically touching the director's right shoulder. His ribbon had three vertical stripes, in contrast to the solid color of the others.

"You will make a fine detective, Ben."

We "removed to the balcony." I told Dr. Westley how Dr. Gordon Taylor had described me as "cannon fodder" and had joked about making me "take the King's Shilling."

"What does it mean, 'to take the King's Shilling'?" I asked.

"It goes back to the days when impress gangs roamed the English countryside, looking to Shanghai – if you'll pardon the anachronism – unsuspecting country bumpkins for service of the King, as lowly soldiers and seamen. But in a groundswell of liberal fervor, Parliament passed a law that the recruit must first accept a shilling – hence, The King's Shilling – before the recruitment would be binding. Then the press gang captains resorted to hiding the shilling in a free mug of ale. As a countermeasure, the innkeepers introduced pewter mugs with glass bottoms."

So I'd accepted the King's Shilling twice: once for regular duty under Dr. Taylor and once for irregular duty under Dr. Westley. Were both officers serving the same king?

"Dr. Westley, I know that your job is to solve murders, and that the politicians are giving you trouble. But I sense that you have a more compelling reason for investigating this case."

"Yes, indeed. A knowledge of science enables one to create great good or great evil. It would simply not do to allow a rogue scientist to get away with bloodless murder." The Old Man uttered these words like a prayer.

He should have prayed to deliver me from my interviews with the next two profs.

– VI –

Interviews

MY KAFKA'S CASTLE ANALOGY CAME to mind the next morning, Friday, August 29th, when the guard behind the semicircular desk refused to let me in.

"If you are going to be working here regularly, you need to get a picture I.D. and access card," he said.

I protested, "I'm supposed to interview all the profs." He just shook his head. "Coming Tuesday, they are going to process me for induction," I assured him.

These proved to be the magic words. While he wrote me a four-day pass, I watched his television monitors switching from hallways, to exit doors, to parking lots, to the loading dock and back again while the radio blasted with official cop talk. It felt more like a police station than an institution of higher learning.

The first open door on the fifth floor belonged to Dr. Grant Johnson, Associate Professor. From the brochure, I deduced that he was older vintage, having received his Ph.D. in physics at Ohio State in 1968, followed by a post-doctoral stint at Florida State in "quantum photochemistry" between 1968 and 1972.

His lab door was open but bore a sign warning, "CAUTION, LASER LIGHT." Dr. Johnson was leaning over a thick, steel plate on a large bench positioned in the middle of the room. Attached to the plate were several three-foot-long, V-shaped metal rails with clamping devices holding lenses, prisms, optical grating and modular light detectors. It was a homemade setup on an "optical bench."

"You can't come in for a couple of minutes," he said. With a small hexagonal wrench, he adjusted a lens. "I've been working all morning on lining this gizmo up."

Dr. Johnson hummed to himself as he leaned his thin, fiftyish torso over his project, revealing a bald spot on the top of his head of dark straight hair. His skin was pale, as if he had spent too much time in the lab. Taped to the wall over his gizmo was a cartoon of a German professor. The cartoon prof looked like Albert Einstein after someone had sat on his violin – hopping mad. The caption read:

> *Diese Machine ist for Science-Experimenten und nicht for Finger-Poken und Button-Pushen und Knobben-Turnen. Venn diese Rubber-Necken-Dummkopf-Sight-Zeers gepoken und gepushen und geturnen, zenn geht die Machine KAPUTT. Just relaxen und gelooken zu die Blinken-Lights.*

A Germanophile! A Swarthmore prof once told me that all scientists are supposed to know a little German and that some regard proficiency as a mark of distinction.

After a couple of minutes, Dr. Johnson looked up. His bench optics might have been straight, but his thick plastic glasses were not. The wire frames were crooked and a large lump of solder bulged over the bridge of the nose, the obvious result of an in-lab repair.

"Now my gizmo's lined up pretty good. Can you give me a piece of paper from your notebook?"

"Sure," I said, stepping up and tearing out a sheet. He took it, then gestured me back.

"Just stand back until I do my test shot."

Dr. Johnson knelt at the end of the bench and looked through a small hole in a metal disc.

"Yeah, looks like the lineup is pretty good."

He tore off a strip of paper and fixed it on the disc with adhesive tape.

"Now watch, but stand back. Five, four, three, two,

one, zero!"

Then I heard a click, zap and slap. For a split second, thin rods of bright red light flashed over the setup. The paper gave off a small puff of smoke. Dr. Johnson leaned over and inspected the burn hole carefully.

"Well, it looks like I got the right hole! Here, you can have it back as a souvenir. Now, what can I do for you?"

"I'm Ben Candidi. I'm starting next week as a graduate student. I wanted to talk with you about your research."

"Well, Candidi, here it is," he said with a sweeping gesture that took in the whole lab. "You just saw my laser excitation system. I stick fiber optic cables into that little hole and pure monochromatic light comes out the other end. So my laser can pump photons into any experiment I've got going here. Hell, I could pump photons to Stampawicz down the hall if he'd get me a cable that's long enough!"

He rattled off this string of jargon in an easy Ohio twang. He pointed to a large black box with an irregular array of precision dials, identifying it as a "fluorescence lifetime apparatus." He identified an instrument-encrusted microscope as his "fluorescence microcytometer." I asked him what he used the microscope for.

"To tease secrets out of a single cell using photons without blasting its head off," he said, as if that were the simplest thing in the world.

"How do you do that?"

"I focus a strong pulse of laser light through a microscope to blast the fuck out of these dye molecules holding calcium in the cell. So the dye releases the calcium into the cytoplasm. Then, a millisecond later, I switch on a weak beam of light and measure calcium binding to the proteins in the cell – you know, molecules like *calmodulin*."

I didn't know. But I kept asking him "intelligent questions" and he told me what's calmodulin and how he measured calcium with the fluorescence of an entrapped dye molecule called Fura-2. He concluded by saying that his experiments told "a helluvalot" about the molecular calcium pumps in the cell membranes.

"It sounds like you can do a lot of interesting experiments," I said, in genuine awe.

"Yeah. Some of the guys around here say I do too many different experiments on too many different types of cells. But I get out a good number of publications each year and the granting agencies seem to like me. So what t' heck!"

His smile reminded me of my old friend Richard Bash after he'd just pulled off a foul-smelling prank in the Swarthmore chemistry labs. Dr. Johnson shared much of my old pal's personality. I could have spent hours with him. He just couldn't be the one who killed Dr. Cooper. Taking advantage of his accessibility, I asked what effect the loss of Dr. Cooper would have on the Department.

"I'm as sorry as the next guy to see anyone leave us that way, but as far as his effect on the Department, good riddance!" His candor took me completely by surprise.

"Did a lot of faculty feel the same way?"

"Sure. Probably half of them. The old-timers like myself. That guy was the Mummy's Curse."

"Which of his policies caused – "

"Hey, stop it right there!" Johnson said, surprising me like his rods of laser light. Behind his nerd glasses, his eyes locked onto me. A notch appeared between his eyebrows, nicely lined up with the lump of solder, as he drew a bead on me. "Let me tell you this, kid. I figure you came here to do research – not to get yourself into a lot of political shit. So let me give you a word of advice. Once you start getting into this political shit, your science is fucked. I mean, *fucked.*"

He made a gesture like he was shooing a fly from his face.

"Just get through your courses as fast as you can and start working on a project."

His initial blast jolted me like the laser pulse knocked the calcium off the dye molecule. But his weak beam of brotherly advice was gentle. I figured he would appreciate a millisecond-quick answer.

"I agree with you perfectly, Dr. Johnson. It's just that these political manipulators can sometimes make life pretty hard for working scientists."

"You can say that again!" He shook his head in silence for several seconds, then took a step toward the door. "See you around, kid. Come back if you decide to do some photocytology in living cells."

So Dr. Johnson was one of the "Old Timers," and this group didn't like Dr. Cooper. George Ashton, neurotoxin specialist, was also an Old Timer. After a couple minutes in the brochure, I had identified the Old Timers and verified that they had been in the department a long time before Cooper came. Cooper probably made himself unpopular with the Old Timers by changing things around. I could imagine a lot of political shit hitting the fan.

And Dr. Johnson as the culprit? I smiled, picturing a group of professors standing around Cooper's smoking corpse on the hallway floor outside Johnson's lab . . . and Johnson putting away his laser while it was still warm!

My next visit was to black-bearded and bespectacled Dr. Gary Stampawicz. He had the sinister look of a bomb-throwing anarchist, but he didn't have any murderous pharmacology. Rubbing his hands together in anticipation of great delight, he ushered me into his laboratory, parted the blackout curtains and said, "Voila! My *microspectrofluorimeter* . . . or should I call it my *video fluorescence microscope* . . . I really should finalize the name of the gadget."

On a stone table was an enormous microscope with a video camera mounted on top. Hanging on the blackened wall was a large color television screen showing the ovoid shape of a cell. Stampawicz looked a little ovoid himself. He said that the blue, green, yellow and red colors mapped regions of different calcium concentrations within the cell. He worked with smooth muscle cells that line arteries and veins and control blood pressure.

Our discussion lead to a comparison of his setup with Dr. Johnson's. Dr. Stampawicz told me in plain and serious tones that he didn't need Dr. Johnson to pipe him laser light from down the hall because he, Stampawicz, had a "state of the art laser from General Defense Technology." He also made it clear that he knew a hell of a lot more than Dr. Johnson about control of cell activation by calcium.

Having successfully defended his turf, Stampawicz adroitly turned the conversation to me, quickly extracting 80 percent of my job description at the M.E. Office. Out of fear that he would blow my cover, I quickly excused myself, claiming to be late for another appointment. Probably, no harm was done.

After retreating down the hall, I gave Stampawicz a lot of thought. Although he couldn't have been a year under 40, he was only an assistant professor. From the dates in the brochure, I deduced he was hired by Cooper and was a member of the New Guard.

He probably didn't have any reason to kill Cooper, and he certainly didn't have any super poisons. Scratch him.

I couldn't get any more interviews that day, because everyone had left for the long Labor Day weekend. I decided to enjoy it, too, because coming Tuesday, I'd be very busy checking out profs by day and studying by night.

– VII –

First Class

OVER THE LABOR DAY HOLIDAY, Coconut Grovites drank a lot of beer. And I did my part. I felt like an enlistee having one last fling before going to boot camp, saying goodbye to the old gang and looking forward to new friendships with my fellow recruits. Tuesday rolled around quickly. Although Sergeant Major Gordon Taylor said the first event would be a luncheon, the bulletin board stated that Membrane Biophysics 669 would meet at nine o'clock that same morning. When in doubt, go by the duty roster. So I reported for duty in the classroom at oh-eight-hundred and forty-five hours, a respectful 15 minutes early.

The otherwise empty room contained a pleasant surprise: a strikingly good-looking, slim blonde about my age. Not bad for a fellow recruit! Our conversational preliminaries revealed that Cindy Larson had just received a B.A. in biology from New College in Sarasota. It's Florida's answer to Antioch, with a high ratio of faculty to students, and no tests or grades.

Unfortunately, Cindy wasn't interested in hearing about Swarthmore. And she quickly proved too rich for my blood. Her wealthy parents lived in Palm Beach. Her leisure time was spent water skiing, horseback riding and snow skiing. A few seasons ski bumming in Vail were the probable explanation why she graduated five years later than most students.

Cindy said she did a senior thesis titled "An Assessment of Meta-Analysis Applied to the Biomedical Sciences." It was one of those "hot new topics."

A Chinese student sat next to me. Then two Chinese students sat behind him. Some more students sat toward the back of the room. Then the lecturer hurried in.

"Now listen up everyone, 'cause we don't have a lot of time. And I don't like to repeat myself. I'm Dr. Grant Johnson, and I've been assigned to give you guys the dope on cell membrane structure. They make me give these lectures so that you'll be set up to learn that more complicated stuff from *them* – about membrane potential and gated ion channels – and all that nerve-firing stuff. Get the basics from me, and you can learn the complicated stuff later. Anyway, I'm going to give it to you straight. If you don't get this simple stuff that I'm telling you now, when they get around to doing their stuff, you are going to be *screwed up*. And I mean, really *screwed up*."

Today's "screwed up" sounded just like last Friday's "fucked up." Perhaps he would have used the stronger term if part of the class hadn't been female. His foreboding message was delivered in an almost friendly manner, like an older brother who knew he could tutor you out of an "F" in algebra if you'd only pay attention.

Dr. Johnson drew a large circle on the board, called it a cell membrane, and started telling us how the cell membrane is "damn thin" and how it "keeps the good stuff in and the bad stuff out." He said that if you tear off the cell membrane, the cell will be shot.

"*Shot . . . kaputt . . . fucked!*"

The Chinese students nodded in understanding and agreement. Cindy smiled like she'd received new and useful knowledge – on this prof. Dr. Johnson glanced from one student to the next, satisfying himself that they were still "listening up."

He presented lots of scientific details, but his only enduring message was that the membrane is "damn thin" and that even the slightest pinhole prick would "screw it up royally."

Yes, cell membranes are made from "phospholipids" that look like old-fashioned clothes pins and line up like slats in a picket fence to form a "hydrophobic" barrier that is only four nanometers thick. But to me, Dr. Johnson's lecture sounded like my old Swarthmore friend Richard Bash expounding on the significance of a pinhole leak in a prophylactic.

Dr. Johnson wrote "4 x 10^{-6} mm" on the board and looked around, as if seeking out anyone who did not know that the "-6" made it 0.000,004 millimeters. His didactic technique vacillated between the Socratic Method and plain old browbeating. He asked Cindy a direct question and she got it backward. During the exchange, which lasted a couple minutes, they both became visibly upset. Dr. Johnson's right hand made an involuntary gesture like he had a fly buzzing in his face.

Dr. Johnson told us the membrane acts as a "hydrophobic barrier" that keeps the potassium from flowing out of cell and keeps the sodium from flowing in. That was easy enough: It keeps the cell from getting fucked. He told us that the certain protein molecules sit in nerve membranes and act as channels, letting the potassiums and sodiums flow across the membrane.

Dr. Johnson turned to a Chinese student a couple of rows back and asked about the ion permeability of a "hypothetical cell membrane which didn't have any ion channels." The student didn't understand what was meant by "hypothetical" and gave the wrong answer. Dr. Johnson harangued him pretty badly. The student persisted, saying that was what his professor had taught him back in Shanghai.

"One thing you've got to learn right away, if you're going to survive here. What they taught you back there doesn't necessarily mean shit. Now listen up. You've got to understand this stuff for pharmacology. Now Mister – what is your name?"

"Chen."

Addressing Mr. Chen by name, Johnson slowly went through his argument, step by step, carefully applying the Socratic Method. The guy got it backward again, and Johnson rolled his eyes to the ceiling and muttered under his breath something that sounded like "Jesus-honkers."

Next, Dr. Johnson launched into a mini-lecture on how uncharged "hydrophobic" molecules can easily cross membranes. He said that's the way most simple drugs get absorbed in the gut. This seemed to calm him down. Then he changed topics. He wrote on the board an equation describing the relationship between the membrane's "electrical capacitance" and its thickness.

"Now, someone tell me what this means," he demanded, looking around the room. There was no answer. "Well, didn't any of you guys have any physics when you were in high school? Candidi, tell me what this means."

It wasn't an easy question. I straightened up and looked carefully at the equation. It was analogous to the equation of an electrical capacitor which I had learned in physics, so I ventured a guess which turned out to be right. Johnson's frown turned into a smile.

"Bulls-*eye* and no bull-*shit*! You know how to give right answers, Candidi. Now that's the way the rest of you guys should be answering these questions. Now what happens when we make the membrane thicker?"

"The capacitance decreases."

"Do the rest of you agree − ?"

And so it went for the rest of the "lecture." Dr. Johnson was Don Quixote, and I was his Sancho. In fluid sentences, he described how the cell is like a battery that gets charged up by Dr. Fleischman's discovery, a protein called the "sodium-potassium ATPase" that sits in the membrane, tossing sodium out of the cell and potassium in. And he got through the rest of the lecture without using any four-letter words. But it was also clear that the best way to handle the course was to know all the stuff already!

Around 10:30, Johnson's digital watch started beeping and he abruptly ended his lecture by saying, "Now you guys get busy with those references in the syllabus and get on top of this stuff. I've got only two more sessions to spoon feed you."

Cindy tried to detain him, but he shrugged her off saying, "I've got to get back to my experiment."

"What a jerk!" Cindy exclaimed, seconds after Johnson left the room. "And we don't even have any syllabus or references."

An older student in the back said, "It's not all that bad. You've just got to read Stryer's textbook."

Chen, the guy who got harangued, and his friend Zhang

looked unsettled. They began comparing notes in their native language. One played back a hand-held tape recorder. Cindy looked over for a minute as if she wanted to borrow it.

We milled around, getting acquainted. The guy who knew about Stryer's textbook was named Grant Shipley. He had been a practicing pharmacist for the last seven years. That experience might explain his quiet manner and sad eyes. Drugstore pharmacy can be hectic. Grant Shipley told me he was rusty on biology, but it would all come back to him.

I talked to an attractive girl with dark curly hair who sat in the back. Maria Mendez was freshly-graduated from Barry University in North Miami where she said, "The sisters taught us most of this but not so mathematical." She had a serene, pleasant manner and spoke openly and with only a trace of accent.

The stubborn Mr. Chen and his friend huddled around the tape recorder like victims of a shipwreck trying to start a signal fire.

The guy who sat next to me remained calmly seated, putting the finishing touches on his lecture notes. The better I got to know Dr. Sheng-Ping Chow the more I admired him. In halting, muddy but enthusiastic English, he told me about the Peoples Republic of China. Whether or not to call him "doctor" became a source of continuous confusion for many of us. In China you become a physician when you receive your Bachelor of Medicine Degree, usually at the age of 23. The younger the better in a country where physicians make house calls on bicycles!

But Dr. Sheng-Ping Chow was much more advanced than a barefoot physician. He had attended Peking Medical College, graduating at the top of his class. He stayed on to earn a Master of Medicine degree, working with sophisticated equipment to determine the pharmacological effects of an herbal compound.

"It be diuretic," he explained. "It interfere with the sodium ion pump in kidney and make urine. It also have tissue-specific cyclic nucleotide effect. Be interesting for Western Biomedical Science."

Studying this ancient Chinese nostrum using modern techniques was a part of his argument for getting permission to come to America. The other part of his argument was half of his life savings placed in the hands of the appropriate functionaries.

"I bring ten grams of purified compound to use for dissertation," he said seriously.

Considering that Western influence had been actively suppressed for most of Sheng-Ping's lifetime, he spoke English quite well.

"We have English Club in University for better translating English science for use in our country."

He punctuated the words "use in our country" with a twinkling of the eye, followed by a nervous laugh. I laughed too, and we hit it off very well. Sheng-Ping had a flat forehead, rough peasant-looking features but a great deal of physical dignity. And he was quite muscular.

"Did you participate in a sports program?" I asked on a hunch.

"Oh, I be captain of Peking Medical College Volleyball Team."

"That sounds pretty demanding."

"It rough. I have to throw *self* on floor harder than other team member," he said with a demonstrative gesture and a laugh.

"I understand, Sheng-Ping," I said with a smile. "Good Communist leaders have to be ready to throw themselves down." This cracked him up and he slapped me on the shoulder.

"You understand Peoples Republic good!"

"Were you in Peking during the June 5, 1989 Tienanmen Square Uprising?"

Sheng-Ping glanced to both sides and his face clouded over. "Yes. But I not be in it. I work in first aid station for students," he told me with a steady gaze.

"I understand. It was very good of you to set up that station. It was heroic of the students to try to change the government."

"It very bad government run by old men," Sheng-Ping said solemnly.

Sheng-Ping had adapted himself quite well in the past two weeks. He had moved into a two-bedroom apartment already occupied for a year by two Chinese grad students from Biochemistry. He paid one-third of the rent and had the use of the kitchen. After 11:30 in the evening he could sleep on the couch. He said that when one of the Biochemistry students graduates next year, he would get his bedroom. This is how the Chinese underground worked.

"But if my wife get permission to *come visit*, maybe I get own apartment," Sheng-Ping said with a twinkle of the eye – this time without a laugh.

A graduate student "lounge" was located several doors down the hall. After buying a soda from a machine outside, I went in. It was furnished with a beat-up couch, a computer and printer, a lettering machine for making graphs and a telephone on the wall. In the center of the room was a large table surrounded by four straight-backed chairs with chromed legs. A student in green hospital scrubs and white rubber-soled shoes was leaning back in one of the chairs, with his feet propped on the table. He held a copy of the *New England Journal of Medicine.*

"Hi. I'm Ben Candidi. First-year grad student."

"Glad to meet you. I'm Dave Franklin," he said, pointing to his shirt where "Franklin" had been crudely lettered. "I'm in the combined M.D., Ph.D. program."

"It looks like you're doing the M.D. part of it now," I said, looking at his scrubs. Under the name was printed indelibly:

"Property of Dade County General Hospital. Unauthorized use constitutes theft by conversion."

"Ah, the scrubs," Franklin said. "Nah, I just got off of a summer job as an orderly down in the Emergency Room. It's the best way to learn medicine, Dad always says. He's Chief of Nephrology at the Veteran's Administration Hospital. Kidney specialist in plain language. No, I'm just wearing the scrubs 'cause they're comfortable and so the Honeys don't get mixed up about who I am."

He delivered his boast in a country club drawl and ended it with an ear-to-ear grin. His bare arms were well tanned, suggesting that he'd spent a good portion of the summer poolside. He was blonde, short, about my size, but better looking. Needless to say, he irked me.

"You're right," I said. "Everyone will know your name when you write it on your shirt with a felt-tip pen. Say, if you're doing the Ph.D. part now, then what year are you in?"

"First year, like you."

"Then you missed the first lecture in Membrane Biophysics."

"Was that today? Taylor told me the first thing was this luncheon spread that's coming up in half an hour."

"The course schedule was announced on the bulletin board," I said, neutrally.

"Well I don't go around reading bulletin boards. I've got other 'Boards' to worry about," he said with a condescending smile.

I didn't give him a reaction. He wouldn't be ready to take Medical Board Examinations for a few years. Why acknowledge second-rate puns from the likes of him?

"So what class did I miss?" he asked.

"Dr. Grant Johnson on the cell membrane," I gambited.

"No sweat on that one. That guy's an easy psych-out. I've got a friend in the Junior Class who told me all about him."

"Dr. Johnson got some of the students worried."

"Who?"

"Cindy Larson, Maria Mendez and . . . a couple of guys named Chen and Zhang."

"Well you can forget about your Chens, Chows and Chews. Those guys shit rice balls every time you show them something new."

"You might be right about Chen and Zhang, but you're wrong about Chow. He didn't even fart."

Franklin gave me no reaction. "Ben, what's this Larson like? Is she cool?"

"You'll see her in half an hour. Don't let my opinion prejudice you."

"Interested in her yourself, huh? Well, as Dad always says, let the best man win. Especially if he's a doctor." Once again, The Grin.

"You didn't ask me about Mendez."

"Nah, I got to see a lot of them around Dade General this summer. I'm sort of Cubed out."

"That's right. The chances are that they've got some scuzzy Cuban boyfriend in the background," I said, in mock agreement.

"Yeah! A scuzzy boyfriend who picks her up in a hot-rod Trans Am after work and wants to fight you when he finds you've been messing around. A guy could get himself killed. Say, Ben, you're all right. We should think about getting together on a two-man note service, you and me."

"Sure, Dave. I'll keep it in mind. But you might be disappointed. I'm not very good at psyching out profs." Franklin's grin slowly vanished as he began to understand.

"Sorry, Ben. I thought you were a fun type of guy. Where did you go to school? Miami-Dade Junior College and Florida International with a part-time job?"

"Swarthmore, 1986," I said, heading for the door.

"Oh! That explains it. See you around, Ben."

I waved at him, not looking back.

The luncheon was more surreal than the first class. Everyone stood around self-consciously in the conference room waiting for the luncheon to begin. Grant Shipley and I made some small talk. Chen and Zhang hovered on the periphery. Dr. Gordon Taylor, designated master of ceremonies, chatted with Maria, occasionally saying a word in Spanish, but looking all the time at Cindy Larson who stood near the buffet, aloof and petulant. Then Dr. Gary Stampawicz stepped in, stroked his beard and headed straight for the buffet. He rubbed his hands and looked at Dr. Taylor, as if waiting for a signal to start eating. As if on cue, Dr. Taylor bellowed out:

"Ladies and Gentlemen, it is my pleasant duty to welcome you to your first and last 'free lunch' at the Pharmacology Department." It came to me as no surprise when Taylor punctuated this comment with a loud predatory laugh. "Before the feast begins, it is my equally pleasant duty to give you a few words of encouragement and advice."

Stampawicz put the bun back on his plate and feigned attention to Taylor's words. Dave Franklin appeared in the doorway, then blended smoothly into the crowd.

"It was once said that the process of becoming a Ph.D. is like the metamorphosis between caterpillar and butterfly. In the first stage you voraciously devour everything in your path . . . (that is the first two years) . . . then you sequester yourself and undergo an intellectual metamorphosis . . . (that is your third and fourth years) . . . bursting forth into a butterfly!"

Few of us saw the humor in his analogy, but most of us laughed politely, anyway. Stampawicz nodded in approval while nibbling a piece of carrot. Dr. Robert Sturtz came in, sporting his insouciant smile and a polo shirt. Dr. Robert Gunnison followed, wearing a distracted frown and a Hawaiian shirt.

"The metamorphosis is aided by the able assistance of the dissertation mentor whom you choose, under the watchful eye of the graduate committee."

Once again, his witticism evoked nervous laughter. Sturtz and Gunnison smiled, and Taylor gestured to them, indicating that they *were* the graduate committee.

"And in absence of other words of advice, let the feast begin!"

Gunnison looked like he wanted to say something, but Stampawicz had already turned his back and was creating a sandwich at the buffet. There was some cautious applause, followed by an equally cautious general movement toward the buffet.

After loading my plate, I talked to Maria. Then Cindy came over and said, "I think we should all get together and complain to Dr. Taylor. Dr. Johnson told us there's a reading list, but there really wasn't any."

I said, "Cindy, that professor with the beard standing by the buffet is Dr. Stampawicz. He's the course coordinator."

Dave Franklin came up, slapped me on the shoulder, and said, "Ben, old boy! Why don't you introduce me to your two charming friends."

Before I could open my mouth, Franklin had already

turned to Cindy and launched into a spiel about how he was a combined-degree student. Cindy was quite taken with him. She started telling him about New College and in-depth education. After a couple of minutes, it became embarrassing that Maria had not been introduced.

"Cindy and Dave, may I introduce Maria Mendez."

"*Como frijoles?*" Franklin said to her. Neither Maria nor I understood what he meant.

"What did you say?" Maria asked.

"*Como frijoles?*" repeated Franklin. "How you bean? It's a joke." Cindy laughed and Maria looked distracted. "It's a joke we had going around General last summer. How beans? How you bean? How you been? You translate it and then transmute it, and then it makes sense."

"Yes," Cindy chimed in. "It's nonlinear thinking." Maria looked perplexed.

"Say, Dave," I said, "Cindy was just telling me about a big foul-up with a reference list for the class. Why don't you both go over to Dr. Stampawicz and get to the bottom of it." This got rid of them.

"Am I missing something or what?" shrugged Maria.

"*No . . . nada. El muchacho se piensa que es muy listo, pero en realidad es stupido. La muchacha tambien,*" I answered.

We continued in Spanish for a while until Sheng-Ping Chow drifted over, followed by Mr. Chen. I learned that Chen was also from the People's Republic of China, but from the less prestigious medical school at Shanghai.

Towards the end of the luncheon, Dr. Taylor announced that we should check our pigeonholes for the reading list for the Membranes Course, which was "hot off the press." Then he handed out interdepartmental requisitions and sent us to the Security Department to get our photo I.D.s.

If the entrance to the Med School was like a police station, the I.D. operation was like a driver's license office. Cindy complained because she was allowed only one pose. I didn't care about my picture, which was just as well, since the finished product showed as much of my chest and polo shirt as it did my face. Attached to my I.D. was a magnetic card which I could press against a sensor at the door to let me in and out of the buildings after hours.

With this formality out of the way, I found my pigeon hole and picked up the reading list. Across the street at the library, I made copies of the articles and even managed to check out Stryer's *Biochemistry*. I used the rest of the afternoon to interview some more profs.

The brochure said that Dr. Pennington's lab worked on sea urchin eggs. There was no doubt of my having walked into the right lab. It was dominated by several aquarium tanks with sea urchins hanging all over the bottoms and sides. Dr. Pennington sat next to a bubbling tank, staring intently into a microscope. She looked up, and I introduced myself and started asking "intelligent questions."

She described the major events in sea urchin egg fertilization.

"Contact with the sperm sets off a cascade of ion permeability changes in the egg membranes. This leads to chemical signalling by phosphate esters of inositol sugars."

She looked every bit as attractive as her picture in the brochure. The shot, taken through a lab shelf, revealed a smiling face, framed between two large reagent bottles. I was pleased to see that the cute smile, reminiscent of the young Shirley MacLaine of *The Apartment*, was not just a chance event captured by a lucky photographer.

I reached deeply into my bag of questions, and she responded by telling me everything I wanted to know about the cellular mysteries of the prickly creatures.

Dr. Pennington herself wasn't the least bit prickly. She was intelligent but not needlessly critical, attractive but not vain. She was also New Guard, and the last person I would suspect of Cooper's murder. I could check one more prof off the list that would end with Ashton.

Acting Chairman Peter Moore was very prickly. Yes, he had time to speak to me, but, no, he didn't really have time to speak to me. Earlier that day I saw this burly guy with a large

head, heavy-framed glasses and flat-top haircut running down
the hallway with an administrative assistant, looking like a fire
chief responding to a three-alarm fire.

Dr. Moore politely but impatiently asked me if there was
anything special about his work I wanted to know. The brochure said he worked on "pharmacokinetics," the study of what
happens to the drug in the body, how the liver chops it up and
the kidneys piss it out. I told him pharmacokinetics was an important part of pharmacology that I hoped to learn more about.

"What are you really interested in, Mr. Candidi?"

I echoed the language in the brochure, saying something
about "biological control at the cellular level."

He slowly shook his head.

"Well, Candidi, that's probably broad enough to cover
everything from here to the Missouri River."

"Dr. Moore, to be truthful, my interests are still sort of
undifferentiated," I said, with some shame.

"If you want to learn some more *practical* pharmacology,
you are welcome to come back. I've got a good technician in
the lab, and I've got some grants from industry and from the
PMA." He made a point of telling me that PMA stands for
*P*harmaceutical *M*anufacturers *A*ssociation and not *P*horbol
*M*yristate *A*cetate. I laughed, like this was a good joke. He
volunteered some advice.

"Work hard on your courses. Especially the Membrane
Biophysics course and the Biochemistry course. Sometimes
the Young Turks on the faculty get overambitious and flunk
out some guys that could have made it. You're about six years
older than most of our graduate students, which can be both
bad and good. Just don't watch too much *Monday Night Football.*" He gave me a knowing wink which made me uncomfortable. "Work hard, and I'll see you around the farm."

With these words, Dr. Moore ushered me out the door
and closed it before I could even thank him. A gruff, no-non-
sense type. I sure wouldn't want to have him catch me in his
watermelon patch after midnight. Yes, he was Old Guard all
right. The brochure said he received his Ph.D. from Iowa State

in 1962, which made him the second oldest member of the Department and much senior to the deceased Cooper. But somehow I couldn't imagine him as the murderer, although I could imagine him punching Cooper in the mouth. So I checked one more prof off the list that would end with Ashton.

Time to call it a day. The bike ride home gave me a chance to reflect on what a strange day it had been. Back on the *Diogenes* with a good homemade meal under my belt, I sat down in the open cockpit, leaned against the cabin, and reflected further. Feelings began to well up. No wonder the Department accepted my application so readily: They were hard up for students! Otherwise, they wouldn't have gone all the way to China to get them.

Yes, they needed graduate students to get their research done. Cheap labor, that's what I was. Or "Cannon Fodder" as Dr. Taylor had half-jokingly said during our first interview. Well, at least he was honest. Except for Dr. Pennington and Dr. Johnson, all the profs, old and young, seemed inhospitable. Sure, I would survive in this program. But I was disappointed that they didn't make even a pretense of scholarly idealism. Trying to put my finger on the problem, I found myself pacing back and forth in the cockpit, eventually breaking into a monologue.

"And the whole program is carried out haphazardly, with two Young Turks who are jockeying for leadership . . . which is held by an expatriate Englishman . . . who carries on more like a sergeant in the Foreign Legion than like a college prof. And there is this acting chairman who SEEMS MORE LIKE A FOOTBALL COACH THAN A COLLEGE PROFESSOR!"

An echo of "College Professor" bounced back from the old Pan Am seaplane hanger.

"Hey! You all right, Ben?" called a voice from a few yards away. It wasn't me. It was "Frenchie," my friend and neighbor, rowing by with a load of groceries and giving me a funny look.

"No, Frenchie. It's okay. Just blowing off a little steam." Frenchie waved in dismissal and rowed on to his *Mon Roi*, Montreal.

Yes, Old Candidi *was* going nuts, holding loud conversations with himself. I went below searching for the proper remedy. Coming topside with glass and bottle of wine in hand and finding Frenchie out of hailing distance, I blew off the rest of my steam, shouting to the wispy tops of the tall Australian pines.

"And you are on this *secret mission,* masterminded by another expatriate Englishman, who is just as nutty as the English prof except that he has better manners. And you can't even *talk* to your mastermind/controller except in a twenty-questions guessing game. Ben, it's time to haul anchor!"

But I didn't. As the wine rose in my head, I pulled out my reading light and sat down with the articles and biochemistry textbook. I would have to master this stuff quick if I was going to nail Ashton. Tomorrow, I would check all the other profs off the list, and then get a rotation in Ashton's lab.

– VIII –

Second Class

COVERED BY WHITE, RED AND BLUE beads, it resembled a coral snake coiled and twisted on itself. Maria Mendez, sitting close to me, shuddered. We all peered at the screen, spellbound. The keyboard clicked and the protein molecule turned slowly on the unseen spit of a rotisserie.

"Looks ugly enough to make you sick, doesn't it?" said Dr. Al Kozinski, Professor of Pharmacology. He stood at the side of the computer screen, surveying the class through thick, heavy-framed glasses. He was small but of muscular build, particularly in the shoulders and forearms. "I still can't get used to looking at molecules. This is a single subunit of the hemoglobin molecule. Of course, the little white balls are hydrogen, the blues are nitrogen and the reds are oxygen. Carbons are black, but you can't see them well. Now, you will remember the hydrogens, carbons, nitrogens and oxygens are combined to make amino acids. There are twenty types of amino acid, and they are linked into chains to form proteins."

Dr. Kozinski related this in a quiet and friendly voice, with a strong Brooklyn accent. He must have been approaching 60, and it was very clear that years of experience had made him master of the situation.

"Each amino acid has subtle differences in shape which affect how the protein chains fold. How the chains fold is important, because it determines its overall shape and what the protein does. Dr. Alverez, could you change to 'ribbon format'."

Two clicks, and the snake's body changed to spiral twists

and loops of green ribbon.

"Ribbon format is better to see the backbone of the protein. Notice where the ribbon is thicker, it's twisted in an alpha helix. It looks like a spiral staircase and it's stiff. Where the ribbon is thinner, there are flexible loops. But to appreciate the subtle twisting and folding of this molecule, you have to look at its carbon backbone. Of course, to really appreciate protein architecture, you need a master of molecular modelling, like Dr. Alverez. Juan, could you give me the stick representation?"

Dr. Alverez, a handsome man about my age, typed in some instructions that turned the ribbon into a skeleton of sticks, showing tight spiral staircases and wide loops.

"In this representation it's easy to see the heme group which contains the iron atom and which binds the oxygen."

The "heme" looked a little like a trampoline suspended between four mangled New York fire escapes. Then Kozinski showed us what happens when the oxygen binds. A stubby dumbbell representing an oxygen molecule came down from the top of the screen, and sat on the "heme" trampoline. As the dumbbell and trampoline touched, one of the fire escapes twisted subtly. Hopefully, I wouldn't have to understand all this perfectly to solve the murder, because it was getting pretty darn complicated.

"Wow," said Maria.

Dr. Kozinski lectured from a personal viewpoint that made us more comfortable while being force-fed with protein structure. He told how, back in the 1950s when he was at Brooklyn Polyscience High School, biochemists broke up red cells, purified the hemoglobin and crystallized it. Back when he was an undergrad at NYU, they were just beginning to solve the structures of simple proteins using a method called x-ray crystallography. A few years later, while a grad student at Columbia, the structure of hemoglobin was published. The computer picture was a playback of this data.

Smoothly and patiently, he went on to describe how four hemoglobin molecules bind together in so-called allosteric interactions, so that either four oxygens bind simultaneously, or none at all. He told us that this was Nature's way of making every breath count.

"When the hemoglobin molecules pass through the lung, *all* of them bind a full load of oxygen. When the hemoglobin molecules pass through oxygen-starved tissue, *all* of them give up all their oxygens. If allosteric interaction were missing, some of the hemoglobins wouldn't give up their oxygen to the oxygen-starved tissue – which wouldn't be good."

We had a lot of questions on this. Kozinski told us that we would first have to learn the mathematics of binding and molecular affinity, which would be taught later by a biochemist.

"Let me show you what happens to hemoglobin in sickle cell anemia. Watch these four hemoglobin molecules closely, while Juan mutates only one amino acid in the chain."

Juan clicked the keyboard and at least two of the four molecules moved subtly.

Dr. Kozinski said, "This small change, when you have it from both your mother and your father, can give you painful and damaging circulatory crises, which will reduce your life expectancy to less than fifty years."

We were all very impressed.

"The subtle change in these hemoglobin molecules disturbs their packaging in the red cell. So the cell can't change shape easily when it has to squeeze through the blood capillary. And the cells break easily, and this starts painful blood clotting in the small blood vessels – all because of *one* bad link in the chain of amino acids."

Dr. Kozinski told us how there are thousands of different "receptor" molecules in the body, and how each receptor has a specific molecule, like a "neurotransmitter" or hormone, that binds to it – just like oxygen binds to hemoglobin – fitting just like a key fits into a lock – to unlock cellular functions. He told us how drugs bind to these receptors and change all this.

"The tighter and more specific the binding, the better the drug. Tetrodotoxin, the puffer fish poison which plugs up the sodium channel, is an example of this. Of course, tetrodotoxin is too effective, so it isn't a good drug."

Grant Shipley had a gem of a question.

"Dr. Kozinski, I read about all these biotechnology companies that are making these short pieces of protein . . . uh . . . polypeptides. The article said that they bind tightly to specific receptors. But then I read there's some reason why most of them can't be used as drugs. But I don't see why they couldn't, if the polypeptide could bind tightly to a specific receptor and change its function. So why can't polypeptides be used as drugs?"

"They can," Kozinski answered. "The companies are making all sorts of polypeptides – strings of amino acids linked together. They would look like little strips of ribbon in the pictures I have been showing you. If the drug company finds the right little strips of ribbon, it could have a very powerful drug. But Dr. Johnson probably told you, yesterday, that they can't cross membranes. And, unfortunately, there's no way of getting these polypeptides into the bloodstream without injecting them. People don't like to inject themselves. And doctors don't want them to do it either. Especially intravenous injections."

I nodded in agreement. This confirmed the information from Dr. Westley and the *Scientific American* article.

"Well, class, I've talked enough. You have your reading assignments. Study hard and take care."

When the students were finished with their informal questions, I followed Dr. Kozinski back to his office and he granted me a get-acquainted interview. Over his desk was a photograph of him as a curly-headed young man in a white lab jacket and standing in a hospital parking lot by a 1956 Chevy, staring into the camera intensely through thick glasses. Today, his light brown hair was so thin that I could see his scalp.

Kozinski's lecture identified him as a *mensch* who was probably incapable of killing anyone. He immediately took me under his wing, offering encouraging advice on how to deal with graduate study. I asked about his research. He told me that he studied "regulatory phosphorylation" – how one enzyme kicks another into high gear by tagging it with a phosphate.

As I started to ask a question, Kozinski gave me a pat on the shoulder.

"Don't feel that you have to learn it all in the first week.

You will just get frustrated. And the longer you are around here the more Kafkaesque it is going to seem. Sometimes things get pretty surreal around here, even for me."

"Do you mean that I made a wrong choice in coming to this department?"

"No. Things are crazy in every department, everywhere. They are crazy in academic science in general. But I hope you knew what you were getting into when you chose science for a career. There aren't many real jobs out there in academia." He glanced at the door, indicating it was the end of the interview. "Take care," he said, patting me gently on the back as I got up. I checked him off the list.

I went to lunch with Maria Mendez and Grant Shipley. He had a lot to say about pharmacy school in Georgia and little good to say about drugstore pharmacy. I expressed similar feelings about the M.E. lab. Maria was 23 and had always been studying full time. She lived with her extended family in Kendall, in the "Southwest."

That afternoon, I was back at work with the list of suspects. Sturtz and Gunnison, who interviewed me before acceptance, were not suspects. They were New Guard and didn't have any murderous pharmacology. Neither did Taylor. The remaining profs were Drs. Fleischman, Ledbetter, Manson, and, of course, Ashton.

Dr. Donald Fleischman, Professor of Pharmacology seemed least suspect and the easiest to start with. Reference to the brochure identified him as the oldest member of the Department, having received his Ph.D. in 1961 at the University of Wisconsin and coming to Bryan Medical School in 1965.

It was surprising to find the discoverer of the sodium pump in a tiny lab with a single technician. He was working on a manuscript at a cluttered desk, writing in longhand in large rounded letters on a pad of paper with blue gridlines. As I approached, he turned his large head and looked up over his large, rimless glasses.

Speaking in a nasal voice, high-pitched but friendly, he asked me about Swarthmore. Then he rambled on about his graduate student days at the University of Wisconsin and the intellectual ferment of yesteryear.

How had he discovered the sodium pump?

"Oh, it just all came together one afternoon while I was a post-doctoral, sitting on a canal bank in Amsterdam." He leaned back in his chair and recited a number of present-day textbook facts – how each enzyme has a specific purpose, how cells are finicky about sodium and potassium, and how ATP functions as the dollar bill of the cell. "So I just put two and two together and guessed that there was an ATP-splitting enzyme that pumps sodium out and potassium into the cell."

"So your discovery was putting different unexplained facts together."

"Exactly. Plus a little pinch of teleology. The cell couldn't go around wasting its valuable ATP like this department has been wasting money." Dr. Fleischman hesitated for a second, as if he had said too much.

"You make your discovery sound so simple."

"All significant discoveries are simple, once they are made. Just don't be too bothered by lack of precedent."

He was so engaging when talking about science. I said something about him being illustrious.

"Illustrious?" His face clouded over. He shifted his short, ovoid body in his chair and ran his hand through his big head of graying brown hair. "Well, Mr. Candidi, quite a few years have passed since my initial discoveries . . . and Miami has plenty of ways to remove one's *luster*. And I don't mean tarnish from the salt air." He spoke with a trace of anger and a touch of resignation.

Not knowing what to say, I stared at the poster of a European castle over his desk.

"*Neuschwanstein,*" he said. "One of Ludwig the Second's Castles. Of course, there's a plastic version of it in Orlando. Plastic replicas seem to be the norm in Florida, even in science. Some people treat science like a hobby, others treat it like a business, and others treat it like a game. For me, science has been a religion."

Obviously, Cooper had not treated him well. But why was he telling me this? I asked about his present research and he showed me a giant chart on the opposite wall, covered by small penciled-in squares, circles and triangles labelled with terms like "cAMP," "cGMP," "protein kinase," and "protein phosphatase," connected with arrows. Some arrows were thick; others were drawn with thin dotted lines, noted with question marks.

He waved his hand at the chart. "I'm working out a rigorous and systematic approach to the problem of 'second messenger regulation.' I still have some tricks up my sleeve," he said pugnaciously. "I recently discovered that the body produces its own circulating digitalis-like compounds which regulate the strength of heart beats. But I made the mistake of presenting it at a departmental seminar. By some sort of magic, one of the late Dr. Cooper's friends from another institution managed to come up with the same thing a short time later."

He noted that I looked older than most students. I told him I was 28 and had worked for six years in the laboratories at the Medical Examiner's Office. He took this without batting an eye, and asked, "Is that outfit still run by Westley?"

"Yes."

"Well, I used to know him before he became famous. I read about him in the newspaper every so often. Back in the middle 1960s I helped him with some biochemistry. In those days there was a great spirit of cooperation around here. But many things have changed."

He told me that Cooper had run the Department like an "East-Bloc Managed Economy" and that he hoped it would now "revert to a community of scholars." Although it was too late for him to learn the "new molecular genetic approaches" and keep up with the younger scientists who were "marching through biomedical science with Seven League Boots," he assured me he still had a few tricks up his sleeve.

What a strange interview! Although he had the motive for murder and at least fifty compounds at his disposal, I couldn't imagine him doing it. He didn't seem sufficiently devious.

I could not check off two suspects because they were unavailable. Both were Old Guard, but a quick check of their publications did not reveal any super poisons. Dr. Howard Manson was "still up in Woods Hole." They said he'd packed his whole laboratory into a van last June, drove up to Woods Hole and worked like a fiend the whole summer. Dr. John Ledbetter had also been out of town for a long time. His Chinese post-doctoral fellow wasn't very communicative about his date of return. Dr. Westley would have to tell me if Manson and Ledbetter were absent on the day Cooper was poisoned.

So I had checked everyone off and was now ready for my prime suspect, George Ashton, M.D., the guy who worked with neurotoxins – the guy whose papers Westley had found interesting enough to have Doris order them. The brochure informed me that Dr. Ashton had an M.D. from Harvard Medical School, 1967. He worked on "neurotransmitters" in relation to Parkinson's and Alzheimer's disease, using neuro-toxins as tools. One of his earliest studies showed how a deadly scorpion toxin binds to a neurotransmitter receptor in nerves.

I had already observed the aristocratic Dr. Ashton in the hallway a number of times. He was tall, with a large-boned muscular frame and dirty-blond hair. He walked around with proud, self-absorbed aloofness, accentuated by his thin-rimmed, thick-lensed glasses and by his hand-tied yellow bow tie, fluffed stylishly under his chin. He reminded me of a movie in which a Providence, Rhode Island, aristocrat put his wife into a coma with an overdose of insulin.

Ashton's office was entered through his lab. Outside his door were reproductions of paintings by Monet. Or was it Manet? As I stepped over his threshold, he looked up from his tidy desk, slowly and curiously, offering no greeting.

"Hello, Dr. Ashton. I'm Ben Candidi, first-year graduate student. We are supposed to talk to . . . that is . . . to have an interview with each faculty member."

After letting me dangle a while, he said, "Yes. I'm in perfect agreement. In fact, I am the author of that policy. We initiated it back in 1969. So please sit down. Tell me a little about yourself."

"I graduated from Swarthmore in chemistry six years ago, and I have worked in the clinical laboratory of the Dade County Medical Examiner."

Did I detect mild surprise?

"Is . . . Westley still there?" he asked, gazing at the window.

"Yes, but I hardly ever saw him."

"I guess he's getting up there in age. About to retire, maybe?" he asked smoothly. He might have seen my application and mentally rehearsed for this interview.

"There were several layers of bureaucracy between him and me," I answered. "I hardly knew him. Did you know him?"

"We exchanged notes on snake venoms back in the early days. Miami was a lot smaller place back then. Not many scientists. Everyone knew everyone."

He delivered this information in a bored, cocktail-party voice. Was this an Ivy League reflex or a calculated move to throw me off his track? Where would he steer the conversation at this point? Ashton's gaze drifted from the window to me, and he said, "And you, Mr. Candidi. What do you want to do, now that you are getting back on track with science?"

"I want to do research, either in academia or in industry. I'm not sure what I want to specialize in."

"Well neuroscience, my field, is quite specialized, but also quite rewarding, and certainly well-funded. If you consider it, we could talk again."

"Would it be possible for me to have a few selected reprints of your work?"

"Most certainly. Help yourself to anything in my collection," he said, pointing to an expanse of shelves, just outside the door. "Browse to your heart's content."

He resumed work at his clean, well-organized desk. What a phony. If I'd said neuroscience is the science of the future, he'd probably tell me I was the smartest graduate student to come through since 1969.

The shelves held multiple copies of over ninety-some papers, some dating back to 1965. Yes, he had published as a Junior in medical school. He'd used cobra toxins to characterize the acetylcholine-activated sodium channel in nerve cell membranes. It was the same sodium channel that the wife-murdering anesthesiologist had targeted with succinylcholine.

The reprints revealed that Ashton had worked with dozens and dozens of potent toxins. He had toxins that could stop you from breathing, stop your heart, drop your blood pressure, throw you into convulsions or to make you hallucinate. Some were natural toxins and some were man-made.

My heart raced as I turned his papers over in my hands. Out of the corner of my eye, I noticed that Ashton was observing me. The deeper I dug into his collection, the longer his glances became. At the end of my dig, I looked up and caught his eye. He pretended to be looking up from his work, as if for inspiration. Did I detect curiosity, pride, suspicion or fear? With 10 papers under my arm, I returned to his office, thanked him again for the interview and told him I'd like to come back.

"Please do."

That evening on the *Diogenes*, I went through Ashton's poison papers. Yes, he had a lot of ways to poison Cooper. Many of the marine toxins in his early work seemed to be simple molecules that would be effective when taken by mouth. But his later work seemed to concentrate on proteins and peptides that would have to be injected.

I opened the brochure and revisited my Old Guard/New Guard theory. It checked out. All the full professors had received their Ph.D.s in the 1961-1968 period and were well-established at Bryan before Cooper came. Those older profs must have resented him. Cooper received his Ph.D. in 1971 from the University of Delaware, making him the youngest of the old ones. All the assistant professors received their Ph.D.s in the 1985-1988 period, were obviously hired by Cooper and were undoubtedly beholden to him.

In an attempt to remain objective, I made a little chart listing the personality characteristics and possible motives and means of each of the suspects. I didn't know much about Manson and Ledbetter, but their publications contained no examples of potent toxins. The more I stared at the chart, the more I became convinced of my initial impression and Westley's inadvertent hint: It had to be Ashton.

Now to get the Old Boy to confirm it.

– IX –

Psyching Out The Profs

VIOLINS DANCED PLAYFULLY AROUND the Old Boy's ancient phonograph. Reflected rays of the setting sun sparkled from an ensemble of crystal in his China cabinet. The first movement came to an end just as we clinked our glasses in a toast.

"You are putting me on the spot, Dr. Westley. But if you make me guess, I'd say it was Mozart."

"Correct."

"I appreciate music, but I don't have an active understanding of it. I never played an instrument or sang in a boy choir, like you."

"Of course, exposure at a young age is very important. But Mozart is so pristine, so accessible to everyone. And he has a certain spriteliness."

The Old Man, himself, revealed a certain geriatric spriteliness, as he chortled on about Mozart. He compared Mozart's move from Salzburg to Vienna, to his own move from Devon to Cambridge, where he studied medicine. Tonight the lesson in parable was "finding your talents." Young Westley had been impressed with the Cambridge biochemists but was uncertain that he had "skills for the science of the general." He had discovered greater skills in the "science of the particular," such as determining cause of death.

While serving the British equivalent of a residency in internal medicine, he "apprenticed" himself to the Coroner of London. As a sideline, he carried out certain x-ray examinations of mummies for the British Museum. This led to his "little project for the Egyptian chaps."

Margaret announced dinner. After we were seated with food on our plates, it seemed natural for me to ask how they happened to come to Miami.

"Oh, it was such an *improbable* series of coincidences!" exclaimed Margaret, turning towards Westley, who continued the story.

"As I was telling you, I had earned myself a modest reputation in forensic archeology at the museum but hadn't yet persuaded them to pay me. I had a semi-secure position with the coroner with a modest salary. We felt that we owed ourselves a little Caribbean holiday, did we not?"

"It was a most *marvelous* cruise," affirmed Margaret.

"Justin Waddington, an old friend from Cambridge, was doing something or other for the Consular Service here in Miami. And when he learned of our planned Caribbean holiday, he telegraphed that I simply had to stop in Miami. He scheduled me for a lecture on my Egyptian caper at the Miami Museum of Science. They had an Egyptology Society – still do, I believe. So I packed some slides in the bags, and off we went."

It was nice to glimpse the human side of Dr. Westley.

"Wessie gave a most *brilliant* lecture," added Margaret. "The audience were *most taken* with him."

"But I must say, they were quite easily bedazzled. I rather suspect I could have told them that the pyramids were built on the advice of visiting Martians, and they would have been none the wiser for it."

"Now Wessie, that is quite unkind of you. The ladies were so appreciative – and *so* helpful."

"It was farcical," the Old Man persisted.

Margaret cleared her throat and turned, with great effort, to face the Old Man. "You are being most unkind. And smug, snobbish and ungrateful. Have you lost *all* capacity for humility? You owe a debt of gratitude to those ladies, Jean-Ann in particular." Margaret was trembling.

The Old Man's face flushed and he stared for a long time

at the tablecloth and played with his dessert spoon. "Yes, love. You are quite right. I do owe a great debt of gratitude to Jean-Ann. Bless her soul," he said almost prayerfully. We were silent for a long time. Then Dr. Westley turned to me.

"But in the beginning of the evening it did seem rather farcical," he quietly explained. "The lecture was given in the 'Space Transit Planetarium.' As if it were some sort of way station to Mars! And then that silly buffoon insisted on turning on his planetarium machine and revealing to us the 'Heavens over the Nile, Today, 2,650 BC!'" Westley was back to full volume.

"You shouldn't speak of him like that," admonished Margaret. He's still – "

"Yes. He's still to be seen on public television around midnight with that bloody awful synthesizer playing Debussy's Arabesque Number One," Dr. Westley exclaimed theatrically. "That particular evening promised to be such a farce that I nearly quit before I began!"

"But you didn't," Margaret said, half in contradiction, half in applause.

"No. I presented my lecture, and managed to farce it out for them – in the sense of stuffing the fabric with wool, not in the sense of adding to the farce or pulling wool over their eyes, mind you – and my lecture was quite well received."

The Old Boy could be so irrelevantly eloquent when he got up a good head of steam. He described the cocktail reception, the conversation with a Dade County commissioner who mentioned that the Dade County Coroner had just passed away, how one of the ladies proposed that he fill the position, how everyone magically agreed, how the Dade County Attorney was rousted out of his bed by telephone to affirm that the post required neither American citizenship nor a license to practice medicine in Florida, and how he was offered the job the same evening.

Dr. Westley turned this into fatherly advice about how it can be necessary to move on, how one must recognize one's skills and to be ready to seize opportunity. "Miami was a boom town back then, ready to make up for its deficits with 'cash on the barrelhead.' As with their recent choice of a symphony director, they wanted to import some first-class talent. Fine young man, he is, incidentally! In the best English musical tradition."

"People have told me Miami has always been crazy," I said. "Some old-timers told me that in the late 1960s there was a guy studying dolphins at the Miami Seaquarium. Half of the people said that he was discovering that they had a humanlike language. The other half said that he was teaching them how to murder Viet Cong frogmen for the Navy."

"'Twas probably a good measure of both," Westley said with a nod. "But craziness can be useful, if it pays the bills. Miami was, in fact, founded on craziness. Did you know that the City of Coral Gables was inspired by the lush "Barcarole Scene" from the *Tales of Hoffmann*? That's why that Merrick chap dug his canals – to make it the 'Venice of the South.' And enough philanderers took it seriously to make Coral Gables a real city!"

He recited a short history of Opa Locka. "Glenn Curtiss' phantasy of an Arab city – minarets on every rooftop." He described it as South Florida's contribution to the Roaring Twenties, with hordes of libertines acting out their fantasies of "A Thousand and One Nights" with the aid of free-flowing gin, money and sex. "But if we had been spared this sorry history, there would have been no Opa Locka University, and the Bryan Medical School might not have seen the light of day."

I was glad when we finally "repaired to the balcony," where I could put an end to this cultural indoctrination session and tell him about my interviews with the profs.

I told him about Dr. Gordon Taylor, making fun of his English parade-ground manner, but concluding that he was really a gentle soul. I conveyed all the important things in double entendre, enabling me to deny under oath having discussed the profs as murder suspects. Concluding with Taylor, I said, "He doesn't seem to have much ability in *applied pharmacology*, if you know what I mean."

"Yes, 'applied pharmacology.' What a nice turn of phrase," Westley said, raising his bushy eyebrows to indicate that he understood my newly designated codeword for "toxin."

The ex-choirboy proved a capable reader of nuance, readily learning my concept of Old Guard/New Guard. He tacitly agreed that Sturtz, Gunnison, Stampawicz and Pennington were of little interest.

"Yes, Ben, one could agree with your impression that the ranks of this 'New Guard' are less likely to contain a *brigand*." Moving on to the Old Guard, he seemed to agree that Al Kozinski, the *mensch*, wouldn't hurt anyone. His only reaction to our Acting Chairman, Dr. Peter Moore, was that he didn't pronounce his name properly. Westley thought it should rhyme with "poor." He described Dr. Donald Fleischman as "a fine chap" whom he'd known "back in the early days."

I told him of the absence of Dr. Howard Manson.

"Yes I remember his picture: long scraggly beard, unkempt hair, wild-eyed look, rather like a bloody Irish terrorist from Belfast! But looks can deceive. And probably no 'practical pharmacology.' Still down at Brighton, is he?"

Next came Dr. Grant Johnson, the laser jock. The Old Man raised a fuzzy eyebrow and pretended to not understand the expression 'jock.' This sent our conversation off on a tangent, with the Old Boy testing linguistic connections between jockeys, jock straps, disc jockeys, Scotsmen throwing the caber with kilts flapping in the breeze, Australian dialect, and cockney reverse slang. Finally, he dismissed Grant Johnson as "not having much 'applied pharmacology' either."

The Old Man really got carried away, playing the irrelevant Englishman. And he drank a good deal of sherry and started dropping syllables. Maybe the Old Man wasn't as upper class as he pretended.

"I wanted to interview Dr. John Ledbetter, but he's been out of town on some kind of business."

"I see." The Old Man glanced down at his glass, and then said slowly and thoughtfully, "Well, I suppose that it is not possible to interview someone who is not here. You will of course interview him when he returns."

In code, I asked him if Ledbetter and Manson were there

on "D-day," the day of the deed. Westley reacted with frivolous chatter about "Monty's invasion of Normandy." He finally agreed that "this intelligence could be delivered in due time."

For some moments, Westley was pensive and quiet. Then he burst forth, saying, "Pray tell, my dear Benjamin, what other characters lurk in Madam Tussaud's Chamber of Horrors?"

"The last man is George Ashton," I said neutrally.

A glow of recognition came to the Old Man's face. "Well, what do you make of him?"

"That's the question I'd like to ask you."

"That may not be appropriate, Benjamin," he said stiffening. This told me what I needed to know. "You should give me *your* impressions."

I described Ashton's aristocratic demeanor, his hand-tied bow tie and how he always maintained conversational dominance. "He reminds me of a character in an old movie I once saw, the *Scarlet Pimpernel.*"

"Oh yes . . . Leslie Howard. Fine British actor. Much better than that New Zealander, Flynn, who was such a rake. Howard did a quite credible job for the British cinema." Why did the Old Boy keep getting off track?

"Ashton has all sorts of 'applied pharmacology.' He works with snake venoms which act as neurotoxins."

"I know."

"He knows you, too," I challenged. Westley showed no reaction. I let a few seconds pass. "He said you and he 'exchanged notes on snake venoms back in the early days. He said — "

"I should hope that he did not — " Westley broke his composure and gave me a searching look.

I recounted the details of our conversation and assured Dr. Westley that we had not dwelled on his history with Ashton or my work at the M.E. lab.

It was now time for the Old Boy to tell me that Ashton was the one to zero in on. He stared for several silent moments towards the lights of Key Biscayne across the Bay. A small craft with a bow-mounted gasoline lantern had been slowly crisscrossing the Bay, half a mile out. Amateur shrimp fisher-men. Probably Cuban-Americans supplementing their income and having a little fun on the side. Westley finally broke the silence.

"Well, Ben, since Ashton is the only motivated 'applied pharmacologist' available to us at present, perhaps you should give his research some more special attention. Cautiously, of course."

"Aye, aye, sir."

It was time for me to go. Margaret had apparently re-tired, and Westley showed me to the door.

The next morning I was standing in Dr. Ashton's doorway, telling him how I'd read his papers and was definitely interested in neuroscience. He rewarded me with a phony smile and told me he had a special problem just for me. I should report to his lab the following Monday morning at nine o'clock.

I made the mistake of being punctual.

– X –

Basic Training

"WHAT DO YOU MEAN, HE WON'T be in 'til noon?" I asked in exasperation. "I had an appointment with him for nine."

Margo Davis half laughed and half frowned. "You didn't have an appointment with him. You have an appointment with me."

A girl who talks to me like that rates a second look: about 35, curly, dark-blonde, middle-length hair framing a reasonably attractive and sympathetic face. She wore tennis shoes, faded jeans, and a thick, oversized T-shirt commemorating "Sunburst 1992, Montego Bay." Outwardly, she was a female version of me.

"Did Dr. Ashton tell you what project I will be working on?"

"No. But it don't make no difference!" she retorted, apparently using the double negative for emphasis, although she did sound a little Cracker. "You don't know the techniques yet."

"Why won't it make any difference?" I asked. "I know a lot of analytical techniques already."

"But you don't know how to 'Grind 'n' Bind' yet, and that's what I've got to teach you." My mouth dropped open. "I teach everyone that comes in here – the high school students and the visiting professors." With that kind of repartee, she could have doubled as a bar maid at Captain Walley's.

I acquiesced and let Margo Davis teach me the "Grind 'n' Bind." We took a couple of mice out of a cage, put them in a plastic tube full of carbon dioxide to make them lose consciousness, cut off their heads, opened their skulls, took out their brains, and ground them up in a miniature Waring blender. That was the "grind." Then we centrifuged the soup to get nerve membrane fragments, incubated them with a radioactive drug and then caught the membrane-bound drug on filters. That was the "bind." The drug bound tightly to certain "receptors" in the nerve membrane and to nothing else. We put the filters into vials and took them to the scintillation counter that read the amount of radioactivity.

The experiment was so simple, it felt like going back to kindergarten. Chatting with Margo, I learned that she was a dyed-in-the-wool Miamian and had worked with Ashton for 14 years. Her husband worked for the phone company. She was Ashton's only technician and was responsible for everything from his daily experiments to mothering his graduate students.

Over the years, she'd helped about 30 graduate students, four of whom had stayed on to do dissertations. She indicated that none of them would have made it without her help. With Margo's help, I mastered the Grind 'n' Bind by 11:30, a full half-hour before Ashton showed up.

Ashton politely wished us a good morning and sequestered himself in his office. No welcome aboard, Ben Candidi. No pep talk about how the drug receptors are responsible for opening ion channels in membranes to make the nerves fire. No in-depth conversation about how drug binding to receptors makes it easier or harder for the ion channel to open. No inspirational message about how psychoactive drugs make it possible for people suffering from depression to lead normal lives. Just a closed door.

Margo sensed my disappointment and indicated this was par for the course.

"We usually don't get around to figuring out the project until the student's been here a week. And you need more training. We've got a rule that the student has to reproduce my results in a system I'm working on before they can go out on a new project."

"But I learned the technique today and – "

"Ben, these filtration assays all have to be done the same

way. Now come in tomorrow afternoon and we will do some
experiments on the GABA receptor, and I'll show you how to
use the scintillation counter."

So much for my first day in the lab.

I was upset until it occurred to me that Margo might be a
big help in identifying the toxin Ashton used to kill Cooper.

That afternoon, I checked my box and found a note to
"Call Steve," with no phone number. Steve Burk told me to
come over to the M.E. Office at 5:30. When I reported for
duty, he told me to change some columns on the HPLC, and
give the GC-Mass Spectrometer a shakedown. When I was an
hour into the job, he gave me a bill for service, which he asked
me to sign. It was a nice typeset invoice. Bold letters on the
top proclaimed:

CANDIDI SCIENTIFIC INSTRUMENTS
Repair and Maintenance

followed by my post office box number. At the bottom was
my social security number and "Terms: 30 days net."

They had typed in a statement for 20 hours of work. I
signed it and handed it back without comment.

Burk handed me a couple of pads of blank forms and
said, "Hold onto these for future use. I have to go home now.
Please arrange to come back and do another 'twenty hours'
next week. You can leave any time."

So the M.E. Office was giving me full pay for light duty.

Heavy course work forced me to postpone my next grind
'n' bind session with Margo. But I took it in stride, learning to
give smart answers about "single channel conductance," "channel open probability" and the "Hodgkin-Huxley-Katz Theory"
of the nerve action potential.

I spent many hours in the library filling in the cracks between the lectures and the reference books. Dr. Gordon Taylor
told the class, "As you approach the frontiers of science, the textbooks will prove less useful. And we don't want you whining
about an exam question not being covered in the book."

It wasn't hard when you think of the cell as little factories and proteins as little machines. In Biochemistry, I learned how the class of proteins called enzymes do their jobs efficiently, binding their specific "substrate" molecules, tightly and specifically, and chopping them in two. Some enzymes join two substrate molecules to build a bigger and more complicated molecule. I began to understand how drugs can bind where the substrates should, and block the reactions. I learned from Dr. Kozinski how one enzyme kicks another enzyme into high gear by chemically tagging it with phosphate – social behavior among enzymes. You can't run a factory without someone getting bossed around.

The biochemists admitted that the DNA in the chromosomes is the ultimate boss, the factory manager. Next semester in Molecular Genetics, we would learn the secrets of genes. Kozinski said that some day it might be possible to reverse the mutation in sickle cell anemia and start the cells making perfect hemoglobin.

During these first hectic few days of the Ph.D. program, I got a good study routine going. When not in class, I was in the Medical Library across the street from the Medical School. I picked out a carrel which commanded a good view of the second floor and was also convenient to a pair of couches. I stored my computer in a rented locker. What more could a guy ask for? Books, journals, air-conditioning, a convenient wall socket to plug in my computer and a good perch to watch the girls from. While thinking about perfect fits between substrate and enzyme, I sometimes lapsed into daydreams about the girl who would be a perfect fit for me.

The girls ran the whole spectrum from first-year nursing students, med students, graduate students, through working physicians and assistant professors. The nursing students seemed a little young for me.

The med students were easy to identify. With a little practice, I could even figure out what year they were in. The first year variety were noisy and nervous, and always hung around in groups. It would make me restless, too, having to learn the

Latin names for all those bones, muscles and nerves without any apparent purpose. The second-year med students were more at home, scattered around the library, reading textbooks, silently mouthing words for rote memorization and systematically transcribing pages of textbook onto flash cards. They also mastered the art of sleeping in the library, sprawled out on the couches.

The third- and fourth-year med students were in clinical rotations. They wore white jackets, pockets stuffed with loose-leaf notebooks and file cards for ready access to important information. They entered the library with a purposeful demeanor, usually walking directly into the stacks in search of an article. The more advanced the med student, the more worn out they looked. One night I looked up from my book to see the girl of my dreams walking by. She was probably a medical sophomore. She was gone before I thought of something to say.

One afternoon I dropped into the graduate student room while Maria Mendez was on the phone, talking in Spanish. I sat down and cracked open a book, but it was impossible to ignore her conversation. Her mom was complaining that her sister was causing problems again. Maria ended the conversation early and plunked down into a chair.

"You know, Ben, sometimes I almost feel like giving up. Ilsa is throwing fits because we can't give her a fancy *Quince*. We'll be lucky if we have a thousand dollars at the end of the month."

In Anglo culture it's "sweet sixteen," but down here it happens a year earlier. Special banquet halls are designed to take care of the parties and to take care of your bank account in the process. With the white dresses, the invitations, the food and photographers and everything, a *Quince* can cost $5,000.

"I know what you mean," I sympathized. "It's like the fancy wedding that no one can afford."

"And Mama and I are worrying about Papa. He shouldn't be working with his weak heart. And he won't listen to the doctor and stop smoking cigars."

She stood up and walked over to the window, perhaps to

hide her face.

"Talk to your other sister. You told me she's nineteen. Maybe she can talk some sense into Ilsa."

"Lourdes is just as *loca* as Ilsa. I told her Lazaro was no good for her. She thinks he's going to be a big businessman, but at his rate, it's going to take him eight years to get out of Miami-Dade Community College. And he spends all the money he makes at Dixie Super-Check on that stupid car. He loves that dumb Camaro more than he loves her. Even now."

"Even now?"

I shouldn't have asked. Maria was silent for a long time, then her shoulders caved in with a sigh. "She's two months pregnant."

I got up and steadied her trembling shoulders with my hands, and found some words of encouragement. She should take a hard line on the *Quince* and should give some good-sisterly advice to Lourdes. I turned her around, dabbed her eyes with the collar of my polo shirt and gave her a brotherly kiss on the cheek – which she answered with a kiss on the lips. For an awkward moment, it threatened to become passionate. I'm not one of those guys who can have a frivolous affair with a serious girl. I promised to help her with the Membranes Course, which I did. Several months later, she returned the favor in a big way.

I always tried to make us a foursome by including Grant Shipley and Sheng-Ping Chow. The volleyball champ from Peking Medical College needed lots of help with English, and our conversations served as short tutorials. I told him to spend some time watching television in the medical student lounge. Television makes your brain porous, and he could learn English by osmosis. But he spent every spare moment on a lab rotation. I admired his zeal.

I shared a lot of laughs with Margo during an afternoon Grind 'n' Bind session later that week. She said I was "getting pretty good" and that Ashton might give me a project next week. He was always holed up in his office. That was fine with me – not having him around while I joked his neuro-toxin secrets out of Margo.

106

– XI –

Departmental Seminar

*D*R. GORDON TAYLOR PACED BACK and forth like a drill sergeant. "An additional ground rule that you entry-level students must know about the seminar which will soon take place: The weekly research seminar is the most important intellectual function in the Department. Every one of us, from the Chairman on down to the lowliest graduate student (ha! ha!) is expected to present at least once per year."

This surprised some of us, and Dr. Taylor sensed it.

"The seminar brings us all on the same intellectual level. Ha! Ha! Ha! We are not some big corporation where the underlings are expected to sit silently, nodding their heads meekly. You are *all* expected to take an active part."

We must listen carefully to the seminar, he admonished. Lowly graduate students weren't expected to understand as much as a post-doctoral fellow. An assistant professor might not give as good a seminar as an associate professor or full professor. He digressed, saying, "Post-docs are something like knights errant who have to move from one kingdom to another in search of a regular tenure-earning academic job." (Ha, ha, ha.)

Then he glanced at his watch. "It is but five minutes to the hour and the knowledge-thirsty hordes are at the gates."

He waved his hand in dismissal and opened the door. As members of the department streamed in, professor and lowly graduate student alike, I moved up to claim a seat in the front row. Taylor joked with Dr. Fleischman about "having conducted an indoctrination session."

The seminar room seemed to shrink as it filled with over 40 people. Several faculty took places and spread out their lunches on a large table dominating the left side of the room.

My front row was curiously empty, although people were standing in the back of the room. At Swarthmore, we used to compete for front-row seats. A student a row behind me said that the seminar would be given by "Dr. Cooper's right-hand man."

Dr. Mary Pennington, the designated mistress of ceremonies, sat at the table, talking to the speaker, Dr. Pang Wong. She often looked nervously toward the crowd, as if responsible for attendance. Around five minutes after the hour, she muttered something about waiting long enough, and she stepped up to the floor-standing lectern.

"I am sure that Pang needs no introduction for most of us," she said, nodding in his direction. He nodded back nervously, as if waiting for a cue to get up.

"But for the new students and visitors, Dr. Wong came to us three years ago to work in Dr. Cooper's lab. He received his Bachelor of Medicine at Taipei University in Taiwan, his Ph.D. at the University of California, San Francisco, working on parvalbumin structure, and after several years of post-doc'ing with Saul Goldfarb at Berkeley, he came here as a research assistant professor."

She seemed to be asking the audience for approval as she searched nervously from face to face, nodding her head as she mentioned Saul Goldfarb, as if this would somehow strike a chord of agreement among us all.

Looking down at a piece of paper, she said, "The title of Pang's talk is 'Molecular Genetic Studies of a New Calcium-Binding Protein from Barnacle Muscle'."

She nodded to him, and he approached the lectern somewhat nervously, carrying a sheath of notes. Once behind the lectern, he glanced at the audience and touched his face.

"Today . . . I am going to talk to you about chimera-construct experiments which we did on the protein 'Calbarn' in barnacle muscle," he read, his face buried in his notes. "As you know, this is a new calcium-binding protein with unknown function discovered in Dr. Cooper's lab. These experiments were done in collaboration with Dr. Cooper, who was tragically lost to us a few weeks ago."

Someone coughed in the back of the room. I sensed that people were reacting, but couldn't turn my head to see. It was a bad mistake, not sitting farther back. What had Ashton done? These rapid, knee-jerk reactions could tell the whole story. Who nodded in agreement? Who raised an eyebrow? And who coughed?

Wong attempted some extemporaneous words on Cooper's work, and his presentation got weaker by the second, until he was holding onto the lectern like a life raft. Stiffly, he read long, complicated sentences, apparently lifted verbatim from the introduction of a scientific paper describing the molecule "Calbarn" from the barnacle muscle. His mispronunciation, mumbling and monotone flatness made it difficult to understand anything. I couldn't have been the only person in the room who was embarrassed for him.

"Can I have first slide?"

Someone flicked on a 35-millimeter slide projector in the back of the room. Dr. Wong picked up a hand-held controller hanging by its cable from the lectern and punched the button. The screen lit up with one of those twisted-ribbon diagrams like what Dr. Kozinski showed us for hemoglobin. Wong showed us a ribbon structure with "five alpha helices" connected by four large loops and showed us where he thought calcium binds. When calcium binds, it is supposed to change the shape on the other side of the molecule so that it can activate different enzymes. He wasn't clear about which enzymes were activated.

"The evidence for this is still controversial," he said.

He told us that the Calbarn from rabbit differs in "amino acid sequence" from barnacle Calbarn. He described experiments where he took Calbarn from the rabbit aorta and put it into barnacle muscle. And rabbit protein worked only half as well in barnacle. This was his test system.

Then he played around, redesigning the rabbit and barnacle proteins, constructing Calbarn "chimeras" using molecular genetic tricks. After the seminar, I looked up the word chimera. It is the mythical she-monster of Greek mythology with a lion's head, a goat's body and a snake's tail. Biochemistry has a lot of snobby types like Westley who pride themselves on their classical education. Anyway, Wong had created a lot of monster Calbarns by grafting barnacle "heads" onto rabbit "tails."

It was fascinating that big complicated molecules like this could be designed at will. I didn't understand the technology, but it involved cutting and splicing the genes, and tricking bacterial cells into manufacturing the proteins. I recalled Margaret's words: "It's all so strangely wonderful." It was as strange and wonderful as cutting off the rear end of a horse and attaching it to the front end of a giraffe and testing how good it could run and eat leaves from trees. Wong made and tested 15 chimera hybrids.

Ten minutes into the chimera stuff and Dr. Grant Johnson's hand went up in the air.

"You mean that you have only a factor of two difference in the activity of the barnacle and rabbit proteins?" he asked.

"Yes, we have twofold difference," Wong answered.

"Jees!" exclaimed Johnson in disbelief. His eyes shot to the ceiling and then slowly descended to the floor. Wong tried to go on but was immediately interrupted by Dr. Taylor, who was sitting close behind me.

"I am not clear as to whether you are attributing this *modest* difference in activity to the calcium-binding site or to the protein-binding site."

"We do not know at this point. We need further experiments," answered Wong.

"It would seem to be more a question of *which* experiments than how many," Dr. Taylor persisted. Then he scathed Wong in one long, eloquent, seamless pronouncement, characterizing the hybridization process as "painfully tedious" and decrying Wong's lack of "pivotal experiments." Dr. Westley would have been proud of his compatriot's use of the Queen's

English. It was a blistering condemnation that translated roughly to "Your experiments were a fool's errand."

Dr. Wong defended himself recalcitrantly, citing Saul Goldfarb's work as evidence. Dr. Taylor turned red in the face and growled, "That is just Goldfarb's deduction of the *probable* calcium binding site, based on loose analogies with other proteins. You should have tested for differences in calcium binding first." *So Goldfarb was just guessing.*

Dr. Wong defended himself stubbornly. Livid-faced and halfway out of his seat, Dr. Taylor renewed his scathing attack. He practically shouted when he came to phrases like "to a very modest degree." He ended saying, "Your experiments do not tell us anything more about Calbarn than we already knew. In fact, they raise more questions than they answer."

"But isn't that what scientific research supposed to do?" Wong's rejoinder brought general laughter from the audience – students, post-docs and faculty alike.

"*No!*"

The answer was as cold as it was emphatic. During the last two exchanges, I had moved a couple of seats closer to the wall so I could look at people behind me without being too obvious.

Pointing a finger at me, Stampawicz delivered a quip for all to hear. "Looks like an innocent bystander is trying to get out of the line of fire." The audience erupted in laughter.

"Don't shoot me, I'm only the graduate student," I answered cutely. This brought more laughter.

Taylor was not amused by either of us. He drew in a deep breath and said, "As I have said before in this room, I find it ludicrous to be attempting such a roundabout proof when simple classical binding-and-activation studies would prove the point." Translation: *You should have done the simpler experiment, you dumb klutz.*

Now I could see. Ashton, sitting in the back, seemed aloof. Kozinski, sitting in the middle, glanced from Taylor to Wong and back, with a look that said, "Let's not have any more trouble." On the sidelines, Dr. Fleischman smiled as if to say "I told you so."

As Taylor and Wong launched into another round of argument, Acting Chairman Peter Moore cleared his throat and announced, "Further discussion can be carried out later."

Wong presented a few more inconclusive experiments, ended his seminar and received five seconds of lukewarm applause. Robert Sturtz and Robert Gunnison each asked a polite technical question about the molecular genetic techniques. Then Dr. Pennington announced the end of the session.

My next session – ten times as exciting – started without warning a couple minutes later.

– XII –

Inside Scoop

DR. ROBERT MCGREGOR, RESEARCH Assistant Professor, plodded behind me as I walked to the elevator. He was a tall, heavy guy, with a high, oversized rear end and a pair of observant eyes. Someone said he was a Canadian of Scottish extraction. In his late thirties, he was old for an assistant professor. I pushed the button and quickly thought up some elevator small-talk.

"I'm going to start bringing my lunch to the seminar. My stomach isn't used to waiting to one o'clock."

"The seminar got my juices going, too," McGregor said, semi-relevantly. "Today, we saw what happens when you spend all your time chasing grant money and forget about solving scientific problems."

"I haven't been around here long enough to understand what you mean," I half-lied. Sometimes it's smarter to act dumb.

"You aren't all *that* green. You've been doing chemistry for the Medical Examiner's Office for a long time." He scrutinized me. "The word is that you're a whiz at instrumental analysis. I was there when we considered your application, Candidi."

I tried to not show surprise. "But all I did was some analytical chemistry. I never did anything with chimeric proteins, genetic engineering or anything," I said, stalling for time.

"You worked with HPLC chromatography, didn't you? You know that your choice of column-packing material determines how long a molecule is held back, don't you?"

"Yes."

"Well," he said, leading me out at the ground floor, "let's

say you run your molecule X through a carobowax column and it gets held back for one minute. And, when you run it through a plasto-wax column which binds molecule X more tightly, it gets held back for two minutes. Now, you pack a new column that's half carbowax and half plasto-wax? Now how long does it get held back?"

"It's common sense. I'd split the difference. One and one-half minutes," I answered, hesitating near the front entrance.

"Right on!" he said, leaning his big rear end against the guard's desk. "And why?" he demanded.

The guard wasn't used to scientific discussions in front of his workstation. I took a couple of steps towards the door before answering, "It wouldn't be any use to make guesses with a complicated theory because the difference wasn't very large anyway."

"And that, Candidi, is exactly the problem with Wong's seminar – and Cooper's whole research program. They were chasing factors of two. A real effect has to make something five or ten times larger. Wong's molecular genetics and chimeras was just a bunch of hand-waving. We already know that one end of the molecule binds calcium and the other anchors the molecule. Cooper and Wong's work was a big waste of time – and money – which is getting pretty scarce nowadays. And *that* really gets my stomach acid churning. Candidi, are you going to the Sub Shop? I've seen you there before."

McGregor stepped toward the door, and the guard looked relieved. On the walk to the Sub Shop, I learned about Dr. McGregor's research methods. He didn't need any molecular-genetic tricks like Drs. Wong, Strutz and Gunnison. He determined which molecules "talked" to each other inside a living cell by chemically trapping them while they were bound together. If molecules were people, it would be like seeing a man and a woman together every day at the Sub Shop and suspecting that "something was going on." McGregor's method would be to catch them in the act by *handcuffing* them together.

I told him it was a clever method, and he invited me to do a rotation in his lab under the tutelage of Dr. Kozinski. As a "*research* assistant professor," McGregor couldn't have his own graduate students. That was a shame, because he seemed to be a good teacher.

After the waitress took our orders, I tested my understanding of McGregor's methods. "If you were going to attack Wong's problem, you would probably add your cross-linker to his barnacle muscles and see what proteins get handcuffed to his Calbarn."

"Chemically *handcuffing*! Hey, that's a good expression, Candidi! Yes, I'd handcuff them, put them on SDS gel electrophoresis plates, and turn on the electricity to spread them out. Then I'd use identifying antibodies and molecular weights to figure out who got handcuffed to whom in the *gemisch*."

Another Germanophile.

There's nothing as exciting as a good scientific discussion. Could I channel McGregor's enthusiasm into help with my investigation? I popped a leading question. "The Department seems split on the value of this molecular genetic stuff."

"Right. Until he died, Cooper had a lot of people nervous that molecular genetics might be the *only* type of research you can do here. But without him pushing it down our throats, molecular genetic research seems to be losing a lot of its momentum."

"You seem to be on the other side."

"Well you see, Candidi, I'm one of those researchers who's blessed with a system which runs on brain power, and not on Chinese coolie labor. Look at me: I'm the whole McGregor laboratory! No technicians, post-docs or anything. Well, maybe an occasional high school student. I run my show for $25,000 a year. Now you look at Cooper's ex-empire. He was burning $400,000 a year. Easy! And the Department paid most of it. Like Wong's salary."

Hanging on McGregor's words, I did my best to keep him primed.

"Wong really got raked over the coals today."

"Yeah," McGregor chuckled. "Johnson spotted him on that 'only a factor of two' business and Taylor nailed him to the wall by the seat of his pants. And this time he didn't have

Cooper to protect him."

"I take it that you didn't think much of Cooper."

"The guy really wasn't that smart. And he didn't have much imagination, either. To him, science was doing the same old crap over and over, occasionally with a new twist. And he played politics."

"You mean local politics?"

"He played politics with the Dean and played dictator with the rest of us. But he was good at acting pompous and getting underlings to do his dirty work. He spent a lot of energy keeping track of who would and wouldn't kiss his ass." A middle-aged woman at the next table cleared her throat in protest, but McGregor didn't notice. "Cooper also had this dominance thing."

"How did it work?"

"He'd stare at you, without saying anything, and you were supposed to supply the conversation. He wasn't much of a conversationalist anyway. If you kowtowed to him, then he knew he controlled you. Then he might even be friendly. But if you acted independent, he didn't like you. Saddam Hussein uses the same technique."

"How did Cooper keep control?"

"He was always bringing in new assistant professors and mixing things up. And the Dean of the Medical School thinks that bigger is better. More grants generate more overhead payments from the NIH – the National Institutes of Health."

McGregor painted a grim picture of academic biomedical science. The faculty were forever chasing "soft money," writing grant proposals to finance their labs and pay their salaries. And they had to bring in soft money because the medical school hired five times as many faculty as could be paid from their normal "hard money" operating funds. A newly-hired assistant professor had five years to establish a track record getting grants and to earn the award of "tenure." And he couldn't get tenure without a favorable letter from his chairman. To complete his control, Cooper pitted his new assistant professors against the tenured associate professors and full professors. If a tenured professor wasn't earning half of his salary from grants, Cooper would threaten to reduce his salary, reinventing tenure policy as he went along.

"Guys like me, who are not on the *tenure track*, we had to worry about Cooper all the time. I'm paid by soft money only. If I lose a grant, I'm washed up. I'd be sacked, with one month grace period for every year I've been here. Once that's used up, it's curtains. And they would never have to hire me back."

He told me how the medical school profited from his federal grants by receiving inflated "fringe benefit" and "overhead" payments, using these profits to erect new buildings to be filled with more "soft money slave scientists." He compared the med school with a sugar plantation. Cooper was a brutal overseer, and the scientists were expendable slave labor.

"You make it sound like I signed up for gladiator school. They keep throwing you into the ring, and only the survivors crawl out of the sand to fight again."

McGregor's face clouded over. He didn't answer me right away.

"Yeah, it's a tough career you signed up for, kid."

The waitress brought our sandwiches. I let McGregor get in a few bites before restarting the conversation.

"If the soft money system was so bad anyway, why was Cooper so disliked? You might say that the hardship just goes with the territory."

"We hated him because he grabbed all the hard money for himself. He didn't have enough sympathy in his heart to toss even a crumb to the rest of us," he said with disgust.

Maybe I could learn who disliked Cooper enough to kill him. "I guess that you 'soft money slaves' got the last laugh. You are walking the earth and he's six feet under."

"Sudden death by arrhythmia, they say. He probably didn't know what he was harboring in himself."

Walking back to the Department, we explored the origins of the expression "harboring the seeds of destruction within himself." That brought us to Saddam Hussein, which brought us to the nuclear threat, to its influence on the psychology of the 1950s through the 1980s, to the nature of the Russian soul, to Chekhov and Dostoevski – which almost brought us back to Cooper.

I first worried that Dr. McGregor would dry up like an oil well that's pumped too hard. But I was to learn that he was a veritable artesian well. As we left the elevator, going our separate ways, he said, "Maybe I'll see you for lunch after the next seminar."

"That would be great, Dr. McGregor."

"Call me Rob."

What a contrast between his cumbersome walk and his dancing intellect. He took his time getting there, but he didn't miss a thing along the way. What a versatile conversationalist. In his inquisitive mode, he had trained all senses on me, making it impossible to keep secrets from him. In his briefing mode, he had transmitted valuable information from his deepest memory banks at high baud rate, hardly noticing me during the transfer.

That evening on *Diogenes* I paced the deck, this time in elation. McGregor had explained it so nicely: Cooper the tyrant, Wong his flunkie, the Old Guard's attack on him, and the New Guard's loyalty to their dead master, revealed by their defense of Wong with their polite technical questions. Stampawicz, normally a stickler for logic, had tried to deflect Taylor's criticism of Wong, with his "getting out of the line of fire" comment.

Yes, the Old Guard was the enemy camp and Ashton was its stealth warrior. And if Westley didn't give me strong signals of agreement, I would snatch off his veil of sacred choirboy innocence.

– XIII –

Zeroing On

"*H*ODGKIN AND HUXLEY DISCOVERED nerve action potential right after the war," the Old Boy exclaimed in a cadence that matched the Bach fugue spinning on his ancient turntable. I sensed a mini-lecture coming on. "Brilliant Cambridge chaps! Worked with squid axon. Seems that the fishing boats brought back an abundant supply of squid. You may not know, but Hodgkin and Huxley worked on perfecting radar during the war. Then they used their special knowledge of electronics to analyze the signals from nerve. Of course, they were awarded the Nobel Prize in 1963 for their efforts, along with John Eccles, an Australian who picked up on their singular demonstrations."

The Old Boy should have tried his hand at television quiz shows – preferably the slow-paced BBC variety, which allowed long-winded answers. My mention of the protein structure lectures triggered another historical monologue.

"Yes. Of course, protein structure was a murky business until Perutz – who put it on a rational basis. Used x-ray crystallography with Germanic persistence to study hemoglobin, but made his contribution in England, of course."

I told him about Kozinski's molecular graphics lecture, with oxygen binding to hemoglobin. He told me that Roughton (an Englishman, of course) had studied the reaction on a millisecond time scale using his specially designed rapid-mixing apparatus. To hear him talk, every major discovery was made by an Englishman.

I shifted the conversation to Wong's seminar, but Westley

stopped me when I began to describe the argument.

"You know, these Chinese are *so* dreary! And it is *so* sad when work is misdirected. We must find something more positive."

He also rejected Rob McGregor's diatribe on Cooper.

"Well, I suppose that every place has its juicy little items of gossip. This McGregor chap seems to be a good one to carry it on. Good Scottish name. The Scots seem to gossip only two-thirds as much as the Irish – to the detriment of both, mind you. But the Scots *do* manage to put in a good day's work, unlike their Gaelic brethren. And Scottish gossip tends to be more concise, although this McGregor seems to be the exception which proves the rule."

So, what the hell, I'd let the Old Boy get it off his chest.

"Is Scottish gossip easier to forgive than Irish gossip? Why do the Scots gossip?"

"I have often thought that the Scots' proclivities for gossip come from a certain sense of justice. They do have a very pronounced sense of justice, they do. Although they haven't quite forgiven us for civilizing them. A century longer in The Empire and we will be able to call them English. Of course, with the Irish there was absolutely no hope. We began the actual process too late."

I tried to restart the subject of Cooper's crimes, but the Old Man would have none of it.

"Gossip and idleness are the devil's playground. You will find, Ben, that there are certain things which one learns, but does not communicate. McGregor may be an interesting fellow, but 'a dog which will bring a bone will also carry one away.' We shouldn't want you carried away, so to speak."

At this moment, Margaret announced that dinner was served. And they both served me large portions of delightful Anglophile conversation. Afterward, Westley and I took our places on the balcony. I expressed interest in learning more about orally active toxins, and the Old Man proved happy to provide a mini-dissertation.

"The general principles are quite easy, Ben. If you are a

snail or lizard or some other helpless creature without massive teeth and claws to defend yourself, you may want to incorporate into your flesh some sort of toxin which would persuade your larger predators not to eat you. Usually these animals are brightly colored. It would not do, in the general scheme of things, to have the predators die without knowing why."

"And bright coloring is a way of advertising that they are poisonous?"

"Quite. All manner of reptiles do it. In fact, I have read of the recent discovery of a poisonous *bird* . . . in New Guinea. It is called the pitohui, and it has distinctive orange-and-black plumage. Ingestion of only 100 milligrams of its breast flesh is sufficient to kill a mouse in twenty minutes, the article said. The toxic principle is called homobatrachotoxin. It's a steroid alkaloid, a nonprotein toxin."

"What about plant toxins?"

"Yes, there are more numerous examples and many examples of weak toxins. Of course, half of the molecules made by plants are poisons of one sort or other. Plants, being passive, had to find some way to keep from being eaten out of existence by the animals. So they produce molecules which made the animals sick to serve as a deterrent. The turpentine in pine sap and tetrahydrocanabinol in marijuana are two such examples. Of course, there are spruce hens in Alaska which will eat pine needles, and a starving goat would probably eat hemp. But the point is that these stout little molecules are created by the plants to make the herbivorous animals sick by interfering with one or more bodily function."

The Old Boy radiated such warmth when delivering these monologues.

"So that's why you can't keep yourself alive in the woods by eating leaves," I summarized.

"Quite true. You'd make yourself quite sick. Even grass, you really can't eat, even if it were cooked. On the other hand, the cow has an excellent liver which is well-designed to detoxify itself, so she can subsist on a steady diet of these things. Of course they are just *low grade* toxins. Nothing so horrible that a few mouthfuls will kill you. No poisonous molecules which are strong or specific enough to kill the animal. That would not do! It is not in Our Maker's scheme of things to have animals dropping dead all over the landscape. No, the Good Lord has only allowed his creatures to do a little *prodding*, in the right direction – unpleasant consequences after fair warning. It is a bit like the border collie nipping at the sheep's heels, getting it to go in the right direction without hurting it."

His voice softened and his face seemed to glow as he talked about Our Maker's Scheme of Things. He must have found comfort, believing in a benevolent universe after so many years of examining murder victims. That's what the human flock needs: A gentle British sheepdog to keep them from going astray.

"Understandably, these low-grade, orally-active toxins are small molecules. They are not carbohydrates, proteins or fats, which are easily digested. Their chemical bonds are a little more stout. Rugged molecules, so to speak. They aren't digested by the saliva, stomach acid or by the bile juice. And they are sufficiently hydrophobic to cross membranes and transit the gut lining unchanged. So they can get into the bloodstream. It's the liver that has the job of digesting them."

He reaffirmed an important working principle: The non-protein toxins work by mouth.

Next, the Old Man told me a heartwarming story of the old Cornish doctor who discovered the heart medicine *digitalis* when he noticed that cows dropped dead after eating an innocent-looking flower called foxglove. He prescribed it for his patients – as a fine medicinal English tea, of course. "Today, this simple toxin is keeping hundreds of thousands of geriatric souls in their decrepit bodies," he concluded.

Rejoice! Both the British sheepdog and the English doctor are on our side!

I told him that digitalis works on the sodium pump discovered by Dr. Fleischman, and he cut me off. "Of course, it would be possible to kill a man by giving him a large dose of digitalis, just like the poor cow. And this is indeed what many doctors unwittingly do to thousands of patients each year. But digitalis is rather old-hat. A death from digitalis overdose would present no great mystery to us. Hospital laboratories have antibody-based radioimmunoassays to monitor digitalis blood levels in their patients."

I made him confirm that he also had assays for well-known toxins like the puffer fish poison, tetrodotoxin. He agreed that I should deliver a short list of Ashton's nonprotein toxins. He didn't seem to be interested in protein toxins, which are produced by snakes and other animals that can bite it in.

"Thank you, Dr. Westley. I'm clear on what I have to do."

A few minutes later, Westley was shaking my hand warmly and wishing me well with my "endeavours."

Rowing home, I felt satisfied to give Westley a short list of Ashton's nonprotein toxins. But I still worried about how to decide which neurotoxins to put on the list – and which ones to leave out.

– XIV –

Neurotoxins Galore

MARGO WAS ALL SMILES. "TODAY Dr. Ashton will assign you a project."

"Thanks for finally telling Dr. Ashton that I'm a reliable pair of hands," I replied half-seriously.

"Oh, they're reliable. And you just keep them to yourself!"

I blew her a raspberry. We both liked to joke around.

Margo knocked on Ashton's permanently closed door, went in and told him something in *sotto voce*. Then Dr. Ashton beckoned aristocratically and received me. I would study a "muscarinic" receptor for the neurotransmitter acetylcholine from the brain. It binds the hallucinogen muscarine. It is a cousin of the "nicotinic" receptor which binds nicotine.

My job would be to study the muscarine receptor #5, the "M-5" receptor, from mouse brain. Ashton gave me a scientific paper showing a complicated twisted ribbon picture of how the M-5 receptor was supposed to nestle in the membrane. Margo gave me a sample of a decapeptide, a short piece of protein consisting of ten amino acids in a specific sequence. Against the diagram of the M-5 receptor, my decapeptide would look like a short snip of ribbon. It was supposed to bind in a crevice of the M-5 receptor, fitting like a key in a lock, and activating the receptor.

Ashton said that my decapeptide was a candidate anti-Parkinson drug. I didn't believe him but kept my opinion to myself. It can't be taken orally because it can't cross the intestinal lining. And it wouldn't be practical to inject the patient every day.

Dr. Ashton wanted data on how tight my decapeptide bound to the M-5 receptor. After spending a few crisp and efficient minutes with me, he sent me to Margo to "get set up in the assay." It would be some variation on the Bind 'n' Grind. It was okay that he didn't pay more attention to me. That way I wouldn't feel so bad about turning him in to Westley.

Half an hour later, Margo was free. She gave me a radio-labelled ligand for the M-5 receptor and some general instructions to get me started. Another half an hour later, I was standing in front of an array of test tubes and manifolded filter-holders that looked like a miniature organ, merrily adding the radio-ligand to homogenized mouse brains.

I tried to get excited about reactions in the first row of test tubes, thinking about how the radio-ligand molecules were swimming around in the brain soup, in and about the membrane fragments, until they found an M-5 receptor, binding tightly and staying bound for a long time.

The reactions in the other rows of test tubes were competitions between the decapeptide and the radio-ligand for binding to the M-5 receptor. It was like the competition between two guys for one girl. If the decapeptide bound, then the radio-ligand couldn't. In fact, that was how I measured binding of the decapeptide, which didn't have its own radioactivity.

But the Grind 'n' Bind wasn't very exciting. It left me plenty of time to worry about the large wall chart from Eta Biochemical Company. It listed hundreds of lethal neurotoxins:

omega-agatoxin IVA from Agelenopsis aperta venom, calcisptine toxin, conotoxin, TaiCatoxin, dendrotoxin, apamin toxin, charybdotoxin, iberiotoxin, leiurotoxin, brevetoxin, imperatoxin, imperialine, argiotoxin, bicuculline, fasciculine, ammodytoxin, totexin, liquorine, heliotrine, cardiotoxin, tetrodotoxin, sax-itoxin, separateline − just to name a few.

They had toxins from snakes, spiders, lizards, fish, snails, frogs, toads, sponges and microorganisms. Half of them were non-protein, and many of them actually worked on the acetyl-choline receptor. So the aristocratic George Ashton, M.D. didn't have to stray out of his own field to find the perfect poison.

During the next two weeks, I spent every spare moment in Ashton's lab. During dead time, when the scintillation counter was backed up, I kept my eyes and ears open for clues.

The simple principles of experiments were delightfully similar to Ashton's poisoning of Cooper. My decapeptide toxin bound to the M-5 receptor in a cell membrane fragment; Ashton's unknown toxin bound to receptors in a living man. The binding of my decapeptide to its receptor was extremely tight; Ashton's poison had to bind tight. The decapeptide/M-5 receptor complex had a so-called "dissociation constant" of 10^{-10} molar. The lower the dissociation constant the tighter the binding. Using Avogadro's Number, a 10^{-10} molar blood concentration and the weight of a grown man, I calculated that 14 milligrams of this peptide could kill a man. Fourteen milligrams is the weight of 30 grains of sugar. It takes a big puncture to put that much material under the skin. So here was another reason to forget about protein and polypeptide toxins.

Now, many orally active toxins could bind just as tight. And 14 milligrams would be easy to slip into Cooper's food. And it could have easily escaped detection by my HPLC machine back at the M.E.'s lab. The problem was beginning to get interesting.

The next day, long-absent Dr. Manson generated his own fanfare when he drove his van to the loading dock, returning from Woods Hole. It was impossible to miss him. He and his technician spent most of the morning unloading and hauling his gear to his lab.

Manson was a sight to see, with a baseball cap advertising "Caterpillar Power," a curly red beard and shoulder-length hair. He wore a heavy, oversized, plaid lumberjack shirt and naturally faded jeans. Completing the picture were thick, loose-fitting white socks and Japanese sandals. The thong indented the sock between the big toe and adjoining toe, but there was plenty of slack to go around. Manson slipped all over the place while pushing the wheel-mounted electronics rack, in a whimsically distracted manner, as if he didn't care if the task would take 10 minutes or 10 hours.

His technician, a bookish-looking woman in her late twenties, did most of the work. Manson stopped at the elevator and got into a conversation with a Chinese graduate student – speaking fairly fluent Chinese! He was a colorful, unforgettable character. I scratched his name off the list of suspects.

Post-seminar lunch with Rob McGregor had become a regular thing. After Dr. Sturtz' seminar, I learned that Dr. Cooper had tampered with the recruiting process to hire Sturz. For five years Sturtz had worked exclusively on molecular genetic experiments for Cooper, who paid him with Departmental "hard money."

The molecular geneticists had become the fair-haired boys of biomedical science because they could manipulate genes. They had indirect methods for finding a specific gene, isolating the gene, reproducing it in bacteria and mutating it at the exact point where they wanted. It was like being able to search a whole library for a certain quote – then being able to change the quote and put the book back on the shelf. You could learn a lot with the technique, but you could also create a lot of nonsense with it.

But there were still greater wonders: Like putting the mutated gene back into the right spot in a fertilized mouse egg, producing a daughter mouse with cystic fibrosis or orange fur.

But the most wondrous story was told by Dr. Mary Pennington.

– XV –

More Intelligence

SHE TOLD OF THE BRETHREN OF Lytechinus who, under the full moon, at the gentle urgings of the streaming tide, mutually awaken to a hormonal trumpet call and release clouds of sugarcoated sperm to swim stochastically toward the lure of gradients of their sisters' unknown fragrances, seeking evaginated eggs for the complicated glycoprotein-regulated act of copulation and impregnation so necessary to sea urchin survival.

Actually, Dr. Mary Pennington's research seminar on intracellular events after sea urchin egg fertilization was properly mechanistic and impeccably correct. I must have been distracted by the third-year graduate student two seats to my left. She was one of the cutest gals I've ever seen – short, slim, with dark eyes, China Doll face and nice legs revealed by short skirts. She never seemed to bother with the top three buttons on her loosely fitting blouse, and it didn't bother me, either. Before the seminar she had hit on me in an unmistakable way. Her name was Tsien Tsien, pronounced "Chen Chen."

As the room emptied, we both lingered in our seats. She stood up in unison with me, bringing us face-to-face at very short range. She stood her ground, batted her eyes and asked, "You think cyclic AMP or protein kinase C more important for calcium mobilization process?"

She smiled enticingly as I composed a fumbled answer. I glanced at the blackboard, as if drawing circles, arrows and crosses might rescue my composure. But Tsien Tsien's question had nothing to do with molecules. I stood, frozen and helpless in her tractor beam.

"Maybe we have in-depth discussion some time," she suggested with twinkling eyes and a bewitchingly nervous laugh.

I sensed a hulking presence in the background and then felt a heavy hand grip my shoulder. "We're late for our luncheon." It was Rob McGregor speaking in his all-seeing, all-knowing, big-brother mode. I muttered something as he slowly turned me towards the door.

"Maybe you come visit me in Dr. Gunnison lab," Tsien Tsien tinkled.

"Sure thing," I answered in confusion.

In the privacy of the elevator, Rob looked down on me like I was a four year-old who'd just gotten himself lost at the department store. "Look here, little breeches. She's a student, but she came here on a J-visa as a post-doc. J-visa, Ben. It's an *exchange* visa, and she's run out of time. In one month she's got to go back to her Worker's Paradise – the People's Republic of China. *Or* she can throw away her dissertation research and start over in Canada. Or she can marry a U.S. citizen. Now guess what's her preferred option."

"Marriage-minded?"

"And, how! Watch yourself, little breeches. It's a jungle out there."

"Thanks for saving me, Baloo."

Over lunch, Rob toughened me up for life in the jungle. He told me how they judge grant proposals at the NIH in Washington. He told how a scientist spends three months writing a proposal, to have it spend several months in Washington going from desk to desk, before copies are finally sent to 15 scientists, only two of whom have to read it, spending at most an hour. He told how the 15 scientists fly to Washington to convene as a "Study Section," spending two or three days grading proposals – at the rate of one every 10 minutes!

Two hastily written critiques are retyped onto a "Pink Sheet" and returned to the applicant together with the "priority score." Only one in six proposals is funded. One negative comment can shoot down a proposal, and often the reviewers are competing with you.

"Do you have any chance for a rebuttal?" I asked.

"Hell, no! You just submit another grant proposal and wait another year to hear how it comes out."

Dr. Cooper had tried to use the Pink Sheets to judge the quality of a faculty member's research. Yet, Cooper found the in-house faculty research seminars so uninteresting that they sometimes put him to sleep.

"Rob, I've noticed that you older profs always call a spade a spade, even if it means disagreeing in public."

McGregor nodded in affirmation. Now was the time for me to pop THE QUESTION.

"It's ironic that Cooper died right after meeting with a sizable group of people, half of whom hated his guts. They probably wished him dead. It's almost like someone pronounced a Voodoo curse." I let this sink in. McGregor acted like it was the first time he'd heard anything like this. I laughed and asked, "Were any faculty members capable of casting a Voodoo curse?"

"Yeah, I guess a few of us would have liked him dead."

"Who'd get first prize?" I asked, hoping he'd name Ashton.

"Probably Fleischman. Cooper literally destroyed his career."

"And second prize?"

"Well, Ledbetter hated his guts, and didn't mind letting anyone know – including Cooper himself!"

"Yes, I haven't met him yet. He's been away on a trip as long as I've been here."

"Yeah, he's a real *trip*. But smart! Probably the most cerebral member of the department"

"And who gets third prize?"

"For being cerebral?"

"No. For hating Cooper's guts."

"Could be anyone, including me."

"But Cooper must have really pissed off Ashton. I mean that guy doesn't like being messed with."

"Yeah. But it didn't happen too often. Ashton was a master at outsmarting Cooper and working around him."

It bothered me that Ashton was so low on McGregor's list. We fell silent for a while. McGregor continued to smoulder and then once again burst into flame on the Cooper theme:

"Paying himself $210,000 a year in hard money and then bragging to his friends at other institutions that he was the 'highest paid pharmacology chairman in the U.S.!' That was pretty hard for us to stomach, Ben."

Old Man Westley was probably right: If you get a Scotsman talking about an old unrighted wrong, he won't stop until he has talked himself out – or pulls a knife out of his sock.

Rob recited a litany of Cooper's crimes, including taking a kickback from a buddy who had a company on the side. He ranted about Cooper's wife's secondary appointment in the Department, describing her as a dietician with minimal scientific training. In the Department of Epidemiology she conducted NIH-sponsored research on "the effect of nutritional deficiencies on the mental and physical status of Afro-American homeless." She sent "data technicians" under expressway bridges to administer questionnaires.

"She was testing a rinky-dink hypothesis that homelessness is bad for nutrition, which is bad for health. She didn't bother to factor in alcohol use." McGregor made a fist, crushing his paper cup, ice and all. "Taylor calls it 'a politically fueled boondoggle masquerading as science'."

"I've never seen Cooper's wife around the Department."

"Peter Moore gave her the boot right after Cooper died, and the faculty closed ranks behind him."

With the deconstruction of the Cooper empire, Rob's sense of justice seemed to be satisfied. The fire smouldered and died out. Our chat ended abruptly when I noticed we'd taken 80 minutes for lunch.

I hurried back to Ashton's lab, when luck delivered a breakthrough for the case.

– XVI –

Stroke of Genius

THAT AFTERNOON IN ASHTON'S lab, the global solution to my amateur detective problem jumped onto my lap! I had key-stroked into the computer my decapeptide binding data. The program would analyze it according to simple theoretical equations. The computer was halfway through the curve-fitting session when Margo walked up.

"Ben, can you tell me how long you'll be on the computer?"

Polite but firm. She was a lot of fun, but when it came to getting the job done, Margo was like the female N.C.O. who ran the Colonel's front office.

"No problem. I can break out any time. Here you are," I said, exiting my program.

"Thanks, Ben. I've got to get these orders out today." She slid into the chair as quickly as I slid out.

"Mind if I watch?"

"No, I like it when men watch." Her jokes were becoming more risqué by the day.

She opened up a file called "ORDERS.TXT." The screen showed chemicals they'd ordered, with dates of requisition, supplier, catalog number and price. She said the file contained everything they'd ordered for the last 12 years! I had to keep her talking about it.

"That's pretty high-tech, Margo. And I'll bet you were the one who set it up."

"Who else do you think did it, silly!"

She told me about using the computer to keep track of

the contents of her freezer, containing all their pharmacological agonists and antagonists.

"What do you call the file?"

"FREEZER, stupid."

"That can't be, Margo. FREEZER-stupid has too many letters in it for a file name.

"Ben, you're a real card!" she said, jabbing me in the ribs.

In a jocular mood, I produced a big, insincere grin.

"This Freezer-stupid file must be a great help to Dr. Ashton when he gets a new idea. He can come over here, sit down and find out if you have the right toxin in stock."

Margo burst into smile and threatened to poke me in the ribs a second time.

"You're not a card, Ben. You're a tease. My boss can't even find the power switch on this computer. He sits in his office and thinks. I do the ordering, keep inventory, set up the experiments and even wash the glassware. No, that's not really true. I don't have to wash the glassware when we have a graduate student in the lab."

Now it was my turn to poke her in the ribs. Margo had a winning combination of Old Florida common sense and Annie Oakley humor. And she had just cracked open the Ashton case! Here was the complete list of every toxin that Ashton ever put his hands on!

It took all my willpower to keep still until Margo finished her ordering. Then I asked her an important question.

"Have you ever done any experiments for Dr. Ashton, giving the peptides, like my decapeptide, to animals by mouth. If they are going to be used for Parkinson's disease, the patient can't go to the doctor for an injection every day."

"No, Ben. Our lab has never fed any of the peptides to rats. There's some reason why these peptides may never be used as drugs."

As she exited her program, I said, "Thanks. You don't know how much you have helped me to understand this stuff."

We almost touched hips when I slid into the chair as fast as she slid out. Margo made a funny face and said, "That was awfully fast."

"I crave your warmth, Margo." This earned me another poke in the ribs.

I pretended to computer-fit data until Margo went to the other lab across the hall. Then I quickly called up her file manager program and copied "ORDERS.TXT" and "FREEZER.TXT" onto a small diskette, which I put into my backpack.

Borrowing three supply catalogs from the shelf, I retreated to the library where I played the diskette into my own lap-top computer. I loaded the "ORDERS.TXT" file into memory and flipped through a bunch of screens. It was a 140 KB file in word processing format – no structured data base or anything fancy, but very complete. I clicked through the file, blocking out and copying out into a secondary file every interesting nonprotein toxin. An hour and a half later, I had an 18 KB file from which to select my short list for Dr. Westley.

The three borrowed catalogs listed 95% of the compounds. They were easy to look up because Margo's file supplied catalog numbers. And the catalogs were also quite obliging, supplying a paragraph of description of each toxin, the receptors they worked on and their pharmacological action. And they listed its EC_{50}, the concentration at which the toxin is 50% effective.

Now I could make a back-of-the-envelope calculation of how many milligrams Ashton needed to bind half of the receptors in a grown man. But in some cases the chemical company had made the calculation already by listing the LD_{50}, the dose that kills half the mice or rats. So I could calculate the lethal dose for Cooper by scaling the rat dose to a 70-kilogram man and doubling it for good measure. Rob McGregor would probably agree that Cooper would weigh in at about 280 rats.

And how much did it cost to buy a lethal dose? For some toxins it would cost $50,000. But 13 of the toxins could be purchased in lethal quantities for between $500 and $3,000. That wouldn't blow the supply budget of an NIH-funded biomedical laboratory. So now I had a short list of 13 orally deliverable compounds.

Next question: Could we detect them? Seven of them had chromophoric groups which would absorb light or give off fluorescence for the detectors on our HPLC machines back at the M.E. lab. Three others had chemically or electrochemically reactive groups which could be used for detection.

The remaining three toxins would have been a problem, except that the companies sold "antibody-based radioimmunoassay" tests for them. So old Steve Burk and his helper Jake Brown wouldn't have any trouble testing for these 13 toxins in Cooper's frozen blood samples. Finally, I verified that Ashton had ordered seven of the 13 compounds in the last two years! Mission accomplished.

I was overwhelmed by a feeling of pride while working this information into spreadsheet in my laptop computer. A little after eight, I went back to Ashton's lab and printed it out on his laser jet. I also photocopied the catalog entries for the 13 candidate compounds and stuffed it all in an envelope. Not a bad day's work!

It was around 9:30 as I rode by the *Faire Isle* complex. It wasn't really too late to drop off the information at Dr. Westley's. Straddling my bike by the guard house, with an inevitable line of luxury cars behind me, I was surprised to learn that Dr. Westley wouldn't receive me.

"Please tell him that I have something important to drop off."

The guard repeated my words into the phone, listened for a second and then said, "Yes, sir, I will tell him." He hung up and told me, "You can leave it with the concierge at the first-floor entrance."

The valet parking people sneered as I dropped my kickstand, leaving the bike freestanding in the motor entrance. I took out the envelope, addressed it to Westley, walked past a surly doorman and gave it to the well-groomed and manicured concierge, faster than she could think up a patronizing insult.

Back at the motor entrance no one tipped my bike, and I didn't tip anyone either. I rode away, elated. This amateur sleuth work was an enjoyable application of intellect. If Ashton were the murderer, it would be "bingo" for one of these 13 compounds. Yes, I'd handed the Old Man his answer on a silver platter – a silver platter so worthy of him.

Of course, he'd have to order the compounds, work up an assay and identify one of them in Cooper's blood. But the case should be cracked by Christmas time. Hopefully, Burk and Brown wouldn't screw up too badly, because I wouldn't be available to get them back on track. I had to maintain a sacred choirboy innocence.

The next morning, I devoted myself to my course and lab work in good spirits but found it hard to stay indoors past noon. With book in hand, I sat on a park bench under a tree on the mall between the med school and the medical library. But the book couldn't hold my attention, which drifted to girl-watching.

I treated myself to an evening at Captain Walley's restaurant on the Coconut Grove waterfront. It's one of those indoor/outdoor restaurants in a fisherman's shack motif. To get to it, you have to walk through a boatyard, past the enormous I-beam scaffolds on which they store motorboats, one over another, up to 30 feet high. During the day it was interesting to watch them taking down boats and putting up boats with a tow-motor fork lift the size of a small battle tank.

At the bar I noticed Sam and Lou, a couple of Coconut Grovites who were regulars there. Sam spotted me immediately and made one of his "come over here" gestures, like he was calling back his dog who had crawled out under the fence. Sam was an inboard motor mechanic. Half his clients were dopers who relied on Sam to get that last couple of RPM out of their Cigarette boats for their midnight runs. Lou had a carpentry shop on the edge of the Grove and was making a bundle doing finishing work on town houses.

"Hey, Ben, ain't seen you around for a while," chided Sam, scratching his closely cut blonde beard. Then he flashed me a toothy grin to tell me it was all right.

"Well, Sam, I've been taking a couple of courses. They're keeping me kind of busy."

"Hey, Ben," said Lou in mock disapproval. "I hope you ain't got so serious about them courses that you can't enjoy a good brew and a good puff ever' once in a while."

"You've got a point there, Lou," I said, matching his cadence.

Lou made a big show of shaking his head at Sam, as if this Candidi kid had no sense at all. Sam shifted weight on his bar stool, pulled up on his jeans, and smiled back at Lou.

"Now, Lou, you know that Ben don't puff. He's workin' at the place where they take readings on that stuff in your blood. Ben cain't do nothin' that ain't legal. He'd lose his job."

I felt a Sam-and-Lou comedy routine coming on.

"That's right, Sam," drawled Lou, pulling up his T-shirt and scratching his potbelly. "Now we can't go raggin' and ribbin' Ol' Ben here, 'cause some day we might be dependin' on him to get us out of a jam."

"What kind of a jam's that – that we'd need Ol' Ben to help us outta?" asked Sam, playing the straight man.

"Like when you an' me is having a night on the town and they pick us up and haul us downtown to Ben's medical examining place. And they's got us laid out there. And Ol' Ben here is the one they send in to do the examining!"

"So what's Ben goin' to do for us then, Lou?" asked Sam, already laughing in anticipation of the punch line.

"Well, Sam, what if Ben dips his *co*caine meter in your blood and starts gettin' readings?"

"Well?" asked Sam.

"Well, maybe Ol' Ben could do you a favor and write in some zee-rows on his ree-port!"

We shared a big laugh. The barmaid came over and asked, "Want another round, guys?"

"Sure, I'm running a tab," laughed Lou, waving a finger over a pile of dollar bills and change sitting on the bar under his pack of Marlboros.

While our laughter was still resonating, I took a big breath and said, "Now look, Lou. You've got it all wrong. At the Medical Examiner's we don't examine guys from the tank. We examine stiffs. If they send me over to you with my cocaine meter, there ain't nothing I can do for you."

This cracked them up. When their stomachs stopped shaking, I caught the barmaid's eye and yelled over, "This round's on me." So I drank a couple of brews and shared a dozen laughs with Sam and Lou. Their humor kept me on my toes. They bad-mouthed every institution, organization and sacred-cow belief in the world and then goaded me into defending it.

Lou would say something like, "Now I don't take much stock in that slick-talking president an' his wife. But Ol' Ben, here, he'd probably say that . . ." And then he'd attribute to me a ridiculous political opinion and give me a hard time no matter what I said. But Lou always made sure the result was funny.

When his comic delivery started to sag, I'd pitch him a pompous slow-ball, and he'd bat it out of the park. The second beer gave me a good buzz, and I caught myself looking over at the barmaid. She was awfully cute in her hip-hugging shorts and halter top, and she flashed me back a nice smile. It reminded me that I'd been a long while without a girlfriend. I ordered a "Walley's Catch." I needed food to sop up the beer in my stomach. Then the juke box came on with a series of guitar chords that brought our conversation to a halt:

THUMP, THUMP . . . THUMP, THUMP . . . Thump, Thump, Thump, Thump.

Then came the unmistakable three-part harmonic humming of Crosby, Stills and Nash. It was "Southern Cross." One of those musicians had spent some time around here, and the song had become an anthem for the Old Timers in Coconut Grove. The babble of conversation diminished as people succumbed to the heavy acoustic beat of the hummed entrance. The guys sang about getting out of town on an 80-foot sailboat making for the Southeast Trade Winds on a downhill run to Tahiti. By the time the first three verses were chanted, everything in the bar had fallen in step with the rhythm: Every snap of a cigarette lighter, every smoky exhalation, every pull on a brown bottle, every crack of the pool balls. Lou started

humming along when it got to the part about the midnight
watch and remembering how he'd tried to call his girl from a
noisy bar in Avalon.

Sam joined in on the first chorus, singing under his breath
and looking off in the distance. Suddenly, I understood the
power of this song to quiet the noisy bar. It was *our* song, a
manifesto of masculine independence. It was a story of man-
hood affirmed by the faint light of a constellation of distant
stars seen only from the Southern Hemisphere. And it was a
lamentation on the search for the perfect girl.

The song had now transformed to a majestic vocal pyramid, a three-part, close-in, harmonic declaration of having
sailed around the world looking for a woman/girl. Sam sang
along, audibly now. Yes, larger spirits were calling. Fate may
have tested you and even bested you. But you stay the course.
Hold true to our credo. Someone else will come along and
help you forget.

I swear that Lou was all choked up at the end of the song.
No one looked at anyone or said anything for a long time after.

I bought the guys another round and ate my "Walley's
Catch." "Southern Cross" was followed by Jimmy Buffet,
whose shallow tenor voice and thumping acoustic guitar dissolved the serious mood. It was good music for chugging along.
Chug-a-lug!

After finishing dinner, I excused myself and went over
to the pay phone at the corner of the bar, pulled out a quarter
and punched in the Old Man's number. Called him up from a
noisy bar in Coconut Grove. What better way to cap off the
evening than to receive a favorable response from him. I
couldn't hear him well with the juke box playing and the noise
from the pinball machine off in the corner. And Sam and Lou
slid off their bar stools and started a game of pool. The table
was right in front of the phone.

"Dr. Westley, I'm sorry to have caused consternation with
your help last evening, but I did want to get the information
to you."

"Yes it was quite interesting, and I assume of some relevance," he said. I could barely make out his words over the background noise.

"Yes, indeed," I replied. "It is a list of the compounds in use in the laboratory in which I am now working. All you have to do is assay for them, and you will know whether you have a match."

"Yes. Very well. Proceeding on that assumption, we have already ordered them."

"Good! Then there is not too much for me to do but to wait until you have done your work."

"And you are certain that these compounds are worthy of assay?"

"They have all been ordered and used in the subject laboratory. They all have the desired effect at the indicated doses. They were selected from a longer list which included prohibitively expensive compounds and protein-based compounds."

Lou gave me a funny look and exclaimed, "Well, la-de-da!"

Westley said, "Yes . . . very well . . . quite. Of course, we could fall back on the longer list if need be."

"Of course."

Westley asked stiffly, "What shall be the explanation as to how I came across this remarkable information?"

"You might say I left it at your residence by accident when I came for dinner last time. You took a peek before giving it back to me."

"Very well. Cheers."

"Cheers," I replied and hung up.

Sam and Lou were both eyeing me.

"Hey, Candidi!" yelled Lou. "What kinda courses you taking? Theory of pushing high-grade coke?"

"Yeah," said Sam. "Sounds like he's got a good customer list. Cheerio! High-grade assay!"

"Hey, Ben!" Lou called out brightly. "What's with this 'Cheerio Coke?' Are you selling rocks that's got little O's in 'em?"

I smiled in denial, but it didn't do any good. I had to come up with something.

"Think what you want, guys. But don't come sniffing

around my boat. My pet alligator will get you!"

Lou and Sam broke into raucous laughter, and I broke for the door.

A week passed uneventfully. Burk didn't call me for any work at the M.E. Office, and Westley didn't invite me to his residence. The courses were going well, and I was making good progress on my experiments in Ashton's lab. In fact, I had almost completed the project. I had a preliminary draft of a report, but I wouldn't quit Ashton until Westley told me that I'd done enough sleuthing. With a little luck, Ashton might submit my work for publication before he was hauled away in handcuffs.

Over lunch, McGregor revealed to me the worst of Cooper's sins: crucifying his inherited administrative assistant, Mrs. Epstein. She had difficulties processing his receipts for lunch and had complained to him. Cooper and his cronies had eaten every day at departmental expense. Usually, they sent a work-study student to get $20 from Mrs. Epstein, to go to a sandwich shop and to come back with a receipt. Eventually, the central accounting office refused to reimburse Mrs. Epstein for so many sandwich and grocery receipts.

"It looked like the Department was feeding Cooper five days a week, which it was," McGregor said. "But Cooper still insisted that Mrs. Epstein 'take care of it.' So what does she do? She took some of her own credit card expenses for restaurants. And the University accepts them. Then she takes this money and uses it to replenish the petty cash box so that Cooper can keep getting his sandwiches."

"She went out on a limb for him," I summarized.

"Now get this: When Cooper starts making these sixty-thousand-dollar deals with his buddy's company using NIH money, Mrs. Epstein balks. I mean, this was too much. What he was doing is a Federal crime that you can go to jail for. So Cooper blew his stack and decided to take revenge. He hires a new assistant and grooms her for Mrs. Epstein's job. Then he sics the new assistant on Mrs. Epstein, trying to make her retire.

Mrs. Epstein was sixty-four and was going to retire soon anyhow. Now the new understudy 'discovers' what Mrs. Epstein did with her credit card receipts and brings this 'evidence' to Cooper. And Cooper calls in a University auditor . . ."

"And indicts her for his own crime?" I asked incredulously.

"Yes. And the auditor gives her the third degree. Mrs. Epstein was proud of her seventeen years of service. The University auditor and the Administration kept her in the dark about their 'findings,' and it literally tore her heart out. Then Cooper told her not to report to work, pending the 'outcome of the investigation.'

"She had a stroke in her apartment and wasn't found for sixteen hours. It crippled her, but her mind was still as sharp as a tack. She blamed Cooper for her stroke. Now get this: She has three adult children in New York and Chicago. The son is a neurosurgeon and the daughters are lawyers! So the family wants to sue and demands information on the 'wrongdoing' and the audit. And the whole thing winds up getting settled out of court. It was a large sum for her nursing expenses and plus a sizable restitution."

"Sounds like the University got its hand slapped," I said in encouragement.

"But, you know, the Dean was on Cooper's side the whole time. God knows why. Maybe he was getting kickbacks, too. Several of us were ready to testify for Mrs. Epstein's suit. She was a Jewish mother, in the best sense of the word. We all loved her, even the new hires. Cooper treated her outrageously."

"Beside you, who was outraged?"

"All of us 'Old Timers'."

– XVII –

Rebecca

*W*HY WAS I IN THE LIBRARY TRYING to study that night? My mind wasn't on pharmacology. The burden of the Ashton project was lifted, and I had received A's on my first exams. When I looked up and saw her coming, my heart missed a beat.

She was a cute medical sophomore that I'd seen around. I smiled, she smiled back, and we held each other's gaze as she walked by. She slowed, sat down and sank into the sofa near my carrel. Quick, Ben, she's opening a book. Say something. Say anything.

"Oh, it's so late to be studying."

"Yes. Too late to study, but too early to quit," she said with a resigned smile.

My dream girl. Expressive face, dark straight hair tied up in a ponytail. Slim and about my height. Dressed in stylish beige slacks and a loose-fitting blouse

I smiled and told her, "I know the feeling."

"Well, you see, I have this roommate, and she has this boyfriend, and they are in this hot-and-heavy stage. It would be hard to study there even if I wanted to."

"My place isn't very conducive to study either," I said, quickly thinking up a quip about rocking the boat.

She cocked her head to the side for a second. "It looks like you are pretty well set up with that computer plugged in and with all those books. Are you working on a dissertation?"

Friendly, honest intelligence. I hoped against hope that she wasn't someone's girlfriend.

"I'm not that far along yet," I said.

"What are you studying?"

Fine-featured, open and sympathetic face.

"Pharmacology," I answered.

"We're just starting Sophomore Pharmacology. I'm Rebecca Levis," she said, moving forward in the couch and extending her hand.

"I'm Ben Candidi. Pleased to meet you, Rebecca."

As our hands touched, mine tingled. Rebecca was the type of girl I could get real serious about. Perhaps the feeling was mutual.

"What year are you in, Ben?"

"First year," I answered. Her dark green eyes studied me for a second. I could see the wheels turning, trying to figure out how much older I was than 23. "I worked six years in a forensic laboratory. Came down here after my B.S. from Swarthmore in chemistry and physics."

"I went to NYU in pre-med and anthropology."

Once more, Swarthmore to the rescue!

"The anthropology part sounds interesting," I said.

"Yes. It's been my hobby for a long time – and important part of medicine. I want to go into family medicine."

She explained her preference fluently and genuinely. What a find! Depth. Educated but not bookish. And my type. None of that superficial pre-med mentality.

"I'm interested in a sort of anthropology," I said. "Cultural anthropology. It's been one of my hobbies for the last six years."

"But you can't be taking courses. They don't even have an anthropology department here. I checked."

"I don't need a department. I've been doing field work. We've got it all here – practically on our doorstep."

Rebecca wrinkled her brow and shook her head slightly, as if to warn me not to bullshit her. I pressed on.

"Miami has Spanish culture, several kinds actually. And Haitian – a French Creole with a lot of African mixed in. And Bahamians and Jamaicans – two different kinds of English culture with strong African roots. And we've got all the standard European ethnic groups."

"We have a lot of Caribbean peoples in New York too, but I wouldn't call it 'field work' when I see them on the street." Rebecca said this insistently but politely.

"Seeing a group of Puerto Ricans in thick coats unloading trucks at the vegetable market in New York in the winter is one thing. But seeing a Cuban refugee, not here longer than a year or two, dressed in raggedy jeans and a T-shirt, pushing carts and selling bags of Key limes at traffic lights is something else. The palm trees, the banana trees and the subtropical climate make all the difference."

Pretty long winded, Ben. Hopefully, you haven't blown her away. I smiled and gave her a chance to catch up. She stared down at the floor for a long time and then quickly looked into my eyes.

"Do you speak Spanish?"

"Pretty well, in fact. I speak it every time I get a chance."

Rebecca smiled in approval.

"I studied French. I never got a chance to speak it. One summer my family was going to France, see the cathedrals, Versailles and everything. But things came up, and we didn't do it," she said dreamily.

The girl to sail around the world with!

"Well, Rebecca, you can speak French, a sort of primitive French, right here. That's the interesting thing about Miami – the opportunity comes to you. Try striking up a conversation with one of the janitors . . . or wait for your clinical rotation."

"Yes, its all very interesting. I wish I had more time but . . ." she looked down at her books and notes, "with all this studying . . ."

"I know what you mean – being stuck in a deep hole with orders to keep on digging. That's one of the things that I thought about when I was considering whether I should . . . I mean, thinking about whether I could . . . aim for . . ."

Rebecca was watching me carefully and patiently and, yes, sympathetically.

"I know what you mean. I'm about eighty thousand dollars in debt right now, and this is only my second year. I'm wondering how I'm ever going to pay it back when I go into family practice, especially with the big health insurance mess and the government talking about 'cost containment.' You're looking at a pretty tired and discouraged Jewish girl."

What a combination! Pretty but not vain; intelligent but not overcritical; polished but not afraid to show her feelings. And from New York, but without any kind of an accent. I had to see her again. Inspiration came to my rescue.

"Rebecca, why don't you take this Saturday or Sunday afternoon off, and I'll show you the Versailles, the Hall of Mirrors and a Romanesque cathedral with stained glass. Then I'll show you some Caribbean culture, and we'll make a physical anthropology dig – all within two miles of here."

"And how are you going to do all that?" she asked incredulously.

"Trust me on this one. I can show it all to you – within two miles of here."

"But . . ." She clutched the book to her breast and looked down. Consolidating her feelings?

"Do you have a bicycle?" I asked. "We can do it on bikes. Then you'll get some exercise as well."

Rebecca made me a very happy guy when she said yes. But was it out of interest in me, or was it curiosity about my outlandish promise? The date was for Saturday morning, only three days away. I would meet her at her apartment in the high-rise "Medical Towers" near Bryan.

How exciting to show the secrets of my adopted city to Rebecca. With Miami, too, it had been love at first sight. I thought back to that sunburned, hung over, hectic and sleepless Spring Break in Ft. Lauderdale eight years ago, and the side trip to Miami. After I graduated, I moved down and took the first scientific job available – at the M.E. lab. Over the past six years I had taken enough photographs and assembled enough historical material to write a book. I just never got it organized. Hopefully, Rebecca would be ready and willing,

Dirk Wyle

because I had a heck of a show ready for her.

Thursday and Friday passed slowly. And the minutes passed slowly waiting at the reception desk after the guard called Rebecca's apartment. Then the elevator door opened to reveal a vivacious girl with a good-looking 10-speed – a picture worthy of a full-page fashion ad in the *Miami Standard* – pretty face behind aviator sunglasses, framed by a white stiffened cloth visor, slim athletic torso draped with a thickly-woven blue T-shirt, hips unrestrained in loose-fitting white shorts, slender and graceful legs, and a bouncy step assisted by a combination of thick-soled tennis shoes and abbreviated socks. My ensemble was more military, based on khaki shorts with multiple pockets.

"I should really thank you for this, Ben. It's the first time I've ridden my bike in Miami. The area around the Medical Center is hostile to a girl on a bike."

"We'll get better riding territory when we cross the Miami River."

We mounted up and rode single file, Rebecca ahead, I guarding the rear as we negotiated serious traffic. A few blocks to the south brought us to the drawbridge crossing the Miami River. Rebecca pedaled energetically, cutting a nice figure with her slender legs, slightly broad hips and a bouncing ponytail. Ten blocks brought us to Flagler Street, the heart of Little Havana. Rebecca pulled over.

"Ben, did I read that street-sign right? Did it really say "Ronald Reagan?'"

"*Sí, sí, Senorita. Es la Avenida de Ronald Reagan,*" I said, laying it on a little thick. "You see, he ate lunch in that restaurant."

"The one with the sign that says '*Guarapo*, $1.25?' What is '*Guarapo*,' anyway?"

"I was planning for you to find out, but first you need to get thirsty. We go seven blocks south and then head west."

It was such fun to have Rebecca ride ahead and see her reactions to the new sights on this gorgeous morning. The sidewalks were filled with women making their Saturday morning rounds of the shops, just like in the Old Country, and with men standing around talking to friends and puffing on good, hand-rolled cigars. After a few blocks on S.W. 8th Street, Rebecca called back, "Ben, let's stop here. There's a memorial. What is that torch?"

"An eternal torch of remembrance. 'For the Martyrs of the Assault Brigade, April 17, 1961,'" I translated.

"Oh, yes, the Bay of Pigs."

"To them it's like remembering the Alamo."

The monument was encircled with a ring of chain suspended from the tips of upward-pointing artillery shells. And the memorial filled a broad center strip of 13th Avenue. We walked our bikes down the center, past an enormous tree, to the end marked by a large wall of quarried coral with an enormous relief map of Cuba. I translated "*La patria es agonia y deber,*" quoted from Jose Marti.

"Ben, that tree has an amazing root system, above ground and coming out like pinwheels. They look like *dendrites* . . . I must have too much neurophysiology in my head, but just look! At the trunk, the roots come almost up to my hips."

I told her it's a Kapok tree and that she should look there for Santeria offerings. Rebecca walked around the tree, stepping over the roots with the grace of a ballerina.

"Ben, I think you are making fun of me. There's nothing here but an old pair of shoes, a partially smoked cigar, some kernels of corn and a quarter."

"Yes. Those are Santeria offerings. I hope you didn't touch them, because that would bring you bad luck. You see, a *Santero* gets rid of his bad luck by casting something off as an offering to his favorite god. If anyone takes the offering, it will bring him bad luck."

"And the cigar?"

"An offering of smoke to the god. It was probably just lighted and puffed on once."

"Right. That's how it looked. And the corn?"

"Feeding his favorite god. The *Santeros* believe that the gods have to be continuously fed and be given presents, or they will die out."

"And the pair of shoes? They looked almost usable."

I thought it might be a form of welfare. You offer the shoes to your favorite god, but if some poor guy has such hard luck that he really needs them, he can take them. We talked about the African and Catholic roots of *Santeria* and how it differs from Voodoo – no effigy dolls, and no poisoning people with tetrodotoxin to make them into zombies. Rebecca was interested in the Santeria gods, so I told her about the supreme *Olodumare*. And I told her about his host of *orishas*: *Chango*, *Yemaya*, *Ochun* and many more. We discussed cultural relativism and both agreed that cutting carotid arteries of goats and pouring their blood on your head is not the right thing for human beings to be doing. The thought made Rebecca visibly nauseous.

Around the corner was *Los Pinareynos Fruteria*, a veritable Garden of Eden that crowded the sidewalk with mounds of pineapples, mangos, carambola, Key limes and the usual citrus. I selected two four-foot sugar canes and handed them to the man. He fed them into a rolling press and juice flowed from a spout underneath.

"This, *mi senorita*, is *Guarapo*," I said with a flourish.

A couple of blocks farther west, Rebecca discovered *Maximo Park*, a concrete slab surrounded by a big iron fence. Inside were old men playing dominoes.

"Let's go in and look, Ben."

"The City won't let us. You need a special I.D. saying you're Cuban and retired. And I've never seen a woman in there. Like a fraternal lodge. Supposed to recreate Havana in the old days."

A few blocks farther west we crossed *Avenida Teddy Roosevelt*. We ordered two *café cubanos* at the service window of a cafe and discussed whether Teddy was an imperialist or a freedom fighter. I chatted in Spanish with some loitering *viejos* in straw hats, T-shirts and jeans. A mural on the outside wall of the cafe depicted the street scene quite accurately. We saw two *Mariolitos*, Mariel refugees, both in raggedy jeans and T-shirt, both with hair tied by a bandanna, both were selling limes. But one was in the mural and the other was in real life.

"I see what you meant, Ben, about the environment bringing out the Old Country culture."

Our anthropological date was a success. We biked past some 1950s vintage tourist motels, now used for nocturnal, polyglot affairs conducted in the international language of no words. Then we rode into the Woodlawn Cemetery, which was to be the high point of the tour. Rebecca stopped at another Kapok tree and discovered a Santeria offering – a clay pot, decorated with bits of broken shells, depicting a human face. The Kapok's dendritic roots were chest height at the trunk and radiated 20 feet. One gravestone was completely captured by the roots: "Juan Fernandez, born Dec. 19, 1885, died in Miami Oct. 9, 1920."

Old by Miami standards, the cemetery and its tombstones were a wealth of local history: Of "Dra. Pieda C Bock, 1902," a Spanish-speaking lady doctor, and of Elmer and Carmen Haynes whose love story bridged cultures and decades. And the stones also told the story of snobbish resistance to polyculturalism, trumpeting formal English-sounding names and bearing the inscription "of New England." They reminded me of Goeffrey and Margaret Westley's snobbish resistance to Miami culture.

Along the winding road to the heart of the cemetery, Rebecca discovered the grave of Carlos Pria Sucarras, 1903-1977, who was once President of Cuba. And she found a mausoleum bearing the name Bacardi and another whose archway announced "Somoza Portocarrero." We peered in through the a small glass window in the large iron door and made out six vaults. One was inscribed "*Anastasio Somoza Debayle, Presidente de Nicaragua. 5 de Diciembre 1925, 17 de Septiembre, 1980 'Amo' a su Pueblo.*" Another vault was inscribed "Hope Portocarrero Debayle. Beloved mother of Anastasio, Julie, Caralinas, Carla and Robato Somoza. June 28, 1929-Oct. 5, 1991."

Yes, it was the Nicaraguan dictator.

As we walked our bikes around the last bend in the road, a colossal mausoleum came into view.

"Rebecca, I hope that you accept this as a Romanesque cathedral."

"Amazing! Stained glass and a spire. How did you find this?"

"I'm interested in local history and culture."

It did look like a Romanesque Cathedral, with its high walls of quarried coral stone, its arched entranceway, tarnished copper roof, square tower and asymmetrically placed stone steeple.

The interior bespoke the vacuous elegance of sanitized death followed by heaven. A long hallway with polished white marble floor and walls ended with an intricate, stained-glass window. Lining the walls, the inscribed doors of the vaults told the stories of war heroes, school teachers, millionaires, philanthropists and the plain salt of the earth that we are all destined to become. Studying the inscriptions was a sobering experience. We both fell silent, lost in our own thoughts. The piped-in background music could have doubled as the sound-track of Walt Disney's *Bambi* – just the right stuff to bring tears to your eyes. Rebecca broke the silence.

"You've given me a lot to think about today, Mr. Benjamin Candidi."

We went out through the back entrance and strolled through the Jewish section of the cemetery.

"Now, Ben," she said with spirit, "it's my turn to be the tour guide. What's different about this section?"

"The absence of statuary. Judaism does not allow graven images."

"Hey, you know a lot about religion!" she said enthusiastically. Then she asked thoughtfully, "Are you Catholic? I would guess so with a name like Candidi. Just like you can tell that I'm Jewish from my name, Levis. Are you religious?"

"Yes, privately. My experience as an altar boy forced me to think about religious doctrine at an early age – and I didn't like to hear about 'burning in Hell.' By the time I was thirteen I had everything figured out. I try to live my life as a Judeo-Christian." Rebecca nodded in understanding. "I don't like things that artificially separate people," I said with conviction.

She looked down pensively, then crossed her arms and

hugged herself. My candor had embarrassed us both. Ask me an important question, and you get a direct answer. That's my style. As we returned silently to our bikes, I worked out the implications. With the Mensa girls, things always became complicated at this stage. They shared my proclivities for analyzing everything.

After I unlocked the bikes, Rebecca supplied the needed lightheartedness. Focussing a congratulatory smile several inches over my head, she exclaimed, "Mr. Benjamin Candidi, you kept your promise. You showed me Europe and the Caribbean, all within two miles of that stupid old med school. And I thought that you were making up a line."

"Now wait up," I answered, matching her lighthearted tone, "I haven't fulfilled my promise yet. I haven't taken you to the Versailles and the Hall of Mirrors."

She objected that it was impossible, but a couple of blocks west of the cemetery I showed her the Versailles Restaurant – a flat-roofed squarish building, but painted up to look like the original palace. Mid-Saturday afternoon was prime time at this high-volume, reasonably priced Cuban eatery, but luckily we got a table in the Hall of Mirrors.

The luncheon was like in a fairy tale, with Rebecca my charming princess, an exquisite conversation partner who listened carefully and replied in kind, her pretty and expressive face communicating feeling with her every word, sharing thoughts and dreams, and occasionally rewarding me with her lilting soprano laugh when something I said touched her fancy.

On the way back we stopped at a park on the Miami River. As egrets played pigeon, as pelicans played scavenger, and as the tugboats pulled tramp freighters up and down the narrow river, I told Rebecca about the spring break, my love affair with Miami and the story of the *Diogenes*. Around five o'clock we were standing in the spot where this fascinating day began.

"Thank you so much, Ben, for the nice time."

"Rebecca, I hope . . ." I purposely let my words dangle.

"That we can see each other again? Why, of course, Ben. Give me a call in the middle of the week."

She made me a happy guy. Well, almost!

I would have been happier still, if Westley had called me up and said it was "bingo" for one of those 13 toxins on my short list. Burk must have been taking his own sweet time analyzing them.

– XVIII –

Selecting Selectins

ℱINALLY! THE LAST MEMBER OF the Old Guard present and accounted for. I could check the last suspect off my list. Minutes before his scheduled performance, Ledbetter entered the packed seminar room and sat down at the faculty table. He gazed proudly over the audience and showed no sign of pre-seminar anxiety. He seemed energetic and physically fit for a guy over 50, although he sat with a slouch. Was it an expression of arrogance or the result of too much desk work?

Advanced-stage male-pattern baldness. A detractor might say he looked like a bald man with two large fuzzy ear muffs made of short dark hair. But I attributed it to male vigor – a surplus of androgen in his blood – and perhaps too many decades of high-voltage mental activity.

Dr. Mary Pennington glanced from the clock, to the audience, to Ledbetter, as if wanting to be told when to start. He nodded, and she went to the lectern.

"I am sorry to say that it will not be possible for me to give Dr. Ledbetter an adequate introduction, because then there wouldn't be any time left for his seminar." Her delivery bordered on sassiness. "Dr. Ledbetter received his Ph.D. in Physiology at Yale University in nineteen sixty-nine. From there he went to the Max Planck Institute for Physiology in Frankfurt, Germany."

Dr. Ledbetter listened to her recitation with a patient but bemused expression.

"After three years, he took a position in this department,

where he has been ever since. He has numerous papers, including a patent for selectins as diagnostic devices."

Dr. Ledbetter made an infinitesimal movement to get up, which caused Pennington to cut herself short and sit down. Ledbetter walked up to the lectern, stood beside it, surveyed the audience and launched smoothly into a terminology-packed introductory sentence that blew us all away.

"The topic of my research is 'lymphocytic selectins.' As many of you know, the selectins are a class of adhesion or 'integrin' molecules, which are cytoskeletally attached membrane glycoproteins, which give specificity to the interaction of lymphocytes with the cells of the tissue in which the integrin is located."

Whew!

"Some of you will remember that it was the research conducted in *my* laboratory that showed a tissue specificity among the selectins. This is the probable basis for lymphocyte homing."

I understood only 10 percent of it. He delivered this extremely technical introduction fluently and flawlessly, all the time bathing the audience in the aura of a supercilious smile. To my taste, his bragging was thinly disguised and overdone. Scientists have an odd way of bragging. You're not allowed to say that you discovered the cure to cancer, but it's permissible to say the cure was discovered "in your laboratory." You are not allowed to say that your work is important, but you are allowed to say that it is properly considered a central reference point for everything in the Universe – as long as you mention the elements of the Universe one at a time, and do not use the word "Universe."

So Dr. Ledbetter had just told us his work was the hottest stuff since the Big Bang and that his laboratory was the center of the Universe.

Ledbetter was figuring out how the white blood cells know where to crawl around in the body. The cells in every tissue are coated with a type of "glycoprotein" – proteins with sugar molecules attached – called "selectin receptors." These receptors give white blood cells a toehold when they crawl around in the tissue, looking for bacteria to kill. And the "toes" on the white cells are called "selectins."

Ledbetter told us that different white cells "go home" to different tissues. For a white cell, home is where it can get a toehold. White cells that go home to the liver have selectin toes which make a specially good fit with selectin receptor toeholds in the liver. White cells that go home to the spleen have selectin toes which work especially well in the spleen. If you take white cells out of the spleen and inject them back into the blood, they will return to the spleen – because that's where they can get a toehold.

"So what would a right-thinking scientist do with this knowledge?" Dr. Ledbetter asked rhetorically. "Well, if he were *only* a basic scientist, he might work away on some small aspect of the problem for the rest of his career. But if he were a true biomedical scientist, he would ask himself what is the most obvious medical application."

Ledbetter said this with a thinly-disguised sneer. Authoritarian and critical, he practically told us that he couldn't stand fools.

"The question one should ask is how can we make this homing mechanism do useful work – or at least deliver useful information."

He told how white cells flow in the blood along with the red cells. But when the white cells get activated, they put molecules on their surfaces which make them "sticky" so that they roll along the walls of the small arteries and veins. The walls of the small veins have "manholes" leading into the tissues. The manholes are too small for the red cells but certain white cells can sit on the manholes and squeeze themselves in – like Plastic Man squeezing himself under a door. Special selectin receptor molecules line the manhole and they "tell" the white cell if it has found the right hole. So white cells destined for the liver will crawl into the manholes in the liver. The same for muscle, skin and many other tissues. Once a white cell crawls through the manhole, it can crawl deep into the tissue to fight infection.

Fascinating stuff, I thought. Molecules don't have any minds of their own. They just bind when it feels right. But cells are smart machines, capable of making some decisions.

Ledbetter's self-described "contribution to medical science" was both brilliant and simple. He took the selectin molecules out of white cells, purified them, and made them radioactive. Then he put them back into the blood stream. The liver selectin molecules went to the liver. Spleen selectin molecules went to the spleen. Of course the radioactivity went where the selectins went, since it was firmly attached.

Ledbetter showed us radioactivity pictures of the liver in living animals, visualized by the gamma rays from injected selectins which accumulated in the liver. Then he showed us how the picture was changed in hepatitis, liver cancer and in cirrhosis of the liver. The pictures were taken by an instrument called a "gamma camera" which can be found in every major hospital. Ledbetter made it clear that his imaging technique was destined for widespread use as a medical diagnostic technique.

It was a fascinating presentation of clever experimental work, underpinned by mathematical analysis, driven by medical need and productive of medical application. Masterful! But Ledbetter's presentation was marred by his condescending and sometimes sneering delivery. Like when he started talking about medical applications:

"As many people realize, and as our deceased chairman was never tired of mentioning, biomedical research is an expensive proposition. Someone has to come up with a success now and then to justify the expense of keeping everyone busy. This is not to imply that those who have the power to administer the available funds are those who are the most productive in generating truly useful knowledge, or even recognizing it in its nascent stage. But then, it is heartwarming when something done in one's department proves to have true medical value."

These individually innocuous but cunningly packaged words brought pained expressions to the faces of many of the younger faculty. It was a most extraordinary statement, telling everyone that he, Ledbetter, was the only one who had any medical application and that the deceased chairman had squandered departmental money on medically irrelevant work.

Dr. Ledbetter ended his seminar at precisely five minutes before the hour, leaving what he "hoped would be ample time for discussion of the material."

At first no one had any questions. Ledbetter looked to my fellow student, Grant Shipley.

"I think you wanted to ask a question during the seminar."

"I . . . I just wanted to know if there were selectin receptors in the intestine."

Ledbetter thought for a few seconds before answering. "It is a good question that I cannot answer at this time."

Everyone looked around, wondering who would volunteer a question.

"Are you going to use the proceeds of your patent for a villa in Monte Carlo or a mansion in Palm Beach?" asked Dr. Manson, stroking his beard and staring at his sandaled foot.

"I will buy neither. I will build an adobe hut in Arizona and grow peyote in my rock garden."

Some thought this was very funny, some did not.

"I should not need to remind you, Dr. Manson, that the commercialization of a medical invention is a long, arduous process."

The next person to venture a question was Dr. Pang Wong.

"Does the selectin-lectin specific accumulation of neutrophils in a tissue depend on actin and myosin contractile activity?"

On the face of it, the question sounded halfway intelligent. But Dr. Ledbetter didn't want to hear anything from Dr. Cooper's protégé.

"*Of course* it depends on actinomyosin-mediated contractile activity! The cells have to change shape to get through the post-capillary portals. They have to crawl in the tissue, so they have to use actomyosin to locomote. But that's not the point. The point is that it is the selectins which provide the *true selectivity* that guides the process. Otherwise, the cells would wander around *aimlessly, mindlessly and unproductively.*"

A straightforward scientific answer with a carefully crafted, hidden meaning – telling Wong, to his face, that his research was aimless, mindless and unproductive. And lest anyone fail to perceive his hidden meaning, Ledbetter delivered his answer with a scowl that would blister paint off the wall.

The next member of the audience to put himself at risk was Grant Johnson. Removing his glasses and staring at the soldered joint, he said, "I may have asked this question before, but what t' heck."

"Yes, you did. But what the heck?" Ledbetter was playful this time. He actually seemed to be enjoying himself.

"Okay, then. What's my question?" asked Johnson.

"If you can use your laser."

Hearty laughter erupted and was sustained by the built-up pressure of the seminar.

"Well, can I use my laser, then?" persisted Johnson, unabashed.

"Yes, we can. We just have to find a tissue in a living animal in which we have an optical path into a small blood vessel. Perhaps the Clark chamber in the rabbit ear would work. I would like to see neutrophils rolling in the arterioles. I would like to learn whether this is influenced by intracellular calcium, which you can so ably control and measure."

"Then why don't you come over and do it with me?"

"Because it would be a major undertaking, and I have no experience with the Clark chamber. Perhaps one of the uncommitted graduate students might be interested."

As Ledbetter talked about the problem, he warmed to Johnson and to the audience. As he got to the point of recommending it to the grad students, he seemed absolutely benevolent. What a bipolar personality! A snarling attack dog one moment; friendly beagle an instant later. Did this strong discrimination come from his scientific standards, or was there something less objective and more emotional behind it?

Robert Gunnison had his hand in the air. After getting

Ledbetter's attention, Gunnison returned his gaze to the table at which he was sitting, staring as if at some unseen object a couple of feet below the surface.

"I'm sorry . . . but I'm somewhat confused – "

"As you quite often are," interjected Ledbetter.

The audience could produce so many types of laughter. This time it was mildly derisive. I wasn't the only one who was irritated by Gunnison's pomposity.

"That may well be," Gunnison continued, not elevating his gaze above the surface of the table, "but I am confused as to whether the tissue selectivity of the neutrophil specificity is under hormonal control."

The question was a natural for Gunnison, since he worked on hormones. Ledbetter made a show of yawning. Then he shook his head and clicked his tongue.

"You shouldn't be confused, because I didn't say anything about hormonal control of neutrophils."

Gunnison squirmed.

"Then, perhaps, I should have said that I would have liked to have known what influence hormones have on the tissue-specific neutrophil homing phenomenon."

Typical Gunnison – unnecessarily complicated grammatical constructions describing nothing. But he didn't sound so pompous this time. He sounded like a croaking teenager. The force of Ledbetter's personality had flailed away his sophomoric, mature-beyond-his-years veneer.

"Dr. Gunnison, the primary phenomenon is not hormone dependent. Of course, it is well known that the immune system can be up- and down-regulated by hormonal status. We even teach that to our medical sophomores. Perhaps it is *I* who should be confused as to whether you have even articulated a question."

With a broad smile, Ledbetter had just told everyone that Gunnison wasn't even up to the level of a sophomore medical student. Ashton was smiling, obviously enjoying himself immensely.

"Well, is the tissue specificity of the neutrophils changed

with hormones?" Gunnison asked meekly, hoping to salvage something.

"Categorically, no."

"Thank you," said Gunnison, shaking his head and looking away.

Dr. Kozinski's hand went in the air. Would Ledbetter mistreat a *mensch*?

"My question is quite specific: Does genistein inhibit the homing behavior?"

"An excellent question, directed at whether tyrosine phosphorylation plays a role in exposure of selectin receptors in the tissue or affects selectin density on lymphocyte membranes. The answer is 'yes' on both counts, although we can apply genistein only to tissue culture. It is too toxic to do meaningful experiments with living animals."

Just like Westley. Push a button and get a mini-dissertation! Dr. Ledbetter was once more benevolent as he delivered this highly technical information. Dr. Kozinski nodded back.

Dr. Gordon Taylor had been listening to the exchange carefully and seemed to be nodding in approval. Peter Moore blurted out, "What was the 'alpha constant' and volume of distribution when you injected the gamma-radionuclide labelled lymphocytes back into the animal?"

Dr. Moore was an expert at pharmacokinetic jargon.

"Lymphocytes don't behave like simple drugs. It's not a simple case of alpha redistribution and a beta phase elimination. If pressed, I'd have to say we have a 'bravo' phase when the lymphocytes go rolling along, a 'charlie' phase when they dig into the tissues, and then a 'delta' phase when the specific ones return to the lymph."

A forthcoming answer, but Ledbetter had put spin on it, making it sound like a military skirmish on the Mekong Delta. "Bravo" and "Charlie" are military terms; scientists would use the Greek letters "beta" and "gamma." For his part, Moore didn't bat an eyelid and seemed to be quite satisfied with the answer. He thanked Dr. Ledbetter and turned his head slowly to Dr. Mary Pennington. As if on cue, she stood up and turned to the audience.

"All of us are either completely informed or completely overwhelmed."

Way to go, Pennington!

"There being no further questions, we can now consider the seminar to be adjourned."

Quite a performance! In fact, if Ledbetter's selectin system had any lethal possibilities, I might have suspected him more than Ashton. The seminar was a natural topic for lunchtime conversation with McGregor.

"Well, Rob. I guess Ledbetter didn't like Cooper very much."

"So you picked up on that, did you?"

"But, Rob, he practically spelled it out to everyone."

"Yeah. Cooper had this funny thing about money. He couldn't get enough of it. Ledbetter got some commercial sponsorship of his patent. According to University policy, half of the royalties should have gone to Ledbetter as a bonus. But when Cooper got wind of it, he forced Ledbetter to pay a bigger fraction of his base salary. This freed up an equivalent amount of Departmental hard money. And what did Cooper use it for? He raised his own salary. Ledbetter was pissed to the gills."

"You mean Ledbetter's medical diagnostic invention brought in some money, and Cooper celebrated it by squeezing Ledbetter and paying himself a raise?"

"Yeah. And the two fought like cats and dogs. They were firing confidential memos at each other for over a year. Of course, what really set off the shooting match was what Cooper did to Mrs. Epstein. Ledbetter's shaken up lots of people around here, but when it comes to old ladies he's a real gentleman. And he almost succeeded in getting Cooper tossed out over the Epstein issue and the finance irregularities. He would have succeeded if the Dean hadn't stood up for Cooper and told Ledbetter to back off. Boy, was Ledbetter pissed!"

"Doesn't sound like a very conscientious dean."

"No, the guy's just interested in control. This joint works on rhetoric, broken promises and 'funny money.' But what do you expect for a place called Bryan Medical School? It's named after William Jennings Bryan. Check your local history and you'll learn it was his loud mouth that got Opa Locka University started in the first place. The medical school thrives, operating by his methods.

McGregor tucked his thumbs in his armpits in a parody of a crackerbarrel orator.

"They say you can drive an ambulance through one of the Dean's speeches without scraping a fact," he said, in an accent as broad as the Great Plains.

"What was going on between Ledbetter and Manson today?"

"Manson doesn't like Ledbetter telling everyone his work is medically relevant. Ledbetter doesn't like to be reminded how Cooper grabbed his royalties. But Manson had it coming."

"I wonder about Manson."

"Yeah, the guy's crazy, all right. Once he had a prolonged brain-fade in front of a whole class of medical sophomores while he was lecturing on anesthetic gases. The medical sophomores started a legend that Manson prepares for his anesthetic lectures by sniffing halothane! They even built the incident into the Senior Class Graduation Play last year. What a roast!"

"And how do you explain what Ledbetter did to Wong?"

"Hey, look, buddy. This is a meritocracy. Ledbetter doesn't put up with dumb shits."

"And Gunnison?"

"That guy pisses even *me* off."

Our conversation meandered on, finally settling into a discussion of Ledbetter's science. It didn't reveal any special knowledge which would be helpful to Ledbetter as a poisoner. But somehow I didn't feel right about checking him off the list, just yet. Damn old Burk and his flunky Jake Brown for being so slow on those neurotoxin assays!

– XIX –

Animal Tracking

"STOP THE TORTURE. DON'T BLIND the rabbits. Animals have rights, too."

There were only two dozen of them, but their picket line blocked the main entrance, holding back a hundred employees. Four security guards, not the usual two, stood at the top of the steps in front of the main door. This time the door was closed. The guys looked worried. One was talking into a hand-held radio and the other three were looking warily into the crowd and fingering their night sticks.

I'd griped before that Bryan Medical School looked like a police station, but today the security precautions were paying off. The demonstration was both threatening and ludicrous. Mounted on some rather formidable pieces of lumber were pictures of sorrowful-looking animals – monkeys with wires protruding from their heads, cats looking desperately out of cages, and a close-up of a rabbit with something wrong with its eye. Crudely lettered placards spelled out demands, like "Stop the torture." A couple of especially noisy male protesters might have enjoyed crashing their placards, cardboard *and* lumber, on someone's head.

Not that all of them were threatening. There were housewives, a few with children, a handful of middle-aged men you might classify as eccentric intellectuals and their long-haired female counterparts. Under other circumstances, I wouldn't have viewed them so critically. In fact, they reminded me of Coconut Grovites and people I'd seen on Jazz-and-Yoga Nights

at the Unitarian Church. But organized protesting brings out
the worst in all of us.

They marched in a 30-foot oval, screaming their slogans
and looking at no one in particular.

"They're killing innocent animals in there!"

"Stop the torture!"

"Cats and dogs and rabbits have a right to live, too!"

"Stop the murder for profit!"

They had to scream it, because it would sound too ridiculous chanted in a normal voice. When one started to falter on
"stop the murder," the others shouted back, "Yes! Yes! Stop the
murder. We have to stop the murder. Please stop the murder."

A throng of laughing, joking medical students shared my
perceptions. One medical student was a real mesomorph, right
out of a bodybuilding magazine. He called out at the protesters, "You ever heard of penicillin, you morons?"

One of the protesters stopped dead in his tracks, balled
his fists and glared into the crowd. He reminded me of Oregon eco-terrorists I'd seen on television, chaining themselves
to a bulldozer. Perhaps it was his plaid shirt, blue jeans and
ankle-high work boots.

"Yes, we have, snot-nose," he shouted back. "And I'm a
nurse, you fuck-ass."

"So you're a nurse, and you just named yourself," shot
back the Medical Mesomorph.

Eco-Terrorist broke ranks but was restrained by a grand-
fatherly protester. Grandpops scooted around in front of him,
whispering admonitions, shaking his head and glancing furtively into the crowd. The chanting stopped, and the mood
became serious.

Medical Mesomorph was joking with his buddies, but he
kept his eyes on Eco-Terrorist. "If you're a nurse, you should
be able to tell me what a GOMER is."

Eco-Terrorist looked confused.

Another med student yelled out, "Maybe he's just a bed-
pan nurse and doesn't even know what an ER is."

Some members of the crowd laughed. The expression

GOMER had been making the rounds of Dade General. It stood for *Get Out of My Emergency Room*, and was applied to lower-class rabble.

While Eco-Terrorist fumed, Medical Mesomorph delivered a new taunt.

"Okay, then, Mr. Nurse who doesn't know about GOMERs and doesn't believe in antibiotics. I know what you are. You're a *fecal peri-anal!*"

Laughter caught fire among the critical mass of clinical types who could translate this as "shit ass." Eco-Terrorist shrank visibly. Medical Mesomorph stepped towards the door, clearing a path through the protestors and coming dangerously close to Eco-Terrorist.

"Now if you'll just excuse me and let me by . . . I've got to go in and practice brain surgery on the computer. You see, tomorrow I'm operating on my first patient."

Eco-Terrorist strained unconvincingly against Grandpop's hold, but it was nevertheless a tense moment.

One of the guards seized the opportunity and shouted with authority, "Now, if you people could just move over a little and let the students get to their classes."

Like a cop directing traffic, he signalled "halt" to the protesters with his left hand while his right hand made a "come on" motion to the employees who streamed in behind the med student. The guard was a little shy of six foot and must have been over 200 pounds, most of it muscle. Like many Cuban-Americans working in law enforcement, he looked like the type who enjoyed working out, shooting guns and injecting steroids.

A frail-looking fiftyish lady protester beseeched, "Please don't, please don't torture the cats. Please don't blind the rabbits."

But it sounded so ridiculous, since about half of the people walking past her were office types. The two med students had Parthian shots:

"Do you think he's a canine shithead, or a feline shithead or a murine shithead?" asked the buddy.

"I think he's a gerbil intra-anal," replied Medical Mesomorph.

The guard probably didn't understand the words, but he did understand the tone. He put his hand on the guy's shoulder – one mesomorph to another – and moved him gently to the door.

"Now guys, just chill out and go to your classes."

In the elevator, I overheard a middle-aged woman with a sympathetic face telling her companion that she didn't mind them working on rats. But they shouldn't work on cats. She proclaimed herself a cat lover, with a pair of Siamese and a tabby who were "just darling." A graduate student from Physiology/Neuroscience butted in, telling her that his dissertation research was on the cat brain. He said putting in electrodes is the only way you could study visual processing. The woman asked how you could move electrodes in the brain while the cat was awake and could see. The student said the cats were heavily sedated with sedative/hypnotic drugs. The two became disgusted with each other.

I worked hard that day and didn't leave the building until after six. Just as I put my ID card into the sensor to open the door, I noticed, behind the desk, the guard who broke up the demonstration. I stopped to congratulate him.

"You did a good job this morning. You said just the right thing at the right time to keep them from fighting. You brought in the crowd just like you were breaking up a traffic jam."

He glanced up only for a second. Then his eyes returned to his monitors, and he crossed his heavily muscled arms over his enormous chest that merged seamlessly with his shoulders, neck and head. After a few seconds, he looked up and broke into a big grin.

"So, you *was* there!"

"Yes, I was there. And I thought you handled a tense situation very professionally."

It might have been the nicest compliment he'd received in months.

"Oh that's *no-thing*," he said with a smile. "I've had a lot tougher things out in Hialeah."

He seemed to be in the mood to chat for a while, and so was I.

"I worked for Hialeah for a while," he said. "Hey, out there everyone's got a gun, and it don't take much for them to pull it out."

"Hey, that's what I heard, too."

"When me and my partner, we have duty on New Year's Eve, we just stay in our car and get under a bridge, man! The old Plymouth, he have nine bullet holes before the evening is done. Hey, when those people celebrate, they don't stop for shit!"

"Yeah, it's a tough turf, just like Opa Locka."

"We had a lot of drog work. And they's *real* bad guys. They used me undercover when I first joined the force. But that gets old fast. I mean it gets old like you can't stand it. Not like *Miami Vice*. And after a while everyone on the street gets to know who you are. And then you got to get your lieutenant to give you something else to do, if you want to get old yourself!"

He shrugged his heavy shoulders, and his head moved slightly.

"You were undercover?"

"Yo. But not always for drogs. Sometimes they put you on stakeout on top of a warehouse for them hijackers. Burning or freezing your boat off all night, waiting for some bad guys to come up with a van and knock over some warehouse. Boy, those roofs get hot in the summer and cold in the winter. And when them drain spouts get fulla leaves and they have a thunderstorm that day – you've got six inches of water on those babies. Have to give the owner a free roto-rooter job just to get a place to sit!"

"I guess it's a lot better job working here and guarding the medical school."

"Yo! Every once in a while we get a bum outside. Maybe a mugger. But it's no-thing like Hialeah. Yo, Mr. Candidi, this is a lot better job. But you got to use your brain here. Lots of paperwork, and the boss don't like it when you foak up."

"How did you know my name?"

"Oh, when you put your card up to that machine, your name come up on the screen and that puts you in the log. You stuck it in the box on the exit side, so the computer knows that you went out."

"So, it's not a dumb system. It really keeps track of people."

"Oh, yeah! They say one boss, he want to use the system to check up on a professor that says he is always having to work on weekends! But we don't use it for that. But it comes in handy sometimes, like when a piece of equipment is missing. We've used that computer to get some bad guys here, too. One guy working here, he get his boat kicked out of here because of that computer. Stole a lot of shit before we got him – student doing cocaine – but we got him! Followed his tracks back to his lab."

"You put fluorescein powder on the floor and traced his tracks with a black light?"

"Hey, you know that story? Maybe you go down to the Cop Shop, too!" he said with a grin.

"No, I don't know that story, but I know a little bit about everything."

"Hey, are you some kinda student?" he asked scrutinizing me this time.

"Used to be a technician, now I'm a beginning graduate student."

"So you are one of those guys that are working with those animals that they woes complaining about today."

"I'm just in the first year, and I'm not doing any animal lab work yet."

"Yo. I guess you have to get yourself pretty advanced before they let you work on them animals. Some of them doctors get pretty upset when someone messes around with their animals and does the wrong thing. Some of those animals are pretty valuable too. That's what we got this one hundred thousand dollar computer system for. To keep out guys like those guys this morning, so they don't come in and take away some animal that you got twenty thousand dollars worth of work in. Them folks would have to steal your card. But between you and me, I don't think they has enough brains in their heads to figure out how to use the card and get in the animal room. They'd need a regular key for the door, too."

"You mean that the computer keeps track of who goes into each animal room?"

"Night and day. Hey! If you don't got no authorization from Veterinary Resources to go into that room, the computer don't let you in."

"That seems a little restrictive. You have to get some sort of authorization."

"Hey, if you got animals in that room, and you and Veterinary Resources knows that you got to get in that room, then they program that computer to let you into that room any time you put in your card, day or night. But if you don't have no animals in that room — and you don't have no business going in that room, then you don't get in that room, I don't care if you're the boss of this place. Since we got this computer, it stops a lot of stupid shit from happening."

"What kind of stupid shit?"

"Like one scientist takes a rabbit from another scientist and kills it to study its muscles. But the other scientist, he's been injecting that rabbit every day for a whole year to make a special serum in its blood. Boy, was he mad when he find his rabbit was gone! But the computer told who it was. Because there was just two guys that go into that room that night! And one was working with rabbits and the other was working with cats. Hey, that computer clears up a lot of problems. We keep the tapes on everything that goes on here for a year. Yeah, there ain't nothing that somebody do with those animals that we don't know about."

"Sounds really interesting. Nice talking with you."

"*Tú tambien, amigo,*" he said with a flourish.

"*Bien gracias para la cuenta y hasta luego,*" I replied.

This prompted another searching look. He shook his

head, smiled and said, "I never know about you scientist guys! You're hard to figure out."

I biked to the Westley's in anticipation of a decent dinner. It was now October. The days had changed from steamy to bearable, and the evenings changed from sultry to room temperature. This made the English cuisine much more attractive. During sherry, Westley played a Brahms symphony.

"It somehow expresses both the romantic and the darkly emotional side of the German character," he said.

At dinner Margaret was ebullient. Our conversation started with the "more civilized weather," moved to her attendance of meetings at Fairchild Tropical Gardens, to English gardens, to "little patches of garden" with roses, to the natural politeness and decency of English people, to the centuries of tradition and good breeding which make this possible, to the poor state of American manners.

"Mrs. Westley, why do you think that the Americans became less polite than the English?"

"Ben, you are so clever at turning the conversation around! Gracious me! I feel as if I am now being called upon to come up with a theory!" She thought for a minute, and then began slowly: "Perhaps it is because there were so many other groups which came – Germans, Polish, Irish, Italians – that they just lost their sense of what good manners were."

I became sufficiently irritated to ask, "What about the Australians? They were mostly Englishmen. They didn't get a lot of Germans, Polish, Irish and Italians."

"Oh, Ben, I fear you are much too sly for an old woman like me. I really do not know what to say in answer to you."

She returned to American manners, commenting on American table manners at fast food restaurants which she had observed among rednecks on their "motor trip through Florida, Georgia and the two Carolinas." I semi-sarcastically asked what would Queen Caroline think about her two colonies. The Old Man frowned and quickly interjected that Carolina is derivative of Charles under the proper rules of English grammar, although he could not recall if it was Charles I or II.

Margaret started to deliver a mini-treatise on the decline of manners, with special reference to portable telephones. But in the middle, she stopped abruptly and said, "But I must be boring you both to tears. An old English lady, crippled with arthritis, fluttering on about things which couldn't be of the least use to a young man. I'll return to the kitchen."

I hastened to assure her that it was not so. The Old Man acted embarrassed and suggested that we "repair to the balcony." Outside, he said a few scrambled words of apology, to which I offered some inarticulate words of assurance that no apology was necessary.

Seated comfortably, I started my debrief, telling the Old Man that I had not learned any new applied pharmacology but had now had a chance to observe Ledbetter. I described the rip-snorting seminar and the verbal thrust and parry during the question-and-answer period.

"Well, this Ledbetter would seem to be a most interesting fellow," Westley said, arching his eyebrows. "Can you tell me more about him?"

I said that Ledbetter was truly brilliant, that he devised ingenious experiments, and that he had little tolerance for people who misinterpreted his work.

The Old Boy said, "It sounds as if he can divine gold from baser metals. You say that he is a real master of his art, but also a bit of a Toscanini."

"Toscanini?"

"Yes, Arturo Toscanini, the famous conductor. He threw fits on the podium."

"Yes. Ledbetter seems to be quite a prima donna. He's very arrogant with those who are not up to his level."

"'Up to his level?' Would that make him a good Mensa candidate?" the Old Man asked, never seeming to tire of a good jest.

"He would get in to the Society based on his IQ. But he would have little patience with our foibles. The guy is very purposeful and seems to live for his science. As if he has everything wrapped up in it."

"Does he have no friends among the faculty?"

"He seems to get along with all of the Old Guard except Manson. Ledbetter reveals something in everyone. He reacts to each individual in a different way. He makes fools out of some and praises others. Ledbetter seems to take everything to its logical conclusion, even if it means telling people in public that they are hopelessly stupid."

"Do you think that he could take a very serious thing to its logical conclusion?"

Neither Westley's voice nor his face yielded the slightest indication that he was asking a most important question.

I answered, "He'd be emotionally capable of it, particularly if he were threatened or impeded in something important to him."

"Then it will be interesting to hear more about him," Westley said.

"Okay, but I thought that we were considering Ashton."

"One should always remain open-minded."

"Ledbetter was out of town for as long as I've been here. Do we even know that he was here for . . . I called it D-Day last time and you didn't like the expression. So please tell me, was Ledbetter present at the Last Supper?"

Dr. Westley liked that expression even less, and it took me a while to get him back on track.

"Was he here or was he out of town on the day in question?" I asked.

"I am not sure I can tell you at the moment," was the evasive answer. "But he seems like a very interesting chap. Does he have a good command of 'practical pharmacology,' as you so deftly put it a few weeks ago?"

"There's no 'pharmacological principle' that jumps out at me. His selectins are useful as diagnostic devices because they get accumulated in different tissues."

"Well, he sounds very interesting. Perhaps you should give him a closer looking over." It didn't sound like a marching order to me.

"I suppose. But how are you making out with the information I 'inadvertently' left here at your apartment a few weeks ago?"

The Old Man became agitated, as if I had been too direct. "Ben, you must simply be patient," he chided. "The wheels turn slowly. It might be a few weeks more."

"Then I will keep my eye on Ledbetter but try to drag out my rotation with Ashton until you are done. But Ashton made me turn in a written report on my work a couple of days ago. Once I leave Ashton's lab, it would be awkward to try to come back on a hands-on basis."

"I quite understand, Ben. One must do what one can."

After leaving Westley's, I thought of how solidly I had served the ball to his side of the court. Why was it taking them so long to analyze Cooper's blood for the 13 lousy compounds? It wasn't my fault if Burk had lost his touch and Brown was no help. And I didn't want to waste time looking into Ledbetter. His seminar clearly showed that he had to inject his selectins for his diagnostic applications, and the Old Man was clear that there were no needle marks in Cooper. And the selectins weren't toxic anyway. Why waste time on him?

I needed the time for Rebecca. We were now seeing as much of each other as her demanding med-school regimen would permit. She seemed to carry gracefully the burden of the 16-hour med-student day, pacing herself with a certain quiet self-confidence. Our frequent lunch dates around the medical center confirmed my first impressions: She was beautiful but not spoiled, intelligent but not overcritical, serious but not moody, and practical but not harsh. Sitting down with a sheet of paper, I wrote down her lovable qualities, jotting down 15 adjectives without even trying. Rebecca was a "fifteen." I became fairly confident that she didn't have a boyfriend in the medical school.

We had our first dinner date a week after the bicycle date. We took a cab, since neither of us had a car. Rebecca voiced her astonishment at my nonchalance, as the meter topped $15 while we rode along the causeway with three miles to go before reaching Miami Beach. I remarked that money is to serve us, and not the other way around. How did she like the ocean liners going out Government Cut? Did she know that amphibious planes from Chalk's Airline take off and land within yards of us? As the meter topped $20 at the South Beach, I told Rebecca that I sometimes rented cars.

"Just like we do up in New York City," she said with a smile.

Ocean Drive in the "South Beach" has a 10-block row of art deco hotels. The district starts at 5th Street with the Bentley, the Monaco, the Paradise Beach, the Park Central, the Avalon, and so on, all the way to the Netherland Hotel up at 14th Street. Most of them have outdoor dining on terraces overlooking Ocean Drive and the Atlantic beyond.

I had updated my wardrobe with a white unstructured sports jacket and a collarless shirt. Rebecca wore a black one-piece sleeveless dress that reached mid-thigh. She walked slightly ahead of me with light, bouncy grace as we filtered through crowds of hip people and around the occupied tables of sidewalk cafes, stopping only to read the menu placards and squeezing by the valet parking peoples' boards, bristling with BMW and Mercedes keys. Rebecca's beauty was like her voice – subtle, slightly fragile and best revealed when she was in motion. As sea breeze blew through her hair and lights sparkled in her eyes, I felt like walking beside her forever.

We stopped for dinner at an outdoor restaurant in a big courtyard, halfway up the Art Deco district. It was a real cosmopolitan scene, with Latin Americans and Europeans outnumbering the Americans, two to one. Entertainment was supplied by a jazz violinist, about my age, accompanied by a guy on an amplified keyboard. They played "Cinnamon and Clove," a bossa nova with a persistent beat and bittersweet melody. As Rebecca grooved to the rhythm, I remembered the exciting lyrics describing the magical essence of love on a tropical night. Every sense was shifted and blended into another. Moonlight warmed the sand, a seagull sailed in the air like a sailboat across the cove. A dip of the hand transformed the water into sparkling crystal, and the air carried a scent of spice. I sang along softly.

"I know that one, too," Rebecca said. "'Brasil Sixty-Six,' back in the nineteen sixties. Two women and two men. Did a lot of bossa nova."

"My folks had the record," I said. "Told me they bought it when they first got married. Used to play it a lot. I developed an adolescent fixation – a fantasy of love in an exotic, romantic setting."

"Well, we sure have that here, with the palm trees, tropical sky and sea. And I would have missed it all, cooped up in that Bryan Medical School, if you hadn't whisked me off my feet." She tapped my elbow, and kissed my cheek with an innocent Victorian charm which was magically in rhythm with the bossa nova beat.

The set came to an end. Rebecca and I struck up a conversation with the violinist. She played second violin with the Florida Philharmonic and was getting well-known in the South Florida jazz scene. I bought a tape from the duo and gave it to Rebecca as a present.

After dinner, we crossed Ocean Drive, took off our shoes and strolled across the sand, away from the art-deco neon and toward the dark shore. We stopped to gaze at a tall palm tree whose tasselled crown glistened in the light of the full moon. Rays of reflected moonlight seemed to jump between the gently arched and twisting fronds, each silhouetted by moon glow, as the tasselled crown gently swished in the wind. It was at once a rustling wind chime and an enchanting kaleidoscope in black and white. I could have lived this moment for eternity.

We walked along the beach at the waterline. The gently surging and ebbing waves splashed our feet and sprinkled Rebecca's face with reflected moonlight. Cruise liners, all white and lit up, large as office buildings, exited through Government Cut. Rebecca stumbled on a pile of seaweed, and I caught her in my arms. We shared a long kiss.

Our next evening date was dinner at Captain Walley's in Coconut Grove. I warned Rebecca to dress down. We went in through the restaurant without bumping into Sam or Lou, passed the outdoor bar and tiki hut, and spent two delightful hours at a table with a good view of Key Biscayne, four miles out.

Afterwards we walked arm in arm along the Dinner Key Marina. I presented my little travelogue about the seaplane hangers, the Pan Am Clipper and its Art Deco Terminal, which now serves as the Miami City Hall. Then we passed my skiff, chained to a tree.

"Ben, you mean that you have to row in this little boat every day?"

"Come rain or come shine."

I hadn't realized how awkward it would be. Although the *Diogenes* lay 400 yards off shore, the skiff was like the front-door of my apartment. As much as I wanted to make love to Rebecca tonight, it was too soon. But inspiration didn't fail me. I played the British seaman.

"That is to say, when it's only me-self to transport, I row out come rain or shine, blowing or calm."

"Well, it probably wouldn't be practical for the young officer to show me the HMS *Diogenes* tonight," Rebecca said with a trace of an English accent herself.

Laying it on thicker, I said, "I must admit to Her Lady-ship that I am but a bosun's mate. And the Lady would find the liberty boat a bit small and wet, and the ship difficult to tour at this late hour."

Rebecca rewarded my wit with a musical laugh in so-prano register, worthy of an operetta. She cocked her head and said, "Then perhaps Her Majesty's worthy seaman could suggest a time during the day."

My next words required a moment's thought.

"HMS *Diogenes* is scheduled to sail for the faire isle of Elliott Key on Thursday in less than a fortnight, on the day which the colonial Americans call 'Thanksgiving.' The Goode Ship will ply the waters about Elliott Key for three days, re-turning on the following Sunday eve. Her Ladyship would be provided her own quarters but would be most welcome at the Captain's table, which captain is a perfect gentleman."

Now Rebecca needed a moment's thought.

"Her Ladyship would be most grateful to accept the Captain's gracious invitation. She will bring her parasol and hopes the Captain can be counted on for food and amenities."

And, thus, the Thanksgiving weekend was planned. It was a meditative cab ride back to her apartment as we silently reconsidered what we'd agreed to. But Rebecca's goodnight kiss by the elevator told me she'd worked through all the implications. The taste of her kiss lingered through the bicycle ride to Dinner Key. Rowing to the *Diogenes* under a sky full of stars, I said an evening prayer: Dear Lord, let it be true.

The Old Man agreed to reschedule the dinner for the Tuesday before Thanksgiving. He said he might have some news by then. The days to Thanksgiving vacation went so slowly, yet so quickly. Upcoming exams in Membrane Biophysics and Biochemistry had me worried. And there was work to ready the "goode ship" for the presence of a woman on board.

The worthy sailing vessel had doubled as my bachelor apartment. Papers and books clung to its walls, in addition to the normal cabin barnacles which collect when a vessel has been too long at anchor. And regular barnacles and a coat of algae required me to grab my mask, fins, snorkel, brush and paint scraper. I worked like a madman, scrubbing and scraping to unfoul the *Diogenes'* bottom.

The next evening I learned that my investigation was fouled.

– XX –

Tragedy of Science

SHERRY WAS POURED WITH AN undercurrent of seriousness that Tuesday evening. The Old Man rambled on about his experiences in medical school and the state of their knowledge of physiology and biochemistry in those days. Lurking below the surface was the message that one must be ready to change old habits, theories and courses of action.

At dinner, Margaret had me describe my cohort of first-year students and showed surprise at the high proportion of girls. No young ladies went into science in her days. A lady's place was tending hearth and home. But she had been a "sub-lieutenant" in the searchlight corps north of London during the Second World War. "'Twas many a time the sirens wailed but never once did the Jerries fly over my sector. We would have singed their tail feathers with our hot lights, we would have! Then the boys from the flak company would have shot their tail feathers off!"

To please her, I saluted the great English thinkers, Hume, Hobbes, Locke, Toynbee, Huxley, and the great 'doers' like Disraeli and Churchill.

"Yes, we have always had a sense of mission, haven't we, Wessie?" He nodded. "When we first came here, I told Wessie that it was like being in civil service in India, with the heat and with so many dark-skinned people. Not that the Americans were all coloured, mind you."

She complained about the lack of cultural amenities in Miami. "It was as if we were always giving culture but never receiving it. But I do feel that through the years we have left some sort of impression on the native people. Don't you, Wessie?"

"Yes," said the Old Man. "I should say that we did, although I would rather agree with Orwell that they can never really be changed. The migrations, the street drugs and the carnal breeding are much stronger influences than a few human good examples. One needs a much more controlled environment for a better sort of thing. Like England."

For some reason I became irritated, and I countered, "But England has its share of problems – soccer rowdies, skinheads and teenagers joyriding in stolen cars."

"That's all in the North," the Old Man said, coming to the defense of The Realm. "And much is due to American influence, with their fascination for motor cars, rock and roll music, drugs and the like."

"Well," I said, feeling a little argumentative and cocky, "it was before my time, but my folks told me that the original American rock and roll was pretty harmless. My dad said it was the Beatles and the Rolling Stones who brought in the drugs. He also told me that because the Beatles made so much money with their records and LSD lyrics, the Queen knighted them."

The Old Man's chin stiffened.

"No. It was the Order of the Empire. A tragic mistake, and I know many a chap who turned back his medal when that was announced."

Margaret returned to the subject of "lady scientists," asking me if I had found any of them particularly attractive. I told her about Rebecca, my "lady medical student" friend. Then Margaret committed a *faux pas*, declaring that Levis was a strange name, and could it be Jewish?

The Old Man and I "removed" quickly to the balcony.

"You mustn't mind Margaret, she sometimes . . ."

"It's quite all right," I said. "What I'd really like to know is how you are coming with your assays.

"I am sorry to say, Benjamin, that the picture is not so rosy. In fact, it would appear to be a complete bust."

"You mean that you can't assay blood specimens with

sufficient sensitivity. Perhaps I could help."

"No, the assays went along quite fine and dandy. We had sufficient sensitivity to assay blood concentrations lower than ten percent of the LD_{50} for each of the compounds – less than ten percent of what was necessary to kill Cooper. If any of those thirteen compounds had been the cause of death, they would have been detected."

I was flabbergasted. As his message sank in, I was over-whelmed with dejection. Had I picked the wrong compounds? Or the wrong man? How in hell could I do a better job than I'd done already? And who else should I investigate?

"What I gave you was a short list," I protested. "Maybe it was one of the toxins on the long list."

"Benjamin, I am afraid that our resources are too limited to look under every rock, so to speak. Our funds, our person-nel and the quantity of original sample are not limitless."

Sensing my disappointment, he tried to console me with a nautical analogy, advising me to take another tack. But I felt like I was navigating in the foggy Arctic Sea north of Hudson's Bay with winter coming on, the compass not working and the ice floes closing in. And I was sick and tired of communicat-ing in double-entendre.

"Which prof should I be looking at?"

"I cannot say."

"You'll have to give me more hard information. Give me the real cause of death . . . I'm sorry to be getting upset . . . I mean the 'cause of the demise.' Give me the symptoms. I sim-ply can't pull the whole thing out of thin air."

"Well, Ben, I had tacitly agreed with the neurotoxin theory since the nerves and the heart are, to be sure, the most sensitive targets in the human body. But you will remember from our ini-tial discussion that there were other very singular observations. For example, there was a most curious general swelling of the tongue – the purple color and a generalized disseminated arte-rial thrombosis. It would appear that almost every small artery of the body contained blood clots. This is not the sort of thing one finds in a garden-variety cadaver – no pun intended. And there was hyperkalemia. One doesn't find such high blood potassium, particularly in sudden death by heart failure. It was as if potassium had leaked from every cell in his body."

"Do you have any idea what sort of agent can cause this type of thing?"

"Well, the thrombosis indicates a derangement of the clotting system . . . activation of the blood platelets. One exogenous source would be endotoxin from bacterial infection in the blood. Naturally, we checked this out and found none. But there are many other proteins and glycoproteins which can cause these symptoms. But how could toxin proteins be administered when we didn't find any needle tracks?"

"What other symptoms should I concentrate on?"

"There were also many indications of an allergic shock which could be triggered by a massive dose of histamine. However, he could not have received a lethal dose of histamine by mouth, because it will cause massive stomach acid secretion and immediate vomiting. I'm afraid that I shouldn't say more than this."

I expressed my regrets for wasting his time by not doing a better job.

"Ben, the time was not wasted," he said soothingly. "You have worked systematically, checking the most obvious first. Your investigation did make some progress by eliminating the possible."

"And whatever is left over, no matter how strange, has to be the truth. Is that correct, Mr. Holmes?"

"Why, yes!"

"But I don't like playing Watson – always one step behind you."

"I'm sorry, Benjamin, but I'm in just as thick a fog as you. You'll just have to buck up and keep a stiff upper lip. Or as the old Cockney expression goes, 'Keep your pecker to the grindstone'."

"Well, just to be sure that I'm not wasting blood on the wrong grindstone, could you please answer one question?"

"Possibly."

"Were Manson and Ledbetter present at the Last Supper?"

"Manson wasn't; Ledbetter was."

As I said goodnight to Dr. Westley, I tried my damnedest to "buck up."

"One of my Swarthmore profs used to say that the tragedy of science was a beautiful theory destroyed by an ugly fact."

"Yes, he was quoting Huxley. *Thomas* Huxley, of course."

So the Old Man couldn't resist one-upping me, even now. Alone inside the elevator, I kicked the door. So much work still ahead of me. One prof down and several more to go. And it wasn't clear who was the next candidate.

Damn this investigation! It was just like a damned science project – starts out looking simple but turns out complex and downright bewildering. I would have to construct a new list with all 12 suspects.

It took me a long time to fall asleep, and I woke up early. I had to be sure I could eliminate Ashton. At my carrel in the library, hunched over my computer, I scoured Ashton's order files for any agent which would give thrombosis or histamine shock. And I found nothing in his files. Sure, he had lots of orders for crude venom that contained enzymes which would chomp on clotting factors in the blood and initiate thrombosis. But he would have to inject them. And Cooper had not been injected.

Or did Ashton have specialized knowledge that would allow him to deliver protein toxins by mouth? How could I question him without creating suspicion? I remembered the old television detective, Columbo.

I stowed the computer in my locker, went to Ashton's lab and puttered around, as if tidying up odds and ends. Finally, he noticed me.

"Mr. Candidi, I read your report over the weekend. Nice piece of work. Actually, it was the nicest piece of work I've seem from a rotation in the last ten years."

"Well, thank you, Dr. Ashton."

He sounded and looked sincere. The bow tie was gone, perhaps in anticipation of Thanksgiving vacation.

"Yes, you seem to have mastered the material very quickly. I think you could do quite well in neuroscience."

Did he mean this, or was I just thirsting for praise? He looked me right in the eye this time instead of gazing past me.

Then I put on my Columbo act, asking dumb questions about how poisonous were the toxins in the lab and asking about the warnings on the package inserts and how they could be lethal to a human being. He listened to this patiently, showing no mistrust or agitation. I laid in a long pause, trying to create tension. Then I blurted out the question.

"But if you put it into a man's bloodstream it would be *sudden death!*"

I couldn't have asked it any more directly. We were eyeball to eyeball, and I gave him a dumb stare. He stared back – no pupil dilation, no blink.

"Mr. Candidi, what you say is absolutely true but – "

"So what keeps a cobra from killing itself with all that poison in its glands?" I blurted out.

A guilty man should have experienced an explosive release of tension. But Ashton showed no reaction to my dumb question – no nervous laugh, no sign of relief, no change of posture. He told me the glands secrete the poison into poison sacs, which are lined with an epithelial layer that acts as a barrier, just like the skin. The poison can't cross the epithelial layer into the blood.

I asked him a lot more "innocent" questions, and he answered them all without suspicion or emotion. Finally, he glanced at his watch and excused himself.

Ashton's last words were a thinly veiled invitation for me to come back and do my dissertation research with him.

Call it 20-20 hindsight. Ashton couldn't have been the murderer. He was too well focussed and self-contained. It was written all over him, even in his handwriting. He'd probably walled off Cooper, like the snake's poison sac walls off the venom. He'd probably talked to the Dean. He couldn't have killed Cooper if he'd wanted to. He couldn't even find sodium chloride in his own laboratory.

– XXI –

Elliott Key

*T*HE LAST MINUTE PROVISIONING of the *Diogenes* helped get my mind off the Ashton debacle, and the wasted two months of effort. At 5:30 in the afternoon, Rebecca appeared at the fuel dock where I had temporarily tied up. She grimaced as she strained to carry a zippered diving bag full of books. Her lighthearted mood immediately rubbed off on me.

I noted some nods of approval from Dinner Key salts tied up in neighboring slips as I hefted down the bag and helped Rebecca on board. With the push of a button, my 24-horse Yanmar diesel snorted to life. With some pride, I strode the dock, casting off lines and pushing off, finally hopping on board and throwing the motor into gear. The *Diogenes* cut through the water nicely as we made our way through the marina. The boat rocked gently as we slipped between the spoil islands and into Biscayne Bay. As my body became attuned to the throbbing of the engine, it felt like I'd left my problems sitting on the dock.

Outside the channel, I headed the *Diogenes* straight into the 10-knot easterly wind and asked Rebecca to steer according to my hand signals. Stepping lively around the boat, I removed sail covers, attached halyards and hoisted main and jib. An active body can nurse back to health a damaged soul. Dropping back into the cockpit, I took the wheel, setting course for a starboard tack and pulling in the flapping jib. Throttling the Yanmar down to idle RPM, I pulled the decompression knob. The motor died with a shudder. Now it was just us and the wind. With the wheel clamped down and the boat sailing as steady as a lifelong friend, I hoisted the mizzen and moved around on the deck, optimizing the set of the three sails – with a touch of understated theatricality.

We made good a true course for Elliott Key at about four knots. I told Rebecca to take the V berth up front and that I would take the main salon. She unpacked her bag below, re-emerging in time to enjoy with me a beautiful sunset slightly to starboard. As the sky slowly darkened, Coconut Grove glowed in a thousand points of light to our stern. The wind picked up to 15 knots, and the boat swished through the water at five knots. I asked Rebecca to go to the galley and pull out some sandwiches. I ate mine standing at the wheel. Rebecca sat on the port bench. As Coconut Grove fell away to stern, darkened Biscayne Bay seemed incredibly vast.

"How do you know where to go, Ben," Rebecca asked with curiosity and a touch of disquietude.

"I've got the compass. The charts tell me that the course is 'one ninety-three.' Another mile and we should pick up marker number two. It's a four-second red flashing. We have to stay slightly to the left of it, because to the right is a shoal called Black Ledge. The next marker after that will bring us to the Featherbed entrance of the Biscayne National Monument. It's really an underwater park. That's where we're dropping anchor tonight."

"Can you see the red marker now?"

"No, it's still below the horizon. It's only sixteen feet high and can be seen for four and one-half miles. Right now it's about six miles away. We should start to make it out in about twenty minutes."

"Then how do you know that you're going to it right? Right now, that is," Rebecca asked with a trace of distress.

"I plotted my course, and I have stayed my compass course. So I know that the marker will come."

"And what if it doesn't?"

I told her what you do if rotten weather degrades your visibility. I explained how you favor the safe side if you can't find the marker. I told her about triangulating on landmarks, and how we could fall back on the Loran if everything else failed.

Rebecca asked nothing more for long time. How ironic. What I'd just been telling Rebecca was so similar to Dr. Westley's "take another tack" advice of an evening ago. After a few moments, Rebecca touched my elbow.

"It's so beautiful. Trusting a weak magnetic force to steer you in the right direction, keeping track of your progress and looking for a light you can't always see."

"That's the story of my last twelve years, Rebecca."

Ten minutes went by silently but for the gentle swishing of the water on the hull and the wind in the sails.

"Ben, show me how you find the light."

"The chart says the light flashes every four seconds. You look until you think you see a flash. It might be ever so faint. At the instant you think you see it, you count 'two, three, four, one.' If it keeps appearing on 'one,' you mark its direction and steer for it. If it's real, it will get stronger the longer you run towards it. When you really have it, no storm cloud can take it away from you as long as you trust your compass."

Rebecca stood silently next to me for several minutes, peering into the distance: a dark and empty universe – except for the light of a half-moon, the constant pressure of the wind, a gentle rocking and the streaming of the water along the *Diogenes'* hull, sounding like a forest brook. I felt so in love with her.

"Ben, finding the marker in the dark is like me leaving NYU as a bright biology and anthropology major – and heading down to a medical school in Miami. I have a weak background in math – I'm getting deep in debt and rained on with course work – and sometimes I wonder how I'll make it to my senior year."

"Yes, Rebecca. I understand. But you've got charts. And a lot of people have done it before – you know what direction to head in – and you are good and solid in biology and anthropology. So you can steer a little to the safe side and give yourself some leeway with the math and chemistry. Then if things do get stormy, you'll still have some sea room to spare."

"I'm glad I met you," she said softly.

Rebecca stood silently by me at the wheel, looking off into the distance for a long time. The binnacle compass before the wheel gave off a gentle, red glow, revealing a beautiful face in a meditative mood. Her hand rested on mine, and she nudged the wheel to the right, shifting our course slightly to starboard and downwind.

She whispered, "Two, three, four. One, two, three, four. One." Her tentative whisper grew to a clearly spoken count. "I think I have it. Yes, I am sure I have it. We're right on course. I know I'm on the right course with you, Mr. Ben Candidi."

"So do I. And you are now certified for the midnight watch."

Rebecca's musical laugh was interrupted by a fluttering noise. We'd just surprised a floating cormorant. We could barely make it out in the weak light of the half-moon as it splashed and flapped its wings in an amphibious take off. The cormorant flew to port, its wing tips almost touching the wavelets, using ground effect to get the most out of each wing beat.

"Ben, this reminds me of the song the violinist was playing at the South Beach. The song where a seagull sails across the cove." She sang the first verse in a clear voice with just a trace of vibrato. For some reason she ended a trifle self-consciously. But inspiration was at hand, and I improvised and sang a new verse in my warbling sophomoric tenor. I made up something about a flashing marker leading us there and our compass casting a reddish light – which I rhymed with "sultry night."

Rebecca squeezed my hand ever so gently and said, "This Jewish girl from New York is becoming strongly attracted to you, Mr. Ben Candidi."

I started to mutter something about it being mutual, but Rebecca interrupted me with a kiss. I clamped down the wheel, braced myself and slipped my arms around her. Moonlight played on her hair and danced between our cheeks, as her mouth melted into mine and we infused each other with passion. For a magical hour, the polite and discrete *Diogenes* held a course five degrees upwind of '193,' making no demands on us as we quenched our thirst for each other. Four-second flashing Red Marker #2 glided by to the starboard. The compass card assured us our course was true.

As flashing Green Marker #2 rose before our bow, it came time to loosen our embrace and tack to the Featherbed Channel. I gave Rebecca the helm. The single flashing marker for the narrow channel grew large before us. The three unlighted markers defining the channel were barely visible. Impassable shoals lurked unseen on either side.

"Ben, is the flashing green one the forward left one? Is there one unlit marker in front and two in back?"

"Yes, darling."

"Then we must be lined up straight with the channel."

"Yes, darling, and I love you," I said.

"Falling in love with you is like the channel markers. The closer I get to you, the more I know I'm in the right place." Rebecca steered a true course through the Featherbed Channel, and we glided into the first anchorage by Sands Key, north of Elliott Key. I dropped the sails as she steered. The wavelets lapped gently on the side of the boat as I folded the last sail on the boom. My two anchors caught quickly and firmly. The splash of each anchor triggered a bioluminescent reaction, with thousands of tiny organisms adding their luminous green magic to the enchanted evening. Soon we were below deck, captured in each other's arms, sharing whispers and sensations rendered no less intimate by the thin layer of latex between us, as we declared our love in moans and gasps of rapture that seemed to last an eternity.

Awaking 15 minutes before sunrise, I lit the alcohol burner and put on some water. While waiting for it to boil, I went topside and sat on the deck, leaning against the main mast. A lazy five-knot breeze out of the east gently rippled over my naked chest. The *Diogenes* tugged insistently on its two anchor lines. Except for two boats anchored a few miles to the south, the Key was ours alone.

But my head was not mine alone. The Ashton debacle

kept creeping back into my thoughts. Did I have any chance to solve this case?

The pan rattled, and I went below to pour the boiling water over the coffee filter setup bought especially for the occasion. I boiled a half-dozen eggs with the remaining water.

An arm's length away, slumbered the new love of my life, stretched so gracefully under a sheet on the double berth we'd hastily transformed from a dinette cove the evening before. She was like a sleeping princess from a fairy tale – delicately beautiful, peacefully smiling, lightly breathing, uttering an occasional faint, high-pitched sigh – the princess whose kiss transformed Frog Candidi into a prince.

As I daydreamed about Rebecca as a princess, she yawned melodiously and opened her eyes. "Ben, did I smell coffee?" She cast off the sheet and stretched her arms to me in invitation.

The exciting view of her slender, naked body confirmed a princess as charming by day as magical by night. We shared a brief, gentle embrace. Then Rebecca took a quick sip of coffee, then danced up the companionway ladder to the cockpit. A second later, I heard a gentle splash.

"You come in too, Ben!" her voice echoed over the starboard gunwale.

"But – "

"But nothing! Come on. The water's fine, and we've got it all to ourselves."

"But – "

"But you're just looking for an excuse to not dive in."

"But – "

"Come on, scaredy-cat! Right now."

"But if I jump in before setting the swim ladder, we'll never get back on board!"

"I can just see it in the newspapers. 'Catholic altarboy graduate student and Jewish girl med student arrested for indecent exposure in Biscayne Bay. Their crime was discovered by the Florida Marine Patrol whom they flagged down for assistance reboarding their yacht. It seems that they forgot to set the swim ladder.'"

I quickly wrapped the jib line around a portside cleat and let it dangle over the side. Tossing off my swimming trunks, I dove from the far side of the boat, swam under the rudder and launched a submarine attack on Rebecca. We splashed around for some time until she decided to get out.

"Ben, you didn't set the swim ladder."

"No, you said that we would get the Florida Marine Patrol to help us."

"But, Ben, how are we going to get up?"

"Well, we can climb one of the anchor lines."

"But, Ben, the front of the boat is so high and pointy."

"Well, we could braid the two lines together and make a rope ladder out of them."

"But the rope is too high to tie knots. Oh! Here's a line that you left hanging over the side. And it's lower."

"Wait, that's the jib sheet." I got one of my flashes of inspiration. "No, you can't touch that line! It's for controlling the jib. It isn't supposed to get salt water on it."

"But it's the only . . . wait, Ben!"

I swam up to it and threw the bitter end inboard.

"Ben!" she half-screamed. "Now how are we going to get back on board?"

"Well, I'm not so sure."

"But, Ben!"

Concentrating on treading water gracefully, I took a deep breath and launched into a mini-dissertation.

"It seems that I saw a TV piece on the U.S. Marine Corps Officer Leadership Course where they had a problem like this. The officer had to figure how to get across a mud pit with two men using a ladder without touching the wire, and – "

"But, Ben!"

"And seeing how you're so aquatic and daring, I just figured – "

"Ben, you are a *tease*!"

I carried on like this until we both got tired of it. I made her play the officer, while I played the enlisted man. She determined that I didn't have enough upper body strength to haul myself three feet up the negatively-sloping hull near the cockpit. And she didn't have enough "swim energy" to push me up. We finally settled on me hanging on the rail and her climbing me and stepping on my shoulders. This worked very well on the second try, but the timing was a little off: One of the yachts had weighed anchor and was just gliding past our stern as Rebecca hauled herself into the cockpit. She received some loud wolf whistles and Rebel Yells. There are a lot of Southerners among the boaters down here. I yelled back at them that sailors do not 'yahoo,' only power boaters.

"Okay, Bosun Candidi," Rebecca said, putting a loop in the end of the jib sheet and tossing it back over board. "You have ten seconds to get yourself on board under your own power, or I'll cut this rope. And that yacht also has women on board."

She stood in the cockpit, hands on hips, giving both me and the yachtsmen a full frontal view – defiant towards me and oblivious to them. In the allotted ten seconds, I pulled myself up the jib line, hooked my heel over the winch and clumsily wrestled myself aboard to the accompaniment of female catcalls from the other boat.

By the time the boat full of Good Ole Boys and Girls was half a mile away, we were eating breakfast in the morning sun. Afterward, Rebecca went below and reemerged wearing sunglasses and carrying a four-inch-thick book titled *Goodman and Gilman's The Pharmaceutical Basis of Therapeutics*. She searched through the pages, marked her place with her index finger and got my attention with a winning smile.

"I thought my new captain and navigator could help me work up some 'leeway.' It's this damned pharmacokinetics. All these equations. And the lecturer was a perfect ass. We've got a test two days after we get back. You said you were good in math," she said, half demanding, half pleading.

"Sure, I'll take a look at it. Specifically, what's the problem?"

"They have the drug going into body compartments that are three times as big as a man! And then these alpha constants and beta constants. It's enough to drive me to tears."

I sat down and started to skim the chapter. Rebecca sunned herself on the other side of the cockpit, looking off into the distance and occasionally glancing at me through her shades. It was distracting, trying to interpret equations with a topless girl sitting across from me. Rebecca's breasts were small but infinitely charming. After 10 minutes of deliberation, I had it figured out.

"Rebecca, there's only one problem with the volume of distribution. The concept is *counterintuitive.*"

"You can say that again!"

"But, mathematically, it checks out. Look at this equation," I said, turning the book around and leaning forward. "This C term is the concentration of drug that you would measure in the blood after you inject x grams of drug into the blood and after the drug distributes throughout the body. And the equation says C is equal to x divided by V_d, the volume of distribution."

"Okay," she said, leaning forward herself.

Topless is not the best format for a scientific discussion. We worked the equation, assuming a blood concentration of 0.01 grams per liter and 7.0 grams of injected drug. The V_d came out to a ridiculous-sounding 700 liters, a volume ten times as large as a man. Then I assured her that the math is correct but the concept of volume of distribution is awkward and counterintuitive. The trick was recognizing that not all the drug was dissolved in the body's water. In this case the drug had to be hydrophobic, with ninety percent of it bound to fat and muscle.

Rebecca pursed her lips and thought for a minute or two. Sensing a struggle between logic and intuition, I waited patiently.

"You're right, Ben! It's just that – " Then Rebecca smiled as she realized that she understood.

"It's just that you have to be a real stickler for definitions and trust the math." My Swarthmore physics and chemistry had taught me that.

"Well, thanks. You're a good teacher. You didn't seem to have any trouble explaining it to me, Ben."

"Well, I actually did have a little trouble explaining it to you."

"Why?" Rebecca asked, pretending to be offended.

"It's hard to explain this dry stuff to a topless girl!"

"Ben, you've probably had lots of topless girls on this yacht!"

"But none as charming and intelligent as you."

Rebecca smiled.

"Well, now that the white knight has rescued his charming, intelligent and topless damsel from the ivory tower of pharmacokinetics, perhaps he could show her a real coral reef." She had such verve. "My last reef dive was our family vacation in Jamaica, three years ago."

"Sure, Rebecca, but it will cost us a day's sail."

So, we weighed anchor and headed down the length of Elliott Key, transiting Angelfish Creek, out past the Ocean Reef Yacht Club and into the Atlantic. Navigating around shoals cost us some time, but kept me from mulling over the Ashton debacle. By four o'clock we were hooked up to a mooring ring 100 yards to the lee of Turtle Reef. The wind died down just as we arrived. Although the November water is not as pristine as in the summer, the visibility was good, and we had the whole reef to ourselves.

After asking whether we were securely moored and extracting a promise to set the swim ladder, Rebecca jumped in *au naturel* except for the mask, snorkel and flippers. This left me no choice but to follow her example, although I'm always squeamish about dangling my most tender parts for fish bait. Once a five-foot barracuda, with fish hooks piercing his nasty jutting jaws, stalked me back to my boat, said jaws often coming within two feet of my flittering fins. Under such circumstances I feel more comfortable presenting a smooth dolphin-like "tank-suit" surface to the sea creatures. But later, Rebecca told me she knew all about 'cuda, and that I was just suffering from a male "castration complex."

Reef snorkeling is a vivid experience, fulfilling our childhood Peter Pan dream of flapping our arms and flying out the bedroom window over familiar houses and around the church spire. The reef offers a landscape of mountains overgrown with forests of coral, canyons populated with fish and plains of waving sea fans.

In the nursery tale, the secret to flying was "to really believe." In reef snorkeling, it's holding your breath. Rebecca must have learned a lot about that on her Jamaica trip, because she made one-minute dives. An Aquarius. What a beautiful sight it was, to see my mermaid passing under a coral arch 25 feet below and then rising, fins fluttering, breasts gently dancing in a thin stream of bubbles, ascending and readying her snorkel and jackknifing at the waist as she broke the surface, transmitting a pattern of concentric ripples playing with the rays of the sun, sending the vibrant message that life is fascinating, limited only by your imagination and love for it.

This ecstasy lasted for an hour, before impending darkness forced us to return to the boat. The wind was gone, and the weather radio predicted calm, so I decided to stay tied to the mooring ring. The icebox was stocked with 30 pounds of ice and 10 pounds of shrimp from a place on the Miami River. Together with some precooked rice and vegetables, and a little help from my alcohol stove, I was able to create a very presentable dinner. *El Sol* put on a most incredible dunking performance in orange and red.

Soon it was dark. A blinking white marker became prominent, two miles out to sea. To our stern was a narrow patch of glow from the Ocean Reef Yacht Club. I imagined 100 people representing several hundred million dollars net worth sequestered individually in their condos, watching football games and docu-dramas. We were wealthier and better entertained. Sipping a French wine, sitting on the port side of the cockpit, my back against the wall of the cabin, with Rebecca on the starboard side, our hands linked across the companionway. I felt peaceful, contented and fulfilled.

"Ben, you're so lucky to be able to come down here for a weekend and be so close to Nature."

"Yes, but it's never been so nice as with you."

"Oh, I bet you say that to all your girls."

"I don't have any others, and there haven't been that many."

"Oh, I bet you had a lot. Tell me now," she coaxed.

"There was one that I sailed the Bahamas with a couple of years ago. But it didn't work out. She wanted flash and glitz. I wanted peaceful nights out on the water. She made me put in at a lot of places so we could go dancing."

Rebecca clicked her tongue and shook her head.

"Too bad for her. Quiet nights are just fine. Growing up in New York, I never got away from the honking horns. The City is lit up all night. All those people walking outside while I slept. It still feels so unnatural. I've probably not spent more than fifteen days with Nature in my whole life! Human beings were made to be close to Nature. Take them away from Nature, and you get socio-pathology."

"I agree."

We passed a few minutes in silence, just us and the gentle tugging of the tide on the hull. Rebecca turned around and looked over the bow.

"Ben, what is that red light and green light?" she asked with some agitation.

My heart skipped a beat. An oncoming boat that I didn't hear? Grab signal flashlight from side pocket. Anchor light on? Yes, burning nicely atop our mast. Rapid scan. Where's the boat? Not anywhere close.

My adrenaline level slowly went back to normal, and my pulse followed suit. Scanning the horizon, I finally saw what Rebecca was asking about: A red light on the right and a green light on the left. But they were coming *closer* together.

"It's two freighters out in the Gulf Stream. The one showing the red navigation light is going northeast, probably up to New York. The one showing green is going Southwest, probably to New Orleans. They'll pass each other in a minute."

"'Two ships passing in the night.' How lonely."

"They may say a few words on Channel Sixteen."

"Channel Sixteen?"

"The hailing channel. You can say a few words on it."

"Only a few words?"

"If you have more to say, you can arrange to switch to another channel, but not too many do."

"Like daily life. You can say a few words to people on an official channel. But if you want to say more, you have to find a special channel. And most people don't want to switch to it." She paused for a long time, looking at the floor of the cockpit. "Like talking with my mother or father. I can't talk to them both on the same channel. They are both wrapped up in different things. I have to find special ways to talk to each of them in their own way."

It was hard for me to reply to this, so I said nothing.

"Ben," she continued, "do you talk much with your mother and father?"

"We haven't talked much since I was eighteen."

"Do they talk much with each other?"

"No. Not at all. They're divorced."

"Oh, I'm so sorry."

"When I graduated from high school, they gave me two presents: College at Swarthmore and a divorce. Mom got herself transferred to Phoenix, and Dad sold the house and moved into a condominium with his girlfriend. I felt pretty lost, and there wasn't much to talk about."

"You probably felt betrayed."

I loved Rebecca's understanding and empathy.

"I probably did," I understated.

"Do you have any brothers or sisters?"

"No, just me. Found out later they'd been sticking it out for my sake. Four years so Ben could finish high school and get off to a good start. Overheard them once worrying about my 'socialization.'"

"Ben, I'm so sorry."

She squeezed my hand.

"I've had quite a few years to come to grips with it, Rebecca."

This time there was a long pause on her side.

"What made you so idealistic? I mean you're really not the normal American guy! You think about things. You ride a bicycle to work when you could afford a car. You live on a boat when most people would live in an apartment. You learned all about Miami, and all the different people that live there. Why are you doing this instead of . . . watching television at night?"

"Because I want to see things as they really are and not the way the advertising people want to make me see them."

"I agree. What people *do* that is really important, not what they say or try to fool other people into believing. Man-made things have become more powerful than things of Nature."

I squeezed Rebecca's hand.

"Ben, that's why I'm so interested in anthropology. In anthropology we try to find the things that are common to *all* men and women. In Africa, they might sit around the fire and the old men tell stories of the hunt. In America we have TV shows about Texas oil millionaires."

"Where did you get your idealism?"

"Oh, I don't know, Ben. When I was growing up, everything was so narrow and competitive. One summer, when I was fourteen and the other girls were chasing boys, I took up psychiatry as a hobby. Wanted to be a doctor, anyway. Started reading Freud. But I saw through him right away – that stuffy, secretive old stinker. But Freud led me into Jung, who was very deep. That led me into anthropology, and I've been hooked ever since."

"But you are not going to be a psychiatrist."

"No, I'm going straight into family medicine. Phooey to the specialties! You should use what you know – what you can see with your own eyes. Like seeing how the mothers treat their kids when they bring them in and how husbands relate to their wives. There are lots of cues you can observe. It doesn't make much difference whether they are East Indian, Latin American, Catholic or Jewish. A doctor should observe and find out what her patients hold dear, what they are afraid of, and show them how to take care of their children and themselves. The doctor should recognize their misperceptions and readjust them. Sometimes she can do it with gentle persuasion, sometimes the patient needs a fast twist, like from a chiropractor. Sometimes a good metaphor or a good story might help."

I'd never known a girl with such depth of understanding and feeling.

"But, Rebecca, you just described a psychiatrist."

"That's right, Ben. But that used to be part of the job description of a GP, back when people used to live in small towns. Like the doctor in the Norman Rockwell painting. Now the doctors don't know their patients. By the time the patients get to the psychiatrist, they're all messed up – the kids are all messed up and they can't afford the bill anyway. It's like not taking care of your heart for forty years, and then going in for triple bypass surgery."

I couldn't stand it any longer. I crossed over, took her in my arms and kissed her.

"You're the most wonderful girl in the world," I whispered.

"That's a real compliment, coming from you, Ben," she whispered back, "knowing all those intellectual people in Coconut Grove."

"The Grove is lower-brainstem."

"Hero to *las muchachas* in Little Havana?" she teased, snapping her fingers like castanets.

"Most of them called me *El Anglo*."

"I'll bet you knew a lot of nice Jewish girls from New York," she said coyly.

"I liked them all, but none as much as you," I whispered in her ear.

Whispers became moans, and our bodies entwined in a constant but ever-evolving knot, which would not be untied until deep in the night.

Once again, I woke up first and fixed breakfast. Friday morning. Three more days to live as man and wife in a state of natural grace. In a slack tide we languidly re-explored the reef. Around eleven o'clock Rebecca swam back and opened her books. She worked hard for about three hours making charts and shuffling flash cards.

Memories of the Ashton fiasco kept welling up. I pulled

out some papers on nerve action potential and tried to study. Rebecca ate the lunch I brought her without looking up from her books. She was engrossed in rote memorization of drugs, their effects and side effects and therapeutic concentrations. Around two o'clock she shook her head and uttered a definitive sigh.

"Well, I guess I've packed my cranium with everything it can hold today."

I was in the mood for some fun.

"Now's time for a pop quiz! Can you name a drug which blocks presynaptic alpha-2 adrenergic receptors, inhibiting their down-regulation of norepinephrine release?"

Rebecca looked at me quizzically and then answered, "Yohimbine."

"Right! Now for two additional points, can you tell me whether this drug has any abuse potential? And, if so, what abuse?"

"Ben, you were looking over my shoulder!"

"Well, are you going for the two extra points or not?"

"Do you think that the instructor would ask *that* question on a test?"

"I don't know who the instructor was. But you must have memorized it because I saw it on your flash card."

"Ben, you've got a dirty mind!"

"Well?"

"The answer is 'Increasing the local norepinephrine concentration at certain nerves innervating certain smooth muscles, serving certain organs. The abuse potential lies in increasing the blood supply to the male organ.'"

"Good, Rebecca. Absolutely erect! You get two points," I said, mimicking a quiz show announcer's voice. "Now, for an additional point and a comfortable pair of operating room shoe covers, which of the Pharmacology profs was embellishing his lecture with this sexy information?"

"Let me see. It was smooth muscle, but it wasn't Dr. Stampawicz. No it was . . . Dr. Grant Johnson."

"Oh, yes! The laser jock from Ohio. Did he tell you how he loads the cell up with a calcium-binding dye and then 'blasts the fuck' out of the dye to release the calcium?"

"No, he didn't tell us that, but he was very colorful and knew what he was talking about."

This led to a discussion of the profs, whom we compared one by one. We agreed that Dr. Gunnison was pretentious. Rebecca said that Dr. Moore didn't make enough effort in teaching pharmacokinetics.

"He didn't help us to understand it. I don't think he had enough self-confidence to be really honest with us. He probably doesn't understand it intuitively."

"I had the same feeling. When Dr. Ledbetter gave a seminar on distribution of a lymphocyte protein called selectin, Dr. Moore asked about its 'alpha' rate constant for redistribution and its volume of distribution, as if it were a drug."

"Who gave the seminar?"

"Dr. Ledbetter. Did he lecture to you?"

"Yes, it was on nonsteroidal anti-inflammatory drugs. You know, Tylenol and aspirin, inflammation and arthritis. Wow, was he a character!"

"How so?"

"Well, he was supposed to be talking about these drugs, but he kept getting off on his protein. What did you call it?"

"Selectin?"

"He said he'd developed a diagnostic test using selectins. He hinted that it was going to make a lot of money. The more he talked about it, the more excited he got. It was like one of these old movies about a mad scientist. Then he said he'd discovered how to use selectins to deliver drugs and how it was going to revolutionize medicine."

I sat up with a jolt.

"I'm telling you, Ben, some of us thought that he was going off the deep end! And he let on that none of his colleagues were capable of understanding the implications of his great discovery!"

"What did he say was his new principle of drug delivery using the selectins?" I asked, trying not to be too interested.

"He didn't say. But he did say that he had a patent application on it. He said that the biotech industry has a lot of protein drugs that they can't deliver. It was something about oral delivery. Whatever it was, it would revolutionize medicine."

I was pacing the cockpit. This was just the sort of thing I'd been looking for and couldn't find – drug delivery for proteins – proteins as drugs.

"Did he say that he was going to use his selectins for *oral* delivery of proteins as drugs?"

"I don't know, Ben. I don't exactly remember him saying that. But you see, it was all going so fast, and I wasn't taking notes because we knew that he wouldn't use this personal stuff on the test. We just sat back and listened to his performance."

"You said he was kind of strung-out. Kind of weird."

"He was like . . . one of those weird atomic-bomb scientists. Like Dr. Strangelove."

My brain was racing. Rebecca, please don't stop now. Give me all the information, while it's fresh in your mind. Quick, Ben, quick! What's the next most important question?

"Did any other professors attend Dr. Ledbetter's lecture?"

"No, I don't think so, Ben, but I wasn't looking around."

"But it would have been embarrassing if another prof had been there."

"Yes, he made it pretty clear that he didn't think they were real pharmacologists. He couldn't have any real friends in your department. I doubt that he was ever properly socialized. Maybe he had an anxiously avoidant relationship with his mother – and competed with his father. What sort of reputation does he have in your department, Ben?"

"All I know is what I saw when he gave a seminar. He seemed to hate the younger half of the faculty and tolerate the older half. Does he really take the Dr. Strangelove prize for my department?"

"Yes, Ben. There was no one weirder than him teaching the Pharm course up to now."

"No one more ready to blow up a whole country to prove a point?"

"You've described Ledbetter to a tee, Ben."

We were red hot, but I needed one final confirmation of it.

"What about Dr. Ashton?"

"He taught us the central nervous system. He's okay, once you get over his stuffiness. He went to some Ivy League medical school and still can't get over it. He lectured us in a blue blazer and a yellow bow tie."

"And hand-tied! I saw it at close range. I was in his lab for six weeks on rotation. Who hasn't lectured yet?"

"Dr. Kozinski is going to do most of what's left of the course. Anti-psychotic, anti-Parkinson drugs, antibiotics, diuretics and anticoagulants. It's a catch-all collection starting after the exam next Tuesday."

"You'll like Kozinski. He's a '*mensch*.' He worries a lot about the students' welfare."

"Well, that's just what this Levis girl needs after those other characters."

Rebecca stowed her books and notes and we went diving again. Except, this time, I wasn't thinking about the fish. I was thinking about Dr. Ledbetter. *Motive*: McGregor told me he hated Cooper's guts. *Concealment*: Westley told me that protein toxins would be the most clever murder weapon because they were so hard to find by purely chemical means. *Method*: Rebecca had told me that Ledbetter bragged to the medical students on what seemed to be a method for oral delivery of proteins to the blood stream. *Corroboration*: He bragged about it to the med students but kept quiet about it in front of his colleagues at the Departmental seminar.

In an excellent mood, I served Rebecca a shrimp dinner and then uncorked a second bottle of wine – a German one this time. As sun set and as the sky, between the silver-lined clouds, transmuted through shades of reddish-orange, violet and blue, we settled down to a second evening of talk.

She told me about NYU; I told her about Swarthmore. I told her about my blue-water experience as a crew member on an Annapolis-to-Bermuda run, the months I'd spent as hand on a charter operation in the Bahamas, the salvage of the

Diogenes and my lifestyle as a live-aboard yachtsman. She said it was beautiful, silently gliding from one place to another using only the power of your mind and the wind. I offered to take her across the Gulf Stream and cruise the Bahamas next summer. She liked the idea.

When she asked me about my friends, the Mensa Society had to come out. After you tell someone you're in Mensa, they'll never look at you the same. It's like saying you're a shrink or an intellectual snob. Not that it's wrong to be snobbish about money, luxury cars, membership in exclusive clubs, good breeding, good looks or even the size of your pectoral muscles. It's just considered bad form to be proud of your intellect.

"Had you ever thought of studying medicine, Ben?"

"Yes, I did, but I didn't think that it was for me. Firstly, I'm not personable enough to be a good doctor. Secondly, rote memorization of other people's 'facts' goes against my grain. I like to think things out for myself. Thirdly, a medical education is somewhat out of my price range. Fourthly, I don't like pompous doctors."

"Well, I can agree with you about the 'facts,' the expense and the pomposity. Especially the expense. How did you decide to go for your Ph.D.?"

So there it was: "If you're so smart why aren't you rich?" If you're so smart, why aren't you getting an M.D.? Most med students considered biomedical graduate students to have made a second-best choice. The M.D. is the power degree that will guarantee you $80,000 per year and can easily get you $180,000. I swallowed and answered honestly and politely.

"Rebecca, for six years I was knocking around trying to find myself and what I really liked. It was suggested to me that my real aptitude was science and that now was the time for me to jump into it."

"Who suggested it to you?"

She probed so softly and gently, yet relentlessly.

"My boss at the Medical Examiner's Office."

The truth wouldn't hurt.

"And was he right?"

I told her how biomedical science gives you a real intellectual workout and how it lets you explore questions in depth. I do my best thinking on systems that can be understood like clockwork, with no slippage, no fudge factors. I can't stand Rube Goldberg mechanisms. Rebecca told me a saying: "A medical education is like a Western river – two miles wide and two inches deep." I laughed and said that education for a biomedical Ph.D. is like an Oklahoma oil well – two feet wide and two miles deep. We laughed.

But then Rebecca resumed her gentle probing. She noted that a lot of the graduate students are foreign-born Chinese. I answered that Chinese and Japanese are overrepresented in the hard sciences because it's "dirty work," requiring hard work and patience. And correct answers are hard to come by in hard science. My head began to fill with ugly thoughts of Jake Brown with his how-to books on climbing the corporate ladder, and of Steve Burk with his 200-word executive summaries.

Rebecca tactfully pursued the question of what I would do with my Ph.D. degree. I didn't have any quick, enthusiastic answers.

A female Diogenes on board – holding a lantern to my face – blinding me by the light. What did the light reveal? A cowering teenage boy sickened by the thought that he has to fight tooth and nail for everything good in life – including the girl he loves? That evening our bodies did not entwine in magical knots. I had my own knots to unravel.

The next day was Saturday. We explored another reef, did some studying and then took the *Diogenes* back through Angelfish Creek to the Biscayne Bay side. The wind had picked up, and we made a rapid passage. We anchored in the lee of Long Arseniker Key.

After a glorious sunset, darkness descended and Venus became prominent. The nuclear power plant at Turkey Point, four miles away, emerged as a glowing seven-story high, mile-wide scaffold of yellow lights, whose glow obscured all the minor-magnitude stars in the sky. It's a fact of life: Power speaks loudly, drowning out the weak. Twenty miles behind the power plant was the city glow of Miami, the consumer of its electricity. A dozen of the tallest buildings blazed in a white, glowing cluster of gaudy self-advertisement.

But to the west remained the large black patch of the Everglades, God's reminder of what Florida was created to be. Stacked in three dimensions over the silent garden by unseen air controllers were five jetliners. The big birds descended on Miami International Airport like a small band of hikers with lanterns, descending a mountain trail. Would the spoonbills and anhingas living on the fringe of human activity perceive a disturbing roar or a gentle whine?

Was it the Everglades or Miami which exerted the greater attraction on the compass needle of my soul? Yes, I had been living on the fringe of human activity, sitting in the *Diogenes* for several years, a few hundred yards off of Coconut Grove, hovering there in a neurotic approach-avoidance reaction trap. Westley had said it, and Rebecca's questioning had affirmed it. But now I could focus my intellect and passion.

As we sat silently in the cockpit of the *Diogenes*, sheltered in the lee of Long Arseniker Key, we talked from the heart. Rebecca's hand found mine. The *Diogenes* rocked us in the cradle of love. Thesis, antithesis and synthesis.

Sunday morning treated us to no glorious sunrise. We awoke to gray overcast sky that merged seamlessly with gray water two miles away. The icebox yielded some eggs and a box of Danish that smelled like shrimp. I scrambled the eggs and made extra-strong instant coffee. No time to mess around filtering gourmet coffee. A 30-knot north wind was kicking up two-foot waves in our anchorage, and the boat was rocking. The open waters of Biscayne Bay would have four-foot waves all the way back to Miami. Feminine sensibilities are fine in good weather, but foul weather demands a masculine response.

I donned my foul-weather gear and tossed Rebecca my second pair. At 9:30, I fired up the diesel. With Rebecca's help at the wheel, I pulled up the anchors and hoisted a storm jib, a reefed main and the mizzen. We headed up the channel into Biscayne Bay, slicing water at seven knots on a close-hauled port tack with considerable heel. A southbound "deep V" Bertram had to share the channel with us, but we showed him, hauling ass and barely noticing his bow wake. Seven miles and a little over an hour later, we shot through the central Featherbed Channel and into the open water of Biscayne Bay.

Our speed impressed Rebecca. The *Diogenes* galloped through the four-foot seas like a spirited stallion jumping hedgerows on a fox hunt. The upwardly curved bow dove and rose over the waves, deflecting their upward splashs. But the wind picked up the smaller droplets, accelerating them across the deck, producing a nearly continuous spray. And every tenth wave splashed over the bow and doused the cockpit.

I stood at the helm. Rebecca sat in my lee, protected from the spray, but looking uncomfortable and withdrawn.

"Concentrate on the horizon, Rebecca. Hang loose like in the New York subway."

Rocking at the helm with the wind blowing in my face, I started hearing the music of Richard Strauss' *Hero's Life* in the crashing waves. Was I ready to follow the advice of Nietzsche, that crazy eccentric genius, and perform a moral tightrope dance that would transform me from techno-nerd to Wagnerian hero? Yes, I would focus my skills, courage and determination to win the charming damsel and slay the dragon. I would swoop down on Ledbetter, discover his guilty secrets and bring the evidence to Old Wizard Westley up in his ivory tower overlooking the Bay. And he would know what to do with it. Justice would be served. Act Two: I would repeat my prodigy act of high school, finishing a four-year Ph.D. regimen in three years. Then Rebecca and I would graduate together and live happily ever after with our respective degrees.

But during the 150-minute run up to Miami, my Wagnerian mood subsided into self-examination. What about my moral dilemmas? The future would certainly confront me with more Jake Brown types and tassel-toed lawyers to test my resolve.

During my philosophical brooding, the high-rises of the downtown Grove grew larger, looming slightly to port. As we approached the Dinner Key Channel, I ordered Rebecca to the helm, turned on the VHF, fired up the engine and took down the canvas.

"Ben, that was impressive. Taking down all those sails in such strong wind."

"Ain't nothing. I've often done it single-handed in much stiffer breezes."

As we passed my mooring place outside of the spoil islands, the VHF crackled:

"*Mon Roi* to *Diogenes*, *Mon Roi* to *Diogenes*, please come in."

I picked up the mike and transmitted, "We read you loud and clear, Frenchie. Over." I waved in the direction of the *Mon Roi*.

"You had me worried Wednesday night. I thought for a moment that the *Diogenes* was being stolen. I hailed you but you didn't respond. Over."

"Sorry, Frenchie. I was a little preoccupied. Over."

"So I see. You've got a passenger! Over."

"Correction: First Mate. Thanks for your concern. *Diogenes* to *Mon Roi*, WAR 7142 over and out."

"I copy 'Mate.' Wishing you a *bon jour*. *Mon Roi* to *Diogenes*, WK 35087 over and out."

Sometimes Frenchie was a good guy to have around, sometimes he wasn't. We passed the spoil islands and bore down on the docks of the Dinner Key yacht harbor.

"Rebecca, bring up your gear," I said bruskly. "I'm setting you off on the dock. Here's ten dollars for a taxi. They usually hang out at the parking lot."

"Ben, you showed me such a lovely time."

"Yes, it was for me, too. Today I've got to secure the boat and do some things. Maybe we can have a quick lunch together tomorrow."

"Yes, I'd like that – very much."

"Good, I'll meet you at twelve noon outside the third floor amphitheater." Our goodbye kiss started tentatively, but quickly grew passionate. I maneuvered the stern along the end of the dock and tossed up Rebecca's bag. Abandoning the helm, I quickly helped her onto the dock, then threw the

Diogenes into gear and headed off to my anchorage, looking back only once. It was a class act, done briskly, accurately and single-handedly. The boat hadn't even touched the dock. Like in the song on the juke box at Captain Walley's, I have my ship, and her flags are flying proudly. With or without the perfect girl, a good man will follow his compass needle.

Hopefully, Rebecca could stay serious about a guy who wasn't going for the 'power degree.'

After mooring the boat, I devoted the day to working out my plans. Then I grabbed a pair of scissors, went to the head, took one last look into the mirror, said goodbye to my moderately hip life and cut off my ponytail. I tossed the hair over the side. A short time later I had to toss myself overboard: While acting out my Humphrey Bogart disembarkation scene, I forgot that my dinghy was ashore, chained to a tree. I swam ashore to retrieve it.

My next step in the investigation wasn't any more elegant.

– XXII –

Phase Two

$\mathcal{O}$ WALKED SLOWLY INTO LEDBETTER'S lab, taking measure of the place: On the right was his office and on the left was a "wet lab" similar to Ashton's. Ledbetter's post-doc, Dr. Dong Chiu, intercepted me immediately, like I knew he would. Basking in Ledbetter's glory made him feel important.

"I help you with something?"

"No, thanks, Dr. Chiu. I've come to see Dr. Ledbetter."

"He very busy today."

"That's okay, I just wanted to make an appointment."

We were but a few steps from Dr. Ledbetter's door. He looked up from his desk and said, "It is all right, come right in. What can I do for you, Mr. –"

"Candidi. Ben Candidi. I'm a first-year graduate student."

"Yes, I know. I am sorry that I haven't been able to meet you until now. I was away most of the summer, and I returned to find the Department in disarray, for reasons which you undoubtedly know. I do remember seeing your file. You came to us with considerable prior experience."

"Six years in a toxicology laboratory, mostly instrument maintenance," I filled in, quickly and preemptively.

"Yes, I remember now. You were the one who graduated from Swarthmore six years ago and applied to us rather late."

"I decided that there was more to life than improving the signal-to-noise ratio on a standard assay."

"Yes. So what can I do for you? You probably need to check me off for the initial interview."

"Yes, and I would also like to investigate the possibility of doing a rotation in your laboratory."

Ledbetter's jaw twitched. "Perhaps you could tell me a little about your career goals."

I didn't have a prepared answer.

"Well, I'm interested in biological recognition in general," I stuttered. "I think that yours is an ideal system. Your seminar was impressive. I thought that your demonstration of specificity between the selectins and their receptors was most elegant. Your system has many theoretical and practical applications."

Ledbetter turned in his chair, locked his eyes on me and asked, "Which aspect of the work interests you most, Mr. Candidi? The theoretical or the practical?" The guy was so intimidating.

"The practical," I said and immediately realized it was the wrong answer.

"I'm afraid that the *practical* aspects of my work are what take the longest time to come to fruition," he said, leaning back and frowning. "The FDA is very particular about what compounds one would put in the human body, even as a diagnostic. Getting FDA approval is an expensive and time-consuming proposition."

Ledbetter dropped his voice and raised his eyebrows as he said "proposition." What did this mean?

"I thought you might have some rat experiments on how one of your selectins distributes in the body. Some problem where I could make a small contribution."

"Well," he said, ever so slowly. "We may have a project in the works that would be suited to a new pair of hands – in a few weeks. I'm sorry to have to express it this way, but there is so much foot work to be done, scutt work actually. We *really* can't reorganize the whole lab effort around a . . ." He was all suspicion and irritation. "I will check with Dr. Chiu and see whether we have space and time. When would you like to start?"

"In a week or two, if possible."

He first showed surprise and then said, "I'll get back to you."

Had I blown my chances for a rotation? What about my chances with Rebecca? I studied until five minutes before noon and walked to the third-floor amphitheater just as the class was streaming out. Rebecca walked out purposefully and smiled when she spotted me. I didn't move a step.

"Ben, you got a haircut!"

"Yes, I thought I'd turn over a new leaf."

"Well, you look just great!"

She punctuated the compliment with a swift kiss on the cheek. Not bad for starters – kissing me with all her fellow students streaming by.

"Sally," she called to a blonde about her size and age. "Come here. I want you to meet Ben Candidi."

"Glad to meet you, Sally," I said shaking her extended hand.

"Sally's my study-mate. Sally, Ben's the guy who got me straightened out on the alphas, betas and volumes of distribution. He also showed me a very nice time over the weekend."

"Well, thanks a lot, Ben," Sally said. "The information helped me out, too. And it looks like you did a lot to improve Rebecca's mood."

Sally gave me a nice smile and stepped back into the stream of students.

"Sally's a really nice – "

A chunky guy tapped Rebecca on the shoulder and said, "Hey, Levis, you've got the Note Service – this afternoon."

Rebecca turned to him and said, "Yes, I remember. – Ron Harris, I'd like you to meet Ben Candidi. Ben's – "

"Haven't seen you around," Harris interrupted. "Are you a Freshman or a transfer?"

"Neither," I said. "I'm a graduate student in Pharmacology."

A knowing smile came to Harris' face.

"You're going for the Ph.D., huh?"

"Yes. And I take my own notes," I added curtly.

"Fine," he replied, and turned to Rebecca. "Now, Levis, don't forget. We're counting on you."

When he was out of earshot, Rebecca said, "Ben, don't mind him, he – "

" – hardly rates my notice."

"Ben, I think that I should ask you – "

" – whether we're going to eat in the student lounge or go over to the Institute cafeteria?"

"Ben, what's gotten into you?" Rebecca asked incredulously.

"You! As Frank Sinatra might croon, 'I've got you under my skin.' Now where is it going to be, the lounge or the Institute?"

"The student lounge, if you don't mind."

"Not at all. Actually, I'm quite pleased – "

"You see it's just that – "

"You've got to do the Sophomore Note Service on Kozinski, starting at one o'clock sharp."

"Well – "

"It's okay. You've already got him psyched out. No sweat. He's a '*mensch.*'"

Rebecca shook her head in astonishment. She started to look away. Then her eyelashes fluttered, her head tilted back and out came a string of pearly laughter.

"Ben, you seem to have developed a case of *witzelsucht.* You aren't letting me finish a sentence. Now give this *schoene maedl* a listen, she has something to say." Rebecca glanced to one side, pulled me closer and looked earnestly into my eyes. "These last four days, you showed me a very beautiful time. I'd like to invite you to dinner at my place tomorrow night."

"I'd be delighted. What can I bring?"

"Your toothbrush." I must have shown surprise. "Your toothbrush for the next morning, big silly!"

Later that afternoon, I attended Dr. Gordon Taylor's lecture on "calcium channel flickering." It was my attention that did the flickering.

Before leaving for home, I checked my pigeonhole and found a hastily-written note from Dr. Ledbetter. In gracious language, he expressed his regret that he would not have a slot open in his laboratory until next May.

Might have been next millennium! Shitty luck. No chance to observe him at close range. Why? Because he was rightfully suspicious of me. No use trying to appeal his decision. That would just make matters worse. Hopefully, he wasn't already destroying evidence and covering his tracks.

What to do now? Old Man Westley would probably say, "Muddle on through as best you can. There's no turning back after you've taken the King's Shilling. Duty of Honor and that sort of thing. Tut, tut. Try to put on a jolly good show."

Standing in the narrow room with his note in my hand, I struggled to formulate a counterplan. First item: No further oral communication with Ledbetter. I pulled a piece of paper out of the feed tray of the photocopy machine and hastily jotted down a note informing Dr. Ledbetter that I could understand how he was constrained by schedules, that I would seek a rotation in another lab, and that there was no guarantee that I'd be free in May. That might help to put his mind at ease.

Aboard the *Diogenes*, I thought about what to do next. At the age of 14, during a couple of lazy summer days at the Newark Public Library, I'd added graphoanalysis and graphology to my bag of tricks. As I flattened Ledbetter's handwritten note on the dinette table, the truth virtually jumped off the page. His l's and t's had the high loops of an idealist, but they were often twisted. It was the uneven hand of a troubled or thwarted individual. Career frustrations? His angular m's and n's confirmed the intelligent, critical mind I'd experienced in his seminar. His firmly crossed t's, with upwards slants and sharp, spear-like points, bespoke optimism combined with sarcastic wit.

Analysis of the letter's cadence revealed negative feelings toward me. Beginning with an extraverted forward slant, it quickly resolved into a standoffish vertical hand. And the words "will not be able to" and "hope that you can appreciate" were written in recalcitrant backslant. And he made such secretive, tightly-closed o's, a's, b's and d's. Yes, I'd been right to reply immediately in writing to put him at ease.

I stretched and took a sip of tea. Yes, it all checked out – McGregor's stories of Ledbetter's hatred of Cooper and the frustrated, perfectionist idealism revealed in the seminar. Ledbetter's several-week absence after the murder was both convenient and necessary. He could learn the "news" over the phone. There would be no eye contact and no need to act surprised. No need to improvise a part in the chaos of the first days.

But how was I to conduct my hindered pursuit of Ledbetter? If I couldn't get into his lab, perhaps I could get *near* his lab. Rob McGregor's lab was just down the hall from Ledbetter's. The 20 hours per week would allow me to walk past Ledbetter's lab hundreds of times without arousing suspicion. In Ledbetter's absence, I might even be able to engage his assistant, Dr. Chiu, in conversation.

The next morning, I asked McGregor about doing a rotation. He was quite delighted and immediately described a "bite-sized research problem." He pulled a folder out of the file cabinet and said, "Read the papers and see what you can make out of them."

I proposed to start with four hours per week until finals were over and then work harder during the Christmas break.

"Fine," he said. "Evenings, holidays and Christmas are the best times to get things done in the lab. All the bureaucrats are away and can't hassle you. So you, I and the Chinese get the centrifuges and scintillation counters all to ourselves."

That evening, Rebecca served dinner with tablecloth and candles. She confided that she'd ordered her roommate to "go out and study." The candlelight sparkled in the wine glasses and in her eyes. She was charming, relaxed, contented and happy. I remained seated between courses but helped her to clean up after dessert and coffee. In the kitchen, washing up under the glare of the fluorescent light, her hand found mine and we suddenly found ourselves in each other's arms. It was a short step to her bedroom. An hour later, as we were lying on her bed, whispering endearments, we heard the key turn in the outside door.

"Don't mind her," Rebecca said. "I've already laid down the rules. You'll be coming here quite often, and she's not going to disturb us. Did you bring your toothbrush?"

"Yes. I bought one before coming over."

"Good, we'll hang it up on my side."

And so it was decided. I stayed the night, and was invited over for a study date and sleep-over every second evening.

It had been a most productive weekend. Now, to report my findings to Westley.

– XXIII –

Winter Break

DINNER CONVERSATION AT *FAIRE ISLE* started with the historical origins of Thanksgiving, shifting to my holiday sail, with all three of us omitting mention of my "lady friend," and skipping gracefully to the art of sailing, which was, of course, an English invention.

"Wessie has a nautical background. He was born in Cornwall," Margaret fluttered.

"Yes," I said, turning to him. "You were at Exeter. Is that in Cornwall?"

"Close. Devon, actually. Exeter is on the Exe River which flows into the English Channel at Exemouth – like Ply*mouth*. There's a certain logic in these things."

With the help of Wessie's gratuitous pedantry, we had no difficulty moving to Sir Francis Drake ("sailed out of Plymouth, you know") and to the nautical origins of the British Empire. And from there we retreated to the safe territory of our agreed-upon Anglophilia. Thus, the Old Boy and the Old Girl artfully avoided confrontation with the fact that their little Italian protégé and his Jewish girlfriend had shacked up on a sailboat for four days.

After dinner, the Old Man and I took our stations on the balcony. In code, I told him how I had given up on Ashton. Dr. Westley nodded.

"At the time, Dr. Ashton was a logical first choice, whom we have now eliminated."

"Dr. Westley, I have some new information on Dr.

Ledbetter which seems very interesting."

"Really!" he said in surprise. "I see." He wiggled in his chair, and then slowly got up. "If you could excuse me for a second, Ben. It is a little nippy out here, and I would like to get a sweater."

He popped into his study. A couple of minutes later he reappeared, wearing a heavy, rumpled blue cardigan, made of dyed Shetland wool, no doubt. He did not sit down.

"Actually, Ben, if you don't mind, we might be more comfortable in my study."

He gestured me to the overstuffed leather chair near his desk and perched himself on the edge of his Pharaoh Chair. So someone really could sit in that monstrosity! A squeaking sound issued from his bookcase. An ancient reel-to-reel tape deck was running. I casually gazed around the room until I found two microphones, well-positioned to pick up my words.

I told the Old Man what I had learned from my "lady friend," Rebecca, about Ledbetter's lecture to the medical pharmacology class. Speaking in double-entendre as code, the Old Boy told me he was very interested. He expressed disappointment that Ledbetter denied me a rotation in his lab. He compared the lab to an orchestra.

"Incidentally, what sort of orchestra does this maestro conduct?" Westley asked.

"Just a three-man combo. He plays piano, carries the melody, provides harmony and calls all the shots. He has two side-men: one Chinese post-doc and one technician. Drums and bass, if you will. In terms of creative contributions, he could just as easily be a solo act. He does all the thinking, and they do all the hands-on work."

"*All* the thinking? Perhaps the maestro doesn't want you in his jazz trio because he doesn't like to 'give up the lead,' as a beatnik jazz musician would say."

We agreed that I would "listen in on his jam sessions." It was surreal, speaking in double-entendre as the wheels of the old tape recorder squeaked, with the Old Man perched on the edge of his Pharaoh Chair, talking about beatniks in the room decorated in Order-Of-The-British-Empire, with choir-boy Westley staring at me from a 55-year-old photograph.

Something else proved surreal: The 18 days between Thanksgiving and Christmas break went by like a video on "fast-forward." I had to prepare for finals, buy Christmas presents for Mom and Dad, and check the boat every second day. Rebecca and I didn't have enough time to turn our nascent love into a committed partnership that could endure all challenges. In fact, her love seemed to be fading away.

Our first reality check was the phone. Rebecca didn't want me to answer it. This meant that someone important to her wasn't supposed to know about me. Slowly, it became clear that an invitation to New York for the holidays was not in the works. The unspoken question grew on the horizon like a navigation marker on the bow. Something would be decided in New York. Our hectic schedules didn't leave us much time to reflect. Then came the final exams, which sapped our last ounce of strength.

Could a post-exam tour of Coral Gables breathe magic into the last two days before Rebecca left for New York? I showed her the crown jewel of Merrick's vision of the Venice of the South: The Venetian Pool, carved from coral rock in the 1920s. We swam around barber poles, under arched bridges and aside low-lying Mediterranean-style buildings. We swam along the coral rock walls and into a grotto where we played prince and mermaid until Rebecca got cold.

Then, sitting at a table overlooking the pool, we drank cappuccino. Lightheartedly, we studied the photographs of the 1920s bathing beauties. Rebecca discovered the plaque that told how William Jennings Bryan, namesake of our medical school, had "lectured" there on the virtues of Florida living.

My narrated bicycle tour of Coral Gables took us past the old Biltmore Hotel with its Renaissance Italian tower with a spiral staircase. We rode past iron gates guarding Mediterranean-style mansions, and along coral-lined canals. But the City Beautiful worked no magic.

That night at South Beach, the violinist was gone – the

fiddler had fled. She was replaced by a saxophonist accompanied by his pre-programmed synthesizer. He played a lot of aimless riff jazz interspersed with some Latin hot. A pair of German tourists offered us some comic relief. During the break, the husband Klaus reached into his bag, pulled out a boom box and played a Euro-Pop tape, booming at German march tempo, pseudo-Italian melodies, punctuated by heavy-handed percussion, with the accent on the first beat of every measure. His wife Inge – blond, sunburned and about 25 pounds overweight – became animated, and they danced a spirited polka.

We talked about the German couple the next evening, in the charming French ambience the Cafe Place St. Michel in downtown Coral Gables. We compared the French and the Germans with the Franks and the Teutons who preceded them, 60 generations earlier. I proposed that certain ethnic characteristics can persist for many generations. Rebecca didn't like the idea that human behavior couldn't be made over in one generation. Was human nature intrinsically good or just perfectible?

"You know, Ben, there's a school of anthropology that interprets all human behavior in terms of biological theories – as if we were just animals! The males are supposed to be driven by their hormones to get power over each other and impregnate a lot of females."

"I know who you mean – Napoleon Chagnon. He did his field work on the Yanomamo Indians in the Amazonas. He makes a pretty good case for that theory."

"How disgusting!"

Yes, I thought, many things in life are disgusting. But the Yanomamos are our last "unspoiled" example of mankind. And primitive emotions have been around for a long time. Classic Greek literature recorded for us the whole gamut.

But Rebecca didn't like the idea. She argued for love, charity, altruism and sacrifice for the good of your fellow man. Suddenly it occurred to me: This wasn't an abstract conversation on theoretical anthropology. This was the question of Ben Candidi versus the boyfriend back in New York. Rebecca was watching me carefully. It was my turn to answer.

"Rebecca, when it comes to fulfilling my life with the woman I love, I can't afford altruism. I've thought hard about this question since meeting you. I won't subjugate my needs and creep away for the 'good of the tribe.'"

Our eyes locked across the table as my words sunk in. There was nothing more to say. At her apartment that night, my body delivered the same message as my words.

The next morning in the cab, Rebecca put her head on my shoulder and sighed, "Oh, Ben." I kissed her cheek and tasted a salty tear. She cradled her head on my shoulder, and I held her hand, wordlessly.

The cab stopped. I quipped about the unreliability of curb-side agents as I unloaded the trunk and carried her bags to the counter. We walked together to Concourse C until we reached the metal detectors and x-ray machines. Then I pulled Rebecca over to the side, pressed a wrapped Hanukkah/Christmas present into her hand and said, "I can't read your thoughts, but I can sense your feelings. I've given you a lot of things to think about."

"But haven't I given you a lot of things – to think about too, Ben? A lot of questions?"

"Yes, Rebecca, but I know the answer. I love you and want to build my life with you. It's a lot simpler for me because I don't have to please my father and mother." Rebecca's eyes moistened. "And because I don't have anyone else in my life."

Face to face, holding hands, the truth could not be suppressed any longer. Rebecca looked down, and when she looked back up, her eyes were wet with tears.

"You can sure see through a girl, Mr. Ben Candidi."

She choked on my name. I sensed that people were starting to stare.

"Rebecca, I want to talk to you every other day. I understand why I can't call you at your folk's house. So please call me at the lab. Think whatever you have to think, say whatever you have to say, do whatever you have to do. Just remember that I love you. And come back to me. In January, I want you back in my life."

I started with male stamina and conviction, but by the time I got to "in my life," I was all choked up.

"I will. Goodbye, Ben . . . 'til January," she said, kissing me lightly on the lips. She turned and walked through the metal detector. I didn't say any more for fear of blubbering. When Rebecca reached a bend in the corridor, she turned and waved just before passing out of sight.

A soft baritone voice to my right was addressing me: "Sir, it would be okay if you want to accompany the passenger to the gate – "

It was a middle-aged African American who worked at the metal detector – sincere and well-meaning.

"No . . . Thanks," I said, as his slow, placid eyes searched me persistently and sympathetically. "I couldn't go through saying goodbye to her again."

"My guess is that you'se gonna get lot'sa chances to say hello and goodbye to that little lady. Now you have a good Christmas vacation."

"Thanks, you have a good one, too."

My tears belied my Yanomamo Indian Theory. The cab ride back proved I couldn't play a hard-shelled Humphrey Bogart. The driver played an oldies station. Bertie Higgins sang wistfully about how he and his girl once had it all, playing Humphrey Bogart and Lauren Bacall, true to life, while sailing away to Key Largo. I felt sure he had lost the girl. Entering the med school, I steeled myself by remembering the song about sailing under the Southern Cross.

"It's great to see you here," McGregor said with some sarcasm. I had not really gotten started on his project.

"Sorry, Rob, but I just put my girlfriend on the plane to New York."

"Look," he frowned, "you've been saying goodbye to her for the last week. Now you won't have anything to distract you. Rejoice!" McGregor lightened up. "You are working over Christmas vacation, and you've got everything to yourself – the centrifuges, the scintillation counter and me. Now, are we going to get this project done by New Year's Day or aren't we?"

"Let's do it, Rob!" I said, feeling like I'd joined the French Foreign Legion.

So Rob and I chemically handcuffed proteins and enzymes, catching them by surprise like adulterous couples while they were "doing business" in the living cell. We busted the cell walls like divorce detectives busting down motel doors. And we grilled the handcuffed molecules on the gel electrophoresis machine and identified them by molecular weight, using identifying antibodies.

I reverted to my old Swarthmore routine of working hard to keep from feeling sorry for myself. I had no complaints about Rob except that he wasn't a good enough sport to leave the room when Rebecca called. It was a subdued conversation, with our feelings deep below the surface. She was spending most of her time getting a head start on pathology and visiting relatives and old friends. She promised to call me every third day, which she did faithfully.

An envelope containing the semester grades appeared in my pigeon hole: A's in both courses, and a note of congratulations from Dr. Gordon Taylor. For form's sake, I did some routine maintenance on the instruments at the M.E. lab, preparing their cocaine, narcotic and alcohol equipment for that peak load of human self-abuse that accompanies the holiday season.

I looked up all Ledbetter's recent publications and found nothing useful. He had published 34 papers in the last 10 years, a prodigious output. But they were either scientific studies of selectins or reports of their use in diagnostic applications. I found nothing that would revolutionize the field of drug delivery – none of the stuff that he had bragged about to the medical students but had concealed from the members of his own department.

The Old Man was clearly disappointed when I called and told him I had no news. He said that we wouldn't meet until early January and that I should work hard on the Ledbetter investigation.

"While the cat's away, the mice will play," goes the

expression."

But how was the mousey Ben Candidi supposed to play? Sure, I'd scampered up and down the hall often enough to get a good picture of Ledbetter's lab operations. The angle between his office and laboratory doors allowed me a split-second glimpse of him as I walked down the hall. It was just long enough for me to see him, but not long enough for him to look at me. I mentally averaged three days worth of glimpses and constructed a moving picture of Ledbetter's daily routine.

Ledbetter was always working hard at his desk, usually typing on his personal computer. People said that he was always getting something ready for publication. He had the best publication record in the department. Occasionally, his assistant, Dr. Chiu, brought a sample that Ledbetter would scrutinize. Sometimes I caught a "sound bite" about sending a sample to a company or a fragment of a discussion on "time of release," "bioavailability," "secondary and tertiary layers" or "first pass effect."

Then, Dr. Chiu would hurry out to the lab and give some instructions to the technician while Ledbetter made a notation in the computer on his desk. The outer laboratory had no computer. All their record-keeping was done in old-fashioned, bound laboratory notebooks with carbon paper and detachable duplicate pages. There were shelves and shelves of these notebooks.

Ledbetter conducted a lively trade in samples from and to industry. The samples were received in styrofoam boxes packed with dry ice. Dr. Chiu unpacked them into a Revco liquid-nitrogen-temperature freezer out in the hallway. It stood like an oversized casket, and when they opened the hinged door, a cold mist spilled over the sides. Chiu carefully reached in with rubber-gloved hands and removed or replaced precious samples from the witch's brew, while the foam insulation and aluminum foil wrappers crackled in response to temperature changes, sounding like the samples were coming to life.

They processed many of the incoming samples with their homogenizers, spray dryers, freeze dryers and coating ma-

chines. My spot-checks of Ledbetter's mail slot verified a steady
stream of correspondence with industry, but an end-of-the day
sifting of the paper recycling bin down the hallway failed to
turn up any evidence that they were dealing with toxins.

After a few days, Ledbetter's door was closed: He had
taken off for Christmas vacation. Dr. Chiu and the technician
worked two days longer, and then they too were gone. All I
could glimpse was a solid, locked door. It was like a sailboat
race when the wind suddenly dies. Everything was put in stasis. My life was on hold.

Rebecca called, telling me they had a foot of snow in
New York. Miami's cold snap arrived the next evening, with
the mercury plunging to 40 degrees. The 30-knot north wind
sweeping through Coconut Grove didn't kick up terribly high
waves in my anchorage, but it was hard to row against the
next morning. My wind generator turned at a good clip, and
my batteries were always topped off, allowing me the mindless luxury of limitless 12-volt, small-screen television.

Next, I would look up Ledbetter's patents. After some
calling around, I found out that the Dade County Public Library is a repository for the U.S. Patent Office, with everything since 1970 on microfilm. After a hard but productive
day in McGregor's lab, I rode my bike downtown to the library. The quadrangle, consisting of the library, an art museum and an historical museum, is an example of something
Dade County has done right. The walls of the complex are
high, both inside and out, reminiscent of a Spanish fortress,
an impression that is reinforced by its large blocks of quarried
coral rock and wrought-iron barred windows some 15 feet
above ground level. I took the main approach to the edifice,
walking through fortress-like gates and carrying my bike up a
long stairway running parallel to a water cascade.

I locked my bike to a post on the tiled quadrangle next to
an ancient English three-speed. It was eight o'clock, three hours
before the lowering of the fortress gates. Passing a sleepy cir-
culation desk clerk, I found the business section where the
patents were located. It was staffed by a single librarian, a

short guy of about 25, who was slightly heavy for his size. In a high-pitched voice and friendly manner, he told me that his name was Robert and asked me what I needed. He got out a compact disk, put it into a computer near the counter, brought up a program, showed me how to bring up the "inventor option," and then left me to do my search.

I punched in "Ledbetter, J" and got two patents, granted one and three years ago. Selecting the "print option" from the menu, I got a hard copy that I took back to Robert.

"I got two citations, Robert. Can you show me how to look up the patents." He preferred Robert to Bob.

"Sure, Benjamin. We should have it on microfilm."

He took a bundle of keys to a 15-foot row of filing cabinets and opened drawers, each containing 50-some boxes of microfilm. He handed me a box labelled 4,897,323-4,898,133 and went to another drawer and got a box from the 5,000,000s.

"Wow," I said, looking at the cabinets, "that's a lot of patents."

"Yes, there are over five million of them now, Benjamin. You can take these spools to the microfilm reader, but first I need your driver's license. It's library policy that you give it to us as collateral, to be sure we get the microfilms back. These things are pretty valuable, and Washington doesn't like to send us replacements."

"Just one problem. I don't have my driver's license with me. I generally don't have it."

"You'd better watch out, Benjamin. They can be pretty rough on you when they pull you over."

"You don't need a driver's license to ride a bicycle," I answered.

Robert's face lit up.

"So you ride around on a bicycle!" he exclaimed, in an excited voice an octave higher than before. "I ride a bicycle, too."

I said, "The fuel is cheap, I don't need to buy insurance, and I can park it anywhere for free."

"And it doesn't kill people and pollute the environment."

"Was that your English three-speed out there?"

"Yes, my Hercules Royal Prince, built in Sheffield, England. It used to belong to my dad."

We continued to chat for a while until I realized there would be little time for my patents. I gave Robert my American Express card, which impressed him, being as how I was a bicycle rider like himself.

I read both patents in projected negative image on the screen. Unfortunately, they had nothing to do with toxins or with oral delivery of a protein. They were the same stuff as Ledbetter's seminar – imaging the liver and other organs using radiolabelled selectins.

Robert found me in a dejected state when he announced five minutes to closing. He suggested that I make copies. When I asked how much it would cost, he said they would be free because the cash box was already locked. He rotated the spools and pushed buttons with considerable dexterity, producing in short order, 10 chemically fragranced and slightly moist pages comprising the two patents. He looked at the face page of one of the patents where it said:

John Ledbetter of Miami, Florida.

"That's a coincidence!" Robert exclaimed. "He lives right here in town!"

Robert replaced the two spools and returned my credit card. I followed him out, and we talked bikes, bike routes and neighborhoods for a while. Robert lived in the north end of Coconut Grove in a garage apartment behind the house of a "nice couple." I could imagine his apartment in the second story of a freestanding garage, accessible by an outside wooden stairway, tucked in behind a charming two-story Coconut Grove house. His monthly rent was probably between $150 to $300.

Robert was a native Miamian with an interest in local history. I agreed to follow him on his "favorite bike route," which took us south through the commercial marina, boat yard and warehouse district. We stopped at the center of the bridge over the Miami River at Second Avenue. Several 80-foot, wooden, island freighters were tied up side by side along the shore. The upper decks were covered with bicycles, stacked 10 high.

"Do you know where all those bicycles are from, Benjamin? They were *stolen* from people here in Miami. And do you know where all those bicycles are going? Haiti! And what do you think those freighters bring back from Haiti? Refugees to steal more bicycles! Sometimes I feel like jumping into that river with my brace and bit and drilling a few holes in those boats."

"The river's pretty dirty, Robert."

"But it didn't used to be. My father used to swim in it!"

The ride home was along the Atlantic Coastal Ridge, a long coral ridge running parallel to the Bay, four blocks inland. Although only 15 feet above sea level, the ridge served to hold the water back in the Everglades until commercial man invaded in the first quarter of this century.

Despite darkness and cold wind, Robert provided interesting narration, pointing out historic houses along Miami Avenue, the neighborhood he knew as a boy, and griping about the long string of high-rise buildings lining Brickell Avenue. He pointed up to a high-rise condominium building.

"Of course, you know what TV program made that one famous, Benjamin."

It was The Atlantis, with its famous hole between the 25th and 30th stories, filled with a palm tree, a spiral staircase and a jaccuzzi. We pedaled past the Museum of Science where Westley got his start and where Robert used to go as a kid. As we passed the John Deering Estate, Robert told me all about Deering's Viscaya Mansion – the European art treasures, the social-climbing "Viscayans" who jealously guard it, and the wedding ceremonies held in its formal garden.

We passed the high-rise Mercy Hospital where he was born. When he was 12, the taxes got too high and his family had to move out to Kendall. Several blocks later on Tigertail

Road, Robert told me it was time for him to turn off. He said he hoped to see me again. I thanked him for his help and rode alone the last mile and a half of my everyday route.

I was not in good spirits, rowing to the *Diogenes* with a strong, cold wind in my face and with the hard-sought yet worthless patents folded in my jacket. On board, I tossed them on the dinette table and fixed dinner. Over a cup of after-dinner tea, I studied the patents. What else to do but study, when the boat was rocking, when a cold and persistent wind was blowing, and when the cabin was so cozy inside? If the patents wouldn't give me the answer, perhaps they would give me a clue. So I read them from stem to stern, from abstract to claims – as if they were fine literary works. Ledbetter's diagnostic invention was well-described. His working examples were virtual recipes for making his injected selectins deliver radioactivity to the targeted tissue. He defined his field of application in grandiose terms, claiming every selectin, discovered or undiscovered, and every conceivable diagnostic application.

"I CLAIM: 1. A radiological method of obtaining a two dimensional or three-dimensional image of an organ, which method consists of attaching a gamma-irradiating radionuclide . . ."

None of his 13 claims said anything about oral delivery of proteins.

So he hadn't yet patented his world-shaking drug-delivery system. Could the funny listing of references on the face pages give any clue? Most of the cited documents were U.S. Patents, identified by number (like 4,876,194) and by the date when it was granted. But what was the meaning of the numbers and letters in second listing, called "International Priority"?

At the end of the second patent was a stray page, the face page of a pharmaceutical patent to an English scientist working for a British drug company. Robert had apparently copied one page too many. Under foreign priority, it had a "PCT" number followed by "GB" and another number, both with dates. These dates were slightly less than one year before the filing of the

U.S. Patent. Does an inventor file his patent in his native country first, and in foreign countries a year later? Did Ledbetter have foreign patents? Who could answer my question?

The next morning, I stopped by the library with my patents in hand. Three clerks manned the desk where Robert had worked and the place was busy. I browsed the latest issues of the *Patent Gazette*, searching for a listing of a recent Ledbetter patent which might not yet be microfilmed. Nothing. I returned to the desk and addressed the most senior-looking lady, explaining that I needed information on a U.S. patent, one that couldn't be found in the microfilm or in the *Patent Gazette*, but that might come out in one year.

"If it isn't in one or the other, you can't find out anything about it," she said authoritatively. "The patent is a secret in the U.S. Patent Office until it gets published in the *Gazette*."

I showed her the British patent and started to ask about the "Foreign Priority" numbers, but she cut me short.

"It must be a *foreign* patent office number. We do not keep any foreign patents here. The U.S. Patent Office keeps its patents secret until they are published."

"But – "

"But, young man, when this patent collection was installed by the Department of Commerce, I attended a three-day course on patent librarianship. I know that whereof I speak."

A grammatically tortured sentence from a snippy school-marm. Probably a transplanted Bostonian, like we read on those old tombstones in the Woodlawn Cemetery.

"Is there anyone else here at the library who could – "

"I am the head of this Department."

But she grudgingly affirmed that Robert would be back that evening.

At the med school, my mail included a small package from Rebecca bearing the warning, "Do not open until Christmas." After a productive day with McGregor, ending about eight-thirty, I rode back down to the Dade County Library. Robert seemed glad to see me. I posed my question about whether foreign filings could give any advance information on the contents of a U.S. Patent.

"Yes, they can. But you have to special order the foreign applications."

"Great! Can you tell me how to do it?"

"You just write the World Patent Service. I can get you the address."

"And they can give me a copy of a foreign application at the same time that the U.S. Patent Office is keeping the U.S. application secret?"

"Sometimes," Robert said with a smile.

"Why do you say 'sometimes,' Robert?"

"Because it depends on whether the American inventor filed for a patent with the European Patent Office under the PCT."

"It sounds great, Robert, but I don't quite understand."

Robert uttered a childishly innocent laugh, tapped me on the shoulder like I was a schoolboy friend and said, "It's really simple, Benjamin. It works like this. Say there's an American inventor and he files his invention with the U.S. Patent Office. Now, they have to *examine* his application. They keep it secret until they give him the patent. That might take two or three years. Now, if the inventor wants to have patents in other countries, he has to file patent applications in those countries. And to make things simpler, all the countries got together and signed this *treaty* that says that the European Patent Office will examine it. And part of the treaty says that they will respect each other's priority dates. So the American inventor has exactly one year to file his application with the European Patent Office."

I nodded to Robert after every sentence, to keep flowing this stream of expert information.

"Now, Benjamin, the European Patent Office doesn't keep the patent applications secret. Right after the patent is filed, they give it to the World Patent Service, and they publish the title. And they'll sell a copy of the whole application to anyone who wants to order it. It's crazy, Benjamin. The American Patent Office is trying to keep the patent application *secret*

and the European Patent Office is letting people *publish it!*"
His hearty laugh could have come from a 13-year-old.

"So, Robert, what you're saying is that anyone can order a copy of a patent application about one year after it was filed in America."

"Yes, Benjamin. As long as the inventor filed an application in Europe."

"Boy, Robert! That's great news! You sound like a patent lawyer." I said this in genuine appreciation.

"No, I'm not smart enough to be a patent lawyer. But I know a patent lawyer. Mr. John Barnaby, *Esquire.* He's a real nice guy. I helped him with some microfilms, and then one evening he taught me all about the numbers on the front page of the patent. Once, he paid me to do a special project in my spare time. But don't tell anyone here at the library about the money."

"I won't tell anyone, Robert. Can you tell me how to order the application?"

"Just a minute." Robert went to a shelf, pulled out a reference book and copied out the address and telephone number of the WPS. It was in Berlin, Germany. I thanked him and left for the *Diogenes.*

I awoke the next morning at first light, fixed a cup of coffee and ate a doughnut. After a brisk row to shore, I was standing at a pay phone along the bayside jogging path. With pen, paper and credit card in hand and the chilly north wind blowing in my face, I put in a trans-Atlantic call to the WPS. It was already two o'clock in the afternoon over there. The number was bad, and I had to get international directory assistance. Thank goodness the operators speak English, because my college German was rusty as hell. My second call connected.

"*Guten Tag. Firma Hansjoachim Vogel,*" answered a businesslike female voice.

"*Ich kann nicht gut Deutsch reden,*" I said with great difficulty.

"Zen ve kann speak Englisch. How kann I help you?"

"I want to order a patent application by John Ledbetter."

"Zen I kann give you the address, and you can make in writing your request."

Letters would take too long, so I turned on the charm, telling her I'd never used the service before and would follow their procedure with my next inquiry. And would it be possible for her to just check if there was at least one application by John Ledbetter.

"Vun minute please." I heard some clicking of a keyboard for a minute or two. I prayed that we wouldn't get disconnected. The wind was cold as hell. "Yes, ve have one from this inventor. It appeared before three months. 'Improved drug delivery using zelectin gleeko-proteins.'"

"Yes! That is exactly what I want. Can you tell me how to order it?"

"Certainly, but there are also two more. One is seven years past. One is eight years in the past."

She told me titles corresponding to the two American patents which I already had. I told her that I needed just the recent one. She told me the identifying number of the patent application, how much it would cost and how to order it. I thanked her and hung up.

Was I shaking from the cold or from excitement? A second cup of coffee at a greasy-spoon restaurant on the fringe of the Grove warmed me up. Sitting at the counter, I hand-printed a business letter ordering the patent application. After giving the waitress five dollars and saying "keep the change," I mounted up and pedaled to the Coconut Grove Bank and purchased a cashier's check.

Next, I pedaled north, up McDonald Avenue to U.S. 1, west to Ponce de Leon Boulevard and then a couple of miles north. The Federal Express drop station was on Alhambra Circle in the fashionable downtown section of Coral Gables. A pleasant, uniformed woman gave me an envelope into which I put the letter of request and the check. I carefully filled out the paperwork and gave the woman $28.

Thus, I ordered the European patent application on "Improved Drug Delivery Using Selectin Glycoproteins" by John Ledbetter of Miami, Florida: Undisputable Mad Scientist, Braggart Before Medical Students and Suspected Murderer. Now there was nothing to do but wait three or four weeks. Too excited to go to the lab, I biked around the downtown Gables, stopping before fountains that lost their charm in the cold. Taking refuge in the Cafe Place St. Michel, I ordered a croissant and cappuccino, sitting at the same table where Rebecca and I had our last date. Well, Rebecca would really be proud of me now. But I couldn't tell her. And maybe she wouldn't even be mine when she came back.

To be truthful, intellect had not been pivotal to my tentative success. It had been persistence and curiosity – and my good luck to have met Robert, that nerdish little library clerk with the open manner and the high-pitched voice. I owed no thanks to his boss.

What a shame when style wins out against substance and when naked willpower wins out against good manners. These "power people" were the personification of the Yanomamo/Amazon Indian theory of the human condition. What a horrible world it would be if everyone acted that way. Jesus was right: The world does owe a lot to the meek.

I said a little prayer for Robert. If he had grown up in Washington and had found a mentor, he might have become a patent lawyer. But he grew up in Miami, and it didn't happen. Was there any way to repay his kindness? No. If this thing panned out, I'd have to hope that Robert would forget me and the patent by John Ledbetter from Miami.

I saddled up and rode north, past the Woodlawn Cemetery and through Little Havana to the med center, where I devoted the rest of the day to the McGregor project. After three days of patient investigation of calmodulin and tyrosine phosphatase, I caught the two molecules *in flagrante*. I handcuffed them together and made them confess that the calcium-calmodulin complex had been kicking tyrosine phosphatase into high gear.

Over the holidays I almost got handcuffed, myself.

– XXIV –

Cool Yule

'THE MIAMI CHAPTER OF THE Mensa Society was having a Christmas party. I had sorely neglected them, having missed every monthly meeting since July. I had gotten tired of going to a Chinese restaurant in Coconut Grove and listening to everyone talk about their hobbies (usually exotic), their jobs (usually dull) and their relationships with their colleagues (usually problematic).

The party was two days before Christmas in the Coconut Grove townhouse of Arnie Green, a 37-year-old psychiatrist and Mona, an artist. She's his third wife and he's her second husband. I RSVPed and showed up at 8:30 – unfashionably punctual. A small number of guests were sitting in a "conversation area," a setup I'd known from previous visits. It consisted of four overstuffed sofas boxing in an oversized coffee table on which sat Arnie's "quadravision," which he had "invented."

Arnie's quadravision consisted of four smallish TVs, the type you can buy for $150, arranged in a quadrilateral fashion, so that the screen of each faced outwards towards its respective sofa. The screens were set low and were angled slightly upward so that you could get a comfortable view of both the picture and of your fellow viewers on the other side.

Arnie's thesis was that TV is too much of a solitary pastime, and that it's more interesting when you can see other people's reactions to what's happening on the screen. His friends had mixed opinions on the experience, but he swore by it. It wasn't only sitcoms that he played. He also played video tapes of art movies and other "visual materials." So what kept him from installing four video cameras to track his guests' eye movements and pupil dilation for subsequent analysis?

"Ben!" Arnie called from his sofa. "Long time no see!" He put a flattened hand to his forehead like an American Indian peering into the distance across the Great Plains.

"You're right, Arnie. Hi, everybody! Sorry I haven't been around. I'm in graduate school now. Pharmacology at Bryan Medical School."

"I see you don't have your ponytail anymore."

"I see you've still got yours," I replied.

Arnie was pretty "hip" when it came to dress. Evenings, he pulled four inches of curly hair from the back of his head, and produced a ponytail. Mornings, he let it pop back and none of his patients noticed. He had a well-proportioned face with a Sephardic nose and an athletic body. His major flaw was his wise-guy, know-it-all attitude. He was a compulsive *sacher macher*, Yiddish for a guy who's always putting together deals.

"Well, well, well, Ben. It sounds and looks like you are getting *quite professional.*" Arnie had a dual personality with respect to "hip" versus "professional" life. He was something of a Dr. Jekyll/Mr. Hyde.

"Yes, pharmacology has been keeping me busy. I've kept my old job at the M.E.'s Office part time, and the Pharmacology Department lays it on pretty thick during the first couple of semesters."

Arnie let out a big yawn, telling all that I wasn't conversationally clever enough. Clever monologues and verbal sparring were his hobby. What a bore, this Candidi, walking in and falling flat on his face. In self-defense, I quickly thought up a gambit:

"I think that the profs make it extra hard in the first semester in order to weed out the mediocrities."

"If they don't want any of *them*, then why do they accept them in the first place?"

"Because it's not legal to ask for an I.Q. score for entrance into graduate school," I said. Realizing that this wasn't witty enough, I added, "And because too many of them have gone to Stanley Kaplan courses to raise their Graduate Record Examination Scores – just like the medically oriented mediocrities go take courses to raise their MED-CATS."

My reference to this medical school applicant screening device hit Arnie pretty close to home, causing some titters among the guests. I pressed on.

"And some of the graduate students are People's Republic Chinese who speak such bad English that it takes ten years to figure out anything about them." The "house" started to warm up.

"Well, Ben, how do you like your studies?"

Now I had shifted him from his jocular sarcastic mode to a more conversational mode.

"My studies are very interesting, Arnie. It is all very molecular and mechanistic. It keeps both your hands and your brain busy all day. It gives you a good all-around workout."

"Well, that sounds great, Ben," Arnie said with a sly look to the guests sitting around the couches. "Is there anything else that gets a 'good workout?'"

"It isn't atrophying," I said, without a pause. Now our audience was hot.

"Well, it sounds like you're fully satisfied on *all three points*," Arnie said with a grin, apparently visualizing the use of my anatomic third point. "Are you looking at this pharmacology stuff as a career or as an interesting pursuit?"

You always had to defend everything you did with this Mensa group.

"A bit of both. I'm not sure about the career path, but it's very interesting. Back at the M.E.'s, I was hitting my head against a glass ceiling. Old Man Westley was always calculating the cost of keeping me to service his instruments, versus bringing down some square-head factory-trained repairman from Atlanta on a case-by-case basis."

Anti-economic, antiestablishment quips usually played

well with this crowd. As if looking at his watch, Arnie pulled up the sleeve of his unstructured Italian sports jacket.

"Oh, yes! Westley. I read about him in the *Miami Standard* about fifteen years ago. He did some medical archaeology thing with the Egyptians a long time back. And he solved a big murder case for an upstate coroner."

Now we were on firm ground, with real Mensa stuff: the out of ordinary, the romantic, the occult. As if on cue, I told everyone about Westley, his Egyptian caper and his Rolls Royce. I even described his piece of England on the 43rd floor of the Faire Isle complex. My verbally rambunctious psychiatrist friend even started to show genuine interest. Gradually, everyone was smiling. Ben Candidi was back in good standing in the Miami Chapter of the Mensa Society.

More guests came, and the party livened up. Alcohol flowed freely, and everyone was drinking or smoking himself down to the detested level of mental mediocrity. The Christmas tree was jokingly referred to as the "Hanukkah Bush." Merry Christmas became "Have a Cool Yule." All three levels of the townhouse plus the back patio filled up. Where had they parked all the cars? Circulating, and trading stories with a dozen old acquaintances, I started getting back into the groove of "us-against-them" camaraderie. We really were a crazy bunch.

The last four months, I'd struggled hard in the outside world and had earned this chance to unwind. After my second gin and tonic, I had a funny feeling that the townhouse was a coral reef, with all different types of fish swimming around taking stock of each other. The townhouse layout did actually resemble a coral reef, with its three levels and wide open space under a cathedral ceiling. Some guests sat on the stairs. Some lurked in nooks like Dr. Gordon Taylor in his mop-closet office. Some sat backwards on desks and tables. Some sat on convertible guest bed/sofas. And some stood in doorways leaning with one hand on the casement so that I had to swim under them to pass by.

A coral reef has grunting and clicking fish noises; the

townhouse had a continuous babble of conversation. How interesting it was, just to sit and listen to two or three conversations simultaneously. Invariably, Mensa people are good talkers: No inarticulate Rambo types are allowed. Everyone was working hard on being different. Woe be it to the poor soul who was just ordinary, with ordinary tastes, routines and desires.

Coral-reef fish display every conceivable color and marking pattern; Mensa people display every intellectual and sartorial stripe. As I made my way down to the bar for my third drink, I saw hats of all types, exotic earrings, incongruous combinations of brass belt buckles and velvet jackets, business suits with pony tails, unstructured jackets over designer T-shirts, and Oshkosh bibbed working clothes (washed and starched) with a Boy Scout neckerchief. One or two guys came with just a pair of slacks and dress shirt, but they were musicians.

Why are we under this compulsion to prove ourselves different and brilliant? It must have begun when we were "gifted" kids in school, head and shoulders above our classmates. Our teachers loved us, our parents fawned over us, and we got by in school without having to work too hard at it. Intellectually gifted and socially retarded.

The magic spell lasted until we graduated from college. Outside of academia, we commanded less respect and no one came around handing out gold stars. What you got was what you grabbed for yourself. Our erudition, which went over the heads of most people, was treated as quaint and irrelevant. In the real world, you had to get an angle and play it through tenaciously.

Many of us had our careers blocked by loudmouthed Southern-drawling Good Ol' Boy types who didn't know Shakespeare from Socrates. We got the A's in advanced courses, they took the easy courses and still got C's. But if we were so smart, why weren't we rich? The Game of Life turned out a lot different from what they taught us in school. We could beat them in chess, but not in poker. And many of them came to the game with a sleeve full of cards and a killer instinct for bluffing and reading faces. The only thing we excelled in was mathematical formulas for calculating the odds.

I drifted back to my dark Nietzschean mood, last experienced at the helm in the storm with Rebecca. Measured by normal standards, most of us Mensa-ites never made an all-out try for success. Instead, we cloaked ourselves in our individuality, collectively decided we were too good for this world and practiced communal commiseration at monthly meetings. As I finished pouring myself another stiff gin and tonic, I felt a light tap on my shoulder and heard a female voice.

"I hear you are Ben Candidi . . . that you live on a sailboat, ride a bike and are working for a Ph.D. in pharmacology, while working part time for the Medical Examiner's Office."

I turned slowly to face a thin, medium-height, dirty blonde about my age.

"Hi," she said. "I'm Alice McRae."

"Alice McRae – who lives in an apartment, drives a car, gets by with one job and has all her formal education behind her," I replied, without a second's hesitation. The two drinks had not yet driven my I.Q. down to a mediocre level.

"Right on the first three, but wrong on the fourth," she said, offering her hand. "Working as a journalist is a formal education in itself. And a never-ending one."

She punctuated her last sentence with an almost masculine handshake. She had what my grandfather called "umph" and wasn't bad looking, in a slightly tomboyish way. She was sensibly dressed and slightly made up. Did I detect freckles under a touch of powder?

She definitely rated a second look. If I hadn't been in love with Rebecca, I might have been quite interested in Alice. But could I count on Rebecca? Why go back to worrying about that right now? You go to parties to meet like-minded people and have a good time, don't you?

"You're a print journalist. Right?" I asked on a whim.

"Yes, *Miami Standard.* How did you know?"

"Just my masculine intuition, I guess. What's your beat?"

"County government. Where did you pick up the lingo?" She spoke with an educated Southern accent. She moved a step closer.

"I had some journalism in high school. I was in Quill and Scroll and wrote for the school paper. So I know about beats, leads, the five W's, scoops and that stuff."

"Well, professional journalism's not much different from high school journalism, except that the deadlines are tighter, the bosses are meaner and the management is stingier. And your most important subjects don't want to be interviewed on the things you want to know." Alice spoke with a self-confident optimism that I had to admire.

"So you're an investigative reporter."

"That's what I'd like to be, Ben. But if you get too *investigative* at the *Standard*, you find yourself without a job."

We continued talking about journalism. Alice liked her job, but she suffered a lot of the same frustrations I did back at the M.E.'s lab. Then she got off on Dade County government: their stupidity, their blundering, their kickbacks and their political infighting. In a certain way she was a mirror image of me, with my low opinion of lawyers, pompous bureaucrats and people who try to get something for nothing.

Alice told me she was 27 years old − four years out of Emory. She had worked for two years on the *Atlanta Constitution* and then had "graduated" to the *Miami Standard* two years ago. As we talked, I realized Alice was the most levelheaded woman that I'd ever met in Mensa. She probably hadn't been blessed with fawning parents. She'd probably pulled herself out of the red clay around Atlanta.

"So, all in all, how do you like Miami, Alice?"

"It's an interesting city, but it's kind of a shame with all these Latin Americans. Things are pretty chaotic."

Here, she had trouble seeing the forest through the trees. *Dios Mio!* Dade County *is* Latin. Over 50 percent of the population and over 70 percent of the growth is Spanish-speaking. If you don't understand that, you're lost. The few Miami-born, die-hard Southerners who you still might find here are all planning to move to Tampa – as soon as they can line up a job there.

Alice proved a spirited conversation partner who didn't give me too much time to reflect on her background. She was an intelligent extrovert who listened carefully, interpreted quickly and gave an appropriate response. It was like a friendly tennis match with a spirited woman who gives her best and expects the same from you. Was it out of mere curiosity that I found myself wondering if she was also spirited in bed?

While talking about Miami, I lost concentration and dropped the ball. Alice picked it up and started asking me about my science, interviewing me in typical journalistic fashion, using a checklist of the five W's and one H. *What* molecules? *Where* are they? *When*? *Why* do they do what they do? *How* do they work? *Who* works on them? But you can't learn science from a journalistic interview. So I gave Alice a short course.

"*How* a molecule works is probably the most important part of the whole business. *Who* or *what* a molecule is depends ninety percent on what it binds to. Binding of two molecules is biology in action. It is also important what the molecules do when they bind."

We were leaning against the wall, facing each other. Alice was smiling, but I didn't know why. I sipped hard on my third drink and continued:

"Does one molecule bind to another and just tie it up and keep it unavailable for another molecule? Or does it cut the molecule or attach another molecule to it? The *when* can be any time when the two molecules are together. It depends upon how fast the molecules vibrate and what different shapes they can assume. But if the molecules are separated by a barrier or are chemically modified, the *when* can be controlled until other molecules determine that they are ready."

Alice sidled a little closer and continued to listen to my spirited monologue:

"The *where* is simply where the molecules happen to be.

Sometimes there are 'hot spots' in the cell where certain molecules are kept so that they will have a greater chance to interact with each other. That's the problem I'm working on in the lab right now. The question *why* is not relevant, because the molecules themselves never question why."

"Theirs is but to do and die," Alice summed it up quickly. She punctuated her Tennyson quote with a pat on my shoulder, but she did not remove her hand. She laid her head on her hand. I broke out in goosepimples as her hair whisked my arm to the accompaniment of her laughter. She'd caught me by surprise, but I didn't disengage. I stayed on track with my lecture, hoping to cool her down.

"Yes, Alice, there are some molecules in the blood, called thrombin, whose only function is to carve each other up as soon as they get the signal that a blood vessel is broken. After thrombin gets done with his work, he leaves a big pile of dead *'fibrin'* molecules filling up the wound. That's the clot that stops the bleeding."

Alice looked at me like she though I might be kidding.

Putting on a mock English accent I quipped, "Bloody awful mess, 'tis. But that's the price of soldierin', they say. And they tyke care of us well when we is at garrison."

It was a good answer to her Tennyson quote, but it didn't help to calm her down.

"Oh, you scientists are so quaint," she said, turning on the Southern charm.

This time she punctuated her words with a kiss on the cheek. She was hitting on me hard. Maybe she had interpreted my lecture as a complicated flirt. Well, her signals were clear enough. I tried to throw some water on the fire.

I told her that individual molecules are mindless but that their hierarchies and collective behavior had been worked out by evolution over millions of years to fulfill a definite purpose. Every cellular reaction is under tight control. "For example, a protein molecule is synthesized as a long chain, but it has to be correctly folded to be useful. Its folding and movements are controlled by a *'chaperonin'* molecule. This keeps it from binding to the wrong molecules."

"So the chaperone molecule keeps the belles separated from the beaus. Ben, you're a funny guy! What are you going to tell me next? That there are 'parson' molecules who perform wedding ceremonies?" She sunk her head on my shoulder and laughed.

"Well, we do have '*reporter*' molecules," I said, quickly scanning my befogged memory for examples.

"What do *they* do? Bind to the scientist molecules?"

Alice was far out on the limb. Luckily, Arnie Green walked over.

"Well, Ben. I see you've met Alice." He turned to Alice and continued, "And you two are hitting it off well together. Maybe you didn't notice, but Charlie has brought his sax and joined Steve. George is setting up his drums. Maybe you two could go over there with Ted and Carol and help set an example for the rest of us by dancing."

The little combo played a cha-cha, which we correctly danced at arm's length. The amplifiers were loud, which gave me an excuse not to talk and get myself into more trouble. We both knew the steps and set a pretty good example for the other guests. But after two fast numbers, the combo tired and got into a groove with slow fox-trots, which filled the floor with other dancers and forced us into each other's arms.

Do people select mates like the molecules select binding partners? When an antibody finds its antigen, they make a tight fit. They have good molecular compatibility. The streptavidin-biotin binding reaction, taking place on cell surfaces, holds the world record for molecular compatibility. That pair of molecules has a dissociation constant of 10^{-15} molar. When bound, they stay together for about 110 days. If you had that type of affinity for a girl, she would last a lifetime. You might call her a "15." For me, Rebecca was a "15."

On that scale, Alice would rate a "12," with her pleasant, extroverted personality and positive attitude. Her charm was different from Rebecca's. She was direct where Rebecca was subtle and aggressively inquisitive where Rebecca was patiently meditative. But Alice knew what she wanted and, at this moment, it seemed to be me. She was also the second-best woman who had shown any interest in me over the last six years.

I awakened from these musings to find that Alice had taken the lead in our box step. Yes, she was quite adaptable. I sank back to my thoughts while she kept us clear of the other dancers. My bonds with the other girls had been weak, with dissociation constants of 10^{-4}. For me they were only "4s." The lower the affinity, the shorter the time until the two molecules dissociate and diffuse off in their separate directions. And my liaisons with the 4s had not lasted long.

Now I was in love with a "15" who had dissociated and might not diffuse back to me. And I was being challenged by a "12" with some pretty good sticking power. Oh, the fickle mathematics of love!

My Swarthmore roommate, Richard Bash, had once formulated the situation most elegantly and crudely:

"When you aren't getting *any*, you can *never* get any. Conversely, and when you *are* getting some, then you've got girls buzzing around you like flies around a shit house."

Bash came from Eastern Tennessee, and he prided himself on his crude homilies. He even codified them as "Hypotheses," "Theories" and "Laws of Nature," and had given them pompous and deliberately ambiguous names. This one he had christened "Bash's Bipolar Female Parts Access Probability Theorem." One night at the dormitory, we spent a good part of an evening discussing this verity.

To be fair to Alice, I tried to maneuver our conversation to reveal the existence of Rebecca without being too obvious.

"How long have you been with our Mensa group, Alice? I don't remember seeing you before August."

"My first meeting was in September."

"That was when I stopped coming to meetings. I got very busy with graduate school, and then I got another major distraction."

This was a sufficient hint.

"What sort of distraction?"

"The human sort," I said. Alice's lead stiffened. "It was a hot-and-heavy affair. It's still unresolved."

Alice glanced around the room.

"So where is the distractor?"

"She went back to New York for the holidays."

"Maybe that's part of the distraction."

"You're right, Alice. But it's unresolved, and I have to see it through to its conclusion."

This relaxed her a little more. She told me she understood. We danced a few more numbers, got another drink, went out to the patio to get away from the music and chatted to the point where the unspoken question started growing.

"I've got to leave, Alice. You might say I have a long row home."

"I'd like to see you again, Ben. Here's my card. If you hear about anything newsworthy at Bryan Medical School or Dade General, call me and give me the scoop."

"I don't know much that happens there that is newsworthy. We were picketed by some animal-rights demonstrators a couple of months ago, but I wouldn't want to see that in the newspaper."

"Well, Ben, sometimes we get science stories over the wire, from AP and UPI, and sometimes the science writer needs some background information. Maybe you could be one of my 'resource people.'"

I gave her the phone number of McGregor's lab and said goodbye. She squeezed my hand as she said goodbye. I was two steps away when she called back at me.

"Say, I just thought of something that might interest you. Your ex-boss, the Medical Examiner, the Englishman. The word around the County Commission is that he's in trouble. His contract is up for renewal next month, and some of the Commissioners are talking about replacing him."

"That's a real shame, Alice. He's a good man. What's the scoop?"

"Something about him not being able to solve cases as

well as he used to."

"They're all wrong. He's as sharp as he ever was. Let me know if you get any new information."

"Sure. I'll give you a call if there are any breaks in the story."

I made my way to Arnie Green and thanked him for the good time. He raised his eyebrows in surprise.

"What? Leaving so early? And alone? Hey, you and Alice were *schmoozing* pretty good when I came by."

"Got to thank you for that one, Arnie. I always knew you were a *sacher macher* but I didn't know you're a *shadchan* too!!"

"*Shadchan*! What's that?"

"Yiddish for matchmaker. Alice told me that you gave her the scoop on me. Thanks, Arnie. She's great gal, probably a 12. It's just that – "

"You've got another one and you're H_2!"

"Right. Hot and heavy," I affirmed.

Arnie gave me a big, conspiratorial grin. Arnie was great friends with any guy who was doing big things or had a lot of girls on the side. Had he ever had this analyzed? Did his mother encourage him to be a *sacher macher*? Or was it a male-bonding thing?

"Thanks again, Arnie. Alice gave me her card and asked me to be one of her 'resource people.' Professionally, that is. So we may be seeing some more of each other."

Arnie's broad wink slowly blossomed into an ear-to-ear grin. Then he burst out laughing and slapped me on the back.

"See you later, you wild-and-crazy guy."

During the ride and row home, I thought about my molecular *spiel* with Alice. With the three drinks in my system and the fourth being absorbed in my stomach, I had a pretty good buzz on. A quick mental calculation using my weight and the stiffness of the drinks gave me a blood alcohol of 0.14 percent, which was legally drunk and unfit to drive.

But I wasn't unfit to row a boat, so I rowed back and forth around my cold, windy anchorage. Movement is good when you have something to think through. Was it just an innocent science lecture, or had I given this girl the wrong signals? Had my eyes, voice and body language been telling her something else? What did she see in me?

The fourth drink must have made it into my bloodstream, because my thoughts came fast, fuzzy and loose: profound but meaningless mediations on the search for the perfect girl, my Quixotic quest for 15s and 12s in a world of 4s, and imaginary conversations with my long-lost college pal, arguing the relative merits of Richard Bash's Stochastic Molecular Fucking Theory versus Ben Candidi's Unfolding Molecular Compatibility Theory.

I'd lost touch with Richard a year after we'd graduated. His last letter told me he was working as an analytical chemist at Dupont. In the chilly darkness, sophomoric theories gave way to feelings. What did Rebecca feel for me now? Did I have feelings for Alice? What would I feel when I learn that Rebecca is returning to her boyfriend in New York?

The wind finally chilled my alcohol-flushed skin, forcing me to row to the *Diogenes*. Stumbling aboard, I tied the painter onto a cleat, opened the cabin, flopped into my berth without removing my clothes, let loose a primal sob and cried myself to sleep.

I survived December 24th by working in the lab. Christmas Eve found me walking through downtown Coconut Grove and along Main Highway, the historic two-lane road lined by giant ficus trees. I slipped into the candlelight service at Plymouth Congregational, the second church on the right. Then I wandered back to the *Diogenes* and went to bed.

The next morning, I opened the package from Rebecca. Wrapped as a Christmas gift was a homemade tape cassette of the 27-year-old Brasil 66 album. Inside the plastic case, she had enclosed a miniaturized color photocopy of the album cover. Sergio Mendez and his four singers stood before a backdrop of palm fronds. She labelled both sides of the cassette with the track titles. I found our song, "Cinnamon and Spice." Her Christmas card showed a snowy, turn-of-the-century Greenwich Village scene. Under the standardized greeting she wrote:

"For salty days and sultry nights. - R."

Mom had given me a tie, and a silver-and-turquoise tie clip, both from a shop in Scotsdale. Dad gave me an assortment of tapes and a book by Tom Clancy. Curled up in my berth, I read about the nuclear submarines, the satellite link-ups, electromagnetic propulsion and cruise missiles with ternary warheads. The technical world offers good escape when the human world becomes too complicated. Oh! to be an Annapolis graduate, an ex-Marine officer and a CIA officer, working on dangerous, exciting and important cases. But, come to think of it, I was working on an important case.

A few weeks later, I would complain that my life was becoming Clancy-esque.

– XXV –

New Year's Revelations

"BEN, I CAN'T TALK VERY LONG because Mother's waiting."

"I'm sorry. But I have the lab to myself today. I thought we could really talk."

"I'm sorry, Ben."

"Thanks for the lovely present. You put so much into it."

"Thank you, too, Ben. I'm sorry. I really can't talk."

"When are you coming back?"

"The late Delta flight on Saturday, the fourth of January. But you don't have to meet it."

"But I want to."

"Ben, I have to go."

Ten minutes later, the phone rang again. "Ben, this is Alice. How'd you like to do the South Beach with us on New Year's Eve."

"I don't know, Alice. It's just – "

"You haven't made any other plans."

"No."

"And you probably won't, either," she said with irrefutable certainty. "We'll pick you up in front of the Grove General Store at nine."

What could I say? At nine o'clock New Year's Eve I was waiting in front of Coconut Grove's foremost convenience store. Two minutes later Alice drove up. We picked up another couple, a woman she worked with and her husband. In their presence, Alice acted like we had a long-term relationship based on deep-running sophisticated familiarity. I went along with her on it. I did my best to be charming, but memories welled up as we crossed the MacArthur Causeway and skirted Government Cut where I'd first shown Rebecca the cruise ships. An hour later we were bar hopping as a foursome, standing in noisy crowds listening to noisy music. Alice had no news on Dr. Westley's plight. Her head found my shoulder a number of times.

The witching hour found the four of us strolling barefoot in the sand within a hundred yards of where Rebecca and I had shared our first long kiss. Signal flares from the yachts off shore made a nice, impromptu fireworks display. Alice kissed me on the lips. I answered with a whispered message that she accepted intellectually, but not emotionally. Around two o'clock in the morning, Alice stood on my landing and watched me row off.

Tom Clancy helped me through the next two days, and lab work got me through the third. When I arrived on the fourth of January, McGregor handed me a message from Rebecca:

> Something has come up.
> Delta Number 935.
> Sunday, 11:30 p.m.

That Sunday was the longest day of my life, and then the flight was delayed for half an hour. Waiting anxiously at the entrance of the Concourse C, I finally identified the first New York passengers. Rebecca walked in the middle of the stream, looking tired, upset and small. I waved and smiled. She quickened her pace, looking at me carefully as if to read my face. With each hurried step, her expression became less worried. She grasped my arms and kissed me lightly on the lips. I started to throw my arms around her, ready to declare my love like an Italian tenor. But Rebecca took one step back and held me at arms length.

"You have to be very nice to me for a long, long time, Mr. Ben Candidi. I just broke off my engagement because of you."

My mouth dropped open and my brain whirled.

"Rebecca," I cried out. "I love you! You won't be sorry.

I've never met anyone like you before. You're my *fifteen*. We'll be like two molecules with a dissociation constant of ten to the negative fifteen power – as tight as two molecules can get. We won't dissociate for a lifetime!"

My biophysical declaration of love brought a big smile to her face, but just as quickly she became serious. She started to say something but it came out as a sob. She threw her arms around me and buried her face in my neck.

"Oh, Ben," she whispered. "It was so hard for me, and I was afraid you might have a change of heart over Christmas. I had been together with him for three years. We have been engaged for the last year. He's going to be a lawyer. He's very self-centered and proud. He's not subtle and considerate like you. After you, I *knew* that I really didn't love him."

"Rebecca, I knew it had to be something like this."

"Oh, Ben, I had so much to resolve. Sometimes I didn't think that I had the strength for it. He tried to use his love for me as a hook. It was like he tried to handcuff us together. And he tried to argue me back to him. Dad took his side and Mom tried to arbitrate. They all wanted to know about you. They used the guilt thing on me. I was destroying four thousand years of tradition. What kind of grandchildren would I give them? Then Mother started telling me about how Dad is getting sick, and he may not live too many years more."

Magically, our embrace wasn't disturbed by worldly problems such as walking in airport crowds, retrieving baggage, hailing taxis and opening the door of Rebecca's apartment. Our embrace continued through a long night, when time was marked by whispered endearments and declarations of love, flooding and ebbing in streams of shared consciousness and tears of joy, interspersed with whispered dreams of a shared future, dissolving into sleep just before dawn.

We ate a hasty breakfast and walked together to Rebecca's lecture. With her classmates filing into the amphitheater, Rebecca kissed me a passionate goodbye and danced up the three steps to the entrance.

I had an important errand to do before going to the lab.

In the hospital gift shop, I selected a card with an appropriate text – "SORRY" in big letters.

I addressed the envelope to Alice, care of the *Miami Standard* and wrote:

> My situation has clarified in the way I told you it
> might. I regret that I will be free for you only as
> your 'resource person' (biochemistry).

That evening, Rebecca and I worked it all out. An answering machine would screen my calls, avoiding further conflict with her mom and dad. I would stay overnight at her apartment as often as possible. Her roommate would be giving up the apartment in June, and maybe then I could move in for good. I would use Monday and Wednesday nights for Westley, for my instrument maintenance job at the M.E. and for the boat. I told Rebecca about my social relationship with Westley, but nothing about the detective work.

At dinner, I told the Old Man and Margaret about the Christmas service at Plymouth Congregational and how beautifully the choir had sung.

"Oh yes, the 'Nativity Carol' by John Rutter!" exclaimed the Old Man. "The piece is destined to become an old chestnut. Fine young chap. Nice voicings he wrote, and he is also quite an organist . . . secure place in liturgical music and a fine future, although he did dabble a little too much for my taste in commercial endeavours."

Margaret said they had attended Christmas Eve services at Trinity Cathedral (Episcopal). To round out the conversation, I offered some bland details on the Mensa party.

After dinner, we "removed" to the study. Westley flipped the wall switch and the floor lamp illuminated the oddly furnished room. A second later his old tape recorder started squeaking like it was going to pop a drive belt. He must have thought himself clever, plugging the relic into the floor lamp socket.

"Yes, it is still a bit nippy out there," I said laughingly. The needles on the yellow backlit input meters registered my

voice, and "pegged" with my laugh. The tape stretched badly
at the start, but did not break. Slowly the large spools on the
ancient device settled into coordinated motion.

"Yes, yes. Quite nippy! Please do make yourself comfortable. Yes!"

In double entendre code, I told the Old Man about
Ledbetter's European patent application and that I'd ordered it.

"This is most interesting, Benjamin. The possibilities that
one has in this Information Age! And just in a nick of time, for
I am once again under severe pressure to produce some usable evidence."

I told him what I'd learned from Alice McRae.

"Oh, Ben, that is but half of it. My enemies on the Commission are forming a subcommittee, and they will probably
use all of their pernicious backbiting tricks. The trouble is that
they can talk about this Cooper thing among themselves as if
it were real, but I cannot answer them before I have the facts."

"We should have a rudimentary theory in a few weeks," I
said.

I put the slip of paper with the patent-ordering information
on the side table near my glass. Under white bushy eyebrows,
Westley's eyes followed the paper to its resting place like the eyes
of an Old English sheepdog might follow a straying ewe.

"Dr. Westley, I hate to eat and run, but I have to complete a problem set for my Molecular Genetics course."

"No, I quite understand. If keeping us company is making too many demands on your time we could – "

"You shouldn't put it that way. Could I just call to check
in with you once a week?"

"Most assuredly." He picked up the slip of paper and saw
me out of the room.

Molecular Genetics, Cell Biology and Cardiovascular
Pharmacology did keep me very busy. So did my follow-up
experiments for Rob McGregor. D-day came four weeks after
that dinner with Westley. When I opened my Coconut Grove
Post Office box and saw a German air mail envelope, I ripped
it open, pulled out the patent, sat down on the lobby floor

and read it. "Improved drug delivery using selectin glycoproteins" stated the title.

I didn't need to go past the abstract to know I'd struck pay dirt. It described "a method for oral delivery of proteins and other gastrically and cellularly degradable drugs or biological substances." Protein-containing micro-particles were coated with intestinal lymphocyte selectins which guide the proteins across the intestine and into the bloodstream. The selectin-coated particles were enterically coated to protect them from digestive enzymes while they pass through the stomach.

The abstract stated that the invention allows a patient to take insulin by mouth, eliminating the need for painful injections.

"Or encapsulate a protein toxin," I said out loud, "and sprinkle it on your enemy's food!"

I stood up and paced the lobby. My first inclination was go right over to Westley and show it to him. But it would be better to keep up our game of innocence so that I would not have to lie under oath. I called the Old Man at his residence.

"Dr. Westley, I've received an important publication in the mail. It's really worth evaluating."

"How good is it?"

"The situation reminds me of a cartoon I saw in the *New Yorker* a while back. You know the *New Yorker*, don't you?" I couldn't resist tantalizing the old windbag.

"*New Yorker*? Why yes, of course, although it does not compare with . . . Well, what was in this cartoon? Can you get on with it?"

"One scientist was standing over another scientist who was looking into a microscope. The second scientist says to the first: '*I think I may have a possible Eureka.* (!!)'"

"Well . . ."

"Well, you know how scientists are so tentative and cautious."

There was a long pause. Westley obviously didn't appreciate my humor. "Would you like to tell me about it?" When I said "no," he wheedled and whined. I reminded him we were having dinner together the next evening.

Aboard the *Diogenes*, sipping after-dinner tea, I studied the patent application thoroughly. It had been filed in the U.S. two and one-half years earlier. The "Background" section said that biotechnology had produced a lot of polypeptide and proteins which have drug action, but they could not be given by mouth because they get digested in the stomach. Even when the digestive enzymes are inhibited, there is still the problem of getting the proteins across the intestinal lining and into the blood.

Several pages of graphs, figures and schematics illustrated how he used intestinal lymphocyte selectin "toe" molecules to give drug micro-particles a "toehold" in the intestinal lining, and to deliver them through a system of manholes and alleys called the Peyer's Patch. He tricked the intestine into letting the protein-drug micro-particles through this lymphocyte crawl space. And the proteins got into the blood without being chopped up.

So this was how he got his toxins into Cooper's bloodstream without causing him diarrhea! His toxins slinked in through the Peyer's Patch, guided by his intestinal selectins!

The crown jewel of the patent was the delivery of insulin. He gave insulin in selectin-coated micro-particles to diabetic rats and showed that it got into the bloodstream and decreased their blood sugar. And he presented long lists of other proteins and peptide hormones that could be delivered, and long lists of protective coatings against stomach acid.

His "Examples" section was a literal cookbook for whipping up these preparations. Just substitute "protein toxin" for "insulin" and it was a recipe for murder.

But which protein toxin? The simple, quick and dirty method that I'd used on Ashton wouldn't work on Ledbetter. How could I get into Ledbetter's lab?

As my excitement wore off, I came to an uncomfortable realization: It was just a theory. A *super* theory, but a theory just the same. You didn't have to be a district attorney to know that we didn't have probable cause for a legal search of Ledbetter's lab. The *Diogenes* did his best to rock me to sleep, but it took a long time. So close, yet so far.

The next evening, the Old Man practically had the sherry poured before I closed the door behind myself. A DHL International Courier Service envelope sat on top of his record machine, and no records were spinning. So he had just received his own copy of the patent. He brought up the subject immediately, speaking in our agreed-upon Pig Latin.

"Ben, I have just read a scientific paper which is so exciting I can hardly put it down! It has opened ideas which I must pursue. But, you see, I am at a loss to do so because the range of possibilities is *impossibly vast.*"

"I hear you talking," I replied.

"One must simply shorten the list. I, myself, am at a complete loss as to how to go about it," he lamented.

We kicked this theme back and forth. Westley had received his own copy of the patent and liked the theory that Ledbetter poisoned Cooper by placing selectin-coated microcapsules of protein toxins in his food. But he needed a short list of candidate toxins, like I'd given him for Ashton. I knew it would come to this. I tried to tell Dr. Westley I couldn't get into Ledbetter's lab.

Margaret announced dinner. She was talkative, but we went through all three courses quite briskly. The Old Boy and I retired early to the study. As he switched on the light the tape recorder did not squeak to a start. My first thought was that it might have blown a fuse, but there was no tape on the reel. Westley gestured for me to sit in the comfortable chair while he continued to slowly pace around the room.

"As if by cosmic coincidence, it would appear that we both have the same problem: the need to act."

"I would guess so."

"Unfortunately, Ben, my hands are tied, as you can well imagine."

"Yes, Dr. Westley. But I am in the same situation. I have absolutely no access."

"But you do have the advantage of working close to your subject . . . matter."

"Yes, Dr. Westley. So close, yet so far away."

Westley sat down in front of me, perched on the edge of his Pharaoh Chair. This brought us face to face, but he looked to the side, staring at the carpet.

"Quite!" he said, glancing at me furtively. He began to wring his hands like at our first dinner interview. "If you could just be a fly on the wall, to quote the old proverb, that is."

"I am too big for that. And I doubt that the subject would tolerate me buzzing around. As I was telling you, his research associate Dr. Chiu – "

"Well, if one could not be a fly, one could be a moth. They are nocturnal." His voice crept up to a higher pitch, and he was fidgeting badly in the chair.

"I am not a locksmith."

Westley gasped at the bluntness of my statement. He sat back quickly, bumping one of the jackals with his elbow. It was several seconds before he collected himself.

"But, Ben, you don't really . . ." He let his words dangle.

"That's exactly what it comes down to."

"Perhaps you could find some way to . . ." Again, he dangled his words. So I remained silent and let *him* dangle. "But, you are so clever, you could certainly find some way to . . . I would say . . . well . . . we are so near and, as you say, and yet so far."

He had extracted a handkerchief from his pocket and wrung it in his hands. I stared at the oriental carpet for a long time, my eyes hypnotized by the arabesque.

It reminded me of a scene from the World War II novel *The Sea Chase* by Andrew Geer. I read the book the summer I turned 14. The English destroyer captain had paid a tribe of Pacific Islanders to go out looking for the German freighter hiding somewhere in a group of islands. The freighter's Kapitän Erlich spotted a canoe full of islanders and gave his helmsman orders to run them down. In answer to his crew's silent condemnation of the murderous deed, the hard-bitten Erlich said that for a thousand years of history, it had been the same story: the British hiring *others* to do their dirty work for them.

Quietly, Dr. Westley said, "Ben, one of my remaining

friends on the County Commission has told me that the decision
meeting on my ouster will be on the twenty-seventh of February.
That is three short weeks. If we cannot come up with something
concrete by then, I shall not be able to weather the storm."

Westley, too, was staring at the carpet. So he was at the
end of his tether. My anger quickly subsided into pity.

"Okay, Dr. Westley, I'll give it my best shot."

"Oh, Ben, I am so truly grateful – "

What a curious mixture of emotions I experienced, riding
the elevator to the ground floor. So I would have to burglarize
Ledbetter's office. Should have known last August that I'd have
to break the law to accomplish this mission. Just like I should
have known last August that the project would take three times
longer than I had estimated. Could I get all the information
needed in a single evening? Could I even bring myself to try?
And if I did get the information and they indict Ledbetter,
would I be able to maintain sacred choirboy innocence? Would
they kick me out of the graduate school? How could I keep
Rebecca from finding out? I slept a troubled sleep.

The next morning, I woke up a confirmed mercenary. A
few months ago, I had signed up for this irregular duty just
like the Pacific Islanders in the novel. I had taken the King's
Shilling and had accepted payments of a few paltry pounds.
Now the King was expecting service. See it through, Ben, and
hope you don't get caught red-handed.

It took the rest of the week to work out my plan. On
Saturday morning I pocketed my checkbook and driver's license and visited a couple of computer shops. I bought a tape
backup unit and a selection of cables and adaptors. At least
one of them would be compatible with Ledbetter's computer.
An office supply store sold me an executive hand-held tape recorder and a number of tapes. At a drugstore, I bought a cheap
throwaway camera and five rolls of 36-exposure film. Lastly, I
bought a length of three-pronged extension cord and an adaptor
at a hardware store. All told, the equipment cost me a month's
salary. The gear barely fit into my locker at the library.

Did the Old Man appreciate the enormity of the step I

was taking? It could get me thrown out of graduate program and into jail. And it was immoral. On Monday evening I called the Old Boy at his residence.

"Dr. Westley, about this coming Wednesday. I'm very sorry, but I can't come to dinner. Things are getting very busy, and I am under pressure to collect some data – "

"Yes, Ben, I quite understand."

"Do you understand data collection, foul in the night?" After a long silence, Westley declared formally, "I understand that one must work the night through on some of these scientific projects – in order to gather data efficiently. I can only hope that you are successful and expeditious in your experiment. Godspeed." (Click)

I went back to the Department and waited until everyone was gone. Standing on a chair that I took from McGregor's lab, I probed around the false ceiling outside Ledbetter's lab and found a satisfactory but inelegant solution to the entry problem. A quick check in the basement confirmed that Physical Plant had what I needed. D-Day would be Wednesday, two evenings later.

I was nervous all day Tuesday and Wednesday. At 5:00 Wednesday afternoon I grabbed a sandwich and swung by the library to pick up my equipment. I had to reenter the building before six in the evening to avoid using my access card, which would generate a computerized record of my entry.

I hung around the graduate student lounge, occasionally checking the hallways for activity. Why had everyone picked that night to work late in the lab? Activity dropped off sharply around 11:30, but I couldn't start until everyone was gone. Sheng-Ping Chow was the last holdout, working in Al Kozinski's lab, testing his damn herbal diuretic medicine, no doubt. Kozinski's lab was inconveniently close to Ledbetter's. I'd told Sheng-Ping so many times that when he got too tired to experiment, he should go home and watch TV to learn more English. Didn't he ever get tired?

Sheng-Ping finally left around 2:00 in the morning. Physical Plant still had the two aluminum stepladders. With shak-

ing hands, I placed one ladder next to the Revco liquid nitrogen freezer that stood in the hallway outside Ledbetter's lab. I
climbed up the ladder and opened the false ceiling, revealing
a large gap in the three-inch cinder block wall, made to ac-
commodate water pipes. Reaching through, I opened the false
ceiling in Ledbetter's lab. In such narrow quarters, manhan-
dling the second ladder up and over into the lab was a difficult operation.

I returned to McGregor's lab, picked up my equipment
and stashed it in the false ceiling over the hallway. Just as I
started to crawl through the gap into Ledbetter's lab, I received
the shock of my life: Footsteps coming up the hall. I quickly
dangled a coil of coaxial cable into the hallway below.

"Working late tonight, boss?" the voice asked. It was a
soft French Creole accented voice. What a relief! Only the
Haitian janitor.

"Yeah, laying cable. Got to get the data transferred," I
shouted down through the hole. The janitor made his rounds
along the opposite side of the hall, opening doors, dumping
wastebaskets and doing cursory sweeping. What would I say
when he opened Ledbetter's lab and found it dark with the
other ladder standing under a hole in the ceiling? He approached. A chill went down my spine as he opened
Ledbetter's door with his pass key and flipped on the lights.

"You going be working in here, too, Doc?" he shouted
up at me through the hole in Ledbetter's ceiling.

"Yes," I said. Through the hole, I watched him empty
the lab wastebasket, open Ledbetter's office and empty the
wastebasket there. I pulled my head back into the shadows as
he turned around.

"Then I leave lights on and doors open for you, Doc."

"Thanks," I said, making as if preoccupied with my cable-
laying. After he had moved on, I climbed down the ladder on
the hallway side and walked into Ledbetter's lab through the
open door. I moved the tape unit into place, replaced both
ceiling panels, and stowed both ladders neatly against the wall
near McGregor's lab. Returning to Ledbetter's lab, I closed

the door, pushing the button in the knob to lock myself in. My heart was still racing as I checked the back side of Ledbetter's computer. Luckily my cables matched his I/O ports. I booted up his computer, looked at the directory of executive programs and then typed in the commands to dump his hard disk into my tape drive. Loading one tape would take about 30 minutes.

While his machine was talking to my machine, I cleaned up the ceiling crumbs from his floor and lab bench. Next, I took inventory of loose-leaf binders holding the carbon copies of his notebooks. They were neatly organized by date, but the last two years were missing. The original notebooks were kept in the locked file cabinets, but I found the keys stashed inside a pewter German beer mug embossed '*Hansestadt Hamburg.*' It's funny how you notice such trivia when your heart is fluttering, your head's swimming and your body is in a cold sweat.

I opened the cabinet and read the dates, titles and tables of contents of the notebooks into my hand-held tape recorder, rattling off names of proteins, drugs, coatings and code numbers like a tobacco auctioneer. By the time the hard disk transfer was completed, I had read one year's worth of books into the voice tape.

But Ledbetter had 30-some diskettes on the shelf. So I put a new tape in my drive and played the diskettes into my machine, one by one, running back and forth between the computer and the notebooks. I hadn't worked so hard since the day I had first hauled out the *Diogenes* and went into a frenzy, hosing it down and scraping away barnacles, trying to remove all the nasty critters before they dried and hardened. This time it was a race against dawn.

Around 4:00 I finished with the computer. I unplugged my gear, packed it into a black garbage bag, rushed it down the hall to McGregor's lab and stashed it under my section of bench.

Then I verified that one of the keys opened Ledbetter's Revco freezer in the hallway. I would not enter it tonight because the containers would frost up faster than I could read them. Camera in hand, I stepped once more into Ledbetter's lab and locked myself in. The most dangerous point was past. If someone caught me now, I could pocket my tape recorder and camera and say I was looking for a bottle of methanol. I photographed Ledbetter's bookshelves and took a shot of the notebooks lying sideways in the file cabinet. I photographed the keys on a piece of millimeter graph paper, together with some lab paraphernalia as camouflage for the drugstore film-processing guy. For backup, I made impressions of the keys using aluminum foil.

The household refrigerator inside the lab contained too many bottles and vials to catalogue. But hanging on its side, calender style, were several pages: "Contents of refrigerator, freezer and Revco freezer." I breathed a sigh of relief and sequentially photographed the pages, holding them up with a pencil so my hand wouldn't show.

I went back to the file cabinets and found Ledbetter's "Received" and "Sent Out" files. There were simply too many formulations to recite into the tape recorder. He had been receiving a lot of medicinal biologicals, like insulin, human growth hormones and prolactin. But I didn't find any toxins.

His right-hand desk drawer contained correspondence with Cooper and University administrators, scientific manuscripts and files of his patents. One contained the complete text of the European application that I had ordered from the WPS. None of them showed any evidence of toxins. I photographed the drawer at a 45-degree angle to reveal all the file headings and then took some camouflage shots around the lab.

I looked at my watch and gasped: It was 5:45! Some of the Chinese grad students might be coming in soon. I picked up all my remaining stuff, carefully locked the cabinets and desk and replaced the keys in the pewter mug. Double check. Triple check. Everything was left like I found it.

Just one thing left to satisfy my curiosity. I stepped on a chair and looked through the false ceiling of Ledbetter's office. Just as I'd feared: Solid cinder block all the way. I never would have made it if the janitor hadn't let me in.

I turned off the lights, locked Ledbetter's lab and stashed

my camera and tape recorder in the garbage bag in McGregor's lab. I tied it up with a special knot that would reveal if anyone entered it.

I cleaned the ceiling tile crumbs off the Revco refrigerator in the hall and returned the ladders to Physical Plant. Mission completed, I staggered to graduate student lounge, flopped down on the couch and fell asleep just as the sky was lighting up.

Maria Mendez woke me up at a 9:45.

"Ben, I am sorry to bother you, but we have Molecular Genetics in fifteen minutes."

"Thanks, Maria," I yawned.

"Also, I should tell you that Dave Franklin has been going around making jokes about you. He says that your girlfriend kicked you out of her apartment."

"No, it was nothing like that, Maria. I was working late, and we had some miscommunication. It wasn't practical to go back to the boat."

After class, I had brunch at the hamburger joint. Returning to McGregor's lab, I found the knot in my garbage bag intact. As I started to walk out with the bag in my arms, McGregor eyeballed it and shook his head.

"Candidi, you'd better watch out."

"What?"

"Or you're going to turn into a bag lady!" he exclaimed with a rumbling laugh.

"Right. I need a place to keep my gear," I replied nervously.

"Yeah, you should get yourself a permanent lab."

"Right. Well, just give me a couple of weeks to get our data analyzed, and then we'll see if you will even accept me."

You had to be blunt with McGregor every once in a while to keep him in his place. "I'll be over at the library for the next couple of days."

This turned out to be a serious underestimate.

– XXVI –

Evaluation

I STAKED OUT A CARREL AT THE library, set up my tape machine and lap-top computer and started looking at Ledbetter's files. It was like looking into a disciplined mind. His files were written in WordPerfect and were assigned by alphabetized category. "Mxxxxxxx.xxx" were manuscripts, "LTxxxxxx.xxx" were letters, "N" for notes, "G" for grant proposals, etc.

The manuscripts had lots of experimental detail on selectins. His patent files, labelled "PT-xxxx", were more interesting. In fact, one file labelled "PT-SEL-E" had the complete text of the European application that I'd worked so hard to get.

I spent the whole afternoon playing the tape into my hard drive and scanning files. Around 6:30 I packed my gear into my locker, dropped the film at the drugstore and went to Rebecca's. When I walked in the door, she asked politely why I was unshaven. I made up a white lie about doing an all-nighter in the lab. She fixed me a nice dinner. I fell asleep in her bed around 9:00. The next morning, with classes to attend, I made little progress on the project. Suddenly, it was Friday evening and time to go to a movie. I was too preoccupied to enjoy it.

Saturday morning I was once again in the library. I started a file called "CATALOG" and classified each of his files as I read through them. Classification was tricky because he had a lot of duplication with his backup diskettes, and I didn't dare neglect anything.

His "I-xxxx" files, containing his ideas, were most interesting. He was very systematic with these, too, dating them and cross-referencing everything. Starting about three years ago, he listed the different proteins and biologicals which he would bind to his selectins. He abbreviated the selectins with "Sel." His file "I-SEL-P" had all the useful proteins, together with their prices and cost per human treatment calculations. The calculations were quite similar to my calculations on Ashton's toxins, except that none of the proteins were toxins. They were all diagnostics, or proteins like insulin and human growth factor. Another file "I-SEL-C" had listings and references to all the known microencapsulation systems, patented and common domain. But no toxins.

A series of diary files, designated "DIA-xxx", looked promising. "DIA-COMM" recorded his daily commercial transactions, "DIA-SCI" logged his scientific transactions and "DIA-PT" was for his patenting projects. The diary entries had a formatted date supplied by the computer followed by abbreviated notes that were almost in code:

> Eval. L-sel-coupled 131-I alb. in mouse 24 hr post-gast. lav. w. gamma-scint. Ind. t1/2 approx. 5 hr. for abs., t1/2 approx. 5 hr. for tissue dist. w. 30% degrad. Gave to DC for sectng & autrad.

After studying this for 10 minutes, I managed to translate it as: Evaluating a mouse experiment in which he had forced down the mouse's throat 24 hours earlier a preparation containing albumin (alb) which was labelled with radioactive iodine (135-I) and chemically coupled to a lymphocyte selectin (L-sel).

The remainder of the note said that the coupled albumin went from gut to bloodstream in about five hours. It took another five hours to get to the tissues, in which it was "incompletely distributed." He gave the mouse carcass to his assistant Dong Chiu (DC) to cut into thin baloney slices and lay on top of photographic film to get a cross-sectional picture of which organs picked up the radioactive albumin.

But albumin was just a blood plasma protein – nothing

lethal like a toxin. I practiced deciphering more entries and
became skilled at reading his shorthand. Cataloging his files
kept me busy well into the evening.

Early Sunday morning, I was back in the library. The
"LT-DEPT" file contained a collection of nasty memos from
Ledbetter to Cooper, describing everything I'd already learned
from McGregor, and more. Dr. Ledbetter wrote a litany of
accusations against Cooper – accusations of lack of interest in
the departmental intellectual life; of fostering cronyism; of mis-
advising graduate students; of neglecting pharmacology as a discipline; of replacing senior faculty with junior faculty for important departmental functions; of interfering with mentor/student
relationships; and of instructing his departmental administrator
to give Ledbetter slow service on accounting for his grants.

Ledbetter's accusations got nastier and nastier from one
letter to the next, and he began sending copies to the Dean of
the Medical School and the President of the University. He
accused Cooper of squandering departmental money to pay
his collaborators in other institutions, which was tantamount
to buying publications. But even so, Cooper had fewer publications than Ledbetter. Ledbetter had medically relevant
projects. Cooper published only on medically irrelevant barnacle experiments. I could almost feel the white-hot hatred.

Yes, Ledbetter wanted Cooper dead. Yet, for all his fury,
Ledbetter's memos were still written in elegantly worded prose,
with a steady flow of logic that worked like a geometrical proof,
leading to one final inescapable conclusion: Cooper had to go.
All I needed was an equally logically constructed murder plan.

Next, I scrutinized Ledbetter's commercial files which listed
all the materials that came in and left in those Styrofoam boxes
and how he microencapsulated them. The formulations were
encoded by date, and sometimes there were notes to himself listing the notebook pages where his assistant had made entries.

Ledbetter had one series of notebooks for formulations
and another series for experiments. He was very meticulous
in his note-keeping, although I did find one computer glitch
where the whole text of a letter to a commercial supplier was

deleted and something in German was in its place. It was all too interesting, and there was too much of it. I wasn't a late-21st Century historian of science looking back on the brilliant Dr. Ledbetter. I was an amateur detective, working against the clock, with less than three weeks to get the answer and save Westley. And there were classes and exams to worry about.

I was overwhelmed. The more I pored over Ledbetter's files, the more I panicked. Damn! It was the equivalent of reading the Harvard Classics, a five-foot shelf of books. I worked well into Sunday evening without success.

The next morning, I told Grant Shipley I was sick and asked him to take notes for me in my courses. Sitting at my carrel, I realized that I'd already covered 85 percent of the most promising stuff. Like a drowning swimmer pulled from shore in a riptide, I felt my strength failing. It was like that time in my freshman year at Swarthmore when I'd foolishly gone out drinking during the first three days of the exam week and tried to do an all-night cram for organic chemistry.

What if Ledbetter had recorded his best stuff on the backs of envelopes and had burned them in an ashtray? My handwriting analysis showed he was secretive. Why would he trust his secrets to a computer?

Now came stomach cramps – a psychosomatic reaction, no doubt, but very real. I skipped lunch, half out of fear that someone would see me walking to the hamburger joint and partially out of fear that I was wasting valuable time. By 2:00 in the afternoon, I had finished 100 percent of the best stuff and still had nothing. So I started working on the unlikely files: the personal letters, his collection of memorable quotes, his address file and various junk files of about 4,000 bytes.

Ledbetter was not completely orderly. He left a lot of abstracts and short summaries scattered around, unconsolidated. There were also many little projects that didn't get finished. I started going though his directory from A to Z, reviewing these. I didn't find anything until I got to V. Here I came across a curious file named "VERGELTU". If it was some sort of a *gel*, then what did the prefix, *ver*, and the suffix, *tu*, mean? Or was it the *verge* of *ltu*? The contents of this file were the quintessence of his cryptic note-taking. Skimming quickly I saw this had to do with a "canine subj." This was interesting, because usually he never worked on anything larger than a rabbit. Reading on, I came across the words "cyanotic" and "tox." This sparked my interest, and I went back and read it carefully:

> Tox expt. 02/03/93: Compounded 50 mg of 930105 w. 10 gm gnd beef, admin. canine subj. (ca. 15 Kg, male, indet. breed) at 19:00 h, 02/03/93. Retd. 06:15 02/04/93, found mort in cage, cyanotic membranes of mouth, pupils dil., est. time of dth ca. 01:00 02/ 04/93 from body temp. upon palpation. (930105: 200 mg KN25 + 200 mg E7532 +100 mg Oregon #35)

I wondered if this could have been a dry run for the poisoning of Cooper. I read on:

> Tox expt. 07/05/93: 50 mg 930105 in syr. + 150 mg H$_2$0, consist. mayo, syringeable 18 gauge. Inj., fast fd. 17:50, adm. canine subj. (ca. 18 Kg female, indet. breed) 18:00. After subj. satiated remved. uningest. veg. mater. frm. floor. Est. > 75% dose inj. Retd. 06:00 070693, subj. mort (equally cold). Success!

This just *had* to be important. What were those chemicals he used 200 and 100 milligrams of? I felt a surge of adrenaline. I was on the verge of cracking this nut! I remembered what old Grant Johnson had told us he did when he made a discovery: "The bigger the 'discovery', the slower and more cautiously I go. I take a deep breath and try to calm down. If my reasoning is right, the fucking experiment will repeat. If my reasoning is wrong, the experiment may not repeat or I might be somewhere out in left field."

If I could just figure out what company made KN25, E7532 and Oregon #35! I selected the general "find" command in WordPerfect and punched in E7532. I waited 30 minutes, and the computer didn't find anything. I tried the same thing with KN25, waited another 30 minutes, and also got nothing.

My brain was too tired to consider anything but brute force. I selected the general "find" command and punched in "Oregon." The computer started to compile the names of the files which contained the word "Oregon." It was slow going, and the computer was coming up with a lot of files. My psychosomatic symptoms were gone, but I was weak as a kitten.

I asked a student working behind me to watch out for my computer while I went out to eat. I turned down the screen, partially covered it up, and walked to the hamburger joint. It was 7:00, and I was in need of blood glucose elevation. After wolfing down a hamburger and fries, I was back at the library in less than a half-hour, arriving just as the search came to an end.

The computer found 115 files containing the word "Oregon." After checking the first two, it became clear what was wrong with my search strategy. Oregon has a lot of scientists. It was always "Eugene, Oregon" followed by a zip code. The university there is apparently quite famous. Since I was looking for an Oregon pharmaceutical company, I tried again, searching for "{Hard return}Oregon." Using this strategy, I narrowed the 115 files down to two files.

The first file was "I-SEL", Ledbetter's idea file for selectin applications. It contained a letter to Oregon Biologicals of Gresham Oregon, inquiring about their mast cell stimulator product, #35. He wanted to know the EC_{50} for histamine release and the LD_{50} for rats or mice. Since "EC" stands for effective concentration and "LD" stands for lethal dose, he was essentially asking how much of this he would need to kill a man. I jumped out of my chair and took a little walk around the stacks. If I were a hound dog, I would have barked. I'd just crossed Ledbetter's tracks and had gotten a good sniff. Now, to start tracking him!

The second file containing "{Hard return}Oregon" was very interesting. I had seen it before. It was addressed to the same company, but the text of the letter consisted of a single sentence written in German. When I saw a day earlier, I thought it was a computer glitch. But now I *knew* it was substituted purposefully. It read:

Anforderung von Materialien zur Förderung der Wissenschaft durch Sonderexperimente.

Damn it! Why hadn't I taken German more seriously back in college? What was *Forderung* and how did it differ from *Förderung*? Damn those Umlauts! Downstairs in the reference section, I found a *Deutsches Medizinisches Lexikon.* I looked up the words while carrying it up the stairs to my carrel. *Anforderung* meant request. *Förderung* meant advancement. *Sonder* meant special.

So he was requesting from Oregon Biologicals materials "*to advance science through special experiments.*" There was only one way this made sense: His "advancement of science" was killing Cooper, and his "special experiments" were his method of doing it. And he had removed the order information from the letter and had substituted his sarcastic German, to keep it secret. It was all logical and self-consistent. But was it true? Well, the letter was written months before the dog experiment.

The greasy burger and French fries churned in my stomach. The sugars, amino acids and fatty acids were getting absorbed in my gut, providing nourishment. But at the same time, the greasy fatty acids and their free radical fatty acid derivatives were upsetting my intestinal flora. The detergent/surfactant in the milk shake also did its part. So I had to expend mental energy keeping my GI system under control, as well keeping my mind on track. And my thoughts rattled in my skull like a wild monkey in a cage.

– XXVII –

Possible Eureka

TAKING DR. GRANT JOHNSON'S advice, I tried to slow myself down, keeping my feet on the ground with the ball and chain of formal logic:

Where was the *corroboration* for his use of German as a secret language? Could I find more German in his files? He had been a post-doctoral fellow in Physiology in Frankfurt, Germany. People said he was fluent in German. How could I be sure he wasn't using German innocently? I thought up a lot of wild stuff, like programming the computer to look for other German words. But then I realized that the answer had been under my nose for the last hour: The name of the cryptic file with the two poisoned dogs was "VERGELTU", which might be the first eight letters of a German word. Then what did it mean? I searched my memory. *Ver* was a German prefix, so *gelt* had to be the root of the word. It wasn't money; that was *Geld*.

Then I realized that the German dictionary – the one I'd promised to "bring right back" over an hour ago – was still in my lap. So I looked up *Vergeltu*. There was only one word in my dictionary, and that was *Vergeltung*. And it means reprisal! My heart stopped for a second, then I jumped in the air and let out a semi-voluntary shout and an involuntary burst of methane.

"Now wait a minute, Ben," warned the little scientist inside my head. "That's a medical dictionary, full of weird psychiatric terms."

I flew down the stairs and ran to the reference desk, dictionary in hand, and told the librarian that I needed a *regular*

German dictionary. He looked at me funny, thought for a minute, and told me to look in the student collection on the fourth floor. I raced up the stairs. It was a special collection of junk that wealthy medical alumni gave the Med School for tax write-offs: paperback novels, investment books and out-dated atlases. I spent half an hour doing a book-to-book search before coming across a ripped and broken paperback *Langenscheidt's*. The Z section had fallen off, but the V's were still intact. A few minutes of checking, thinking and double-checking convinced me that the German language had only one *Vergelt* and that was *Vergeltung*, which means reprisal. Reprisal!

Running down the road of discovery as fast as I could drag my ball and chain of logic, I took another look at the "VERGELTUNG" file and decided on a global search for Oregon #35. The computer found nothing. Ledbetter had really been clever in covering up his tracks. Either he had not referred to it anywhere else or he used a different name for it. I looked back at the entry:

930105: 200 mg KN25 + 200 mg E7532 +100 mg Oregon #35

I would search the number 7532. I started to search the files, but the computer sorted out too many examples. It registered positive on all sorts of crap like phone numbers, zip codes and page numbers from journal articles. A search of E7532 came out negative. Then I tried E{space}7532 and came up with one example: It was a file "DIA-LAB" where he kept his notes on lab work. The relevant entry had the date Jan. 5, 1993 and read:

930105 = 200 mg KNip 25, 200 mg E 7532 (Eta), and 100 mg O-35, in starch matrix cont. amylase, micronized and coated with std. intestinal selectin/ lecithin, after-coated enterically.

So E stood for "Eta"! That meant that O stood for "Oregon". He now abbreviated Oregon #35 as O-35! Clever bastard. Eta Chemical Company is a major supplier! I ran across the street to McGregor's lab and pulled out the Eta catalog. Number 7532 was bovine thrombin! Put this into your veins and your blood turns to jelly! I ran back to the library. My carrel still looked like a rat's nest; no one had touched anything.

Now I had to figure out what was KN25 or KNip 25. I couldn't search 25. The letters had to be the name of a company. Remembering my boyhood stamp collection and my uncle's stories of World War II in the Pacific, I took a wild guess that the Nip stood for Nippon, which meant Japan. My strategy payed off immediately. In Ledbetter's "Idea" file, I found a note predating the dog poisoning:

Kanazawa Nippon, Tokyo and LaJolla, CA., KN 25 = Mathriotox., potent antagonist of cholinergic ACh receptor, $K_d = 10^{-12}$ M (!), LD_{50} - 0.1 ng/ml (!), rel. inexpens., marine organism.

Eureka! It was a potent neurotoxin. The case was cinched! I could hand over a complete proof.

I played through the whole scenario: Ledbetter looked through the catalog from this Kanazawa Nippon company and found a nice inexpensive killer neurotoxin with a dissociation constant of 10^{-12} M. It has a molecular compatibility score of 12. It had a high affinity for the acetylcholine receptor and would stay bound to it for a long time – long enough to stop Cooper's breathing. And the wily Dr. Ledbetter had even abbreviated it "Mathrio*tox*" so that no one could pick it up scanning his files for the word "toxin."

Then Ledbetter had made a polite inquiry to Oregon Biologicals to find out if their mast-cell stimulator was a 4, a 10 or a 12. Finding it was suitable, he got his hands on at least 100 mg of it. Then he went back to his computer file, found the letter of inquiry and changed the text by substituting that snide sentence in German about an experiment "to advance science." He also got hold of some bovine thrombin to use as a third component of his poison containing microcapsules, just to be sure. He made his preparation on Jan. 5, 1993. If Dong Chiu or the technician had made it for him, there would be a detailed, handwritten notebook entry in one of the notebooks in his cabinet.

With the poison microcapsules manufactured, he probably tried them out on a laboratory rat. After finding that was okay, he went into the animal rooms and tried it out on a dog, his "canine subject." At 7:00 PM on Feb. 3, 1993, he administered it to the first dog by mixing it up with some raw ground beef. The dog must have wolfed it down appreciatively. The next morning at 6:15 he returned (retd.) to find the dog dead (mort) with a purple mouth (cyanotic membranes), pupils dilated (dil.). He estimated (est.) the time of death (dth) as 1:00 AM, which meant that his stuff took about six hours to work.

For his second experiment, five months later and only a matter of weeks before Cooper's death, he devised a more realistic experiment. He mixed 50 mg of poison microcapsules (930105) in a syringe (syr) with 150 mg of water and observed that it had the consistency (consist.) of mayonnaise (mayo) and that it could be extruded through an 18 gauge syringe. He injected (inj.) it into a hamburger (fast fd.) at 5:30 and administered it (adm.) to his canine subject at 6:00. After the subject had satiated herself, he removed (remved.) the uneaten (uningest.) vegetable materials (veg. mater.) from the floor. He estimated that only 25% of the valuable poison had been wasted by the dog's failure to eat the lettuce (Est. > 75% dose inj.). He returned (retd.) at 6:00 a.m. to find his subject dead (mort) and equally cold. At this point, he permitted himself an exclamation mark: "Success!"

I could just imagine his disgust when he had to stoop to clean the floor because the dog didn't eat the lettuce and tomato. (*Schweinehund!*) I could imagine his pleasure the next morning when he found that his formulation worked when mixed with food of the gooiest kind. (*Sieg Heil!*) His ultimate experiment was not described, but this Final Solution was all too obvious.

It was 11:30 in the evening. I could still call Westley. I

pulled a quarter from my pocket and called him on a pay phone near the restrooms. After four rings, I heard a very somnolent but irritated "Yes?"

"Dr. Westley, this is Ben – "

"Ben? Ben. Well, yes, but don't you think it is a bit late? A little past the witching hour?"

"Yes, but I have been doing some witchcraft myself, and I know that we have a definite Eureka!"

"You are quite sure, are you?" he said, in a voice gaining clarity and enthusiasm. "Well, jolly good! I was wondering how you would come out with your late-night experiment."

"The experiment was carried out that night, successfully. Since then, I have been working day and night to evaluate the data. Just this moment I have put everything together. I have a definite and verifiable proof."

"Wonderful!" the Old Man said, with growing alacrity. "I rather imagine your experiment can be likened to an astronomy experiment. The astronomer spends an evening at the observatory making his measurements. Then, with the encroaching dawn, he packs up his data, disturbing nothing, leaving all the lenses in the telescope in place, not disturbing the archives and leaving nothing, not even his footprints."

"Quite," I said confidently.

"Did I hear you say 'quite?'"

"Aye, aye, sir!"

"My Dear Benjamin, I believe we have made an Englishman out of you."

"Well, at least you could call me an English mercenary," I said with irony, thinking about *The Sea Chase*.

"We shall have to celebrate with dinner tomorrow evening! And you say that you have spent day and night literally poring over your data. There must have been reams of it."

"Yes, but it is all stored in computers nowadays." I told Westley in code how I'd give him sample numbers and notebook reference just like one astronomer tells another how to find a star.

"So tomorrow evening, seven o'clock," he enthused. "A

little early so as to allow time. You will, of course, practice your little ditty for a few hours during the day, to guarantee a good performance.

"I'll be a good choirboy. I'll practice singing my solo righteously and with – what did you once say? – with a joyful sound?"

I dragged myself back to Rebecca's apartment and found her sleeping. I tucked myself into bed next to her like a husband returning from a late night at the office.

I had an important day in front of me.

– XXVIII –

Solo at Exeter

*W*AKING AND REACHING, I found Rebecca's side of the bed empty. It was 10:00. I left her a note to not expect me for dinner. Less than an hour later I was at the Purchasing Department, going through a Kanazawa Nippon catalog. Its 50-some pages are a delight to a would-be poisoner. I photocopied out KN 25. I did the same thing for O-35 in the Oregon catalog and E 7532 in the Eta Chemical Company catalog. Back at the library, I copied the relevant pages from the German dictionaries. Then I sat down to review my proof.

Around noon, I rode my bike to the drugstore and picked up the snapshots. Then, back at the library, I inserted a small earphone and listened to my voice tapes of Ledbetter's notebooks. I really did sound like a tobacco auctioneer. Studying the snapshots under my credit-card-shaped Fresnel magnifying "glass" from Edmund Scientific Company, I was able to determine the exact location of the notebook containing the details of Ledbetter's death potion number 930105.

A simple search for that number in Ledbetter's computer files revealed the exact location of the deadly sample in his Revco freezer. Over the phone, the Purchasing Department verified that it would be possible to look up an order placed one-and-one-half years ago. And how would I verify that he performed the canine experiment? I remembered my conversation with the security guard on the day of the animal rights demonstration.

With all of my facts solidly pinned down, I practiced my "Little Ditty" several times until I'd learned it by heart. Soon, it was 5:45 and time to head for the *Faire Isle*.

When the Old Man opened his door, I was overwhelmed by a thick, greasy smell.

"We are having lamb tonight," he said, rubbing his hands together in delight. "Would you fancy a claret before dinner?" he asked, uncorking a dignified-looking bottle. "So you have been making excellent progress. I cannot wait to hear."

Westley's face revealed boyish, indeed mischievous, delight. He looked so much younger and happier that night. I imagined him as a choirboy, getting ready to pull a caper. He played a favorite record for this special occasion: "Requiem, Op. 48" by Faure, performed by the Choir of Kings' College, Cambridge, with John Wells at the organ. As we sat sipping wine, a boy sang the "Pie Jesu" in a beautifully clear treble. It seemed so strange to create beautiful music about death. The Old Man said that he had sung this part at Exeter. I asked if the performance was recorded.

"Tape machines were not as abundant as they are now. Although Mr. Blackwood did attempt a recording, technically it was not of sufficient quality, and the experience was necessarily ephemeral."

Margaret hobbled out of the kitchen looking more frail than I'd ever seen her. But she greeted me warmly and enthusiastically. The Old Man said that she had prepared a "simply marvelous" dinner. We sat down to lamb with mint sauce, roasted potatoes and carrots. For dinner music, the Old Man put on a record titled *Ere's 'Olloway*, featuring Stanley Holloway with a number of English music hall ditties. In the fourth song, he sang the part of a happy vagabond who lived on a park bench in Trafalgar Square. It was written in three-quarter time and had the swing of a beer hall song. It was something of a musical travelogue, with a tongue-in-cheek description of the four guardian lions and Lord Nelson standing on top of the tall pedestal, surrounded by fountains and pigeons and everything. In the boisterous refrain, old Holloway declared that if it was good enough for Nelson, it was good enough for him.

Margaret had hummed along to the first verse. By the

second verse both Margaret and Dr. Westley were singing. After the third verse I sang along at the refrain. The song ended the three of us laughing heartily, Margaret so deeply that tears came to her laughing eyes, which showed the vulnerability and innocence of a little girl.

"Can you tell me about Stanley Holloway?" I asked.

"Oh, he is simply the most *marvelous* music hall singer. Very famous in England, you know," fluttered Margaret.

"You Yanks may know him as the ne're-do-well father in 'My Fair Lady,'" added the Old Man.

Whereas Margaret had prepared a feast of food, the Old Man had prepared a feast of conversation: spirited monologues on the charm of the British Isles in winter and in the spring as they greened — the gardens, the gentle waterways, the country houses and pubs. For dessert Margaret had prepared a "trifle." The Old Man almost popped a gut carrying the enormous lidded glass compote bowl. Rows of strawberries, tangerines and kiwis were pressed against the glass, making a festive pattern. The Old Man stood over it with a large spoon, dishing out portions. I imagined him as Father Christmas, handing out presents to the "wee children." I experienced a cozy, light-headed gaiety and lost all sense of time. Perhaps it was because Margaret had saturated the trifle with wine. Or was it rum?

Finally, the Old Man suggested that we retire to the study. Margaret said that she would "retire to the kitchen, and thence to bed." I thanked her profusely for the nice meal and for her good company. When she trilled something about being an irrelevant old lady and a terrible bore, I felt the urge to hug her. She must have sensed it, because she offered her hand, which I took. Her smile was so warm, but her hand was as cold as death itself.

The Old Boy glanced at me mischievously, drawing me into his study where he flipped on the light switch.

"So you have made great strides in your studies, you tell me, Benjamin."

I paused for a minute to let the old reels get into motion. I coughed and the input meters responded. Were the old vacuum tubes sufficiently heated?

So speaking in our agreed-upon Pig Latin/Double-Entendre, I told the Old Man the whole story. At times he enjoyed it, but at times he became agitated and stared desperately at the old tape machine, as if praying that it would not fail him. I had brought strips of paper with the critical code numbers and dates of the notebook entries. When I laid down the first morsels on the table, he breathed a sigh of relief.

I told him about the dog-poisoning experiments. I told him about the computerized access system for the animal rooms and that the guard said it records all comings and goings. As I told him about Ledbetter's diary entries, and dropped several pieces of paper identifying the file names, the Old English Sheep Dog began to look more like a Border Collie trying to hold together a straying flock. My final words were in plain American English.

"When you take possession of Ledbetter's computer, you should make multiple magnetic-tape copies of his hard drive before doing anything. And copy all of his diskettes. Use skilled technical help. Don't let any police sergeant-type do it."

"Yes, Ben."

"Well, this completes my solo at Exeter. Any comments or questions?"

"No, it is simply enthralling. I had to take care not to sneeze during the performance. It would be a pity to have lost these valuable program notes."

"Be sure to destroy the 'program notes' and all evidence of our conversations. I am prepared for some surprises, but I don't want any big surprises."

"Yes, one can always expect surprises in life. But one should not prepare too much for surprises, because they would then not be surprises, would they?" He delivered this piece of Lewis Carroll logic with a Cheshire Cat grin.

We talked some more in double-entendre about maintaining innocence and how the Old Man had his work cut out for him.

He said, "Some liken me to Sherlock Holmes. But then if this were merely a Sherlock Holmes adventure, we would be close to the end of the story. I would have only to inform the constabulary. But the United States of America is a constitutional democracy, and we have the problem of due process and legal proof. It is much like that popular television crime drama in which the police use the first half-hour detecting the murderer and the attorneys spend the second half-hour trying to prosecute him. So my task has just begun. And your task is also formidable. You must keep your head low, maintain you innocence, and *do your utmost to keep from getting sucked into this thing.*"

I must have yawned.

Westley smiled and said, "I agree that it is getting a little late. Let me see you to the door. You have sung your part beautifully. You are the perfect choirboy. And honestly and truthfully, you have enjoyed coming here and sharing the company of Margaret and myself, haven't you?"

"Yes," I said, with true conviction.

At this moment the Old Man seemed almost fatherly.

"Godspeed."

What a curious mixture of emotions I experienced, as the stout oak door closed slowly behind me: proud, foolish, sad, happy and uncertain. I had handed over my "definite eureka" and the Old Boy had saluted me with a "jolly well done." Henceforth, the King's Shilling would be a memory – a keepsake in my drawer. But I did not realize at the time that I would have so much hell to pay.

Released from clandestine duty, I redevoted myself to my classes. When Rebecca said I seemed more relaxed, I told her a major project had been completed. But there were some bits and pieces to attend to: destroying all the Ledbetter patents, my notes, deleting the Ledbetter files from my computer and overwriting the whole hard drive so that even the cleverest hacker couldn't find the symbols KN 25, O-35 and E 7532.

I dropped the photographs and the voice tapes in a dumpster in Coconut Grove and hid the backup tapes in an inaccessible battery compartment on the *Diogenes*.

"Keep your head down, Ben," I said to myself. "Pray that you don't get subpoenaed in the case. You can't stand up to cross-examination, even when you're telling the truth."

I innocently devoted the rest of the week and weekend to my studies. We even took Rebecca's friend Sally and her boyfriend out for a day-sail that Sunday.

When Monday rolled around, I spent the morning in Rob McGregor's lab, putting the finishing touches on a draft of a manuscript reporting our studies.

Then two police detectives came to haul me downtown for questioning.

- XXIX -

Command Performance

THE POLICE DETECTIVES WERE JUST like on television: A fat one and a thin one, wearing slouchy suits and knit ties, came walking down the hall like they owned the place. Once their eyes locked onto me, they never let go.

"Are you Mr. Benjamin Candidi?" asked the thin one.

"Yes"

"We're with the Miami Police Department. Would like to have a few words with you."

My eyes took refuge in my coffee cup. Little ripples threatened to turn into tidal waves. Mentally half-prepared and emotionally unprepared, I glanced back towards McGregor's laboratory. Luckily, he wasn't in.

"I'm sorry, but I'm in the middle of a timed experiment," I lied, not daring to ask them to state their business out in the hallway.

"That's okay, Mr. Candidi. We can wait as long as it takes." The technician from Kozinski's lab caught these words as she passed by with a rack full of scintillation vials. She looked back curiously. McGregor would be ten times as curious.

"How long do you need to speak to me?"

"It's hard to say, but at least an hour."

"Let me see what I can do about the experiment."

Stalling for thinking time, I went into the lab and fiddled with the knobs of a spectrophotometer, which wasn't even switched on. I thought it through and returned.

"Where do you want to talk? I don't have my own office or anything."

"We can take you to our office," said the fat one. "It's just five minutes away."

It was a silent walk down the hall and a quiet elevator ride. Their unmarked car was double-parked in front of the main entrance to General — one of those big black Plymouths with a handle-activated spotlight mounted on the driver's side. Two wheels rested on the sidewalk, narrowing the hospital entrance way. The trunk blocked the wheelchair incline.

They got in the front, letting me open the rear door for myself. People looked at me funny, like I was a robbery suspect. The car was in motion before I could slam my door. We accelerated across the zebra stripe like there wasn't a pedestrian around for miles.

"I guess you guys don't like to waste time." This elicited a half-grunt from the fat one behind the wheel. "So why don't you guys tell me what this is all about?"

"Later, when we get to the station."

I always did want to play in a B-grade movie. While the detectives discussed their work schedules, I tried to think about the interview. But the erratic motion of the car hurt my concentration. The fat guy drove like it was a chicken race. Blowing the horn was his way of being polite, and flashing his badge was his way of being politely assertive. So I used all my mental energy looking at the horizon and striking poses to not look like a criminal. Occasional humiliation can be humanizing experience.

The police station is a 12-story building rising out of a one-block-square parking lot. Fatso threw the transmission into park before the car was completely stopped. I slammed my door harder than they did, but neither cop seemed to notice.

The room on the 10th floor had a small table, a couple of chairs, no windows, but a large mirror on an inside wall. In the corner, next to a pile of leather carrying cases and her three-legged machine, sat the stenographer/court reporter — about 32, peroxide blond, skinny and a little unhealthy looking, I'm sorry to say. A one-piece pink chiffon dress covered her from shoulder to leg, blooming out four inches below the knee. Her right leg was crossed over the left at the knee, toes pointed to a spot on the floor two feet in front of her, said pointing effect accentuated by a pair of high-heeled patent-leather shoes. Funny how you notice such things on your hay wagon ride to the guillotine.

She didn't return my glance. The two detectives motioned me to sit down. The thin one sat across the table from me, the fat one sat to the side and farther back. The inhospitable environment made me feel defensive and mousey.

"Mr. Candidi, we're doing a routine investigation into the death of Dr. Charles Cooper, who was the Chief of the Department of Pharmacy at the General Medical School."

I let out a nervous laugh, and they looked at me strangely.

"I'm sorry, but he was the Chairman of Pharmacology at Bryan Medical School. Dade County General is only affiliated with Bryan Medical School."

The steno machine clicked away while I was talking and continued for a few seconds, as the Chiffon Lady took down my last words. The detectives waited patiently as if my initial response was not worthy of a reply.

"I'm sorry," I said, looking from them to the stenographer. "I understood that he died unexpectedly, but I never met the man. I wasn't even associated with the Department until after he died." I laid in a pause. No answer. "So I really don't understand why I have been brought down here with this court reporter."

The fat one winked and said, "Mr. Candidi, we can assure you that you are not a suspect in any criminal investigation. The only reason we have brought you here is to help us with scientific information in your department – information that might be useful to us in understanding Dr. Cooper's early death."

"Well, fine, but I can't imagine that I would be of any use to you on that."

The thin one said, "Our questions will have to do with information that you have about substances and methods which are used in your Department."

I tried to keep my mind innocent and sing righteously.

"Do you mean things that he could have been exposed to in the laboratory? You don't mean – "

"Mr. Candidi, if you could please let us ask our questions."

"Yes, please do."

"On the evening of December third, nineteen ninety-three, did you visit Dr. Westley at his residence on Bayshore Drive, Miami."

"I believe so. That was a Thursday, wasn't it?"

"Yes"

"Then the answer is yes," I said, falling into the routine. The steno machine was beginning to click in a smoother rhythm.

"In the course of that conversation, did you state to Dr. Westley that Dr. John Ledbetter was working on a drug system that can take protein-type drugs and put them into pills that can be swallowed, and the proteins go into the bloodstream?" He read the question from a sheet of paper.

"Yes, I think I did tell him something like that . . . Yes, I'm sure that I did. Say! Did you bring me down here because Dr. Ledbetter is a suspect in a – "

"Mr. Candidi, I am afraid that we are the only ones who will be asking the questions here."

Wouldn't my innocent answers and questions make me sound more convincing? Proof that I wasn't a coached witness? I didn't appreciate being reprimanded. But perhaps all they were interested in was a clean steno record.

"Very well," I answered.

"What is your relationship to Dr. Geoffrey Westley?"

"He is my former employer . . . and a good friend of mine. Well, he was really more like a Dutch Uncle. We have kept in touch since I left his organization."

"Are you an employee of the DCMEO?" he asked. I pretended that I didn't understand the acronym. "The Dade County Medical Examiner's Office," he said.

"Oh, the M.E.'s Office! No, I resigned that position when I was accepted in graduate school."

"Then is it true that you have no official relationship to

the Dade County Medical Examiner's Office?"

"That is correct."

"Do you have *any* relationship with the DCMEO?"

"They have paid me to come back there once in a while to service their instruments when they need it. I agreed to do that for them."

"So you are paid to service their instruments?"

"Yes, they have paid me on a per-visit basis. I'm an independent contractor, of sorts."

"Why does the DCMEO call you back to work as an independent contractor?"

I told the detective that Steve Burk and Jake Brown didn't know shit about troubleshooting instruments, and how I was saving them big money on factory-trained technicians from Atlanta. "Besides, its a good moonlighting job for a penniless graduate student. I mean, it beats working in the Seven-Eleven!"

The fat cop chuckled. The thin one asked, "Did your consultant – strike that – independent contractor services for the DCMEO involve investigating or consulting on cause-of-death cases."

He shook his head at himself after saying "strike that." Maybe he was going to law school at night.

"No, I wasn't involved in that kind of stuff – just keeping the instruments working."

"When you made these service visits to the DCMEO, did you confer with Dr. Westley?"

"No, I hardly ever saw him. His office was on another floor and he was usually very busy."

"Did you confer with him on matters of cause of death during your visits to his residence?"

"No."

"Did you confer with Dr. Burk on any DCMEO matters other than the status of the instruments?"

"No."

"Could we turn back to your conversations with Dr. Westley at his residence. Did you discuss the work of other professors in your department?"

"Yes. Probably all of them."

"Did you visit Dr. Westley more than one time?"

"Yes, he and Margaret had me over for dinner five or six times."

"Did your visits to Dr. Westley have any special purpose?"

"No, they were . . . social. I think that they liked having me over, and I think . . . well you know . . . I'm sorry, I'm a little confused right now."

"Excuse me a moment." He got up and left the room.

The Chiffon Lady leaned over, searched in her bag and pulled out a thick paperback book. On its cover was a big-breasted woman in an evening gown, one strap dropped from her shoulder, in the arms of a bare-chested man. The century and setting were indeterminate. A generic romance novel – the type the drugstores sell. It was probably the right reading material for someone who records pain and suffering day in and day out. I wandered over to the mirror. On the other side of this one-way looking glass, the thin detective was probably conferring with Dr. Westley and an Assistant State Attorney. All I needed to get a good look at both of them, was to cup my hands on the sides of my face and put my nose to the glass. What were they discussing? Whether my testimony gave them probable cause to go after Ledbetter – and whether there was sufficient distance between me and the D.C.M.E.O. On whim, I strolled back to the fat detective who had been watching me.

"Did you ever study physics in high school? Transmitted light, reflected light and that kinda junk."

"No, never got that far, fella. But I made varsity wrestling."

"Probably much better training for your job – twisting people's arms."

The stenographer didn't bat an eye. Probably deep in her vicarious love affair. Two minutes later, the tall, thin detective was back. The stenographer looked up at him, and he waved her off.

He thanked me for my cooperation, said I'd answered all their questions for now and said he was sorry he couldn't tell me what it was all about. "I would appreciate your not discussing this interview with anyone. Of course, it would be possible to get a court order to that effect, but then we would have to detain you – "

"No, it's okay. I promise to not talk to anyone."

"Well, once again, I appreciate your cooperation. Joe! Could you take Mr. Candidi back to General Medical School."

Needless to say, it was a silent walk down to the parking lot. Just as I was about to get into Joe's car, he flashed his badge and flagged down a squad car leaving the lot.

"Hey, patrolman, you going north?"

"Yeah."

"Then take this feller up to Dade General as a courtesy, fifteen twenty-seven"

Or was it a "twenty-seven fifteen"? I hopped in the front seat. About ten blocks short of Dade General, the officer received a call for a 13-75 – or was it a 15-37? He slammed on the brakes, ordered me out, made a U-turn and hauled off in a cloud of dust, exhaust and burning rubber, leaving me on the edge of Overtown.

After a good afternoon's work on the manuscript in McGregor's lab, I biked back to Coconut Grove. I ate at Captain Walley's and talked with some old acquaintances. Then I pulled out a quarter and called up Westley, half out of habit.

"Hello, Dr. Westley. I'm just calling to see how you are doing."

"Oh, yes, Ben. Well, we are doing jolly well. Yes, quite fine indeed! How are your classes coming along?"

"Just fine, thank you. But they were interrupted today." I laid in a long pause which was matched with silence on the other end. "I was visited by two police detectives and interrogated for a half-hour this morning. They wanted me to verify that I had told you something about Dr. Ledbetter. They also wanted to know about my social visits to you."

"You have me to thank for that, I am afraid. But when you told me a while back about Ledbetter having an oral delivery system for proteins, I had to pass this information on to the police and prosecutors." His voice sounded as distant and formal as when I'd first met him. "It seems that they had an interest in these things. Lord knows why. It may be one of their police theories, or some sort of bureaucratic make-work scheme, for all I know. At any rate, I had to pass on the information. Fiduciary responsibility, affirmative duty and such things. I wouldn't make too much of it, if I were you. They must have told you as much. I hope you weren't unduly inconvenienced."

"It was like a one-way conversation with a guy wearing mirrored sunglasses."

"Well, sometimes it is better when we do not see everything. The wheels grind slowly, the invisible hand, movement in mysterious ways . . . You are intelligent, articulate and well-educated. You know what I mean. I am very sorry that you were inconvenienced, but I am *quite* sure that you shan't be inconvenienced again. By us, that is."

It was a stupid conversation. They had to interrogate me before they made their move. The Old Man and I were finished, but yet . . .

"I was wondering about Wednesday evening . . . "

His answer came quickly, delivered with a combination of professional brusqueness and whining self-excuse:

"Ben, I am sorry to say that we will not be seeing much of each other for the next several months. Professional matters will be requiring my attention in the extreme . . . and they will spill over into my evenings . . . such that it would be extremely difficult, if not impossible. Perhaps you can see what I mean."

My head told me we were just acting out a script, but my heart felt abandonment.

"Yes, I do understand, sir. Quite clearly." If I could only have retrieved these last words.

"I was certain you would. Also, Margaret has recently taken a turn for the worse and should be having less excitement. She will be disappointed because she did so much look forward to your visits."

"I'm sorry, Dr. Westley. If there is anything I can do – "

"No. I am, of course, a physician. I am attending to matters and everything is under proper control. *All matters.*"

"Then there is nothing for me to do but wish you luck, sir."

"Quite," he said with finality. Then warming to me he said, "Ben, it has been a joy to have had you working with me for all these years. You are a truly versatile young man. It has been a pleasure to *witness* the rapid growth of your professional *expertise.* I wish you the greatest luck with your studies in pharmacology . . . for which you seem to be showing the *greatest aptitude.* Fair weather and following seas. And I hope you will be able to weather the coming storm. Godspeed." (Click.)

So it was a done deal. I would not be allowed to call Dr. Westley for a long time. Within a week I would be longing for his advice on how to weather the storm.

– XXX –

Return Engagement

"*Y*OU BE CAREFUL YOU NOT UNPLUG freezer. It have many important samples," Dr. Dong Chiu admonished the men working in the ceiling. He had draped plastic over Ledbetter's Revco liquid nitrogen freezer. Ledbetter's door was closed, presumably to avoid noise and dust.

I had an early morning appointment with Dr. Kozinski next door. He said my reputation had preceded me, and that he would be glad to have me do my next rotation in his lab.

Outside, I found Dr. Chiu still guarding the freezer. Next, I made the mistake of stopping by McGregor. He suggested some alternative calculations and changes in our manuscript. These tied me up in his lab for a couple of hours. I left just as the workmen were finishing.

I attended a departmental seminar. Ledbetter sat at the table with the other faculty. He seemed to be in an expansive mood, joking with the guest speaker from another institution.

The next afternoon, I wasn't surprised to see the fat-and-thin detectives coming down the hall. They did not return my nod of recognition. They walked right past me and into Ledbetter's lab. I stayed outside, some 50 feet down the hall, pretending to read the bulletin board. After several minutes, they emerged with Ledbetter in tow. He wasn't handcuffed, but he definitely wasn't going of his own accord. As they passed by, I pretended to read the inner pages of a flyer titled *Post-doctoral Research Opportunities at the National Institutes of Health.* And I pretended to not notice Ledbetter's searching glances as they waited for the elevator.

"The questions shouldn't take more than an hour," said the fat one.

"You people must realize that we do not have infinite time. I am scheduled for an important conference call with . . . a collaborator on a manuscript at four-thirty. You must have been over this ground many times with many members of the faculty, months ago. If you want to learn medicine, and if you consider yourselves qualified, you should take your college transcripts down to the Admissions Office and – "

The insult was cut short by the closing elevator door. Back in McGregor's lab, I fiddled with the manuscript. I imagined Ledbetter riding in the unmarked car to his appointment with the stenographer in the room with the one-way mirror.

At 4:30 I got a message to call "Steve." Old Burk told me to come over to troubleshoot the GC mass spec, reporting not later than 5:30. I should finish up at Bryan and take all my stuff with me, because it would probably take most of the night. They were getting phantom peaks and needed to run important assays tomorrow morning.

Before going over there, I grabbed a bite at the hamburger joint. Burk claimed to be doing some after-hours work himself and instructed me to report to his office before leaving. An hour of running baselines didn't turn up even a hint of a phantom peak. I told him there was nothing wrong with the instrument. He said to replace the guard column, repeat the run at several different temperatures and do a calibrating series.

"But that will take three hours."

"Just do it."

Every so often, Burk came in with a copy of *Forensic Pathology* in his hand and checked my progress. At a 10:45, I brought a couple feet of strip chart showing nothing but clean peaks and flat baselines.

"Great job, Candidi. Well, why don't we finish off the evening with a beer at your Captain Walley's. We could throw your bike in the back of my wagon and be there in no time."

This was obviously an offer I couldn't refuse. I was not

expected at Rebecca's that night, so I went along with it. Riding shotgun, as Burk barreled his eight-cylinder Bronco down I-95, I tried a couple of times to jump-start a conversation. But Old Burk just wasn't interested in my material. So what the hell – I just told him what was on my mind.

"I guess these high-rise four-wheel-drive vehicles are pretty good when you get stuck in traffic. All you have to do is hop the curb and drive across people's yards."

This unleashed a cascade of anecdotes about his urban exploits with his gas-guzzling toy. At Captain Walley's, I managed to switch the conversation to pharmacology, Burk's graduate work at Lexington, Kentucky, life in Miami and his golf game. We sat close to the seawall, at the same picnic table where Rebecca and I had our pre-Thanksgiving date. Our "Walley's Girl" was a 19-year-old redhead with the charming accent of the Emerald Isle. We exchanged some small talk when she brought our pitcher of beer. Burk remained fixated on her breasts.

A four-year-old boy was running around and zooming dangerously close to the edge of the seawall. At high tide it was a five-foot drop with three feet of water. At low tide it was an eight-foot drop with bare rocks. The kid's parents, Swedes or Danes in their early 30s, paid no attention. Every time the child ran within three feet of the seawall, I held my breath.

"Awfully late for that little rug rat to be out, don't you think?" Burk remarked.

"Parents are probably Scandinavian tourists."

"Yeah, fits with the blond hair. I hear that those Swedish girls are good fucks. And pretty easy to get in the sack. You know anything about that?"

"Didn't you have any Swedes at Lexington?"

"No. That's why I was asking. You must have had a few at Swarthmore."

"Not really," I said, "but there's a Swedish technician here in the Biochemistry Department at the Med School. I talked with her a month ago. She said she came here to get her freedom . . ." (Burk's pupils dilated) ". . . from taxation." Burk frowned.

The rug rat did another bombing run on the seawall, and I winced.

"You're really worried that the brat will go over the side, aren't you?"

"Yeah. Look, I'll take care of the brat, and you take care of the mother."

"You know, Candidi, you kind of remind me of that guy in a book they made us read in college lit, *Catcher in the Rye.*"

"You might not be too far off, Burk – in more ways than either of us can guess. Look, it's getting late."

Burk looked at his watch. "Right, it's twelve-fifteen. Let me give you a ride home."

"It's just two blocks to my landing."

"Look, your bike's still in my Bronco, so we'll unload it there."

He drove me to the landing and stuck around while I unchained my dinghy and chained my bike to a tree. And then he stood there while I rowed out to the *Diogenes.* I was halfway to the boat before his tail lights lit up, and he pulled away.

Grant Johnson provided the first indication that it was not a typical morning at the Department of Pharmacology. "They'd better not come fucking around in my lab," he said to no one in particular, as he entered the elevator on the fifth floor. I stepped out to find a gaggle of cops blocking the hallway near the Revco freezer. The whole department seemed to be wandering around in a state of shock – students, technicians, post-docs and faculty alike. A couple of University security guards stood on the periphery.

The Revco freezer was wrapped with yellow tape marked "Police Line." A man in a brown work uniform stood on a step ladder over the Revco, his head stuck in the false ceiling. A minute later, he handed down some equipment. One piece looked like a boom box with a radio antenna. Another looked like a diver's weight belt, but proved to be a battery power pack.

"Don, could you hand me up a bag for this last one."

What came down was about the size of a video camera. When he replaced the ceiling panel, I noticed a two-inch diameter hole. Dr. Dong Chiu complained periodically that they were getting dust on the Revco.

The police technicians entered the air conditioning equipment room located behind a louvered, aluminum grating that served to collect the return air at the end of the hall. Two of the grates were bent, making a two-inch gap, which lit up nicely when they entered the room and flipped on the lights. A couple minutes later, they were wheeling out several cubic feet of equipment. Yes, a trap had been set and sprung. And a trap was now retrieved.

If anyone saw what went on last night, it had to be Sheng-Ping Chow. He was practically living in Dr. Kozinski's lab.

"What happened here, Sheng-Ping?"

"Oh, Dr. Redbetter come here last night. He open lab and go to freezer. And creaning man come and say he policeman. Dr. Redbetter, he run away and other creaning man come grab him. Before I can do something, creaning man tell me that he police officer. Then rots of police come. They take vial from Dr. Redbetter and put in dry ice box. They take pictures of freezer."

"What did Dr. Ledbetter do?"

"Oh, first he try to run away. When they get him, he say they can't take vial. It part of important experiment. Then he try to grab it back. Then he scream that they have no right to come here and fuck up his experiments. Oh, he mad! He mad like when technician take wrong vial and mess up two-month experiment."

"What did the cleaning people look like, Sheng-Ping?"

"Oh, they black. You say Haitian. Like regular creaning people. I not believe them either, but they show me police badge."

"What did they do with Dr. Ledbetter?"

"He under arrest. They read him Miranda and put on cuff-hands. Just like in TV. They say he kill Dr. Cooper. Dr. Redbetter say they idiot. He say they use 'fuzzy logic.'"

Hopefully, Ledbetter had grabbed Sample # 930105.

It had been good thinking on Westley's part, keeping me away from the scene with that fool's errand for Burk.

"Thanks, Sheng-Peng."

"Ben, you think Dr. Redbetter kill Dr. Cooper? Some people say Dr. Redbetter very mad at him. But some people say Dr. Cooper just die sudden death. What you think?"

"I don't know any more than you do."

Taking to heart Dr. Westley's advice, I kept my head down. I retreated to a corner of Kozinski's lab and worked hard. Everyone else spent the day in hallway conversation, and I heard it all through the open door.

Ashton told someone, "I'm glad that they didn't decide to go into my lab. They could have made up any story they want with the things I'm working with."

Peter Moore said, "A good working scientist has been victimized by those idiots downtown."

Dr. Fleischman said that it was a throwback to the days of Stalin.

Hallway conversations told me that the police were cataloging Ledbetter's notebooks and making photocopies of everything. And when I left at seven that evening, they were still working. They had their own lock and alarm on the Revco freezer. In the mail room, everyone's pigeonhole contained a memo from Dr. Moore, saying we should not take notice of "recent events affecting members of the Department."

I went home to Rebecca and "innocently" told her what everyone else in the Department had learned. She remembered that Ledbetter was the crazy one, but she didn't say anything about our conversation at Elliott Key.

The next day, the Department was still in chaos. Gordon Taylor was strangely subdued. It would be many weeks before he would deliver another "Sergeant Major" joke.

That evening, I found a thick envelope in my Coconut Grove post office box. It was from the M.E.'s Office and contained a series of predated invoices for service between November and mid-January, plus a check for $9,320 made out to my instrument repair service. When I added this to previous payments, it came to a few dollars more than the agreed-upon $12,500. So we were squared away. A typewritten note requested that I sign and return the predated invoices, which I did.

It was an evening scheduled for the *Diogenes*. I removed the backup tapes from the battery compartment and spent an hour snipping and burning them in a tin can. This, I thought, severed my last physical link with Dr. Ledbetter. Other links, I could not easily sever – links in people's minds.

– XXXI –

Reverberation

*I*T WAS EASY ENOUGH TO KEEP my head down and look busy. I was busy. I'd fallen far enough behind to experience masochistic pleasure in Sturtz and Gunnisons' flagellating Molecular Biology course. They expected us to master the precise details of taking out a gene from human brain cells and putting it into frog eggs. I would have liked to have taken out my brain cells containing memory of Ledbetter, put them into a frog and release it deep in the Everglades.

Our student study group propped me up emotionally. Sheng-Ping mastered molecular genetics more than any of us. He had an excellent analytical mind and was good at manipulating symbols. Grant Shipley, like me, found the subject too nonlinear. Maria fell back on rote memorization and got the answers right most of the time. Cindy Larson arranged for a lot of help from a fourth-year student in Sturtz' lab. Dave Franklin made like he was interested in molecular genetics when Sturtz and Gunnison were around. But he told us that he really didn't need to know the stuff: In the future, physicians will be able to order molecular genetic tests from hospital labs the way they order blood chemistry tests today.

Evenings, Rebecca filled in physiology background for my Cardiovascular Pharmacology, which I was taking ahead of schedule with second-year students. But she had her own courses to worry about. She called to New York quite often and was worried about her father. He had an unexplained illness, was losing weight and was getting sicker by the day.

Any "free" time left for me during the day was spent in
Dr. Kozinski's lab, doing experiments on regulatory phosphorylation. With my head bowed over the lab bench, I might be
spared an eyeball-to-eyeball interrogation on my role in the
Ledbetter affair.

Rebecca was too distracted to pick up all the news from
the active med-student grapevine. Dave Franklin had quickly
established himself as a one-man liaison committee and general gossip monger between the two groups of students. The
med students had an oral tradition that Pharmacology was
always a "problem department." Cooper's predecessor was a
high-flying physician with a reputation for coming in drunk
for grand rounds. In a "Senior Class Play," the students depicted him walking around, pulling a wheel-mounted IV pole
holding an inverted whiskey bottle. And there had been a
"scandal" involving a weight-control clinic in the Bahamas.
Rob McGregor had once told me that Cooper also repeated
these stories to cast aspersions on the Old Guard faculty.

I heard that Ledbetter was out on bail but was legally
restrained from coming back to the lab. He phoned in instructions to Dr. Chiu. One day, the *Miami Standard* carried a short
story, stating that a professor had been arrested "in connection with" the death of a colleague, and that the authorities
were refusing to say anything more at this time. The TV-news
people ignored the story completely, probably because they
couldn't get pictures and sound bites. But I did get a lot of
background in a most curious way.

While eating my lunch in the outdoor mall between the
Med School and the Medical Library, I overheard an extended
conversation between two faculty members. The older prof
told a younger colleague about a recent meeting of the Faculty Senate. A colleague of Ledbetter's, reinforced by one of
Ledbetter's lawyers, argued that it was unfair to suspend
Ledbetter, violating his academic freedom and prejudicing his
case. The University had to let Ledbetter continue his research.
Every day that Ledbetter was out of the lab, his Federal grant
dollars were wasted. The University's "precipitous actions"

were scaring off Ledbetter's financial backers and were inter-fering with his ability to commercialize his medical inventions. He stood to lose several million dollars, and it might be neces-sary to sue the University.

"Then the Dean spoke," said the older one.

"What did he say? Treat me to another parody. My tissue-culture room just got a yeast infection. I need a good laugh."

And the faculty senator supplied one. He took off his wire-rimmed glasses, puffed up his chest, looked into the distance, as if addressing a large group of people, and mimicked:

"Bryan Medical School is a high-quality institution which has made great strides in healthcare delivery and medical re-search, and has lived up to the great humanitarian ideals of our namesake."

This reference to William Jennings Bryan started the younger one snickering. The bearded one broke character and laughed along with him. It was a caricature of a smooth-talk-ing operator who smugly reveled in bullshit. The mimicked oration was delivered in unctuous tones and seamless sen-tences, punctuated only by slight pauses for visual emphasis, with glances cast to the left and then right, as if silently de-manding affirmation from an unseen audience.

"Institutions and individuals must face all forms of strain and unexpected challenges, many of them unjust."

As the character sketch continued, the "Dean" smugly told his audience that although he was enjoined from discuss-ing the merits of the case, he didn't need to tell anyone in the room that he was Harvard-trained as a cardiologist, with a distinguished career in that field. He was familiar with the sta-tistics on sudden death.

"I most firmly believe that professionals who are not en-gaged in healthcare delivery are not entitled to hold expert opinions on such specialized health matters." The Dean went on to further identify the unentitled: Those in professions on the periphery of medical science and physicians who are not engaged in healthcare delivery.

So the Dean didn't think Westley was entitled to an opinion because he delivered corpses and not health care.

The speech ended with the Dean stating that he would present Dade County with a bill for several million dollars after the Ledbetter affair was resolved.

The younger scientist practically howled at his colleague's parody on the phrase "healthcare delivery." Biomedical Ph.D.s will often enjoy a good laugh at an M.D.'s expense.

"Say, George," asked the younger one, "you've been around here longer than I have. What was Old Flannel-Lips' distinguished career in cardiology?"

"He did a thousand unnecessary bypass operations and published one-hundred case reports." They laughed hard enough to rock their bench.

But they didn't think much of Westley, either. The younger one called him "that old fogy of a medical examiner that you read about in the papers every once in a while." They thought Dr. Jane Goddard Cooper was pushing Westley's case, and they had a low opinion of her.

"Supposed to be a dietician, but doesn't know vitamin E from vitamin A. And she thinks free-radical damage is what happens when leftist students go on a rampage!"

Then the bearded one looked at his watch, and it was all over. It bothered me that the Old Man was far out on the limb. Knowing the truth and having evidence is one thing – but proving it beyond a reasonable doubt is harder. Could our case be blown away by a couple of stuffed-shirt Harvard doctors testifying on sudden death? If Westley's case blew up in his face, I would have to do more than just "keep my head down."

The more weeks rolled by, the more cogent seemed Dr. Westley's advice: "*Keep your head down. Maintain your innocence, and do your utmost to keep from getting sucked into this thing.*"

But how could I counter nonverbalized suspicion that grew stronger by the day? Sometimes at seminars, I caught Dr. Moore staring at me. Dr. Taylor acted sulky. Ashton no longer bothered with his phony show of friendliness when we passed in the hall. Thinking back, I must have tipped my hand to him with my goofy "Columbo" interrogation.

McGregor tried to get me to talk about my experience as a lab tech in the M.E.'s Office. Dr. Westley was right: "A dog that brings a bone will also take one away." I soon learned that someone had carried one away.

– XXXII –

Encore

DR. MOORE'S MIDDLE-AGED SECRETARY walked into Dr. Kozinski's lab and told me, "Dr. Moore would like to see you immediately." I went ahead of her and walked through Dr. Moore's open door and into his office. From behind his desk, Dr. Moore scowled at me and indicated I was not to sit down. He lifted the phone and punched four numbers.

"He's here . . . I'll bring him right down." In one continuous motion, he hung up, rose and walked me to the door.

"We're going to have a little chat with the Dean," he said brusquely.

"Can you tell me what it's about?"

"Can't you guess?"

"Well, I suppose. It seems that everyone in the Department is getting involved in this thing about Dr. Ledbetter."

We had no further conversation. As we stepped off the elevator at the first floor, I had the distinct feeling that Dr. Moore wanted to march me out of the building, kick my butt and tell me to never come back again. But instead, he led me to the Dean's office and pushed me through two layers of secretaries, opening the final door without knocking.

It was a large, mahogany-appointed office. Sitting behind a massive desk, the Dean made an interesting picture: Mediterranean features, Oxford cloth button-down shirt and bright, preppy tie. His outermost layer was a hip-length white clinician's jacket. He seemed more like an executioner than the smooth operator described by the faculty senator.

Seated to the Dean's right and facing him was a woman in a business suit. Early thirties. Poor complexion. To her right was a dapper-looking gentleman in three-piece suit. His expensive threads and his thin-soled, tasseled loafers immediately identified him as a lawyer. Such ridiculous shoes. The front cut practically extended to the base of his toes, revealing a lot of sock and upper arch. They weren't shoes. They were god-damned lounge slippers! The things never saw anything more challenging than the pigeon shit on the courthouse steps.

Dr. Moore said, "Dean Alcibides, this is Mr. Benjamin Candidi, entry-level graduate student in our department."

I looked to the Dean, ready to extend my hand. But he didn't extend his. He acted like I was a bag of guano from a Peruvian island.

"Please sit down," he virtually ordered.

I took my time lining up with the chair, and looked inquisitively at the lawyer fellow and the woman sitting next to him. If the Dean couldn't extend me courtesy, at least I could insist on knowing who was in the room with us.

"Ms. Julia Blanco, Assistant Counsel for the University, and Jason Diamond, Esquire," the Dean said.

So the Defense was now in the process of discovery. And the topic of the day was whether Candidi had been sent by Westley to gather information on Ledbetter. If the answer was "yes," they might be able to get the case thrown out. If the answer was "no," they could use me to discredit Westley. I was mentally rehearsed for this interview.

The Dean frowned and patted his well-trimmed, rounded head of gray hair. "Mr. Candidi, is it correct that you were an employee of the Dade County Medical Examiner's Office immediately before coming to us as a graduate student?"

"Yes, sir," I answered.

Then came a sharp click. The Dean's secretary sitting behind me had snapped on a medium-sized tape recorder. I turned around and stared at her. She lurched and looked away.

"We are recording this interview for accuracy," the Dean said. "We hope that you will understand."

"Oh, yes, of course. I do this myself, quite often for exactly the same purpose – accuracy in lectures, that is."

I tried to sound innocent and diffident. This time, Ben Candidi, failed expert witness, was going to enjoy the game of cat and mouse.

"Mr. Candidi, could you tell us why you applied to the Department of Pharmacology."

"Yes. I want to get a Ph.D."

"A Ph.D.?" he asked, as if this were a strange aspiration on my part.

"Yes. I wasn't getting anywhere career-wise."

"So that is the reason why you applied to *Pharmacology*?"

"Yes!"

I looked at him and then at the two lawyers in turn. The power people watched me closely and said nothing. Like I had to justify myself to them!

"Is there more I should say?" I asked, feigning amazement.

"And your choice of *pharmacology*?"

Like my choice was stranger than tropical lepidopterology!

"It's an important scientific discipline. Just like I wrote in my letter of application." Turning to Dr. Moore, I asked, "You must have read it, didn't you?" Dr. Moore grunted an incomprehensible monosyllable. "Like it says in your brochure, pharmacology is a crossroads discipline between chemistry, biochemistry, physiology and *medicine.*"

As I ended with the word "medicine," I threw my face to the Dean, trying to project the mindless gaze of a doe frozen before automobile headlights. He immediately turned his head in disgust, and the room was silent for several seconds.

"How are you enjoying your studies in pharmacology?" he asked ironically.

"Well, my studies are fine, but the *Department* seems to be in turmoil, if you don't mind my saying so."

The Dean wrinkled his nose in disgust, like I even smelled like a bag of Peruvian guano. Then he glanced down at a sheet of paper on his desk – apparently a list of questions.

"Are you in the employ of the Dade County Medical

Examiner's Office?"

"No, I'm a graduate student."

"Do you feel that you have certain obligations to the Dade County Medical Examiner's Office?"

"No," I answered, after hesitating like I didn't understand.

"Very well, but I will note that you did not answer my previous question completely truthfully."

"I beg your pardon, sir! I told you the exact truth. I am not an employee of the Dade County Medical Examiner's Office. I resigned my job when I was accepted into Pharmacology. I'm still doing some instrument maintenance work for them for pay. But I'm not employed by them. I am an independent contractor, and it takes only a small fraction of my time. I have read the Graduate Bulletin and the Department's Welcome Aboard Package, and I know that I am expected to devote full time to my studies."

"Well," Mr. Jason Diamond Esq. interrupted, "maintenance work would be a form of connection, wouldn't it?"

"Call it whatever you want, but I have read the Graduate Bulletin and the Welcome Aboard Package, and neither of those documents forbids me to do some outside work to pick up a little money here and there."

"And did you have an obligation toward them?"

"Only that I feel sorry for them when their instruments break down and they don't know how to fix them."

Dr. Moore chuckled. Tassel-Toe Diamond frowned for a second and then nodded to the Dean, who continued the interrogation.

"When you were at the DCME Office, did your duties ever involve solving cases of unexplained death?"

"No, sir, I was just a chemist. They never consulted anyone like me on such things. I just did the assays. You know, finding certain chemicals in blood samples. The ones that decided cause of death were the doctors."

The word "doctors" caught the Dean's attention. I got a little flash of nasty inspiration.

"You know what I mean: The doctors who are specialized in *forensic medicine*."

He made a face like he didn't approve of this specialty. Ms. Blanco stared vacuously into space. Tassel-Toe got the Dean's attention by clearing his throat, and nodded to him in a prearranged signal. Apparently they had reached the Continental Divide of their strategy. The Dean lifted a pair of half-cut reading glasses to his face and glanced down at a paper. After a few seconds of hesitation, he resumed.

"So it's correct that you did not consult for anyone with the Dade County M.E.'s Office on any cases involving death since leaving their employ? Is that correct?"

Tassel-Toe was nodding in approval of his well-trained physician.

"That is correct. I did not consult for any of them on human death or any other human condition."

"Aside from your moonlighting as an instrument service technician, did you have any contact with employees of the M.E.'s Office?"

"Well, sir, I did see Dr. Westley . . . how shall I say . . . socially."

"Could you tell me the nature of these *social* meetings?"

Of course, this question had to be in the script, but I was offended by the Dean's manner. The guy thought he had the right to ask me anything.

"Sir, may I ask why you are interrogating me on my social relations?"

The Dean fumed silently. The guy wasn't used to having his motives questioned by underlings.

"My only interest is in a possible connection between recent actions of the Dade County M.E.'s Office and your . . . status as a student here."

Tassel-Toe signalled more approval. I tried to act surprised.

"I see. So that's why − " I made as if lost in thought. Then I pulled myself together and said, "He invited me for dinner − I think as a farewell gesture. He invited me to his condo, and I drank tea with him and his wife. He took an interest in me and invited me back a few times. We talked about science, Egyptology and philosophy. A lot of things. He is a really well-rounded, fine gentleman."

Take that, you healthcare-delivery expert!

"Did you talk with Dr. Westley about the expertise and research interests of the faculty in your department?" asked Tassel-Toe.

"Yes, sir, about every one of them. He was very interested in the different research projects that were going on."

Best to leave the courthouse pigeon a trail of bread crumbs.

"Did you speak to him about Dr. Ledbetter's research interests?"

Tassel-Toe stared at me intently. Ms. Blanco showed more interest. Peter Moore watched from the sidelines like his favorite team was just coming out of a huddle.

"Yes. We spoke about Dr. Ledbetter's research, about his work on cell surface attachment molecules, about selectins, lymphocytes homing, and so forth. I told him some scuttlebutt that Dr. Ledbetter had patented selectins as a means of oral delivery of proteins into the blood stream. You know, that proteins like insulin can't be taken by mouth. The word was that Dr. Ledbetter had invented a way to do it."

A bowl of walnuts in front of a squirrel. Put it out there, all at once. Otherwise, the "discovery" might have taken all day. Dr. Moore chuckled and started to say something, but the Dean waved him off.

"Was Dr. Westley interested in what you told him about Dr. Ledbetter's research?"

"Yes. He asked me a lot of questions about it. More than I could answer. You see, I learned about Dr. Ledbetter's invention second hand – from some med students who took Sophomore Pharmacology. They said that he told them parts of his invention in one of his lectures."

Tassel-Toe said softly to Ms. Blanco, "Please check into this." Then he turned to me and asked, "Do you have any opinion or know any reason as to why Dr. Westley was interested in Dr. Ledbetter's research?"

"Well, he has an inquiring mind. He's interested in everything."

Should I lay it on thicker? What did these people deserve? The Dean who wouldn't shake my hand, the manipulative lawyer and the gruff drug metabolism expert? Go for it, Ben! Give them a "jolly good show."
     First tentatively and cautiously.
     "Well, at least I *think* that was the only reason that Dr. Westley was so interested in Dr. Ledbetter's research."
     Like it was slowly dawning on me that it wasn't true.
     "But – " I lingered.
     Acting myopic and engrossed in thought, I focussed on the Dean's University paperweight.
     "But . . . but . . . but, no! I don't think that there was any other reason other than being generally interested."
     "Are you sure?" asked Tassel-Toe.
     "Yes," I said, pulling myself together, acting resolute and looking inquisitively from one to another.
     "Did Dr. Westley give you indications that he suspected Dr. Ledbetter of having murdered Dr. Cooper?" asked Tassel-Toe.
     "No."
     "Did he tell you he was going to use the information in a criminal investigation."
     "No."
     "Then it must have – strike that – then did it come to you as a surprise when you were questioned by the police about statements that you had made to Dr. Westley about Dr. Ledbetter's research?"
     "Yes," I said excitedly. "The whole thing was quite surprising: getting visited by police officers; being taken downtown; being asked a lot of 'routine questions' about things that I knew nothing about. I wasn't even there when Dr. Cooper died. And then when I tried to ask them questions, they told me to shut up. Said they were the only ones asking the questions."
     I paused for several seconds to catch my breath. You could have heard a pin drop on the carpet. I resumed at a slower pace.
     "But when I got back to the Department and asked around, it turned out that the police had asked a lot of people lots of questions right after Dr. Cooper died. So I didn't make

too much of the whole thing. I was a little disappointed that Dr. Westley didn't tell me that I was going to be questioned. But maybe there was some *reason,* some *legal reason* why it wasn't proper for him to tell me what he had told them . . ."

Seasoned interrogators don't interrupt a spontaneous confession. Savoring my temporary mastery of the situation, I pretended to submerge in thought.

"The practice of law is a very complicated thing, and I'm afraid that I don't understand it very well."

"Mr. Candidi, did you ask Dr. Westley afterward about the interview by the police?" Tassel-Toe asked.

"Yes, I called him up that evening. He said that some of the things I had told him might be significant. Yes, those were the words he used! He said it was just a routine matter, but he had to get the information into the record. He was sorry if it had inconvenienced me, but there wasn't any other way to do it."

"Have you visited with Dr. Westley since the interview with the police?"

"No."

"Why?"

"He told me that he was getting very busy with some professional matter." The Dean and Tassel-Toe nodded to each other. "Those were his words. He said he was getting very busy, and also that his wife was getting sicker. He wished me well. There wasn't very much more that I could say but to wish him well and to wish her better health. Perhaps you know Mrs. Westley," I said, looking to the Dean. "She is in your Ladies' Auxiliary. She has very bad rheumatoid arthritis and some cardiovascular complications. Maybe you could recommend a specialist here at the Medical Center."

The Dean gave a weak smile and shook his head at the improbability of his knowing who was in his Ladies' Auxiliary. I stopped talking. The silence was overwhelming. My interrogators exchanged glances, as if checking whether they had left any loose ends. Then Tassel-Toe capped it off.

"Thank you very much, Mr. Candidi. You have been extremely helpful. This must be very confusing to you, having so many people asking you so many questions. We probably won't have any more questions. Here's my card. If more should occur to you, as to *why* Dr. Westley was so interested in Dr. Ledbetter's research, could you give me a call?"

"Sure," I said, making a show of admiring his card and stroking the raised letters: Jason Diamond, Esq., of Emerson, Waxer and Wanker – at a Bayshore Avenue, Coconut Grove address. It was the Mayan Temple-like building that loomed over my anchorage.

"Mr. Candidi, you would, of course, be willing to reaffirm what you have told us with a sworn statement, if necessary."

"Of course, Mr. Diamond Esquire," I said, extending my hand slowly. He took it and shook it properly. Following his example, Ms. Blanco smiled and extended her hand. The secretary returned my nod and clicked off the tape recorder.

Now was time to see what His Deanship would do. I turned slowly to him with a weak, embarrassed smile. He quickly extended his hand one-third of the way across his desk. I reached across the remaining two-thirds, making a show of leaning across his desk. I received half a shake with no eye contact.

"Dean Alcibides, I hope that I have . . . not – "

I let my deliberately inarticulate words hang painfully in the air.

"No, it's okay."

An Untouchable with leprosy dismissed by a Brahman. Dr. Peter Moore followed me out.

As Moore closed the door, I heard Tassel-Toe saying, "This is clearly a case of – "

This time the elevator ride with Dr. Moore wasn't completely silent. He chuckled.

"So old Westley was interested in what's going on in our Department, was he? He should have come to our seminars. Well, we can't blame you for that, Candidi. There was a big cow-pad on the path, and you just stepped in the middle of it and tracked it into the house."

No further reprimand. Would this be the last interrogation? Probably not. They might play cat and mouse with me right up to the trial. Which ever way they tried to make me hop, it would be bad. If they continued to believe me, they might want to subpoena me as a witness as to how Dr. Westley jumped to conclusions. If they didn't believe me, they'd grill me on the witness stand about what was so attractive about those English dinners. I couldn't lie on the witness stand. Right after my last exam, I'd get out of Miami and stay away until the trial was over. I would have to get Rebecca out, too. I couldn't allow her to learn enough to become suspicious of me. It would be impossible for me to lie to her.

That evening, I broached to Rebecca the idea of sailing to the Bahamas after finals. She could study for her Board Examinations on the boat. She liked the idea as long as there was some way for her to check up on her father once a week.

The spirit of the department became Kafkaesque. And a voice from my recent past came back to haunt me.

– XXXIII –

Fallout

"KAFKAESQUE". IT HAD BECOME Dr. Al Kozinski's favorite expression. It took him days to recover after the police interviewed him. "Aren't certain relationships between colleagues 'privileged,' just like client-attorney relationships?" he asked Dr. Fleischman.

Kafkaesque, distorted, surreal. I was sensitized to little things, like the security guards checking our I.D.s at the front entrance in the morning. In the evening, I felt nauseous when I had to walk around a cluster of guards outside the building. They were getting orders in cop talk from a pudgy, cigarette-smoking Miami Police Department burnout who wore a rumpled navy blazer and gum-soled shoes.

And each day was Kafkaesque. The profs were metamorphosing. Stampawicz became perceptively more aggressive. Maria Mendez thought he was wresting control of the Graduate Program from Taylor. Dr. Sturtz' attitude of sophisticated unconcern metamorphosed into assertive superiority. Robert Gunnison, in his Hawaiian shirt, shorts and sandals, held forth like a hallway philosopher, making vague pronouncements about the need for responsibility in science. And Rob McGregor became tenaciously inquisitive.

And the indictment provided a focal point for our collective angst. The *Miami Standard* carried a short story in the local news section. It stated that Dr. John Ledbetter, Professor of Pharmacology at the Bryan Medical School, was indicted for the murder of his colleague Dr. Charles Cooper. The indictment claimed that he had poisoned Cooper and offered professional rivalry as a motive. The article said that the indictment was supported by medical evidence from the M.E.'s Office. But it said that defense attorney Jason Diamond described the case as "fabrication, flimsy beyond imagination." He was very critical of Dr. Geoffrey Westley.

The next day, Dr. Kozinski's technician called me from across the lab and handed me the phone.

"Ben, this is Alice. Alice McRae from the Mensa Society."

"Hi, Alice. How are you doing?"

"Well, that's what I called up to ask *you*, Ben. You know your department has been in the paper. There's something about one of your profs having poisoned another. What do you make of it?"

I heard a click of a keyboard and office conversation in the background. I could imagine Alice sitting at her computer, ready to take down my every word. She was probably also recording our conversation "for accuracy."

"Alice, all this stuff happened before I came to the Department."

"Sure, but you must know something. You're sitting right in the middle of it."

"Alice, I'm sorry, but I can't tell you anything."

"Why?"

"Because: *One*, I don't know anything and *Two*, we are under orders to say nothing to the media."

"It must be very confusing around there now. Do the professors think – "

"Alice, I'm sorry. I can't say anything."

"Bastard." (Click.)

The next day there was another story in the *Miami Standard*. The headline read "Murder or Coroner's Theory?" It repeated the details of the day before, stating that the indictment hung on an intricate theory of Dr. Geoffrey Westley. The story said that the professors in the Department of Pharmacology were in a state of shock, and that everyone was under orders to give no details.

The next day, I received my own shock. Rebecca and I were eating lunch on a park bench outside the Med School and sharing our feelings. Then I looked up to see Alice McRae sitting with Rob McGregor, just a few yards away! Their bench faced away, but they sat sideways. Alice nodded as she took notes and listened. Rob was smiling and gesticulating, like when he was in one of his high-baud-rate information-transfer modes. Occasionally, Rob would stop and then Alice's lips would move, and suddenly he would be talking again. How many intelligently formulated questions would it take to uncover Ben Candidi? What would they do if they turned and saw me? I gasped, told Rebecca I'd forgotten to turn off the electrophoresis and got the hell out of there.

The next day the *Miami Standard* ran a background piece under Alice's byline. "Sources who declined to be named" confirmed that Ledbetter and Cooper had been fighting for some time. Her sources described Ledbetter as a brilliant but personally difficult scientist. She wrote that within days of Cooper's death, an employee of the Dade County Medical Examiner's Office had made application for study in the Department and was accepted. At this time, it is not clear if there was any relationship between the sudden appearance of this employee and Dr. Goeffrey Westley's eventual findings.

From that day on, McGregor avoided me as much as I avoided him.

Luckily, I wasn't named in the article. Luckily, Rebecca didn't see it. Luckily, that day was Good Friday, and the med students got a one-week Easter vacation. Unluckily, we grad students were still expected to work in the lab. The following Tuesday Dr. Moore sent around a memo saying that we were not to talk to reporters or take any actions which "might confuse the public or compromise the legal proceedings."

I started feeling sorry for Ledbetter and had trouble getting him off my mind. Someone said he had a daughter in a college in the Northeast, and that he had divorced his wife several years earlier. He probably didn't have many friends. What was he doing now? Planning his defense? Was I really sure that he was guilty?

I took refuge in the library, but Ledbetter found ways to haunt me there. While browsing the shelves, I opened a volume of the *Journal of Psychiatric Medicine* to an article titled "The Narcissistic Personality." Seven of the nine listed traits described him perfectly: Extreme reaction to criticism; grandiose sense of self-importance; preoccupied with fantasies of unlimited success; pronounced sense of entitlement; lack of empathy for others; pronounced feelings of envy; and elitist attitude. Or had Ledbetter simply been disappointed about not getting proper credit? I longed to discuss my doubts and feelings. But I had no one. Fondly, I tried to recount Westley's English-Sheepdog lectures on the Divine Scheme of Things. Oh, how I longed to check my moral compass against his.

And torpid weather did its part. By Easter it became quite warm. By late April it turned to summer. The cumulus clouds were back, the thermometer passed 80-degree mark before noon, and it was always humid. And in mid-May, two weeks before final exams, came the African dust. It happens in the summer, every once in a while. A big Saharan sandstorm kicks micron-sized grains of sand thousands of feet in the air, and the Trade Winds carry them to the Caribbean. The dust seems to get pulled down when the winds come ashore. The sky became a haze, and the downtown buildings were indistinct.

In the early evening, two hours before sunset, the sun transformed into a large pale sphere. You could almost mistake it for the moon, except for its slight yellowish cast and lack of features. You could look straight at it without hurting your eyes. And there was no sunset. Well above the horizon, the sun simply faded away and disappeared. No glorious sunsets. No clouds with silver linings. Instead, fallout. When it rained, the cars were covered with dirty splotches.

Then Ledbetter invaded my dreams. One night on the boat I dreamt that I was in a Central American jungle. The Aztecs were rounding up people to tear their hearts out. I came across a large pyramid, partially covered with jungle growth and swarming with warriors. By an act of willpower, I was able to float away. Rising up the side of the pyramid over their heads, I floated over a bald priest, with a large feather head-dress, standing at the top. As he slashed the air with a knife, I recognized Ledbetter's face. I tried to float higher. The warriors shot arrows at me and yelled that I didn't have the right DNA sequence.

Then a well-defined Egyptian pyramid rose like the sun in the East, and I had a vision of Westley in his Pharaoh Chair. And Margaret's voice echoed from the clouds:

"We shall have to tame these savages. And we shall give them a real drubbing if they don't behave themselves! And we'll singe their tail feathers in the bargain, we will!"

The feathered priest shouted out, cursing in the voice of Ledbetter, "Yours is the logic of fools, a sacrilege of science."

Awakening in a nauseous state, I went up to the cockpit. It was covered with dust, and there was no breeze. Coconut Grove gave off its ghostly yellow light. I could make out the Mayan Temple shaped building housing Tassel-Toe Diamond's office. I went below and grabbed a beer to wash down my throat and quiet my nerves.

Rebecca's apartment was air conditioned and dust-free, and her sleeping body was warm and soothing, but Ledbetter still attacked me while I slept there. In a dream, I hovered over a cold, starlit desert floor and glided to a walled city. Holding a short thin rope, I floated over the wall and drifted through a moorish arched window into a palace – floating over the heads of sleeping guards armed with long daggers – drifting into a spacious bed chamber. On the bed slept a regal figure in a long robe. Persian slippers on his feet curled up at a ridiculous angle. He resembled a dead Raja on a funeral pyre, ready for the torch. What was I doing?

Behind me an imperious, English-accented voice, exclaimed, "Not in the slipper, Watson, in the chest!"

But I could find no one behind me. I descended to a small treasure chest at the foot of the bed and plugged the rope into the keyhole. The chest sprang open to reveal glimmering plates and strings of diamonds, each of which held the secrets of the centuries of souls who had possessed them. I slowly perceived them to be optical discs and the diamonds to be computer chips. The sleeping sultan began to stir and transform into Ledbetter. I sensed a light step behind me and saw, reflected in the plate, a dark-haired, veiled maiden.

"The plate is crystal in your hand," she sang in an enchanting but lulling soprano.

"Rebecca!" I shouted.

"Ben," she cried, appearing before me. I sat up as if shot from a bolt.

"Rebecca, he's going to find us," I shouted, waking myself in the process.

"Who?" she asked.

"Led – " I said, swallowing my tongue to stop the last two syllables of Ledbetter's name from betraying me. "Lead to crystal to dagger in the back."

Thankfully, inspiration had not abandoned me.

"Ben, darling. You had a bad dream, but it's over now. Would it help if you told me about it?"

"No."

No, I couldn't tell her. No, I couldn't bear to hear a play-by-play account of the trial. No, I couldn't stand up to scrutiny if they subpoenaed me on my role in the Ledbetter investigation. I could act the smart-ass in front of the Dean, but I wouldn't be able to lie under oath for hours. Westley had known this and had offered a last word of advice: *Do your utmost to keep from getting sucked into this thing.* But the pull was getting stronger by the day, and the situation changed from Kafkaesque to nasty.

– XXXIV –

Escape

SEMESTER ENDS ARE ALWAYS THE same – like the middle of a swan dive from a 32-foot platform. You are accelerated into exam week and go crashing through. In that split second between hitting the surface and arching your back 10 feet below, you learn whether your arms are still in their sockets. I just wanted the semester to be over.

Angst had exacted its toll. Would Alice and her journalist friends publish the "real" story of Ben Candidi? Would Tassel-Toe summon me to testify I was the Old Man's unwitting fool, or would he subpoena me as a conspirator? I lived in constant fear of the process server. But finally it was Monday of exam week, the last week in May. The next day Rebecca and I both had finals.

Rebecca was looking forward to sailing the Bahamas. It fit nicely in the two months between the end of the semester and her National Board Examinations. The boat was not yet provisioned, but I did make two important preparations. First, I located a periodical clipping service, gave them a substantial deposit and ordered every newspaper and magazine article on the Ledbetter trial.

The second preparation was relaxing, even if it did involve a six-mile bike ride west on Bird Road. It took 40 hot, dusty and sweaty minutes of pedaling along that ugly commercial strip before I reached ABBA Radio & Video at 93rd Avenue. I had an appointment with the proprietor, Joe Kazekian. Joe had dropped out of Mensa a couple of years ago. But Joe was always dropping out of something. He dropped out of high school to repair televisions back in the days before the Japanese took over. When TV repair dried up, he switched to video, and from video he moved into commercial videotaping. As an Armenian, he had the videotaping business locked up for every Armenian wedding from Key West to St. Augustine. Now he was dabbling in satellite communications. He came out to greet me as I locked up my bike in front of his shop.

"Ben, if I'd known you were going to ride your bike out here, I would've picked you up with my van. You're taking your life in your hands, riding that thing on Bird Road."

We chatted a little about old times before we got down to business.

"Joe, you've got all the public-access channels here."

"Sure. Everything from the School Board to *Wayne's World*."

"A murder trial of Dr. John Ledbetter will start in a week or two. The trial will probably take a month. I want it taped, gavel to gavel."

"Gee, boss, that won't be any problem, but it's going to take a mountain of tape."

"I'm not asking this as a favor. It's strictly business. I want the whole thing taped, no matter what it takes. You just figure how much the tapes cost, figure your time changing and labelling them, and be sure to charge overhead on your equipment. When it's done, just give me a bill."

Like many Middle Easterners, Joe was never satisfied with a deal that didn't involve bargaining. He was definitely uncomfortable with the words "money is no object."

"But, Ben, what if you get tired of the trial a third of the way through? Give me your number, and I'll call you after I get started."

"I'm telling you now that I want the whole thing, no matter what." To prove the point, I took out my checkbook and wrote a check for a substantial sum. "Here's your retainer. I'll give you the rest when the trial is over. As the saying goes, 'Money talks and bullshit walks.'"

Convinced, but still uneasy, Joe asked, "Where can I get hold of you? Are you still living on that sailboat?"

"Yes, but you can't get hold of me. My girlfriend and I are sailing for the Bahamas in a couple of days."

A knowing smile grew on Joe's face. "I see. Well – "

"Well, I'm counting on you, Joe. And just so you don't forget, can I see your 'in and out' ledger?" Joe showed me, and I picked up a red pen and wrote "Ledbetter Trial" for every day for the next three weeks.

Joe wanted to know all about my sailing partner. He had married a sweet Armenian girl 12 years ago, partially to please his parents. Over the years, she had sort of ballooned out, and Joe had developed a roving eye. He popped in a cassette and showed me clips of 20-year-old Armenian beauties dancing and merrymaking at a weddings he'd recently taped. If it weren't for Rebecca, he might have persuaded me to change my ethnicity. After half an hour's gab, I was back on my bike, pumping east on Bird Road.

At Rebecca's that night, I called Dr. Steve Burk at home. I told him I'd be on vacation for two months and hoped he didn't "need anything done" in that time frame.

"That's fine with us, buddy," he said. They hadn't used me since the final payoff.

"Please give my regards to Dr. Westley," I said. Nothing was holding me back now.

The next morning, Rebecca took her final in Mechanisms of Disease and I took mine in Cardiovascular Pharmacology. It was a real bitch, but I felt good handing in the nine pages.

That afternoon, what made me go back to check out the *Diogenes* instead of studying for the next day's Molecular Genetics final? As I rowed my dinghy round the spoil island, the *Diogenes*' masts came into sight. The hull was obscured by a Boston Whaler, apparently anchored behind it. Then I noticed that the companionway was open. Was I catching burglars in the act? Unfortunately, none of my boat neighbors seemed to be home. My heart raced, as I quickly rowed up to the stern of the Whaler. It was tied to the *Diogenes*' stern. And it wasn't a police boat – no siren and too much personal stuff around. Noises from inside the *Diogenes* told me they were tossing the place. I carefully pulled the dinghy, hand over hand, along the side of the Whaler. I wrote down its Florida registration number on a scrap of paper.

"How much longer we going to be looking here, boss? Bet the guy's clean. All he's got here is his log book and some crap that looks like school notes." High pitched. Definite Spanish accent.

"Just see if the notes have Dr. Ledbetter's name in them," answered a lower voice with a trace of Brooklyn accent.

I let the wind and tide drop my dinghy back until we were even with the Whaler's outboard engine, a 260-horse Johnson. My six-foot length of chain made a handy wrap around their propeller and I secured it with a padlock. Then I pulled the dinghy, hand over hand, to the stern of the *Diogenes*. Their knot was easily undone by my unseen hand and the Whaler was set adrift. Pulling hand over hand along the *Diogenes'* starboard rail, I moved to the bow and secured the dinghy to the anchor line. As I lifted myself onto the deck, the dinghy thudded against the *Diogenes'* hull.

"What's that?"

"Probably a board. I'll take a look," said the lower voice.

I made my way along the starboard lifeline, past the forward hatch, rolling my feet Iroquois style until I was in front of the main mast. The bulge of the sail cover on the boom offered some protection against discovery. One of them may have looked out, but neither came topside.

The open cockpit was a mess. Hatches were open and rubber fenders, life jackets and diving gear were scattered all around. A boat pole and my Hawaiian sling rested on the starboard bench. So I had the choice of bopping them on the head or spearing them like a fish. The spear was already set in the hand grip/launcher, and the rubber straps were in place near the blunt end.

"Maybe he's got a secret compartment. We going to start tearing into the 'glass?"

"Might have to if we don't find what we're looking for," answered the Brooklynite.

"Hey, Joe. He's got a funny bulge by the toilet."

"Here's the tire iron, Al. Go pry it open."

My blood started to boil. I jumped down into the cockpit, grabbed the Hawaiian sling, stretched the rubber bands as far as they would go, and pointed the tip through the companionway into the cabin. "Come out of there with your hands up or I'll run you through. You're both under citizen's arrest."

My spear was three feet from the chest of one of them. The other looked out at me from the V berth. We were all surprised.

"Hey, you've got it all wrong, sonny boy," said the close one in a low Brooklyn voice, looking me over and sizing me up. He was middle-aged, fat and wore a dark sports jacket with an open collar. "We're police officers. And you're the one who's under arrest. For criminal possession of narcotics."

"Like hell you're a policeman! You busted my lock and trashed my boat and – "

"Here, let me show you my badge."

Before I could say anything, his hand was fumbling in the right outside pocket of his jacket.

"Don't move – "

He brought up his hand as if producing a badge. The tear gas hit me faster than I could shut my eyes. After a split second's hesitation, I let loose the sling. My ears told me it struck wood, not flesh. As I gasped for breath, a fist jolted my stomach. I tripped over a fender and fell back on an open hatch, my legs splayed open.

"You little bastard. You point that thing at me?" he growled. A bolt of lightning went up my spine and reverberated in my skull when he stomped my crotch. I gasped, sucking the dripping tear gas deep into my lungs. Doubled up in a paroxysm of coughing, I received a roundhouse to the left side of the face. "Did yuh get a good look at me? You good at identifying narcotics officers?"

"No," I croaked.

"Maybe you wanna get another look at me." He sprayed more tear gas around my mouth and nose.

"You dome sheet! You almost killed me," snarled the high-pitched one. Instinctively, I ducked as the skin on the top of my skull was plowed open.

"Don't kill him, 'cause we aren't going to arrest him. We're letting you off this time, punk."

I rolled back, fell over the side and let myself sink deep below the water's surface. I rubbed the tear gas off my face. It's funny how my face was still full of tears, even under water. My skull ached, and a pink cloud floated around my head. He'd tried to spear me in the face with the tire iron.

I spun around, found the hull of the *Diogenes* and swam to its bow. Drowning in my own pulmonary fluids, my lungs felt ready to burst. But a couple of deep breaths, holding on the anchor line, brought me back to my senses.

"Look what that sheet-bird did," whined the tire iron man. "He cut the Whaler loose. How are we going to get to – "

"He's got a dinghy tied up front," said the pudgy one. We'll row it back." The longer he spoke, the more familiar sounded his voice. I'd heard him around the med school.

I swam to the port side of the *Diogenes* and listened to them on the starboard side, climbing into the dinghy.

"We'd better look around. Maybe he's drowning," said the pudgy tear-gas man.

"No. I saw him swimming under water," said the tire-iron man.

As they rowed away, I collected my energy. The drifting Whaler was now about 75 yards astern. Apparently, there was no one in the anchorage to see those guys beating me up. No use to call for help. As the pair reached the halfway point, I got a clear view. Tire Iron was rowing and Tear Gas was sitting in the back, his fat ass hanging over the transom. Under their combined weight, the gunwales were barely an inch above the water. The arrogant bastards were getting away! I took stock. My groin ached, and the left side of my face felt like it had been slugged by a baseball bat. My scalp was bleeding, but I wouldn't lose enough blood to put me into shock. Tire Iron's face was completely blocked from view by Tear Gas. If I couldn't see him, he couldn't see me. Yes, I could make it. I took off my shoes, pants and shirt, and tied them to the anchor line. Then I swam towards the dinghy in a free-style crawl. It seemed to take forever, but after 40 yards I knew I'd intercept them. With 15 yards to go, I hyperventilated, dove and breast stroked towards them several feet under the surface. I was just starting to gray out when Tear Gas's fat ass came into distorted view above me. I ascended and grabbed the transom, pulling it down with all my might. Water rushed into the dinghy so fast that it surprised even me.

As the dinghy sunk, Tear Gas lurched forward. I climbed up, reached around his shoulders and pulled his jacket back over his arms. The dinghy slipped quickly below the surface and so did he, wiggling his straight-jacketed arms. I pushed his head below the surface. Under water I made out a revolver in a shoulder holster. I reached over his shoulder, tore the gun from the holster, and stuffed it in my underpants.

Tire Iron had fewer clothes, but he must have been a miserable swimmer. He struggled furiously to keep his head above water. I took a deep breath, dove and inspected him under water. The outlines of his wet T-shirt didn't reveal a shoulder holster but his ankle-high boots would make a perfect hiding place. Like a drowning man, he kept sinking below the surface and then clawing his way back up. I positioned myself under him, waited for his downward swing and grabbed. For the price of a kick in the head, I gained possession of one right-footed boot and a .38.

I came up for air five yards away, hyperventilated and tucked the second gun into my underpants. The dinghy was on the weedy bottom, 10 feet below. Groping along its floor, my hands found the tire iron. I grabbed it, surfaced behind Tire Iron Man and clobbered him on the head so hard that the metal hummed like a tuning fork. He panicked and started to climb Tear Gas like a tree. I dove down, circled behind Tear Gas, grabbed his crotch with my right hand and squeezed with all my might. He doubled up and let out an enormous burst of bubbles.

Swimming back to the *Diogenes*, I hoped that the two would drown each other. I called out to the neighboring boats, but incredibly, no one answered. As I reached the stern of the *Diogenes* and looked back, I saw that the pair was now making progress, buddy-swimming toward the Whaler. Remembering my swim ladder escapade with Rebecca, I created a foothold by making a loop in the anchor line. After my third agonizing try, I was sprawled on the deck of the *Diogenes*.

Painfully, I let myself down the front hatch and into the V berth, which looked like it had been visited by a tornado. After a nightmare of slow-motion groping, I finally found what I needed: My telephoto lens and 35-millimeter camera. Luckily, it was freshly-loaded with 36 shots.

Through the companionway, I saw that the two gangsters had made it to the Whaler and were helping each other on board. From deep within the cabin, I clicked off several good face shots as they stumbled around and fired up the big Johnson outboard. It made a horrible sound as they threw it into gear at high revs. I swear that sparks flew out of the water. For a full minute, the jerks tried to make the fouled prop push water. Then they came to their senses and freed the prop with a bolt clipper. I got off a few more shots, catching them and their Florida registration number.

I turned on the VHF and hailed the Marine Patrol on Channel 16. They answered and promised to come just as the Whaler limped away. I took some more shots of the trashed interior, the two revolvers and tire iron. Then I set the lens to short focus and photographed my battered face and gashed scalp. The Marine Patrol took their time, and it was starting to get dark. So I set the swim ladder, cleated a 30-yard line to the stern and set out to recover the dinghy.

Just as the sun was setting, the Marine Patrol roared up in a big Cigarette boat. Officer Mike Carter was tall and muscularly built. He conducted business in a quiet, understated, professional manner. I imagined him as a paratrooper in his younger years. He took the registration number of the Whaler and radio-phoned an inquiry. I told him the whole story and gave him the two revolvers after writing down their serial numbers. He gave me a receipt for them. Just as he was giving me some friendly advice about going to the ER, his hand-held radio crackled and his dispatcher communicated the name and address of the owner of the Whaler. I quickly memorized it: Joseph Klouski and a South Miami address.

When Officer Carter left, I went to the head and took a look at my scalp. The gash was three inches long and bled profusely every time I let up on the bandage. Now, the cabin light was on at Frenchie's. After half an hour of signalling him with a hand-held spotlight, I finally got him on Channel 16.

"Frenchie, could you come over with your first aid kit and some sutures if you have them. Over."

"What is it, Ben? You been scraping barnacles without wearing gloves again? Over."

"No, I caught some bad guys burglarizing my boat, and they gave me a three-inch scalp wound. And I don't want to spend the night at Dade County General. Over."

"I don't blame you. I'll grab my kit and row right over. *Mon Roi* WK three five zero eight seven, over and out."

"*Diogenes* WAR seven one four two, over and out."

Frenchie used to be a hospital corpsman on a Canadian icebreaker. When he rowed over with his black bag, he was real apologetic. He had sterile sutures but no lidocaine. He tried to talk me into going to the ER. I grabbed both ends of the table and told him to do it now. Fifteen stitches and 30 minutes later I was thanking him. He pulled a nonprescription antibiotic ointment from his black bag.

"Put this on it three times a day. And you'd better keep that wound out of the water for the next couple of weeks."

"Thanks, Frenchie. I'll try to do that. And could you keep an eye on the *Diogenes* for the next couple of days. I've got the feeling these guys will come back."

I hailed the Marine Telephone Operator on my VHF and placed a credit card call to Rebecca.

"Rebecca, I'm calling you from the *Diogenes.* We will have to speak slowly because it's coming over the VHF."

"What's the matter, Ben?"

"I can't come home tonight. I've got to stay on board."

"Ben, are you okay?"

"Sort of. I surprised a couple of guys breaking into the boat, and I got hit a couple of times before they got away."

I told her most of the story – leaving out the reason for the burglary, my head wound and how I took away their guns and almost drowned them. I'd stay on the boat that night and go directly to my exam the next day. Rebecca also had a final.

"Oh, Ben. Do be careful."

I gave her my love and signed off. It took a couple of hours to put the boat back in order, including splicing back the alarm wires. It took a couple of hard yanks to pull the spear out of the bulkhead. I reinserted it in the Hawaiian sling and put it next to my berth, so it would be close at hand.

My house cleaning uncovered a strange diskette – a brand I never used. My visitors must have planted it. I taped it to a can of beans so I could deep-six it on a second's notice.

A splitting headache made it impossible to study for tomorrow's exam. So I grabbed a can of beer from the warm ice chest and sat in the cockpit, contemplating the lights of Coconut Grove. Sodium-lamp photons bounced around in a low sky full of African dust, immersing me in an ambrosia-orange city glow. A fuzzy outline of Mr. Jason Diamond Esquire's Mayan pyramid building was visible in the distance. Through the terraced shrubs shone lights from several offices. Was this high priest of law sitting up there plotting my ritual death? My visitors were probably reporting back that they hadn't found any evidence for a Candidi-Ledbetter connection so they planted some on my boat.

Westley's *Faire Isle* complex was but a diffuse glow. What had been his last words of advice? "*Do your utmost to keep from getting sucked into this thing.*" But now I was sucked into it. "*I hope you will be able to weather the coming storm.*" I went to bed but tossed and turned the whole night.

An hour after sunrise, I was on my bike heading for Bryan Medical School. Along the way, I put the planted diskette in a plastic bag and hid it in the crotch of a tree. I also dropped the films off at a drugstore, ordering three sets of prints. Arriving at the Med School library a couple of minutes after opening, I went straight to my locker, expecting to grab my notes and do some last-minute studying. I opened the door to find things subtly rearranged. I pulled out my computer, flipped it on and quickly searched the name "Ledbetter." My heart skipped a beat as two files came up on the screen. One contained Ledbetter's hate correspondence with Dr. Cooper. The other was a complete text of his European patent application. I deleted them both and overwrote all the free disk space.

I complained to the head librarian that my locker had been entered. She wasn't a very good liar. She offered to give me a new lock, which I declined. Returning upstairs, I cleaned out my locker and turned in the lock at the front desk. Why give them another chance to plant evidence?

The Med School telephone directory listed Joseph Klouski, all right – Assistant Head of Security! That's where I'd seen him before – outside the Med School puffing cigarettes and debriefing his uniformed security officers. Well, I would deal with him later. Now I had a final exam. I went back upstairs and crammed molecular genetics.

Around noon, I grabbed a bite at the hamburger place and then went over to the classroom. I caught a glimpse of Maria, staring at her notes with a worried expression. When she looked up at me, she looked even more worried.

"Ben! What happened to you? You look horrible. What happened to your face?"

"I caught some guys breaking into my boat and there was a little scuffle." I gave Maria a quick, sanitized version of yesterday's events.

"An what's with that baseball cap? You've got it on backwards, like a teenager."

"It's going to bring me luck on the exam."

"Ben, there's something that I've got to tell you. Some security people have been coming around, asking about you – yesterday afternoon and this morning. They set up in the conference room. Dr. Moore's secretary went around to the labs and brought us in, one by one."

"What did they want to know?"

"They told me there were reports that you'd been acting strange. They said some people felt threatened. They asked me if I had noticed anything strange about you. They wanted to know if I ever saw you going into any labs where you didn't belong."

"What did you tell them?"

"What do you think I told them, Ben! I told them they was crazy. I told them I never saw you do nothing wrong!"

"Sorry. I didn't doubt you. I know you're my friend."

"You'd better believe it, Ben."

"What else did they ask? "

"They didn't ask anything more. They said that it was a routine inquiry. They said that it was confidential, and I shouldn't talk to anybody about it."

"Thanks for tipping me off."

"Ben, do you know that there is a rumor going around that the coroner sent you here to investigate Dr. Ledbetter?" Her voice quavered and her eyes exuded empathy.

"It doesn't surprise me. Dr. Moore hauled me down to the Dean's Office several weeks ago, and they practically asked me the same thing, point blank. I guess they didn't believe me, if they're sending around security people to make a liar out of me."

"Ben, you take good care of yourself," she said softly.

Our classmates were filtering in, and we couldn't say more. Dr. Sturtz handed out the exam, and soon we were struggling with the problem of "clearly and precisely" stating how to find a piece of DNA encoding a target protein of the tyrosine kinase enzyme, using an anti-tyrosine phosphate antibody and standard molecular cloning technology as our "primary tools." The exam question listed a number of "special features" of the target protein. The problem was the mental equivalent of parachuting into the middle of the Everglades, equipped with a pocket knife, collapsible drinking cup and chlorine tablets, and being given three days to trudge your way out.

Two hours later Sturtz came back and collected the exam. Rebecca had one more exam tomorrow, and then we could get out of town. Just one problem: How to inform Dr. Taylor I wouldn't be around, without coming right out and saying it? He was in his mop-closet office reading one of his *Nature* magazines.

"Boy! Do you look a sight," he exclaimed looking at the left side of my face. "What happened to you? Did you run into a locked door while prowling around here at night?"

No boisterous laugh, this time.

"I'm afraid I don't know what you are talking about, Dr. Taylor."

"Well, perhaps it's just my imagination. You look like a street punk, with that hat on backwards. Did you fall off your skateboard?"

"Would you believe that I fell off my bicycle?"

"Well, you seem to be unmitigated and undeterred. Pray tell, what may I do for you?"

"I wanted to ask your permission to postpone my next laboratory rotation for a few weeks."

"I suppose you would like to spend the time in a front-row seat at Dr. Ledbetter's trial," he snarled.

"No way. I've had it up to here with that thing," I said, bringing my flattened palm to just above eye level.

"So precisely how do you propose to use the time?"

"To study for medical pharmacology. They say grad students have a harder time with it than med students."

"So you propose to study pharmacology in the library?"

"No, I was planning to study at home, actually."

"Where *do* you live? You never did give us a proper address."

"I live four hundred yards off of Dinner Key, on my sailboat."

"On a sailboat?" he challenged, like I'd just told him I lived in a whorehouse.

"Yes a thirty-eight foot, two-masted Choi Lee."

"Indeed! And how will we get hold of you?" he asked, as

if this were his constitutional right.

"Get hold of me?"

"Yes, if we need to *communicate* with you."

"Leave a note in my pigeon hole. Or write to my post office box in Coconut Grove."

"And if we need to get hold of you on short notice?"

"I'm moored in the Dinner Key Anchorage."

"And one could find you there any time?"

"Unless I sail down to the Keys for a long weekend."

"Pray tell how we would get hold of you then."

"I'll listen to Channel Sixteen every night at eight."

"Channel Sixteen, bloody hell! Do you expect us to – "

"That's only if you need to get me in a hurry. You just call up the Coast Guard, or better yet, the Marine Operator."

"It seems very complicated and I don't know if I could approve – "

"I do get to call the weekends my own, don't I?"

"Well, yes, I suppose."

Immediately after leaving Dr. Taylor, I put a note in his pigeon hole, reiterating what I had just told him. For my own protection, I made a photocopy. In my own pigeon hole, I taped a note requesting that all my mail and notices be forwarded to my post office box.

Balancing on my handlebars a big garbage bag full of my academic possessions, I must have looked like a homeless person. My first stop was the drugstore. The photos proved well worth the $14. Despite my jittery hands and the blood on my eyelashes, I'd taken the best telephotographs of my life. There were enough photos of Klouski's face to make a holographic 3-D picture. The Florida registration number came out clearly, and you could even make out one of the oars from the sunken dinghy floating near the Whaler's bow. I bought some envelopes and stamps, and I hastily drafted a letter to the Florida Marine Patrol Officer Carter, enclosing one set of photos. I mailed the second set to myself at my post office box and kept the third in my backpack.

Next, I quickly pedaled a mile down the road to the Coconut Grove Bank. They were just closing the lobby, but I pleaded my way in and deposited the negatives in my safe-deposit box. Outside, I made a hefty withdrawal from the automated teller machine. Next I rode my bike to the tree and reclaimed the planted diskette. Then there was some heavy-duty shopping to do at the Super Check, up where the Grove meets U.S. 1. Finally, after a quarter of an hour outside the supermarket, I found the right guy to help me – a construction worker carrying a cold six-pack back to his pickup truck.

"Hey buddy, I'm in a jam. Let me give you twenty dollars for the use of your truck and fifteen minutes of your time."

"What-shu got that needs haulin'?"

"This," I said gesturing to 12 bags of groceries, my garbage bag and my bicycle. "Just need to get'm down to the Coconut Grove waterfront."

"Shouldn'da bought all that stuff if you don't got no car."

"I lost her last week. She threw a rod. Hard times. We live on a boat, and we've gotta get out of town quick."

"I'll back my truck in right here," he said, pointing to a ten-foot open space along the fire lane.

Minutes later, my dinghy was packed solid with groceries and the garbage bag. I laid my bike over the top. It took a little argument to make the guy take even $10 – and then he gave me one of his beers. So we tossed one down together. After we wished each other luck and he drove off, I phoned Rebecca. I'd have to make my move right away. If she couldn't leave tomorrow afternoon, maybe she could take Chalk's Airline and meet me in Bimini.

"Hello."

"Rebecca, I've been tied up with provisioning the *Diogenes*."

There was a long silence, and I knew there was trouble before she said her next word.

"Ben, I can't go . . . Mother called me this afternoon, right after my exam. It's about Dad. His diagnosis. It's pancreatic cancer. He doesn't have six months to . . . to . . ." she broke into a deep sob, "to live."

"Oh, darling. I'm so sorry. I – "

"You see, Ben, I have to *be* with him," she whimpered.

"Yes, darling. Of course." My brain was whirling. Maybe I could get Frenchie to watch after the *Diogenes,* and I'd go up with her to New York. "Go up there right away. Take your books along and study for the Boards. Maybe I could come up for a while."

"Oh, I don't know, Ben. I can't think now. It might be hard for me. Mother and Father haven't accepted the idea . . . And now that Father's going to – " She cried convulsively and then was abruptly silent. She must have put her hand over the transmitter.

"Rebecca, I understand. I just meant that I could get a room in one of those tourist hotels. Or maybe I could stay with Dad and his girlfriend in Newark."

"I just don't know, Ben. Wait. There's someone at the door."

I could hear the knocking getting louder as she walked with the phone to the door. I heard a metallic clank of the security latch and pictured the door partially opened.

"Process server, Dade County. Are you Miss Rebecca Levis?"

"Yes."

"We're informed that Mr. Ben Candidi is living here. I am directed to serve this summons for him to appear in the matter of the State of Florida versus John Ledbetter, as a witness for the Defense. In the name of the Law, I direct you to open your door so that he may be duly served."

"Rebecca!" I pleaded. "Stall, and listen to me."

"Just a minute, please. I'm on the phone." I heard the clank of the security latch.

"Rebecca, listen carefully. I've got to disappear for a couple of months. You've got to trust me. You'll hear a lot of bad things about me. Don't believe them. I can't tell you now. Don't ask why. Just trust me."

"But, B – " She caught herself before pronouncing my name. "But, darl – " She caught herself again, with a desperate sob.

"Miss, you'd better give me the phone now."

"Just trust me!" I pleaded, then hung up in a split second. It was already dark. I pulled out another quarter and called up Western Union. Pacing back and forth, I worked my way through their touch tone routing menu. Finally I was answered by the voice of an elderly Southern lady. I gave her my American Express number and dictated a telegram.

> Dear Rebecca: I love you. I want to spend my life with you. I want to marry you. But I cannot see you for two months. I have done nothing wrong but can't explain. Forever yours, B.

The lady asked, "Can we phone this telegram to your party? A copy will arrive in the mail."

"No! I want it to go to her hands and to no one else's hands."

"We do offer personal delivery service, although it may take an extra day if the party is not home."

"Do it. I don't care what it costs. God bless you and your company."

"And may God bless you too, young man. And always remember – Jesus loves you."

Fifty yards out from shore, I remembered the lady's words. My overloaded dinghy's rail was little more than one-half inch above water level. Twice I came within a hair's breadth of sending the whole mess to the Deep Six. Thirty minutes later, I put one hand on the *Diogenes* stern and took my first deep breath. I tied the painter to the aft cleat and manhandled the bike and bags into the cockpit. I stowed the dinghy on board, lashing it down over the forward hatch.

I fired up the engine and furiously hauled in the two anchors, leaving them in a muddy heap on the forward deck, resting on a bed of coiled anchor line. Time to make things shipshape later. I flipped on the navigation lights, pulled out the spotlight and signaled *Mon Roi.* Frenchie appeared on deck just as I passed by his stern.

"I'm going down to the Keys for a few days, Frenchie."

"Ben, switch on Channel Thirty-two. We need to talk."

"Sorry. Can't talk."

"But, Ben!"

I motored out at full speed towards the southern tip of Key Biscayne. For 30 seconds at a time, I left the helm to stow the grocery bags, bike and anchors. Should have bought that autopilot. Thirty minutes later I was half way to the Stiltsville Channel. I put on a life jacket, pointed into the wind, and hauled up the main. Had to run back from the mast to the helm several times to correct the steering. Really should have bought that autopilot. Repeated the routine to raise the jib. Better to hoist canvas here than risk falling off the boat in the Gulf Stream.

With a 12-knot south wind filling two sails, the *Diogenes* fell into pace, holding course with no help from me. Allowing myself a breather, I looked back at Coconut Grove, wondering if I could ever return. Then I made out a Cigarette boat roaring up to my anchorage. As it came off plane, its spotlight flicked on and began illuminating the boats. Probably the Florida Marine Patrol looking for the *Diogenes*. So I didn't haul up the mizzen sail, hoping they'd take us for a sloop. And I kept the diesel engine running to make full speed.

Ten minutes later, the Marine Patrol boat moved into the Dinner Key harbor and out of sight. I was just making my way through the Stiltsville Channel and out to the Atlantic when he reemerged and headed south with his blue lights flashing. They'd be looking for me down in the Keys like I told Dr. Taylor and Frenchie.

An hour later I was rolling in three-foot waves of the Atlantic Ocean, hoisting my mizzen sail. I killed the engine. The boat held steady while I went below to turn on the VHF and get my spotlight and flare gun. You need them all when a freighter comes bearing down on you in the night. It didn't take much listening on Channel Sixteen before I heard the *Diogenes* being hailed. I tied a rope around my waist and tied it to the helm. Within two hours the Miami skyline was little more than a glow off my stern. Let the process servers search the Florida Keys all they wanted. I had just passed the 12-mile limit, which put me outside U.S. jurisdiction. They probably couldn't subpoena me in the Bahamas.

It was a lonely run, running away from the trial, from the Ph.D. Program and from Rebecca – thinking that all three were probably lost. Rays from the half moon danced on the three sails of my rocking boat like they had danced on the palm tree that night on Miami Beach with Rebecca. The red glow of the binnacle light brought back memories of the enchanted evening when we consummated our love. Now, love would be a memory. My one constant friend would be my compass.

I sailed on through the night without being run down by a freighter, without dozing at the helm and without getting knocked out by a flying fish. Landfall at Bimini came shortly after sunrise. I had to keep slapping myself in the face to stay awake while pulling down the sails, maneuvering in behind the winding sandbar and motoring through the narrow channel to the Bimini harbor. I tossed out the anchor, raised the yellow quarantine flag and then sank into my berth with a sigh of relief which quickly resolved into slumber.

An hour later, I was awakened by a loud roar. Drunk with sleep, I scrambled topside just in time to catch a shower of propwash from an amphibious twin-engined Grumman Mallard of Chalk's Airline, as it "taxied" past me. The horizontal spray washed all of the African dust from the port side of the boat. I had to laugh as the old bird literally waddled its way up the ramp, with its rudder flapping back and forth like a duck's tail, until it stood on solid ground. "The Mallard quacks across the cove." But it wasn't bringing Rebecca.

After a bite to eat, I motored to the Alice Town "customs dock" and filled out a declaration. Then I reclaimed my mooring. I slept deeply through a sultry day and fitfully through a balmy night.

The next morning, computer in hand, I went topside to meet the first rays of the sun. I inserted the planted diskette and read it. It contained the same two files they planted in my hard drive at the library. Hands trembling, I removed the foreign diskette. As soon as I reached open water, I'd deep six the fucker. Half an hour later, a small wooden runabout pulled away from the dock at the Big Game Fishing Club and motored directly toward me. A young black man sat in back, steering with the outboard motor. He was shirtless and shoeless, but wore long black pants. I waved to him, and he smiled. He throttled down and drifted towards me, until his bow was 10 yards off my stern.

"I know I see right from de observation deck of de Club. This is the *Diog .. gen ..es*," he said, referring to a piece of paper. "So you must be Mr. Benjamin Can .. di .. di. I have a message for you from Mr. Jason Diamond."

"Sorry, you've got the wrong boat. This is the *Dionysian* and I am Marcus Lucifer," I said emphatically.

"But he tell me on the telephone to look for a two-masted Choi Lee and here be just such a boat, man."

"The *Dionysian* is a Grampian sloop, retrofitted as a ketch. How do you like my wooden planking? I installed it myself."

"Hey, man, Mr. Diamond is goin' to take it real bad if I do not deliver his message."

"Do you know him?"

"Yeah, man, he come to de Club with his deep V all de time. He take me out to fish and I bait his line and show him de good places and he pay me good. Hey, man, you give me break and take de message so I get what Mr. Diamond promise me! I know *you* de boat he looking for. If I call him back and say you don't take de message, maybe he don't give me de money."

"How much money did he promise you?"

"He say he give me twenty dollar. Say, man! You know of Mr. Diamond?"

"Just by reputation. They say he's a very rich man who is very stingy with his money. Wait just a minute."

I went to the wet locker, pulled out a $50 bill, came back topside and flashed it. It was like waving a steak in front of a hungry dog.

"Look. What did you say your name is?"

"Malcolm, Malcolm Williams."

"And do you remember my name?"

"You say you be Marcus Lucy."

"Right, Malcolm! Now I'm interested in seeing that Mr. Diamond gets his message to the right place, since he's such a big, important man. Now listen carefully. I saw a two-masted Choi Lee named the *Diogenes* heading north yesterday afternoon. So if I give you this fifty dollars, do you think you could set out right now, *without stopping back at the Club*, and motor a ways north, looking for that boat?"

Malcolm stared at me with curiosity. I simply waited until the look of understanding came slowly to his face. I smiled and continued my instructions.

"You could take most of the day looking for him. And then you could come back at four-thirty and call Mr. Diamond. Tell his secretary that the man told you wrong and that there's no *Diogenes* here. And that would be *all you would say*! Think you could do that?"

"Yeah, man! I give him a good search," Malcolm said with a grin.

"Good, here's the fifty dollars. I want Mr. Diamond to get what he deserves. Be sure to call him collect."

"No problem. "Malcolm started to motor away, but then throttled down and called back. "Hey, man. How good you know Mr. Diamond?"

"Well enough that I will find out if you don't do right by me, man! Well enough to call him up and let him know! When Mr. Diamond comes back to visit next time, I hope you have some more good fishing trips with him."

"No problem." Malcolm throttled up and headed north.

– XXXV –

Exile

*S*O MUCH FOR RESTING A FEW days in Bimini. As Malcolm motored out of sight, I hauled anchor and headed south to Vic-
tory Cay. Passing Turtle Rocks, I remembered my plan to take
Rebecca diving there. Couldn't even visit the reef myself. My
scalp was oozing and swimming might make the infection worse.
The first night was spent at Gun Cay. Next, I made a day and
night run at 099 degrees to Joulters Cay, north of Andros Island.
I spent the next several days putting distance between myself
and all authority, sailing by day and anchoring at night.

There weren't many boats around, and those I did see
showed no interest. It was a short jump to Frazers Hog and
Berry Islands. Then I sailed east across the deep water of the
Northeast Providence Channel to Current Isle and on to
Eleuthera, that long strip of coral that extends so many miles.

The sailing was like the dreadful ecstasy of an opium
trance. It served no purpose except to occupy my mind and
kill time. The infection went systemic, and the fever must have
lasted a week. The sailing was a dream of Rebecca at my side,
yet out of reach, with time, like sand, slipping through my
fingertips – no beginning and no end – like the endless expanse of water before me.

As the morning sun rose, I looked over the side of my
anchored boat into my exotic garden of coral, sea fans, sand
and striped fish. Forgetting my festering scalp, I plunged into
the beautiful garden, disturbing it by only a ripple. The plunge
was a daily rebaptism that washed away the memories of Mi-

ami and cleansed my mind of bad thoughts. Every day I moved another 10 miles along Eleuthera and planted my anchor in a new coral patch.

Slowly, as weeks rolled by, I came back to myself. De Maupassant and Dostoevski were on board. Dostoevski fit my mood, and slowly brought me back to reality. As I regained capacity for emotion, I switched to de Maupassant, who made me lovesick for Rebecca. Then my mind slowly wandered back to science. Next, came an outpouring of meta-scientific ideas. How the ship is like a cell, how its master is like its DNA, and how its thin, fiberglass hull is like the fragile cell membrane. Together, master and ship can survive all challenges the sea has to offer.

I have my ship, and his name is *Diogenes*. He's all that I have left, and survival is my game.

My entire life was on hold until the verdict on Ledbetter was rendered.

Uncertain whether I was still in the pharmacology program at Bryan Medical School, I studied halfheartedly from Goodman and Gilman's pharmacology book. My mind often drifted back to sociobiology – like the *Scientific American* article on chimpanzee sociology. Crowded into laboratory colonies, chimps do the same as people crowded into organizations: some start bossing. After the bossy ones achieve control over their cage-mates, aggressive boss chimps have healthy hormone levels. And, of course, the submissive chimps get unhealthy hormone levels. Perverse old Mother Nature! Always rewarding the bad guys.

Paper and pencil in hand, I tried to summon philosophy to the rescue. I wrote down two contradictory theses: Thesis 1: People must suppress selfish inclinations if civilization is to exist. Thesis 2: Society's self-serving manipulators will use the framework of civilization to trap you in a self-destructive spiritual cage. What would Dr. Westley's Old English Sheepdog have to say about this? Was Old Anglican Westley any better than I at fathoming The Divine Scheme of Things?

The philosophical brooding must have drained my lymph, because my spiritual strength gradually returned. I set sail for New Providence and anchored on the south side of the island. For fear of being discovered, I didn't put in at Nassau on the north side. I rowed ashore, chained up my dinghy and set off on my bike. After pedaling over 20 miles of bumpy asphalt and crushed coral, I found a telephone that would accept my credit card number. I spent two full days trying to call Rebecca, but could not get through. Finally, I settled for a lengthy telegram. As the days wore on, I became curious about the trial. New Providence had a newspaper but there was little information from Miami.

My miniature black-and-white TV didn't yield anything useful. There were plenty of AM radio stations to listen to – Island D.J.s and endless rumba from Cuba. I spent a lot of time scanning for a Miami station and finally picked up a news and talk station with a weak, unreliable signal. After many hours of listening to it fade in and out, I was rewarded with something about "another day of expert scientific testimony in the murder trial of – "

Two days later, the trial was the subject of a call-in talk show. The ether was better, but the show was like seeing the world through the eyes of a dimwit.

"All scientists are crazy, anyhow."

"Sure they would poison each other. They poison rats and dogs."

"You can't trust doctors. And scientists are just like doctors. So you can't trust scientists, either."

"They should be finding a cure for AIDS instead of killing each other."

"This ding-blasted thing reminds me of that Woody Allen movie. If they had this guy in the freezer, maybe they should of turned him over to the Deep Freeze Society. Maybe they should of waked him up in a coup'la hundred years when they get cures for them poisons."

The next day, the topic of talk show conversation was lesbian love triangles. So eight weeks after leaving Miami, I set sail for Bimini hoping to pick up a stronger radio signal.

I moored in Bimini Harbor and made occasional forays

into Alice Town, mostly to send telegrams to Rebecca. It was past the point of trying to call her on the phone. If she lost faith in me and went back to her old boyfriend, a phone call couldn't change it. Worse yet, I wouldn't know what to say if she asked about my role in the Ledbetter thing. Better to telegraph my love to her at $2 a word.

Bimini must have had a repeater station because my TV picked up the Miami stations nicely. It was "Tough Guys Week" on the independent channel. For a week of evenings, I compared myself with Chuck Norris, Charles Bronson and, finally, Humphrey Bogart.

Immediately following *The Deep Sleep, Eyewitness News* broke the story:

"The seven-week-long murder trial of Dr. John Ledbetter, Professor of Pharmacology at the Bryan Medical School has just come to an end! After three hours of deliberation, the jury turned in a verdict of guilty of first-degree murder. The trial told a story of professional jealousy leading up to murder by poisoning. Weeks of testimony by expert scientific witnesses told a story of a carefully crafted poison formulation based on state-of-the-art pharmaceutical technology."

The screen showed pictures of the GC-mass spectrometer in the M.E. Lab.

"Through careful and methodical analysis, Dade County Medical Examiner Dr. Geoffrey Westley was able to prove that Dr. David Cooper was murdered by three micro-encapsulated toxins, injected into a hamburger which he ate at a meeting at work. The most dramatic portion of the trial was when the jury was shown actual video footage of Dr. Ledbetter's arrest while attempting to destroy the sample with which Dr. Cooper was murdered. Painstaking scientific analysis was presented by a large panel of scientific experts from universities across the country. The method of toxin release from the preparation was actually patented by the defendant, Dr. John Ledbetter, for use in pharmaceutical products, and may still be used to cure diabetes."

While the male anchor read this, the screen showed footage of attorneys questioning witnesses. Then came a dramatic scene, looking down on the Revco freezer as a latex-gloved hand opened it and removed a vial. Then came a down-the-hall shot of a man approaching with a mop, a couple seconds of animated but mute conversation, and Dr. Ledbetter running away and being tackled by a second "janitor." All three concentrated on the vial like it was a football in play. The screen faded and blended to a courthouse steps interview with Alan W. Smith, the prosecuting attorney:

"It was the high-tech crime of the century. A murder which was as brilliant in its execution as it was evil in its intent. Our office has never had such a complex case. A major share of the credit goes to Medical Examiner Westley, whose expertise and insight identified this bolt-from-the-blue death as the intentional poisoning which it was."

The screen faded and blended to a face and chest shot of the Old Man, sitting in the leather chair in his office.

"It was a murder, most foul," he said in a soft but resolute voice with Shakespearian overtones. "As soon as the case and the details surrounding the tragic death of Dr. Cooper came to my attention, we took the *extraordinary* step of freezing and storing his remains at liquid-nitrogen temperature, together with the remains of his fatal lunch which we were lucky to retrieve from his wastebasket. In this manner, we were able to put the evidence into – to use a fanciful science fiction expression – into *stasis,* permitting us time to conduct a thorough scientific investigation requiring months of effort. I wish to thank the Miami Police Department for some excellent *footwork*, so to speak, and Dr. Ledbetter himself for providing us with a few shortcuts."

The unseen male reporter asked, "Is it fair to say that this is your most puzzling case, Dr. Westley?"

"Well, Miami offers so many puzzling cases. But I should think that my most intriguing case was the one of the opened skull of a 4,000-year-old mummy, which I investigated for the Egyptians a while back. We had considerably greater obstacles in that investigation since the evidence was, as it were, con-

346   Dirk Wyle

siderably more *dusty*, so to speak – "

The picture faded and the screen returned to the studio anchorman who turned in his chair to face his weatherman.

"Well, Jack, after that *dry* performance do you have any rain for us?"

So I now had hope. Hopefully, Joe Kazekian had taped everything so I could know for sure. The TV weatherman showed a tropical wave and predicted some stormy weather.

– XXXVI –

Return

*T*HE NEXT MORNING, A STRONG northerly wind blew intermittent rain through the Bimini Harbor. High seas would make it too dangerous to cross the Gulf Stream. After two days it calmed, and I set out at first light, sailing perpendicular to the wind and making good time. As I reached the middle of the Stream, a dot appeared on the horizon. It grew slowly, eventually transforming into a cluster of skyscrapers. For the rest of the journey, Miami rose slowly from the water like the Lost City of Atlantis.

By sunset, the *Diogenes* was tied up at the Matheson Hammock Marina, a yacht basin carved out of a mangrove swamp, five miles south of Dinner Key. Luckily, the customs inspector was already there for a string of big power boats. I paid the dockmaster for a couple weeks' berthing.

The mosquitoes and "no see-em's" tormented my sleep. The next morning, a Wednesday, I called a cab and went into action. I would need correct answers for everything before I could show my face at the Department of Pharmacology. As I walked into ABBA Radio & Video, Joe Kazekian greeted me with mixed emotions.

"Ben, you'd better not change your mind about those tapes, because I've got a whole shitload for you," he said, ushering me into his back room and pointing to several three-foot stacks. The VCR cassettes were all labelled by date and ready to go.

"Thanks, Joe. I knew I could count on you. Have you put together a bill?"

"Yes, but you'd better sit down before I show it to you. The tapes themselves are about seven hundred dollars."

"Whatever you wrote up, I am sure it's fine. We've known each other for a long time," I said, taking the bill from under one of the stacks. Zeekie had put down $400 for his labor, and, of course, he'd make a little off of the tapes. "This is just fine," I said, pulling out my checkbook.

"Well, it did keep me busy, popping in and out tapes. But that stuff was pretty interesting – some of it. I had the audio playing in the shop."

I continued writing the check, saying nothing. Zeekie fidgeted for a second and then said, "Hey, I know that murder happened at the place where you're studying, but how do you come off spending one grand to tape the trial? I mean a guy could buy a used car for that kind of bread."

"Well, let's just say that the thing is more real to me than a used car. Let's say I have a scholarly interest."

Zeekie looked puzzled.

"You writing a book or something?"

"Let's say I've been thinking about it."

A knowing smile came to Zeekie's face.

"You better get it together fast, because this thing's all over the TV and magazines now. But in a year everyone's going to forget about it."

"I agree completely," I said, handing Zeekie the check. "I hope that the bill covers everything you did for me. Now if you could just get me a box, and maybe I could get a ride."

"Sure."

"And could you give me a deal on a VCR?"

"What kind are you looking for?"

"One that will work on a sailboat and will last long enough for me to run through all this shit."

"Sure. I've got just the baby for you," he said, gesturing to the end of the bench. "I call her 'Ferina.' Found her on a trash pile in Liberty City. Only thing wrong was that they gummed up the drive wheels and broke the belt. I put eighty dollars into her. I'll let you have her for ninety."

I acted like it was a big decision. It was Joe who broke the silence:

"OK, I'll let you have her for eighty-five dollars."

"A deal."

So we got in some Middle-Eastern bargaining after all.

Joe left the shop in the hands of his assistant and drove me by the Coconut Grove Post Office where I pulled several pounds of mail from my box. Most of it was from my clipping service. There was also a letter from Dr. Taylor, postmarked the day after my departure, demanding that I contact him immediately regarding an "urgent matter."

Setting the VCR and the four boxes of tape on the dock at the marina, Joe said, "If anyone wants to make a documentary out of this, remember me. I've got editing equipment."

I loaded my booty into a dock cart and rolled it along the concrete dock to Slip C5. The tapes filled the whole wet locker and part of the V berth. Dripping sweat, I put the VCR in a plastic bag and tied it tightly. On the dinette table, I pieced together the newspaper clippings. As I assembled the journalistic jigsaw puzzle, a low-resolution picture of the trial emerged.

The opening argument of the prosecution described Ledbetter and Cooper engaged in a war. Ledbetter was infuriated to the point where he microencapsulated the three toxins. Minutes before the faculty meeting, he added water to his preparation until it had the consistency of mayonnaise, put it into a syringe and injected it into Cooper's hamburger.

The prosecution described the trial run with the two dogs and linked it to the preparation that killed Cooper. After Cooper's death, the M.E. drained all of the blood from his body. They put his blood, organs and remainder of his body in a liquid-nitrogen freezer. Later, they sampled his blood and tissues and found the same toxins that were in the vial at the med school.

"POISON VICTIM PULLED FROM 'DEEP SLEEP' TO TESTIFY IN OWN MURDER CASE," proclaimed one tabloid.

The local press carried stories every second day. There

were many photographs of Ledbetter, Cooper, Cooper's wife, and the prosecuting attorney. Early on, the trial was reported briefly in *Time* magazine:

"MODERN FORENSIC MEDICINE: INGENIOUS JUSTICE OR HIGH-TECH WITCH-HUNT?"

The *coup de gras* from the prosecution was the video tape of the arrest, which was described in vivid detail in the print press.

"SCIENTIST MURDER SUSPECT CAUGHT BY UNDERCOVER POLICE WHILE REMOVING POISON COCKTAIL."

The defense consisted of a parade of expert witnesses. They asserted that sudden death is not an infrequent occurrence. They argued the M.E.'s proof was a sham and that small amounts of toxins can be found in the body anyway. They debunked the State's case as a harebrained theory of an eccentric coroner who had lost touch with reality. The Defense claimed Westley had seized on a chance observation from an ex-employee of his office to cook up this theory. Their experts were "cross-examined savagely" by the prosecuting attorney.

The defense disputed the assays for toxin in Cooper's blood. They disputed the dog evidence and argued that other people could have used an entrance badge. They said the videotaped arrest was entrapment of the most crass type: Wouldn't a scientist working late at night be surprised when a janitor told him he was under arrest? In fact, they replayed the video tape to bolster their theory of Ledbetter's startled reaction.

Halfway through the defense case, the clippings described the trial as a battle of experts, with everything revolving round whether antibodies are specific enough to assay E 7532, KN 25 or O-35.

The press had major difficulty with the technical testimony, and began calling it "a high-tech Mexican standoff between two bands of hired-gun expert witnesses." But then, in a surprise move, Ledbetter took the stand in his own defense. He testified that he worked with all sorts of toxic principles, so it should be no surprise to find some of them in his lab freezer. But under hours of "grueling cross-examination," he apparently held up badly. When the prosecuting attorney persisted in asking why he had the vial in his hands the night he was arrested, he broke into a rage, criticizing police and prosecutors of "sloppy thinking" and of using "fuzzy logic."

The latest batch of clippings told the story of the guilty verdict of first-degree murder. Sentencing was not yet imposed. After the verdict, the press came down on Westley's side, reporting in more depth on the three toxins and a timed-release microencapsulation. They commented that it had been clever of Dr. Westley to "break the scientific case" and find the particles, caught in the act of releasing poisons inside Cooper's body. Westley emerged as the hero. The *Miami Standard's* Sunday supplement, *The Cabana*, carried a four-page article and interview giving his version of how he cracked the case.

The story mentioned me briefly as the one who'd unwit tingly given Westley a crucial bit of information – that Ledbetter was working on a means of oral delivery of proteins to the blood stream. There was a small picture of me, taken from my University photo I.D. – mousey and unimpressive, ponytail showing.

The article had an impressive picture of Westley pulling an unidentifiable cadaver from refrigerated vault. If it had been of marble and not of stainless steel, it could have been a mausoleum vault. The *Cabana* article had pictures of Westley standing on his balcony and in front of his Silver Shadow. They described him as a "cultivated English gentleman."

The story was picked up by *People* magazine, which ran a shorter version with a more revealing photograph: A strong, determined, yet aristocratic Goeffrey Westley sitting in his Pharaoh Chair, each hand gripping the base of the jackal figures. The article told of his mummy investigation for the Egyptian government. Yes, the Old Boy could allow himself expressions of pride and accomplishment, having persevered and done a "jolly good job": A proper Englishman's answer to the Royal scandals which had been filling the tabloids for decades.

That evening, I called Rebecca's apartment, hoping against hope that she would be there. But all I got was her answering machine.

– XXXVII –

Under the Video Microscope

𝓕UNNY HOW YOU CAN READ A hundred newspaper articles and still have nothing but secondhand slop. I would have to examine the video tapes for answers to two important questions. Was Ledbetter really guilty? What were the consequences of my dodging the subpoena?

The next morning, I pulled the VCR from the garbage bag, plugged it into my portable TV and plugged both to shore power. The VCR had fast forwarding, which proved a blessing. When I heard a defense objection and saw a "side-bar" coming up, I pressed a button, speeding up the two attorneys' march to the bench. The exits and returns of the jury looked like Keystone Cop comedies. When something important was said, I took notes and jotted down the tape-counter numbers for future reference. The defense attorney was Jason "Tassel-Toe" Diamond, Esquire.

It took seven days to watch the whole trial. I fell into a routine of watching all day and calling Rebecca's apartment at night. All I got was her answering machine.

Dressed in a business suit, Dr. Jane Goddard Cooper stepped into the box as the first witness. She told how her husband died in her arms; how she learned from the doctors that the purple tongue and skin symptoms were unusual for a heart attack; and how she began to suspect foul play, and asked for an autopsy. She called up Mrs. Warren, Dr. Cooper's secretary, who "had gotten Charles his food, as usual." She, Mrs. Warren and a detective retrieved the hamburger sack early the next morning, turning it over to the M.E.'s Office.

Mrs. Warren explained how she went to the departmental administrator for a $10 bill and picked up a hamburger, French fries and a malted milk at the fast-food place, "as usual." Five minutes before the faculty meeting, she left the sack on the desk in her office, which was also the anteroom and entrance to Dr. Cooper's office. She remembered seeing Dr. Ledbetter reading the bulletin board in the hall as she left her office to drop off the change and receipt with the administrator.

She returned to find Dr. Ledbetter in her office. She told Dr. Ledbetter that he could go into Dr. Cooper's office, and she remembered his sarcastic response, "No, I would not impose myself on His Excellency. I'll just wait until the other peons arrive." When Dr. Taylor came, Dr. Ledbetter said there was a "critical mass" for the meeting.

Mrs. Warren opened Dr. Cooper's door and followed the two professors in, giving the hamburger bag to Dr. Cooper who was behind his desk, talking on the phone. She had no indication that the bag had been tampered with. It had the same "feel" as when she put it on her desk. And the bag had not been out of her sight except for the one minute she left it on her desk with Dr. Ledbetter in the room. She remembered that Dr. Ledbetter had worn a lab coat – unusual for him.

Dr. Gordon Taylor was brought in to corroborate the secretary's description of his movements relative to Ledbetter. He was a hostile witness, volunteering his serious reservations about "this hamburger theory."

The next witness for the prosecution was a crime technician who examined the wadded-up sack, the cardboard burger box, the French-fry box and milk-shake cup. When the botulinum tests came back negative, he boxed and stored it at liquid-nitrogen temperature under Dr. Westley's orders. In February, when Dr. Westley ordered a closer physical examination, he found a small puncture in a remnant of a pickle and a mayonnaise-like substance in and around it. A minuscule hole in the side of the sack corresponded to the position of the pickle in the hamburger in the sack when all the food items were "packed correctly." They later brought in the manager of the hamburger joint to testify how they trained their counter clerks to pack the sacks.

It was an interesting first day of viewing. Bright and early the next morning, I watched the thin detective who had questioned me. He described Dr. Westley's suspicion that Dr. Ledbetter had "put certain microencapsulated protein toxins into Dr. Cooper's food." With proper attention to due process, they put Dr. Ledbetter's laboratory under surveillance and brought Dr. Ledbetter in for questioning. The surveillance team followed Dr. Ledbetter to his apartment where he was seen "pacing back and forth most of the night." At 12:30 in the morning, he got into his car and drove to the Medical School. Next, the detective brought in a video monitor and played the now-famous arrest scene for the courtroom. They played it three times.

The next witness was a Ph.D. who worked in the Division of Cardiology of the Department of Medicine. It was his dogs that were poisoned. Unluckily for Ledbetter, he had saved some frozen samples of the hearts and could turn them over to Westley. The friendly security guard was right. The scientist did have about $20,000 of work in those animals.

The next witness was the Chief of Security at the med school, thug Joe Klouski's boss. Reluctantly, he described the "computerized access control system" and verified the taped log which showed that Ledbetter had entered the dog rooms. In cross-examination, the defense obtained his willing admission that someone else might have used Ledbetter's access card.

The next witness was Westley. He described the autopsy of Cooper, his suspicions that it was not a normal food poisoning or heart attack, and how he had "taken the extraordinary step of freezing all of the blood and organs of the deceased, indeed the whole body." He explained about chemicals, drugs, toxins and how you assay for them. He said it had to be a poisoning by protein toxins and attributed the long delay in interrogating Dr. Ledbetter to the complexity of the case.

Dr. Westley admitted that, when it came to his attention

that Dr. Ledbetter had invented a means of oral delivery of proteins into the bloodstream, he had focussed his attention on which proteins were available to Dr. Ledbetter. This led to the interrogation of Dr. Ledbetter.

"And that led to Dr. Ledbetter's actions which were so ably recorded by the gentlemen of the constabulary." This concluded the general portion of Westley's testimony. He was cross-examined.

Tassel-Toe got up slowly, glared at Westley and asked, "And in pursuing your theory of murder, you confined your investigation to one professor: Ledbetter. Is that correct?"

Dr. Westley said, "No. We looked for some snake toxins and other agents which were used by other faculty members."

Tassel-Toe looked surprised.

"When did Dr. Ledbetter become a suspect in your mind?"

Dr. Westley said, "I learned from an ex-employee who was a graduate student in the Pharmacology Department that Dr. Ledbetter had told a group of medical students that he could deliver proteins to the blood by an oral route. This supplied the missing piece of the puzzle."

"Wasn't it true that this ex-employee was one Mr. Benjamin Candidi and that you invited him to your home several times for the sole purpose of pumping him for information to prove that one of the faculty poisoned Dr. Cooper?"

"I should like to answer that. Might we repeat the question substituting the word 'partial' for 'sole' and substituting 'one or the other' for 'one?'"

"I don't understand."

"Well, I shouldn't really expect that you would. Please let me state that it is true that this ex-employee was one Mr. Benjamin Candidi, whom I invited several times with the *partial* purpose of pumping him for information which I could use to prove whether one or another of the faculty poisoned Dr. Cooper."

Westley's flawless delivery produced titters in the courtroom.

"And to the extent that the poor lad was an unwitting servant of my curiosity, I would like to publicly apologize to him . . . here and now."

"So then you constructed an elaborate theory of murder based on these findings?"

Westley remained silent.

"Will you please answer my question?"

"My dear boy, if you would have me *answer* it as a question, you should phrase it as a question. As it stands now, it is but an impertinence."

Laughter reverberated through the courtroom.

"Is it not true that if it had not been for your ex-employee Mr. Candidi, you wouldn't have had any information on which to base your theory?"

"That is *not* true."

"Could you please explain?"

"In addition to reviewing every publication of each professor, we also reviewed their public utterances. Dr. Ledbetter's boasting about his oral delivery system for proteins was dutifully recorded by a medical student in their 'Sophomore Note Service.'" Dr. Westley pulled out paper and asked, "May I read into the record a report by sophomore medical student Ronald Harris?"

There was a lengthy side-bar, then adjournment to chambers. When they returned, the judge stated, "Let the record reflect that State's Exhibit number nineteen has been entered into evidence, and that the subpoena of Mr. Benjamin Candidi be negated. Dr. Westley will please return to the stand."

Dr. Westley returned to the stand, picked up the exhibit, and read:

"LEDBETTER SPITS LEAD. November three, the Class of nineteen ninety-five witnessed a great moment in medical history as Professor John Ledbetter announced to the world that he had invented a means of delivering insulin and other proteins to the bloodstream by an oral dosage form which is so ingenious that it can be understood only by him! But don't worry, classmates, this foaming-at-the-mouth material will not upset your stomach and will not be on the exam. Study your aspirin and ibuprofen. Six exam questions from last year are attached."

The next new face to appear on my screen was that of Mr. Ronald Harris, M.D. (to be), who testified to the veracity of his contribution to the Sophomore Note Service. He was the guy who insulted me in front of Rebecca after our Thanksgiving vacation. I wondered if the Dean would haul his ass down to his office and give *him* hell for getting the med school in trouble. In any case, Mr. Harris seemed quite contrite and it was nice of him to take over as scapegoat.

So I was off the hook! My dodging the subpoena had not influenced the outcome of the trial. I called it a day and phoned Rebecca's apartment. Her answering machine gave a message that it was overloaded.

The next morning I called the Florida Marine Patrol. Luckily, Officer Mike Carter was deskbound that day.

"Oh, yes! Mr. Candidi. I'm glad you've called. I need to know if you are going to file a complaint on that B and E. Also, we need to serve you with a subpoena in another matter."

"The subpoena is no longer current. They don't need me anymore. Never really did."

"Well, they should have told us earlier. We've been looking for you and your boat all the way down to Key West."

"Did you try Ten Thousand Islands?"

"South of Sanibel Island?"

"Yes. If it was good enough for Gasparilla, it's good enough for me."

"Right place for that pirate. Mosquitoes thick as black clouds there. Bet you were eaten alive."

"I had a quart of Avon lotion. Mosquitoes didn't bite but the fish did."

We talked for a while about saltwater fishing. Then Officer Carter suddenly reverted to a businesslike manner.

"Mr. Candidi, regarding the assault-and-battery charge, we put the case on hold because we weren't able to get you. Those photos you sent tell a helluva story."

"I'm sorry I left you holding the bag, but we'd scheduled the vacation. Did you get the facts?"

"We checked the serial numbers of the guns. They belong to Joseph Klouski and Alberto Alonso. Both gentlemen work in private security and are deputized by the City of Opa Locka."

Yes, private security for the Bryan Medical School, I thought. "That checks with my sources. I'd appreciate your mailing me this information. Do you know if they reported their guns as missing?"

"We have not actively checked that, sir."

"And you probably have no way of knowing if they have reported the incident to any other law authority."

"That's affirmative, sir."

"Well, for right now I would like to keep the matter in abeyance. I need some further information."

"Just from me to you, the thing could get a little messy if you pursue it."

"It's already been messy for me. I've been parting my hair differently ever since."

This was slightly exaggerated, because my hair grew back with Mediterranean vigor. But my scalp would forever carry a scar as a reminder of the experience. We ended the conversation on a cordial note, and I went back to the tapes.

Dr. Westley resumed the stand. Next to him stood a tripod holding some oversized figures taken from Ledbetter's European Patent Application. Sitting comfortably in the witness box, with pointer in hand, Dr. Westley showed how the microcapsules in the captured vial were identical to what was described in the patent – except that the payload was poison, not insulin.

He explained how the three deadly peptide/protein toxins were nested in core of the microcapsule, coated with a layer of starch, then coated with a lecithin membrane containing selectin molecules to give the particle a toehold, and were then enterically coated with a layer of a polymer to protect everything from stomach acid.

Then he explained how the microcapsules were mixed with water to make a mayonnaise-like paste, how the paste was injected into the hamburger through a syringe, how the microcapsules got through the stomach unharmed and stripped off their protective coat in the gut, exposing their selectin toes, which made the particles stick to the Peyer's Patch, grabbing onto the selectin receptor toeholds and entering the intestinal lymphocyte manholes leading to the bloodstream.

Dr. Westley next described a molecular time bomb ticking inside Cooper. As water penetrated to the starch layer, the amylase enzyme started breaking it down, releasing sugars, building up pressure on the lecithin membranes until they popped, spilling the three toxins into the bloodstream. Yes, Dr. Johnson was right. Those lecithin membranes are damn thin.

Ledbetter had included a small amount of cobra venom phospholipase enzyme to chop up the lecithin molecules and break the membrane, just in case the starch swelling didn't do the trick. Dr. Westley commented that the enzyme serves a similar purpose in cobra venom, spreading the poison.

Dr. Westley described how the released KN-25 mathriotoxin from Kanazawa Nippon blocked Cooper's acetylcholine receptors, making it hard for him to breathe; how the O-35 from Oregon Biological made every mast cell in his body dump histamine, triggering a massive shock reaction equal to hundreds of bee stings; and how the E 7532 thrombin from Eta Chemical Company activated Cooper's clotting factors, making his blood turn to jelly. Dr. Westley showed that any of the three agents, alone, would have been sufficient to kill Cooper.

Then Dr. Westley presented assays which proved that all three toxins were in Cooper's blood, Cooper's gut, Cooper's hamburger remnant, in the captured vial and in the dog hearts. The prosecution brought in a string of expert witnesses from research institutes all over the country. They showed the jury enough oversized charts to paper the whole courtroom. The final compilation was thicker than a Ph.D. dissertation.

Interestingly, the dog experiment provided the most damning evidence: the cryptic record of injecting the hamburger, feeding it to the poor animal and Ledbetter's jubilation at finding it dead the next morning. Like the animal rights people, many folks feel more pity for an abused animal than for an abused human being. The prosecutor brought in a professor of German to translate the passage about the "advancement of science" and to explain the meaning of *Vergeltung*. This gave the experiment a damning Nazi touch.

Dr. Westley was brought back to summarize the scientific evidence.

"The unfortunate Dr. Cooper received a very strong combination of a snake bite and bee sting. It is the most ingenious murder device brought into being by the imagination or hate of a human being."

In cross examination, the defense went to great length to debunk Dr. Westley's description of how the microparticles got into the bloodstream. To this, Westley had one simple answer: "What I have told you is described most eloquently in Dr. Ledbetter's patent . . . for the delivery of insulin."

Then the defense quarreled about how Dr. Westley assayed for the three toxins, objecting to the immunoassays. But Dr. Westley replied that the same technique is used in hospital laboratories to analyze digitalis.

The defense resorted to sophistic counter-arguments. At one point Tassel-Toe pounded away at Westley, finally concluding, "I find your testimony incomprehensible."

Dr. Westley replied, "My dear boy, you must realize that people have to go to school eight years past high school to only *partially* understand these things. I shouldn't be too disappointed if you do not succeed in understanding this, particularly since you seem to have given over most of your attention to . . . how shall we say . . . 'fast and dirty' arguments against the *very things you must learn!*"

High English is an excellent vehicle for a reprimand, and the courtroom responded to Westley's seamless delivery with hearty laughter.

The defense called a long line up of chief cardiologists from famous universities. The prosecuting attorney was very well prepared by Westley, and he made fools out of most of them. One of the cardiologists criticized Westley's immunoassay, but didn't know it was the same kind of technique used to assay the heart drug, digitalis. Some of this went over the jury's heads. From their standpoint, the trial probably *was* a high-tech Mexican standoff.

Another day's viewing, and Rebecca's answering machine was still overloaded. The next morning I called the med school to confirm that her Board Exams would be given Monday, only a few days away. Rebecca would have to return by then. I went back to analyzing the trial.

Ledbetter made a big mistake when he took the stand in his own defense. Sure, he was his brilliant self, debunking Westley's assays and offering alternative explanations for everything presented. But everyone saw that it was self-serving – except him. Under cross-examination, he got caught up in his own explanations and lost all credibility. At one point he threw a tirade at the prosecutor, telling him that he didn't know a damn thing. His argument wasn't that much different from Westley's "my dear boy" pronouncement, except that Westley was calm and Ledbetter was livid.

I viewed Ledbetter's testimony several times, coming each time to the same conclusion: Ledbetter convicted himself. He made it easy to imagine him writing hate letters to Cooper, thinking up his dream poison and putting it into Cooper's food. It was easy to imagine the medical sophomores laughing at his "foaming at the mouth lecture." As Dr. Westley had said to me, "He is a real Toscanini; He went into tirades on the podium." And his tirade in the witness box was one tirade too many.

I completed my analysis of the video tapes at 1:00 Saturday afternoon. It was a week well spent. I was certain that Ledbetter was guilty, that justice had been served and that my non-availability for the trial could not be grounds for an appeal. I could return to the Pharmacology Department holding my head high – although it might get bloodied, running a gauntlet of pharmacology profs.

I walked to the bait shop and made two phone calls. Half an hour later a cab pulled up. I gestured to the dock cart containing my VCR and 15 shelf-feet of video cassettes. "Load it in the trunk and take me to ninety-three twenty-seven Bird Road."

It was a thoughtful and silent ride. In the doorway of his

shop, Zeekie greeted me with a smile which turned to a frown when he saw the cab driver unloading the trunk.

"Hey, Ben, I already cashed the check. A deal's a deal."

"Of course, Joe. But now I want to make you a new deal." Reluctantly, Zeekie picked up an armload of VCR tapes. "You know how wordy these lawyers are. I need only a few tapes for the stuff I really want to keep. Here's a list of the tapes and counter numbers for the video footage that I want. You get the stuff onto four or five tapes, and I'll give you all the rest."

Zeekie shook his head as he studied the list.

"I don't know Ben. It's a lot of work cueing these things up, and – "

"And there's $700 worth of tape that I'll give you in trade. You could use it to build up your video collection. Think of all those porno movies you've been picking up on your satellite dish. It takes an electronic genius like you to unscramble them, but it's all lost if you don't get it on tape."

Zeekie smiled at the mention of this opportunity. Then he frowned. "But why'd you bring back Ferina?" he asked, motioning to the VCR.

"No, she's not part of the deal. I'm only loaning her so you can cue up on the right tape-counter numbers."

This seemed to relieve him.

"She works real nice, doesn't she? Okay, Ben. We've got ourselves a deal. But don't you think we could make a documentary on it?"

"You're welcome to do anything you want with the original. But I don't think the courthouse camera work was good enough for any entertainment value. It's interesting to me as a permanent record of exactly what they said. And it's all very complicated."

"So you aren't writing a book?"

"No, I'm just keeping it as a souvenir."

"Pretty expensive souvenir."

"The best ones are."

"Okay, Ben. Check back with me in a week. I'll have to rig up a programmable counter so that I can get this shit copied off without having to stand over it all day. I've got a repair shop to run, too."

"I know you'll take it in stride, Joe. You're a genius with electronics."

"You're right, I am. Give you a ride?"

"No, thanks. I have some business in the neighborhood." That was a fib, but I needed a long walk to clear my mind.

My slow progress along the mean, dusty, commercial strips fronting Bird Road was anything but pleasant. After three eastward miles, the coral stone entrance arches of Coral Gables finally came into sight. Passing between these markers was like coming into a harbor, out of a storm. Coral Gables was so green and peaceful. I walked through the section where Rebecca and I had our bicycle date just before her return to New York, walked past the Cafe Place St. Michel where we talked about the Yanomamo/Amazon and the biological imperative, walked past the Federal Express office where I'd dispatched my inquiry to the German patent service, and walked along the Woodlawn Cemetery where we discovered the first signs of our mutual love. As the sun set, I trudged through Little Havana, revisiting all the stops of our first date. My feet took me north to Rebecca's apartment building across from the Bryan Medical School. Her answering machine was still overloaded and her windows were still dark.

My feet took me to the hamburger restaurant, the one that sold Mrs. Warren Dr. Cooper's hamburger, the one that gave me the stomach ache when I was deciphering Ledbetter's files that frantic night in the library. Amid a crowd of Saturday night hospital visitors, I ate a silent meal. On the way out, I bumped into Sheng-Ping coming in to chow up for an all-nighter in the lab.

"Oh, Ben! Grad to see you. I worry that you not come back."

"No, I'll be back Monday, Sheng-Ping. Just took off some time to study."

"Oh, Ben, you in big trouble. Dr. Taylor say you like in Army when soldier leave when not suppose to. He say you AWOL. And school police come and ask questions. I think when Dr. Taylor see you he be very, very mad."

"That may be, but I have some reasons to be mad myself. Thanks for warning me, Sheng-Ping, and don't worry. I'll see you Monday."

I took a taxi to Matheson Hammock. The next morning, a Sunday, Rebecca's answering machine was still jammed. But she had to arrive by that evening, because the Board Exams were Monday. I whiled away the day with swimming and daydreams. As the sun went down, I put on my back pack and rode my bicycle north to Rebecca's apartment. She still wasn't home. I locked the bike, sat down on the grass in front of the entranceway, and waited, my brain burning with Dostoevskian fever. Eight o'clock. Nine o'clock . . . Twelve midnight. A few minutes shy of 1:00, a yellow taxi pulled up, and Rebecca stepped out, looking as lovely as ever. I ran up to her as she pulled a second heavy bag from the back seat.

"Rebecca!"

"Ben!" she cried with joy.

I put out my arms to embrace her, but she held me off with a flattened palm to my chest.

"We have some things to take care of first, Ben," she said with a slight frown, her voice quietly resolute.

The meter showed $12. I pulled out two $10 bills and tossed them onto the front seat next to the driver. "Any more baggage?"

"No."

I waved the driver away.

"Ben, we have to talk."

We stood facing each other, our faces half in darkness, half illuminated by the light of the entranceway. She now looked so worried, small and shaky, yet purposeful. She would insist on the truth. A frog stuck in my throat, and I shook all over.

"Ben, it was wonderful, all the telegrams you sent. I'm so glad you did. They kept me believing in you. But, Ben, you ran from the law and left me to cover up for you!"

"Rebecca, I'm sorry," I pleaded. "There was no other way. They wanted to drag me into that murder trial. I couldn't testify. I just couldn't. Security officers from the med school broke into my boat looking for things to discredit me. They planted false evidence on my boat. When I caught them in the act, they beat me up. They tried to escape in my dinghy, and I almost drowned them. I had to hang up on you. I couldn't drag you into it. You have to trust me. I think that everything is all right now. I'll know for sure in a day or two."

I must have blurted this out in a feverish pitch, because Rebecca's expression slowly changed from cool resolution to concern. She reached out and put her hand on my cheek as if to gauge my temperature. She softened, but it would have been a mistake to lean forward and kiss her.

"Oh, Ben. They acted like you were a criminal. A fugitive. All I had were your last words and then that lovely telegram. The next afternoon, I went to your anchorage and the *Diogenes* was gone. I had to go to New York for father. It was so horrible, so lonely."

"I'm sorry, Rebecca. I had to sail the *Diogenes* away and hide for a long time."

"Ben, be honest with me. Was it a coincidence that you came to Pharmacology right after Dr. Cooper died?"

"No, Rebecca. But that's what I'd like to think it was."

"Ben! You are not being forthcoming. Dr. Westley is the chief coroner and your ex-boss. He had you over to dinner almost every week. I know there was a reason for those dinners. If we are going to get back together, our relationship must be based on truthfulness. Absolute truth, Ben. Even if it hurts."

I chose my words carefully. "Rebecca, it has proven true that Dr. Westley invited me over to pump me for information on the Pharmacology Department. He admitted that at the trial. He also publicly apologized to me for it. He said I was 'the unwitting servant of his curiosity.'"

"And what do you have to say to me?"

"Anything I say will complicate things further – for me, for you, and for us. If I have to give you the truth from the bottom of my heart, we have to be married. With the legal ramifications, there's no other way."

"Ben, you're starting to talk like a lawyer. Don't you know I've given up on lawyers?" She said this with a frown, which turned to a smile, which turned to a laugh, which quickly dissolved into a passionate moan as our lips met.

Our embrace may have lasted for five minutes. It may have lasted an hour. I do know it was ended by a polite honk of a car trying to squeeze by us. I carried the bags up to Rebecca's apartment where, once again, our lips met, our weary bodies drew strength from each other and we were reunited in communion of flesh and spirit. An hour or two before dawn, we fell into an equally delicious sleep.

At 8:30 I kissed Rebecca goodbye and wished her well on her Board Examinations. Over a second cup of coffee, I mentally rehearsed my return to the Department of Pharmacology.

– XXXVIII –

Administrative Hearing

$\mathcal{I}$ FOUND DR. TAYLOR SITTING IN HIS mop-closet office, talking on the phone. He glanced up at me and grimaced.

"Our long lost Benjamin Candidi has just resurfaced . . . Here in my office," he said sarcastically into the transmitter. "I'll call you back, Peter." He hung up.

"Second-year graduate student Candidi reporting back for duty, sir," I said, with a mock salute.

Taylor frowned.

"After being two months AWOL?"

"I told you I was taking some time to study medical pharmacology. I've also been working on some ideas for a dissertation project."

He said nothing for a long time. The silly bastard just sat there, glaring at me. Finally he roared, "AND WHAT DO YOU HAVE TO SAY FOR YOURSELF?"

"What do you mean?"

"You made yourself scarce when they needed you for the trial."

"My radio went on the blink, and no one made sufficient effort to contact me."

"For three days they searched for that boat of yours, all the way from here to Key West."

"It wasn't my fault they didn't find me. So what did they want me for?"

"They wanted to subpoena you for the trial. But they later decided that it was unnecessary."

"So there! It didn't make any difference. What else am I supposed to be blaming myself for?"

Taylor's face was red. He continued glaring at me.

"You can blame yourself for initiating the prosecution of Dr. Ledbetter! You were involved in it early on. The tip-off came from you. You told certain things to the Medical Examiner." Taylor was twitching all over.

"I don't know what the Medical Examiner learned from me that he couldn't have learned himself, or from two dozen people around here," I snapped back, indignantly.

"The newspaper quoted Westley as saying that an important part of the solution to the case occurred to him while talking to you. The prosecution wouldn't have happened if it weren't for you."

He kept trying to stare me down.

"Well, maybe you should not rely solely on the newspapers for your information. I heard from the medical students that the investigators got the information from the Sophomore Note Service! They told me that the prosecution even brought a medical student in to testify on the notes he published. Is that right?"

"Yes, I believe so," he said cautiously.

"So why aren't you skinning *him* alive? Why are you blaming me?" I scowled.

"Well — " he temporized, almost meekly. Blood drained from his face.

"Well, the medical student isn't to blame, and neither am I. It was just scientific information. I don't remember you or your two assistants, Dr. Sturtz and Dr. Stampawicz, announcing any prohibition on telling people what's said in lectures."

My upper lip may have curled when I said "Stampawicz." I laid in a long pause, staring at Taylor. He didn't look away for a long time. Then he started to blink. Then he looked past me, raised his eyebrows and smiled.

I renewed my attack. "I didn't tell anyone about the dog-and-cat fights that were going on here, because I didn't know about them. But from what I've subsequently heard, I wouldn't have been surprised if Ledbetter had killed Cooper with his bare hands. I guess it took a trial to bring *that* out."

Taylor looked away, but I was in no mood to let him off the hook just yet.

"If I were mentioned or quoted, or if they had my picture in the paper, well, I don't give a damn! I got sick and tired of the whole affair when Dr. Moore hauled my butt down to the Dean's Office. They grilled me like a toasted cheese sandwich. They treated me like a piece of shit. In fact, I was so god-damned pissed off that I seriously thought about giving up on this Department and transferring my credits to another graduate school."

Dr. Taylor visibly shrank under the onslaught of my words.

"Dr. Taylor, maybe you would be so good as to tell me whether *you* think Ledbetter is guilty."

Taylor squirmed in his chair, and then slowly whined, "Well, I . . . I . . . It is a very complicated case and – "

"Thank you, *sir*, for your expert opinion. Now, as the Director of the Graduate Program, do you have any more questions of me?"

He slowly came to his senses. He looked past me, once more seeming to gather strength, and said, "So you studied pharmacology for two months, did you? Name me an alpha blocker!"

"Yohimbine. Alpha two blocker. Works on presynaptic receptors to give enhanced release of Nor-Epi. Tips the balance towards adrenergic stimulation. Used for idiopathic orthostatic hypotension, and is abused in certain circles to abnormally prolong penile erection."

"And some less *exotic* alpha blockers?"

"Phentolamine, prazosine and phenoxybenzamine."

"Well, enough. You shouldn't have trouble with medical pharmacology next semester."

"No. As a matter of a fact, I'm going to blow the top off of it. Just call off your dogs. And the next time I hear anything from any one of the Faculty on this Ledbetter thing, I'm trans-

ferring out. One more thing, I want to take the preliminary
exam with the third-year students this fall."

"But students are not generally allowed to do this before
completion of the second year."

"I'm ready for it now. I've also got a dissertation project
thought out. I can finish up here in two more years."

"Graduate in three years?"

"Yes. I want to talk to Kozinski and McGregor about a
project I thought up over the last two months."

"By all means."

I gave him a mock salute. This time he returned it, involuntarily.

I turned on my heel, took one step and bumped into Dr.
Peter Moore. He must have been standing there listening to
us for a long time.

"Fine performance, Mr. Candidi. Now we'll give you a
chance to repeat it before the Dean."

"I'd like nothing better."

I marched down there so fast they had trouble keeping
up with me. After we'd penetrated the second layer of the
Dean's secretaries and were standing directly before the final
door, Dr. Moore slipped ahead of me.

"We'll go in first. You can wait here," he said.

The senior secretary gave Moore and Taylor a nod, and
they opened the door and walked in.

"He's impenitent," Dr. Taylor announced as the door
closed.

During the wait, I borrowed the secretary's Medical
School telephone directory and looked up Alberto "Tire Iron"
Alonso. The directory listed him as "Security Specialist 3,"
working directly under Mr. Joseph "Fat Ass" Klouski. I overheard the Dean instructing the secretary to get Assistant Counsel Blanco on the phone. The little light on the phone told me
that the conversation lasted a full half hour.

The light went out, and I waited still another quarter of
an hour. Taylor, Moore and the Dean must have had a lot to
discuss. Finally, the secretary told me to go in. The two phar-

macologists looked exhausted. The Dean looked cool, but I guessed he was silently seething.

"Mr. Candidi, I'm faced with a difficult call."

I showed neither the expected diffidence nor fear. "If you'd like me to go out while you make a difficult telephone call, it would be all right with me."

"A judgment call," he replied frostily.

"I'm sorry, sir. I wasn't expecting to hear slang in a Dean's office. So you are faced with a difficult decision. Can I assume that Dr. Moore and Dr. Taylor have explained to you what I have explained to them?"

"Yes."

"Then I don't see why you would have any difficulty making your 'judgment call.'"

"That is for me to decide, not for you," he said, dropping his voice to a temperature that would liquefy oxygen.

I reached into my backpack, pulled out the packet of photos and tossed them down on his desk. "Perhaps these will help you decide which side of the fence to come down on."

He opened the envelope like he knew it was bad news.

"They were taken after two of your security men, Joseph Klouski and Alberto Alonso, broke into my boat and beat me up. I have a positive I.D. on them. I managed to disarm them. Their pistols are in the custody of the Florida Marine Patrol."

The Dean feigned surprise, but he didn't fool me. He probably didn't fool Moore and Taylor, either. I told him about discovering his two officers on my boat, the tear gas in the face, the struggle in the water, my retrieval of the guns and the record I compiled with the Florida Marine Patrol. I complained about my head wound. The Dean was silent for a long time.

"Of course, this doesn't really prove anything," he said brazenly, but searching for my reaction.

"Then I'll pick up where I left off with the police. Thanks for your time. I'll see you in criminal and civil court."

"Mr. Candidi!"

"What?"

Again, an embarrassingly long silence. The guy had been too long at liquid-nitrogen temperature and was frozen stiff. It was up to me to thaw him out.

"Sir, the problem may be inflated pride. It gets in the way of intelligence, and then people do damage to themselves. When a human being gets away with treating people like shit for too long, it goes to his head. Let me propose a deal: You don't bullshit me, and I don't bullshit you." I let this sink in. "Now, on behalf of yourself and your institution, what do you have to say?"

"I'm sorry."

"That's all I wanted to hear. I forgive you and your institution. Now, let me make one more proposal. You and your people leave me alone, and I'll leave you alone." I turned to Moore and Taylor. "And no more cowardly innuendo and comparing me with a farm boy who tracked cow shit into the house. If I hear any more of this, I'm transferring out to a more respectable institution. Is there anything more to say, gentlemen?" We would have to solve all the details during these golden moments with the Dean.

They were silent.

"Then I'd like to return to the lab. If there are any afterthoughts, you can find me there." I turned on my heel.

"Mr. Candidi," called the Dean, as I reached the door. "The negatives?" The guy had been reading too many L.A. detective novels.

"You'll just have to trust me on that one."

Thus, black sheep Ben Candidi was taken back into the fold, never again to feel the shepherd's crook. I checked my mailbox. There was a note to call "Steve." I used the phone in the med student lounge.

Steve Burk told me that my services would no longer be needed at the M.E.'s Office. "In the last several months we've gotten pretty damned good at extending our assay capabilities."

"Well, goddamn! Westley promised – "

"Keep cool, buddy, and let me finish. The Dade County

Environmental Resources Agency wants you as a consultant on chromatographic methods. They're going to give you a three-year contract at twenty-five thousand dollars a year. All you have to do is visit them several times a year, and be available when they need an opinion. The Old Man put in a good word for you. Congratulations!"

"Congratulations to you, Steve! You did a great job. I know you must have had your hands full."

"You'll never know how much. Say, maybe after you get your Ph.D. and things get back to normal here, we can go down to that beer joint of yours and shoot the breeze a little. And check out the Swedish tits."

"Sounds great. You're on. 'Til then."

I left the Department, took a long walk and then met Rebecca as she came out from the exam. She was in good spirits, and I took her for a nice dinner in Coral Gables. The next morning she went back for the second round. I figured Dr. Taylor and Dr. Moore had enough time to tell everyone to lay off of Ben Candidi, so I went back to the Department. Dr. Rob McGregor and Dr. Al Kozinski were pleased with my idea for a dissertation project under their joint mentorship.

– XXXIX –

Final Chapter

$\mathcal{I}$T WAS EXACTLY ONE YEAR SINCE Dr. Westley called me into his office and made a proposition that changed my life. And the Old Boy was right: I had needed to be kicked out of the house. Thinking back to our balcony conversations, I began to see the method in his madness. He had mentored me into adulthood, closing one chapter of my life and opening another.

If I had known the project would be so difficult, I wouldn't have agreed to it. And I would have been an unemployed HPLC jockey. His proposition was like a scientific project: you get hooked on the original hypothesis – which doesn't hold up. Then it takes ten times longer than expected to get the thing sorted out. But the experience had brought rich rewards.

After accepting the King's Shilling, I had learned many valuable lessons: that being well-intentioned and intelligent is not enough; that you must be willing to act on your beliefs and knowledge; that for the sake of truth you must be ready to cast off an unproductive hypothesis, even if you have spent two months on it; that you can never know from whom you can receive useful knowledge or enlightenment; that you can learn as much from their mistakes as from their successes; that backlash will be your reward for producing knowledge which threatens people; that you must always be ready to fight for the survival of any good thing you have produced; and that if you wish to sustain a stellar love of the 15th magnitude, you must be ready to forswear all love of the 12th magnitude.

Yes, I owed a lot to Dr. Westley for setting the process in

motion. Of course, I'd helped him as much as he'd helped me. My solving the murder removed his problems with the Dade County Commission. They couldn't call the Old Man incompetent. In fact, the Ledbetter case had raised his reputation to new heights. Would he now retire or stay on for a few years? When the dust settled, I would invite him and Margaret out to dinner.

Happily, all of my fellow students had survived the first year. As the month of August rolled along, I completed some promising experiments on my dissertation project. When I told Rebecca about finishing in three years and graduating with her, a Mona Lisa smile appeared on her face. She cast a glance toward a pile of soft-bound books in the second bedroom, which we were converting into a study.

Later that evening, I looked at the books. They were catalogues of residency programs and graduate departments of biomedical science. The family medicine residency programs and the pharmacology programs were marked with dog-ears. The pile was organized geographically: Johns Hopkins, Georgetown, Duke, the Universities of North Carolina, South Carolina and Miami, Tulane, Baylor at Houston and the University of California at San Diego. With the exception of the North Carolina schools, they were all on the water. Good thinking, girl! Can't forget the *Diogenes*.

Two of the catalogues described two-year Ph.D. –> M.D. programs which Rebecca had encircled in red. Why, you crafty little darling! At the bottom of the pile was a list of Caribbean medical schools and a brochure on physician service in the World Health Organization. So we would enjoy a two-year Caribbean vacation on the *Diogenes*, with Rebecca doing her anthropology studies in family medicine, while I get my foreign medical degree! Then she could help me with my "Foreign Physician Licensure Exam" and I could, of course, help her with her Ph.D. dissertation.

Needless to say, I love her madly. After years of being out in the cold, it was Rebecca who warmed my frostbitten soul. And she loved me. She planned to introduce me to her mother and her father – before it is too late.

So what were my career plans? Well, I didn't want to be just another Ph.D. academic biomedical researcher from the mold of McGregor, Kozinski and Ledbetter. They spend all of their time chasing grant money. They put in long hours, and for what? To be "managed" by a corrupt, organization man like Cooper? If I had been in Ledbetter's place, committed to a dead-end career at a medical school run by a dean whose only use for laboratory research was to collect overhead payments from the NIH – I might have killed Cooper myself.

My experience with the Dean and his lawyer have shown me that I *do* have the ability to manipulate verbal symbols and to argue by leaving out certain facts. It seems what you leave out can be just as important as what you put in. Perhaps that's the key to survival in the Information Age. I'm still grappling with the moral questions involved.

If I don't decide to be a physician-scientist, maybe I'll get a law degree and become a patent lawyer. But, to be honest, I would really like to invent something as brilliant as Ledbetter did. Tricking the intestine into letting whole proteins into the bloodstream is nothing short of fantastic. Of course, if we were a nation of Spartans, we wouldn't need his invention. But it is a fact of life that 90 percent of the people don't like to inject themselves, even if it's necessary to avoid premature death. The market for oral insulin is large enough for Ledbetter's selectin delivery system to bring in tens of millions of dollars a year in royalties.

Ironically, it was the publicity of the trial that finally sparked interest in the patent among drug-company executives. One day, McGregor told me that the Medical School had just licensed rights for the patent application to a major drug company and that they'd be paying a minimum royalty of $1 million per year. Of this, about $300,000 per year will go to Ledbetter. After five years, when the company gets FDA approval for an insulin pill, Ledbetter will get millions. But I doubt it will make him happy in prison.

A couple of weeks after I got back, Ledbetter was sentenced to life imprisonment. How much better it would have been if the Dean had reined in Cooper and had given Ledbetter the support and recognition he needed.

I arranged with the dockmaster at Matheson Hammock for a permanent berth. It cost $300 a month, but I didn't have the time to row out every day. The dock proved a convenient staging area for the small parties that we took down to Elliott Key on two free weekends.

The *Diogenes* was retired as my cocoon and was recommissioned as the center of our social life. Our invitees were some of the most interesting Ph.D. and M.D. candidates at Bryan, together with a smattering of Mensa Society friends. The *Diogenes* was living up to his name, discerning honesty from falsehood beneath the rays of his mast light under the open skies. Arnie "*sacher macher*" Green and his wife Mona went with the first group. After Arnie got used to the on-board environment, he was actually able to a hold normal conversation with us. He called a couple evenings later to express his thanks. He said we helped him "untie some knots."

Late one Friday afternoon in the lab, about four weeks after my return to Miami, I received a call from Dr. Westley's secretary, Doris.

"Ben, I'm glad I was able to get hold of you. I have some bad news which I must tell you. Otherwise, you may not have any way of knowing."

"What?"

"Mrs. Westley passed away yesterday morning."

"Oh, dear." My heart rose to my throat and my vision became indistinct. I croaked, "What?"

"She died of heart failure, but she had been failing for a long time."

"How is Dr. Westley taking it?"

"Well you know how *he* is, never saying what he really thinks. He said that he could manage. But for a few hours my husband and I thought that we were going to be the ones to make the arrangements. I notified the Bishop at Trinity Cathedral. He and the Rector are taking care of everything. Dr.

W. is a pillar of the church, you know." She gave me the details on the funeral. "I hope you can come. It's important to him, although he did not say so. They say 'no flowers,' but they are accepting donations to the scholarship fund of the Ladies' Auxiliary of Bryan Medical School."

I called the Alumni Office for the address of the President of the Ladies' Auxiliary. I wrote a check for a generous donation with a short note saying how greatly I had admired Mrs. Westley. I mailed the letter with a little prayer.

The next afternoon, hot, humid, August air smacked me in the face as I stepped out of the cab in front of Trinity Cathedral. Bright sunlight reflected from the white limestone of the charming little church, built to overlook the Bay, but now boxed in on three sides by massive parking garages of the Omni Center and the Marriott Hotel. Like Miami itself, the church is a hybrid: Spanish bell tower, asymmetrically placed over its three arched entranceways, stained-glass rosette window with inlaid stone cross.

I entered the sanctuary half an hour early. The coffin stood before the chancel. Dr. Westley was kneeling in the front pew, head bowed, obviously deep in prayer. Not wishing to disturb him, I sat in the back. The church must have been a mere semblance of his Exeter Cathedral. The walls bore no dark-stained wood, but rather white sparkling alabaster. Yes, there were stained-glass windows with pictures of the saints, organ pipes and choir stalls up front. But how incongruous to sit in this Episcopal church in the middle of the day, with an equatorial summer sun baking the roof and bombarding the stained-glass windows. Perhaps the alabaster interior walls were the Miami architect's concession to indefatigable sunlight.

Dr. Westley's head remained bowed and unmoved. Feeling ashamed of spying on him, I picked up a hymnal and searched for familiar hymns. A few minutes later an elderly couple came in. The gentleman wore a heavy, double-breasted, dark wool suit. His face was broad, his skin white, almost translucent, with the same little red-and-blue streaks as Dr. Westley. An Englishman. He reminded me of one of the organists on Dr. Westley's record jackets.

His wife's clothing was equally dark: a heavy, navy-blue, two-piece dress, a dark silk blouse and a rounded bonnet with small black beads sewn in. She clutched a small purse, also covered with tiny beads. And beads of sweat stood out on both their faces. They must have lived in Miami because they seemed familiar with the church. But did they always dress so heavily when going to church?

They glanced past me as if I didn't exist and walked up to the front pew. They genuflected, she a couple of inches, he with the left knee all the way to the floor. Turning to Dr. Westley, she leaned forward, taking his hand. The husband reached over and planted his right hand on Dr. Westley's shoulder, where it remained for a long time. At arms length, the wife expressed condolence. She nodded alternately to Dr. Westley and to her husband, who punctuated her words with his own slow thoughtful nods and with visible modulation of the pressure of his hand on Dr. Westley's shoulder. Dr. Westley dropped his head as if to cry, and the woman grabbed his free hand and squeezed it to her body, midway between belt and breast.

Then Dr. Westley glanced at Margaret's open coffin, and the couple nodded and walked respectfully toward it. The lady pulled from her beaded purse a small flowered handkerchief and dabbed her eyes. The gentleman remained one step behind her, holding her lightly by the shoulders. After a few minutes, they returned to Dr. Westley's pew, took places on either side of him, and knelt with him in prayer.

Slowly, more people of similar description arrived. All properly genuflected to the altar before paying their respects to Margaret. From their pew, the original couple regulated the flow of condolence and silently indicated the order of seating. Semi-audible air conditioning lowered the temperature a degree or two. Slowly, the organ began improvised strains. English friends slowly formed a tightly-knit group, about 40 strong, on the left side of the sanctuary. Less intimate guests were marginated to the right side.

Doris entered, and I followed her to the front. As we approached Margaret's coffin, my eyes filled with tears and my throat tightened. Thankfully, Dr. Westley's head was still bowed as we turned around. A glance from his two protectors told us that we were not bidden to express our sympathy.

I chose a pew five rows back, just close enough to be part of the congregation but far enough to be properly ignored. Doris sat two arm's lengths away. An usher closed the coffin, and many of the ladies quietly wept. The Rector appeared and read several pages of prayers set out in the *Prayer Book*. Then he announced that we would sing Hymn #680. I opened the red hymnal and found "O God, Our Help in Ages Past." The organ piped up the introductory chords, and the tight knot of Englishmen sang all five verses of the hymn, properly and stoutly.

One of the ladies stepped to the pulpit. She read a Lesson from the Old Testament and something about death being just one step in our journey toward God. Then came another hymn and a New Testament reading. We recited the Twenty-Third Psalm.

The Rector delivered a sermon, telling me little of Margaret that I didn't already know. I found myself thinking of Margaret as a young lady in the suburbs of London, of her education in her adolescent years, of her service in the war, of her life with Geoffrey, their emigration to Miami, and of her love of culture and good manners. The Rector said that Margaret's life had served as a carrier of values. This brought subtle nodding of heads. He said she had borne with grace the burden of a long, serious illness which clouded the last decade of her life.

Then the Rector announced Hymn #208, "The Strife is O'er." The congregation started stoutly, but by the third verse, many of the singers had fallen out. The organist started the fourth verse too early and with a bad chord. Only two singers made the entrance but they quickly faltered. I raised my watery tenor voice and sang with the beat: "He closed the yawning gates of hell . . ." The two singers recommenced, and slowly

we were joined by the other congregants. The flame had flickered, but had not gone out. Toward the end of the verse, I was
all choked up. But the little knot of Englishmen started the
fifth and final verse without my help. Slowly and individually, many of them turned and glanced back in my direction
to see who was the unknown singer in the back row.

The Rector lead out the coffin, borne by six pall bearers.
Doris was not going to the burial, so I requested a ride with
the most approachable-looking couple of the group. They
welcomed me into their car but not into their conversation.
Two uniformed black men on motorcycles escorted the black
hearse into Biscayne Boulevard, playing a dangerous game of
leapfrog. While one secured the intersection ahead, the other
thundered past us, hurling forward at 70 miles an hour, to
claim and secure the next intersection with the authority of
one gloved hand and the urgent flashing of the blue light atop
the seven-foot pole mounted over his rear wheel. My host commented on how difficult it was to keep up with the funeral
train. I had another thought: How ironic that the living were
risking their lives to save time for the dead.

It was such a rush, streaming west on N.E. 14th Street,
through Overtown, that part of town which supplied Dr. Westley with so many cases, then dipping under an expressway
bridge, tires singing as we crossed the S.W. 7th St. drawbridge
over the Miami River, whizzing past the Ronald Reagan restaurant, with the Bay of Pigs Memorial and fruit stand a blur.
Finally, we slowed for the entrance of the Woodlawn Cemetery, and followed the winding road at a stately pace, until
the large Romanesque Cathedral mausoleum came into view.

The hearse drove up the steep motor entrance and the
cars parked on the grass around a circular war-memorial statue.
The coffin was removed from the back and wheeled into the
mausoleum. I followed to where a throng of mourners stood
before an open vault. Beside it lay its marble cover, inscribed:

"Margaret Lloyd Westley, † London, Sep. 10, 1917, ‡
Miami, Sep. 15, 1994. She loved her God, her husband and
her country."

The vault next to hers was not inscribed. It was undoubtedly for Dr. Westley. The vault on the other side was inscribed "NELSON." I remembered the last English dinner and Margaret singing about how Trafalgar Square was good enough for Nelson and "good enough for me." My chest tightened and I could hardly breathe.

Flanked by the protective couple, Dr. Westley stood, gazing into the opened vault. It was just like the picture in the magazine, of him looking into the refrigerated vault at the morgue. Fame, like life, is so ephemeral. At that moment I realized Margaret had been like a mother to me.

My field of vision narrowed, and I remembered how, as a young acolyte standing at attention, I used to faint. The group of mourners became a blur, and I felt myself floating in a sea of piped-in music, gently lifted and dropped by waves of strings and a chorus of voices singing "ah." The music had the sad, heart-wrenching simplicity of the sound track of a Walt Disney movie, like when Bambi's mother dies. As the strings were joined by horns and the music worked up into a slow crescendo, I felt a press of people around me.

Far off, a disembodied Rector's voice echoed words of consecration. The strings and voices disappeared as a solitary French horn made a statement. It was joined by a violin. The two instruments receded and a choir of strings repeated the statement. A brass choir replied. Then a solitary violin resolved the theme in a slowly developing diminuendo. I opened my eyes to find the vault closed. Only Westley, the protective couple and a middle-aged man were left. Dr. Westley looked toward me, his eyes clear, his face dry and resolute.

"Benjamin, thank you ever so much for coming and lending your voice to the prayers and the hymns sung for Margaret. She was truly fond of you. She always looked forward to your visits and our little chats. I am sure that she would have been delighted to know – "

He stopped abruptly as he realized the impossibility of completing his sentence. He was silent for a second or two.

"You were the reincarnation of our lost son." Under his

fuzzy eyebrows, his eyes glistened.

I started to take Dr. Westley's hand but threw my arms around him instead.

"Now, now. You mustn't feel sorry for me. I shall manage. But I do wish that you would drop in on me once a fortnight. Margaret was quite proud of you, but we haven't made a proper Englishman out of you yet."

He slowly disengaged me and held me by the shoulders at arm's length. He looked to the side and nodded to the protective couple.

"Mr. and Mrs. Charles Worthington, may I present Mr. Benjamin Candidi."

Mr. Worthington gave me his hand, and while shaking it said, "Yes, my pleasure. We appreciated your adding your voice to our choir."

Mrs. Worthington extended her gloved hand sideways, a few inches in front of her clutched purse. I squeezed her hand lightly and shook it gently.

Dr. Westley turned to the other gentleman and said, "Gerald, Mr. Gerald Hartley. I would also like you to meet Mr. Candidi. Perhaps you would be good enough to drop him off."

I said goodbye to Dr. Westley and promised to call him. Walking with Mr. Hartley to his car, I learned that he was from Toronto and worked with the Canadian Consulate. I let him drop me off in front of the Ronald Reagan restaurant, intending to walk the rest of the way back. A moving body can pump life into a drained soul.

The sun set over the Miami River just as I crossed the bridge. For some strange reason, my feet took me back to the med school. The friendly guard I met the day of the animal rights demonstration was manning the desk. He remembered me and let me in without my badge. In the elevator, I must have pushed the wrong button, because it took me a floor too high. I got off and walked through the Cell Biology Department and toward a convenient stairwell. It was there that I saw a list on a laboratory door, which I stopped to read.

GHANDI'S DEADLY SINS:
Wealth without work
Pleasure without conscience
Knowledge without character
Business without morality
Science without humanity
Politics without principle
Worship without sacrifice

The card beside the door said "Ragu Parikh." He was a post-doc, a quiet guy. He seemed to be quite intelligent, but never had that much to say in seminars. Why had he put this up on the door to his lab? I reread the page, and then it became clear to me that these were actually seven moral equations. And the simultaneous solution of these seven moral equations could have prevented most of the problems I had seen in the last year: the ruthlessness of Cooper, the white hatred of Ledbetter and the aloofness of Ashton. Trouble had compounded itself because those people had allowed themselves to fall deeply into one or more of these lethal states.

None of us was free of each of these sins. Westley's petty prejudice against Irishmen, wrapped in the sheepskin of cultured Anglophilia, was actually Worship Without Sacrifice. And Ben Candidi? Was he a perpetual Diogenes or a Holden Caulfield, the Catcher in the Rye? Could he turn the lantern to his own face and stop calling other people phony? Yes, my sin had been the worship of my own ideals without sufficient sacrifice to them. I thanked God for sending Dr. and Mrs. Westley to pass to me the torch and for sending me an angel to hold a mirror to my face. My feet slowly took me to my new home with her.

Postlogue

Specific molecules and mechanisms comprising the murder weapon have been fictionalized. To the best of my knowledge, the specific mechanism has not been proposed, although many laboratories have been working overtime to trick the Peyer's Patch. All background pharmacology and physiology in the novel are correctly described. At the time of publication, the search for an oral delivery form for insulin remains an unfulfilled, decades-old, billion-dollar quest.